Best wishes!
Jim Sundlesperger

Escape From Libby Prison

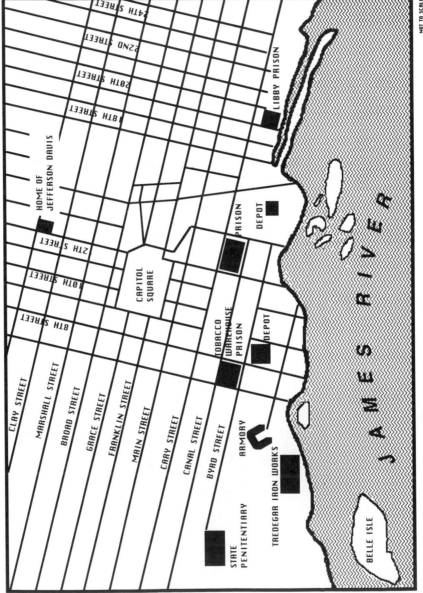

RICHMOND, 1863-64

CLAY STREET
MARSHALL STREET
BROAD STREET
GRACE STREET
FRANKLIN STREET
MAIN STREET
CARY STREET
CANAL STREET
BYRD STREET
ARMORY
TREDEGAR IRON WORKS

STATE PENITENTIARY

8TH STREET
10TH STREET
12TH STREET
18TH STREET
20TH STREET
22ND STREET
24TH STREET

HOME OF JEFFERSON DAVIS

CAPITOL SQUARE

TOBACCO WAREHOUSE PRISON

DEPOT

PRISON

DEPOT

LIBBY PRISON

JAMES RIVER

BELLE ISLE

NOT TO SCALE

Escape From

Libby Prison

By

James Gindlesperger

BURD STREET PRESS

This Burd Street Press publication
was printed by
Beidel Printing House, Inc.
63 West Burd Street
Shippensburg, PA 17257 USA

In respect for the scholarship contained herein, the acid-free paper used in this book meets the guidelines for permanence and durability of the Committee on Production Guidelines for Book Longevity of the Council on Library Resources.

For a complete list of available publications
please write
Burd Street Press
Division of White Main Publishing Company, Inc.
P.O. Box 152
Shippensburg, PA 17257 USA

Library of Congress Cataloging-in-Publication Data

Gindlesperger, James, 1941–
        Escape from Libby Prison / by James Gindlesperger.
            p.   cm.
        Includes bibliographical references.
        ISBN 0-942597-91-5 (alk. paper)
        1. Libby Prison--History--Fiction. 2. Escapes--Virginia--
Richmond--History--19th century--Fiction. 3. United States--
History--Civil War, 1861–1865--Prisoners and prisons--Fiction.
4. Prisoners of war--Virginia--Richmond--Fiction.   I. Title.
PS3557.I488E7   1995
813'.54--dc20   95-43550
                                                        CIP

PRINTED IN THE UNITED STATES OF AMERICA

"Why do men fight who were born to be brothers?"

Lt. Gen. James Longstreet, CSA

To the memories of the 109

Finally the world will know
who you are
and
what you did

Table of Contents

Page

*A*cknowledgements

No research project of this magnitude can be conducted without the support and assistance of many people. This one was no exception, and without this help it never would have been possible.

I must first thank my family for their support, encouragement, and patience throughout the entire research process. To Cheryl, my daughter, whose discovery of the grave of one of the escapees actually started the project, and who provided me with background information, I am extremely grateful. And to my son Mike, who accompanied me on countless trips to the National Archives, and to my wife Suzanne, who gave constant support, I can only say I couldn't have done it without you. Mike and Suzanne did much of the research into the personnel records, and a great deal of the information contained in the Appendix is a result of their efforts. l like to think all three enjoyed being a part of this work, but most likely there were times they would rather have been doing something else. They never complained, though, and it made the whole project much more enjoyable.

The friendship, assistance, and generosity of the staff at Mcllwain Charters & Tours is also deeply appreciated. They made the travel part of the project more enjoyable than I would have ever expected it to be.

Thanks also to Robert E. L. Krick, National Park Service Historian at the Richmond National Battlefield Park for his encouraging words and general support. To James Rodgers, assistant curator for the La Porte County (Indiana) Historical Society, for his efforts to trace the whereabouts of the Danielson barn, many thanks. Thanks also to the La Porte county commissioners who put me in touch with Mr. Rodgers; to Dr. John W. Hamblen, Brown County (Indiana) Historian, who also assisted in trying to ascertain the final disposition of the Danielson barn; and especially to Steve and Donna Toth, present owners of the Danielson property, who seem to love the story of Libby as much as I do.

The help of the employees at the National Archives was also invaluable and I am deeply indebted to them. They went far beyond the bounds of their job descriptions to provide the key information which allowed the list of escapees to be completed. None helped more than Mike Meiers, whose expertise and assistance saved me many hours of valuable time. The friendship with Mike which developed over the course of the two years it took to complete the research is something I value highly.

Much of the research material was located through the tireless efforts of the Interlibrary Loan Department at Carnegie Mellon University. Joan Stein and Geri Kruglak exhibited an amazing talent for locating even the most obscure sources, and I am deeply indebted to them.

Without the help of many fine organizations and institutions the research for this work would have been much more difficult and far less complete. At the risk of omitting some, I must thank the following: The Museum of the Confederacy, The Civil War Library/Museum, Louise Arnold-Friend of the Historical Reference Branch of the U.S. Army Military History Institute, the Rhode Island Historical Society, the State Historical Society of Wisconsin, the Illinois Historic Preservation Agency, the Indiana Commission of Public Records, the Michigan Department of State - Bureau of History, the Alderman Library of the University of Virginia, the Illinois Department of Veterans' Affairs, the Kentucky Department of Military Affairs (Military Records and Research Branch), Dianne O'Shea of the Johnstown Genealogy and Historical Society for Pennsylvania, the Kentucky Department for Libraries and Archives, the Connecticut Historical Society, Gus Stevens and the Lewis Historical Collections of Vincennes University, the Commonwealth of Massachusetts State Library, the Memphis Shelby County Public Library and Information Center, the University Libraries of the University of Tennessee and the University of Illinois at Urbana-Champaign, the Margaret I. King Library of the University of Kentucky, the Ohio Historical Society, the Virginia Historical Society, The Valentine, the War Memorial Museum of Virginia, the Chicago Historical Society, the South Bend *Tribune,* and the State Archives of New York, Missouri, Michigan, and Maine. Many of the reference personnel at these institutions went far beyond their normal duties to ferret out details and provided critical pieces of information which made the story of the escape more meaningful. Their assistance must be acknowledged with sincere thanks, and with apologies to anyone I may have missed.

I must also thank Angela Welsh, my contact in Washington, who unselfishly shuttled requests to the National Archives despite her busy schedule, and Harold Collier, my publisher. Harold's friendly assurances and willingness to take a chance on an unpublished would-be author made the final product possible.

And finally, to those friends who read the manuscript, made suggestions, and generally gave their encouragement, this book is yours, too. I can never thank you enough.

Foreword

During the Civil War the Confederate Army captured nearly 200,000 Union soldiers. Not including the Southern soldiers who surrendered at the end of the war, the Union counted slightly more.

Early in the war these prisoners were exchanged or released on parole, contingent upon a promise by the prisoner not to take up arms against his captors again until an exchange could be effected. However, the Federal government was reluctant to conduct official prisoner exchange negotiations, fearing that would be interpreted as a recognition of the Confederate States of America. As a result, no formal discussions regarding the exchange of prisoners were conducted until early 1862. Even then, there is little doubt that delays would have continued had it not been for the outcry of public opinion on both sides, demanding that some type of exchange program be established.

In July, 1862, after the war had been raging for more than a year, an agreement was finally reached and exchanges were begun. The agreement called for prisoners to be exchanged on a one-for-one basis; that is, a private for a private, a general for a general, etc. A scale of values was also agreed upon, whereby a general was the equivalent of 60 privates, with other ranks assigned lesser values. It was also decided that exchanges in the west would take place at Vicksburg, with those in the east at City Point.

Several problems immediately arose in connection with this cartel, however. The day before the agreement was to be signed, Union Secretary of War Edwin Stanton issued an order which allowed Union commanders to seize property belonging to citizens who were deemed disloyal. In retaliation, Governor John Letcher of Virginia filed a request with his War Department which would have Union officers tried for treason and inciting slave insurrection. Further, Confederate President Jefferson Davis stated that the Union's actions constituted uncivilized warfare, and that any captured officers who carried out Stanton's edict would be considered robbers and murderers rather than prisoners of war, and would be dealt with accordingly. Amid this atmosphere, the exchange cartel nearly died before it got started.

Once the cartel was ratified, it was heartily welcomed by many soldiers on both sides for reasons other than those intended. Those who had become disenchanted with the war saw capture, and eventual exchange under parole, as a means of getting out of the war. They simply would allow themselves to be captured, give their parole, and go home to sit out the remainder of the war. Some, apparently not wishing to go through the formality of capture, went so far as to forge parole certificates and walk into the nearest parole camp. This added an unforeseen problem to a growing litany of complications, and made a bad situation even worse.

For several months both sides bickered, with charges and counter-charges becoming common occurrences. Both sides also violated portions of the agreement, stretching the wording to suit their respective purposes.

Among these violations was a plan by the Union to use paroled soldiers as guards or Indian fighters, which the Confederacy saw as a means of freeing up other soldiers to do the actual fighting. In turn, on December 24, 1862, the Confederacy declared Major General Benjamin Butler a felon and outlaw for his "excessive behavior", ordering him hanged. President Davis's proclamation also ordered that no captured Union officers would be paroled until Butler received his due punishment. Ironically, Butler would eventually be appointed by the Union as an agent to work on prisoner exchanges, negotiating with Colonel Robert Ould, the Confederate Commissioner of Exchange.

The Confederates also felt that any slaves captured while wearing the Union uniform were to be treated as recovered property and were to be returned to their respective states to be dealt with under state law, rather than exchanged. The white officers of Negro troops were to be put to death.

On December 28, 1862, disgusted with the constant problems, Stanton gave instructions that no officers were to be returned to the Confederacy. The New York *TIMES* quickly predicted that this was merely the first step in a plan to eliminate all exchanges under the cartel.

Within a few months exchanges had all but halted, as the news media had suggested. Some sporadic exchanges took place under special agreements, but it was becoming apparent that the problems which continued to arise were placing a stranglehold on the cartel.

After Ulysses S. Grant assumed command, exchanges virtually stopped. Grant believed that prisoner exchanges actually were more beneficial to the South than to the North, considering the superior manpower availability in the North. He would eventually say "...every man we hold, when released on parole or otherwise, becomes an active soldier against us at once, either directly or indirectly."

Under the terms of the cartel, prisoners were to have been exchanged within 10 days of their capture. If this step had been properly carried out, many of the deaths associated with the rigors of prison life would have been avoided.

The reduction of exchanges made it necessary for the two governments to develop more extensive prison systems in order to hold all those captured. Among the several prisons at Richmond was Libby Prison, a building which had been built in 1845 for use as a grocery and tobacco warehouse.

Brigadier General John H. Winder was named to head the Virginia prison system, including Libby. A strict disciplinarian who was not particularly competent, Winder tried to make prison life bearable. As a graduate of West Point, he had been a major in the United States Army when the war began. Following the lead of many Union officers, he had resigned his commission and applied for a commission in the Confederate army.

The commandant of Libby Prison was Major Thomas P. Turner, who showed a marked intolerance and lack of compassion for the prisoners. A cruel and ruthless man, Turner did little to make prison life easier. He was generally despised by the prisoners, and often by his own guards.

Conditions at Libby, whose occupants were all officers, were similar to those in other prisons on both sides. Food was scarce, prisoners slept on the bare floor with no blankets, and conditions were so filthy that visitors were warned not to venture above the second floor because of the vermin. Depression among the prisoners was quite common, and many went insane.

Despite Turner's approach to managing Libby, however, many of the poor conditions were not deliberate. They arose from a number of factors, including human error, overwhelming logistical and distribution problems, politics, war strategies, and often the prisoners themselves, with many of them showing a lack of discipline, low morals, and poor hygiene. In fact, it is generally agreed that it was in the best interest of the Confederacy to take good care of their prisoners if they hoped to gain the support of European nations.

In February, 1864, after several unsuccessful attempts, a group of officers made their escape from Libby by tunneling through the wall and under the street. Their efforts were well documented, but amazingly, no complete listing of escapees has ever been assembled until now. The pages which follow accurately depict their dramatic and heroic feat. The story you will read is true. The characters are shown as they really were, good or bad. Every event is depicted as it actually happened, with no attempt to hide the shortcomings of any of the principals. Their chronicle concludes with the only known listing of escapees, along with other pertinent information, including their ranks and regiments, where they were captured, and whether or not they were successful in their escape attempt.

Mere words could never grasp completely the prison's conditions, the mental states of the prisoners, or what they went through to make their escape. We can only imagine the despair the unfortunate ones felt who were recaptured, knowing that not only were they going back into the prison they had worked so hard to escape, but that they also would probably be treated worse than before for having fled. The author tries to capture the feelings of the moment, but the reader is urged to reflect on what is read, rather than merely read the words for entertainment's sake. It is important that we realize what these brave men did, and do everything in our power to prevent such situations from ever happening again.

Chapter One

"Live Yankees! Live Yankees!" the boys shouted as they ran beside the disheveled group of prisoners marching down Richmond's Cary Street. The year was 1863, early October. The war was into its third year and there was no end in sight.

Col. Thomas E. Rose of the 77th Pennsylvania Volunteer Infantry was a big man, his beard thick and black. He presented an imposing figure, and those under his command sometimes had the feeling that he was indestructible. Now, however, he was limping badly. His foot, broken at Murfreesboro and rebroken at Liberty Gap, throbbed with every step.

He watched the citizens and shopkeepers pouring out into the street in response to the youngsters' shouts. While being transported to Richmond in open flatcars, Rose and his fellow prisoners had become used to the citizens who had inevitably gathered at every rest stop, and eventually had even looked forward to seeing the next group. Now, a new group was assembling, one which included women and children, soldiers and civilians, merchants and shoppers.

Most of the people at the earlier stops had treated them courteously, more as curiosities than enemies, and he anticipated nothing different from the people of Richmond. At some stops the onlookers had even given them water, and in one small town an old man with a full, white beard, apparently a Union sympathizer, approached Rose and pretended to negotiate a trade for Rose's cap. Instead, however, the old man had said in a soft whisper, while putting on a show of examining the Union officer's kepi, "Don't let 'em get you down, boy. As long as y'all are alive y'all got a chance. Never give up hope."

Rose knew the old man had been placing himself in danger and had been impressed with his courage. Now, he mulled over the heartening words. He didn't know what loomed ahead but he certainly hoped he could maintain some semblance of a positive outlook until he was free again.

Rose wiped the sweat from his brow and looked straight ahead, ignoring the dust in his throat which was being kicked up by the hundreds of prisoners marching with him. As he marched he recounted the string of events which had brought him to the capital of the Confederacy. Much had happened over the past few weeks, and he wanted to remember as much detail as he could until he was able to find a pencil and continue the diary he had been keeping. He thought about the horrors of Chickamauga, his capture there, and the excruciating injury to his foot. Smiling slightly, he remembered how he had escaped, only to be hunted down and recaptured while wandering through the dense pine forests of North Carolina. Marched to a stockade, he had been placed on a flatcar and transported to Richmond, a trip that had taken several days.

The train had only moved at about 10 miles per hour, and he had given serious thought to jumping off and scrambling into the thicket, as several others had done. The flatcars were so crowded that he didn't think he would be missed immediately. Even with his injured foot he had thought he might be successful, but when the guards shot two would-be escapees he had decided to wait for a better opportunity. Perhaps at one of the many delays at sidings, he had hoped, but the guards never looked away from their reluctant cargo.

The guards had told the prisoners they were being sent to Richmond to be part of a prisoner exchange. Many of the men had believed them, and even now many of them were talking excitedly about going home. Rose instinctively knew better, although he held out hope that he was wrong. Logic told him his instincts were right, though. After all, hadn't he himself said the same thing in the past to prisoners in his charge, just to keep them quiet?

Now, here he was, walking through the streets of Jeff Davis's capital, although it wasn't exactly the victorious entry he had envisioned when he volunteered for service. Neither a victor nor a liberator, he was here, nonetheless, and only time would tell what part he would play, if any, in this war's history.

The crowd grew larger and louder with each passing minute, and several of the more vocal citizens tried to engage in conversation with the prisoners. "What do y'all think of the rebellion, now, Yank?" shouted a tall, thin man wearing an eye patch.

Rose ignored the man, as well as the other catcalls raining down on the prisoners. Looking neither left nor right, Rose heard an exasperated guard shouting at the citizens, "Y'all get out of the way and leave us through! We brung these men clean from Atlanta and we ain't about to see them escape in the crowd just 'cause y'all want to get a closer look."

The crowd parted momentarily, but then closed again as others, who either had not heard the guard or chose to ignore him, took the places of those who had stepped aside. The pace had slowed noticeably, often amounting to little more than a shuffle. The crowd was not unruly, however, and Rose felt no anxiety. He just wanted to get to wherever it was they were going, and take the weight off his throbbing foot. After what he had been through the past few weeks he felt much older than his 33 years.

From his position near the front of the procession, Rose could see several soldiers standing in formation as the group approached a large building. Their presence told Rose that the march was nearing its end; something was about to happen. What was that building, and why was it surrounded by troops? A huge brick structure, it seemed to consume the entire city block on which it stood. Something did not seem right; Rose could not put his finger on it, but somehow he sensed that this building was going to play some part in the outcome of his capture. Whether it would be good or bad was still to be determined. Would this be the promised exchange? Rose could only hope.

Those hopes were quickly dashed, however. The disorganized group straggled to a stop, those in the rear walking up on the heels of those in front. Rose's eyes were drawn to the large building, and he felt a sickening feeling in his stomach when he saw the barred, glassless windows, wan faces peering out forlornly. Then he saw the sign. "Libby and Son, Ship Chandlers and Grocers," it practically shouted in bold, black letters. He realized then that his intuition had been correct: there would be no prisoner exchange. He had heard of this place from men who had escaped, and none of what he had heard was good. He was about to enter the notorious Libby Prison.

"Y'all split up now," a stocky sergeant with a red beard shouted at the milling prisoners. "Officers on this side of the street, enlisteds on the other."

Several guards prodded the prisoners with their guns, trying to move them to their proper places more rapidly than the prisoners appeared inclined to move on their own. Slowly the two groups formed, each wondering what would become of the other.

The large crowd of citizens had completely encircled the prisoners by now, each person trying desperately to get a better look at these men, their enemies. The guards were doing an admirable job in keeping the crowd at bay, and despite all the jostling, the people seemed to be in a festive mood.

"Why don't y'all go back up North and leave us poor dirt farmers alone?" a man shouted at no prisoner in particular.

Another man shot back, "This prob'ly ain't a good time to make 'em that offer, friend."

The crowd laughed appreciatively.

"Why don't y'all let 'em loose, one at a time?" yelled another, addressing his query to a nearby guard. "My hounds could use some exercise!"

Again, guffaws sounded at the thought of the man's dogs chasing an unfortunate prisoner through the streets of Richmond, doing God only knows what, once they caught up with him.

As the crowd continued to mock the men, Rose was startled by the blast from a guard's musket just behind him. Turning sharply, he could see the dust still rising from the bricks around a window on the third floor of the prison, where the minie ball had struck. "Y'all keep your Yankee heads inside or I'll shoot 'em off, I swear I will," the guard was shouting up in the direction of the window. "There ain't nothin' down here y'all have to see."

Rose wondered if the guard was as angry as he sounded, or merely enjoying some fun at the expense of the poor wretches near the window? "If he plans on using me for a target, he'd better do it within the next few days," Rose vowed to himself. "If this's where they're putting us I'm only going to be here a short time."

Although Rose had never been known as a particularly violent man, even in the heat of battle, he would do whatever he had to do in order to make good his escape. He was already making his plans, vague though they still were.

"I'll give yuh ten Federal dollars if'n yuh let me git a closer look at 'em," a man near the front of the crowd said to a guard. The guard looked at him and smiled briefly.

"I wish I could do that. I surely do," he answered. "But if I got caught takin' your money I'd soon be sharin' a place with those Yanks over there. Now if'n y'all had said somethin' to me aways back, 'fore we got here, mebbe we could've worked a deal."

The first man spat in disgust, fingering the knife in his coat pocket. Conspiratorially, he sidled up to the guard. "My brother was killed at Gettysburg. I sure would like to talk to a Yankee, just to see if'n maybe he was there."

"And if'n he was...?" the guard asked without making eye contact with the man.

"If'n he was, I'm prepared to kill 'im!" said the grieving man sharply.

"Now, y'all know I can't allow that," returned the guard. "It ain't that I'm a bit partial to bluebellies, but killin' a man when he ain't in no position to fight back just ain't right. Not only that, it's almost dead-out sure that none of these Yanks was the one who killed your brother."

"They's still Yankees, and that would be good enough," the man retorted. Seeing he would not be getting his revenge this day, he shoved his way back through the crowd. More prisoners would be coming in tomor-

row, and again the next day. "There will be other chances," he thought, looking at the laughing faces which continued to mock the prisoners. "Maybe these others think this is a time for festivities, but I surely don't."

By now the two groups had formed into their respective areas. Rose looked across the street, trying to spot a familiar face. Sixty-four enlisted men from the 77th had been captured with Rose, along with eight other officers, and he mentally wished them all Godspeed as he watched the enlisted men being led away.

"Y'all are going to get a chance to partake of some of our Southern hospitality," one of the guards said, sarcastically. He and his compatriots began herding the officers into the former warehouse. "Welcome to the Hotel de Libby. Sorry we ain't got nobody to take your bags to your room."

The prisoners shuffled through the doorway and into the building which, despite the brightness of the day, was ominously dark inside. The men entered through a large door, finding themselves in a room which seemed to extend forever. The darkness made it difficult to accurately gauge its size, but Rose was able to see the contrasting brightness of the windows at the far end of the room and determine that it was probably bigger than any room he had ever been in before. It had apparently been one of the storage rooms when the building had been a warehouse, but the Confederates had converted it into offices and sleeping quarters, judging from the appearance. It looked too clean to be a prison, and Rose surmised this area must be for the use of the prison officials.

Once inside the cavernous room, the prisoners were led, one at a time, to an area which had been set aside as an office. Rose could see those in the front of the line entering the office, staying for a few minutes, then coming out and forming a new group toward the end of the room, where they sat or milled about. When this group's size reached twenty or twenty-five, a guard would escort them to their quarters, returning for the next group. Those whose turn to go into the office had not yet come, a group which included Rose, huddled silently, moving forward only when another prisoner exited the office.

Curious about his new home, Rose looked around. Through the shadows he could see the set of stairs leading up to the next floor, but little else. Beyond the windows he could see the leaves of trees wafting gently in the fall breeze. Back in Pennsylvania the leaves would be starting to take on the red, orange, and yellow hues of early autumn, but it was still late summer here in Virginia, and the leaves were still green. He fought back a sudden wave of homesickness, as he thought of his beloved Lydia and their children. Autumn had been the favorite time of year for the Rose family, as they often walked in the woods and enjoyed the smells and colors together. He had only seen his wife and children once in the last two years and he promised himself that they would enjoy autumn in Pennsylvania again, and it would be together. Never again would a walk in the woods in October with Lydia be something he would take for granted.

"Y'all seen much fightin', Colonel?" said a guard standing next to Rose.

Rose looked at his inquisitor. The guard was about Rose's size but younger, possibly not even out of his teens yet. The man smiled, revealing a set of tobacco-stained teeth. "Some," Rose answered suspiciously, not sure what the guard's motive for asking may have been.

The guard apparently sensed Rose's reluctance to speak, and quickly blurted out, "I don't mean yuh no disrespect, Colonel. Honest, I don't. It's jest, well...we're prob'ly gonna be here a while, judgin' from the speed we're movin'. I figger we might about as well get ourselves acquainted."

Rose eyed the man for a few moments. He didn't seem like a bad sort. Friendly enough. Maybe having a friend, or at least an acquaintance, on the guard staff could come in handy.

"I don't guess that would hurt anything," said Rose.

"Where all yuh been?" the guard continued after a short silence.

"Mostly small skirmishes," Rose replied. "Only big ones were Pittsburg Landing, Stones River, Liberty Gap...then there was Chickamauga. That's where you boys got me." Rose looked away, not really wishing to remember the hand to hand fighting in which he had participated.

"Yeah," the guard persisted. "I wasn't at Chickamauga, but I was at Shiloh. That's what y'all are callin' Pittsburg Landin', ain't it? Guess we both lost a lot of good men there, didn't we?"

Rose sighed. It had been a bloody battle indeed. He merely nodded, trying not to see the faces in his mind, the faces of his friends who didn't survive. Ironically, one of his men who had been wounded there, Corporal William Jack from Company B, had been captured with him at Chickamauga.

"Y'all reckon mebbe we shot at each other at Shiloh, Colonel?" the guard went on, now sporting a sheepish grin.

Rose looked back at the man. "Possibly," he acknowledged.

The guard looked down at the floor, then back up at Rose, still grinning. "Reckon it's a good thing we're both bad shots, then, ain't it?" he drawled.

Behind his full beard Rose couldn't repress a grin himself, despite his circumstances. The irony, if the two had indeed faced one another across the battle lines, was not lost on him.

The line pressed forward, bringing the guard back to his task at hand. "Y'all keep movin', move on up, now," he shouted, even though the line was doing just that before he even thought of issuing his command. He took a few steps back so he could survey the entire length of the formation.

When the line stopped again the guard came back to Rose and picked up the conversation as if it had never stopped. "Shiloh the worst fightin' yuh seen?"

"Nope," answered Rose, nodding a greeting toward one of his officers, Lieutenant David Garbet of Company G, coming out of the office. "Liberty Gap was the worst for us." He wandered off again into the privacy of his thoughts. A full one-third of his regiment had been lost at Liberty Gap. In fact, Liberty Gap was where he had taken command of the brigade after Colonel John F. Miller, from the 29th Indiana, had been wounded and unable to continue.

"I don't know much about Liberty Gap," Rose heard the guard saying, his voice interrupting Rose's thoughts. "Ain't even sure what state it's in. This much I do know, though. When it gits down to the serious fightin', a minie ball don't pay no mind to a man's rank. It'll go through a colonel like you jest as quick as it will through a poor ole private like me, and that's a fact."

Before Rose could reply, another guard approached and indicated that it was his turn to enter the office. "Keep yer head down, if'n y'all ever get back to the fightin', Colonel," the first guard shouted to Rose with a laugh, as Rose disappeared into the office.

"You can count on that," Rose mentally retorted. "I'll keep my head down, and I'll definitely get back into battle."

Stepping inside the office, he saw an officer seated at a desk in the center of the room, and two dirty-looking guards near the windows. The room was brighter than the main room, but still there was nothing cheerful about it. It was furnished with only a desk and a few chairs. A Confederate flag stood in the corner, and a portrait was hanging on the wall behind the desk. Looking at the picture, Rose assumed it was a likeness of President Jefferson Davis, but suddenly realized that he really had no idea what Davis looked like. Even though he had spent the last two years of his life trying to defeat him, Rose would not have recognized him if he had been standing in this room.

Several captured regimental battle flags and cavalry guidons adorned the walls, and behind the desk a Union flag was hanging upside down. If it had been deliberately placed in that fashion to raise the ire of the incoming prisoners it was serving its purpose in Rose's presence.

"Come on in, Colonel," said the man behind the desk when he spied the insignia on Rose's coat. The officer gave off an air of aristocracy as he stood and leaned across his desk, extending his right hand to Rose in an unexpected gesture of friendship. Taken aback, Rose hesitated, then took the offered hand. His grip was firm but the hand was soft.

"Adjutant Latouche," he said, as a way of introducing himself. Standing ramrod straight, his resplendent uniform presented a sharp contrast to the shabby attire of the guards, or to Rose's own battle-worn garb, for that matter.

"We're going to give y'all some relief from soldierin' for a while, Colonel," he went on in a soft voice. "I do hope y'all enjoy your stay with us."

Latouche took a cigar from his coat and bit the end off. Lighting it and puffing, he almost disappeared in a shroud of blue smoke. Rose watched him as he walked around the desk, approaching Rose in a manner not unlike that of an old friend. "As a general rule," he said slowly, exhaling another blue cloud, "I don't take much to Yankees. But that doesn't mean we can't be civil to each other, does it?"

Rose nodded his agreement, watching with disdain the adjutant's pompous movements. Was it merely because he was the enemy, or was there some other reason for disliking this man? Rose wasn't sure, but he knew this was not someone he wanted to get to know better.

"I'm sorry Major Turner couldn't be here himself today to check y'all in, but I'm sure y'all will be here long enough to meet him eventually. Now, I'd like a few questions answered so we can fill in the register. Courtesies of war, you know. Then these gentlemen will conduct a search for any contraband y'all may be carrying."

By contraband, Rose knew Latouche was referring to greenbacks, Federal money. At the current exchange rate he was sure anything the guards took from him would never be returned, even though both governments had agreed that prisoners would get their money back in small amounts while they remained prisoners, or in a lump sum when the prisoner was exchanged.

"Your soldiers have already taken care of that matter," Rose said acidly, remembering how his captors had confiscated anything of value almost as soon as he had been captured. Many of the prisoners had hidden their money behind their chaws of tobacco when it had become apparent that their captors were helping themselves to whatever they could find. Rose himself had quickly hidden his money behind his belt buckle, a hiding place that had not yet been discovered.

"Well, we'll just check to be sure," Latouche answered. "After all, we don't want our prisoners bribin' our guards, don't you agree? It just doesn't look good."

Rose knew he would have no choice, and sat down in the chair the officer gestured toward. Anything the guards found, though, they would have to work for. He wasn't going to make anything easy for them. Whatever anyone could say against Rose, nobody would ever have reason to think he had cooperated with the enemy.

Taking his place behind the desk, Latouche asked Rose his name.

"Thomas E. Rose," came the sullen answer. The adjutant entered it in his log as Row, T. E., then continued.

"And y'all are a Colonel, right?"

Rose didn't answer, his eyes drawn again to the desecrated United States flag hanging on the wall.

"Am I right, Colonel?" he repeated, his voice rising slightly.

His eyes returning to the desk, Rose answered with a brusque, "Yes, you are."

Latouche looked up from his writing, fixing a steely glare on Rose. Rose stared back, refusing to be intimidated. "Don't let them get you down, boy," the old man's voice rang in Rose's ears, taking him back to his clandestine conversation at the train stop a few days earlier.

"And would y'all be so kind as to tell me your regiment, Colonel?" said the adjutant, a touch of sarcasm entering his voice.

"I'm with the 77th Pennsylvania," Rose said boldly, sliding to the front of his chair and leaning forward

Not looking up from his register, Latouche pretended not to notice Rose's agitation. "And where were you captured?"

"Chickamauga," came the answer.

At the sound of the word Chickamauga, the Rebel's eyes seemed to light up.

"We whupped you Yanks pretty bad there, didn't we?" he said with a knowing smile.

"We got our licks in," replied Rose defiantly.

"Well, that's one thing y'all won't have to be bothered with for awhile," Latouche went on. "Just think about it. Only a few days ago people were tryin' to kill yuh. Now y'all can sit back and let someone else do the fightin'."

Rose's eyes flashed. Resisting the impulse to stand up and lean across the desk so his face would be directly in front of his adversary, he squeezed the arms of his chair and said as evenly as he could, "If it's all the same to you, being a guest of Jeff Davis isn't in my plans. It's nothing personal, but as a soldier I believe it's my duty to try to escape. Maybe not today, or next week, or next month. But my time will come. And when it does, I won't be lookin' back."

The adjutant stood and walked slowly to the window, giving no indication that he had been surprised or intimidated by Rose's outburst. "I guess I don't blame yuh," he said after a long, uncomfortable silence. "But I can't say that I fully understand why anyone would want to go back to the fightin'. As for me...well, I've had a bellyful of it, and I hope I don't ever have to kill another man again as long as l live. The sooner this war is over, the better I'll feel. But until it is, y'all do your duty as a soldier and try to escape." Then, he turned and paused, allowing his words to take their fullest effect. "But understand, I'll do my own duty and try to stop yuh."

His eyes were now looking directly into Rose's, and neither chose to look away. After a few tense seconds Latouche said to the guards, without looking away from Rose, "Search him."

Demeaning though it was, Rose refused to show any sign that he resented the intrusion on his person, choosing instead to fix his gaze on the Rebel officer. As the guards went through Rose's pockets, Latouche recited the prison rules. "Y'all will be permitted to send and receive mail, but all mail will be censored. Mail goes out and comes in regularly on flag-of-truce boats. You'll be allowed packages from home, which also will be searched. If we find any Union money, either on your person or in any letter or package, we will confiscate it. Small amounts will then be given to you each month, which y'all can use to buy anything you want from the sutler. And...,"he paused as Rose gathered up his pen knife, diary, and few odds and ends which the guards had allowed him to keep,"...you will be allowed a bath every so often to get rid of the vermin."

Rose looked up as he straightened his coat. "I don't have any vermin," he retorted indignantly. The guards laughed out loud.

"You will, Colonel," said Latouche with a demonic smile, looking pointedly at Rose's beard. "You will."

Chapter Two

Rose ascended the stairs to what he hoped would only be a temporary new home. Spying the new arrivals, several of the other prisoners let out a cry of "Fresh fish! Fresh fish!" This signal that another batch of new prisoners had arrived resulted in a throng pressing to get close enough to ask them questions.

Although he had some idea of what his quarters were going to look like, nothing had prepared him for the appearances of the other prisoners. Entering the doorway he was shocked at the sight of hundreds of dirty, poorly clothed men. Their hair was matted, their skin pallid. Sunken eyes peered out of filthy faces. Their barrage of questions, however, indicated a faint spark of hope still existed.

"How's the war going, Colonel?" said a young officer, hardly allowing Rose to enter the room before asking.

Rose turned to the young man and saw in his face the faces of so many of his young troops who were no longer a part of this life. Softly, he answered, "We're holdin' our own, son. I wish I could tell you we were almost ready to put the rebellion down, but I can't. We will though, I promise you that!"

"Can you tell me anything about the 24th Wisconsin, Colonel?" another shouted out.

"No, I can't. I'm sorry, but I just don't know."

"How close are our boys to Richmond, Colonel?" asked a third, placing a grimy hand on Rose's arm to attract his attention. The eager look on this soldier's face begged for some encouraging news, and this time Rose was able to oblige.

"I can't say for sure," he answered, "but last I heard, Meade was about ready to move into Culpeper."

Rose saw the prisoner's countenance light up, possibly for the first time since he had entered Libby. "Did you hear that?" he shouted to no one in particular. "Meade's taken Culpeper! The troops are comin' this way. We'll be out of here soon!"

Rose did nothing to correct this loose interpretation. Feeling only slightly guilty, he rationalized that this man needed some good news, and maybe by now Meade had indeed taken Culpeper. What could it hurt to let him enjoy his delusion?

As Rose did his best to answer the questions, he noticed that the other prisoners who had been brought upstairs with him were undergoing the same type of interrogation. Answering the questions that were being fired at him in rapid fashion, he noticed that those who didn't have their questions answered to their satisfaction worked their way back to the head of the stairs, patiently awaiting the next newcomer. As each new prisoner was brought into the room, the desperate volley of questions began anew.

Finally, Rose was able to elbow his way through the crush and away from the door, believing that if he could get away from the doorway the questions which were coming from all directions would have to be fielded by someone else. When he reached the edge of the crowd he looked back and saw new faces surrounded by those eager for news from the outside world. As he had hoped, the attention was now being directed to the next group of arrivals.

Hobbling toward the streams of light coming through the windows, he took stock of his surroundings. Reaching the end of the room, he touched the smelly brick wall. His hand came away from the cold surface feeling wet and slimy. The musty odor given off by the walls, foul as it was, was overpowered by the stench from the open privy which was overflowing onto the wooden floor, through the cracks, and down into the room below. Rose struggled to suppress the gagging sensation that originated deep in his stomach. The walls and floors swarmed with bugs and lice, and Rose immediately remembered the ominous comment made by the officer who had registered him, almost promising Rose that he would soon have vermin on his body.

The room was dark, lit only by candle stubs. The meager flickers of light from the candles did little to pierce the pitch-like darkness, particularly near the center of the building where the light from the outside seldom reached. Disheveled prisoners, many wearing filthy bandages over still seeping wounds, occupied themselves by reading or playing chess in the dancing shadows. One with no shoes whittled to pass the time, others talked softly, scarcely noticing the newly arrived colonel. Still others, most likely those who had been in Libby the longest, simply sat and stared, despondent faces masking thoughts of better times in friendlier places.

Nor did these men even look like the soldiers they once had been. The Rebels had "traded" clothing with many of them, and the prisoners had obviously not been the better traders. With their filthy and ill-fitting clothes, none looked like the dashing officers they all must have been when they left their hometowns to the cheers of friends and neighbors. Many were not wearing any shoes. Of those who were fortunate enough to have them, few wore a matched pair. In another time and place, the appearances of some would have even been amusing, but here in Libby, Rose breathed a prayer of thanks that his rank had spared him the indignity of having to give up his clothing.

Few even looked up as Rose passed by, and those who did said little. Other than an occasional "Afternoon, Colonel," or "How do, Colonel?", Rose may as well have been invisible. The desolate feelings of these once-proud soldiers was almost palpable. Rose could not help but marvel at the overwhelming silence, despite the crowd.

Walking through the unfamiliar surroundings in the subdued light, he nearly stumbled over a naked man sitting in the shadows, nonchalantly picking lice out of his filthy clothing. The man glanced up momentarily, looking at Rose yet seemingly not seeing him, and then, wordlessly, returned to his task. A flicker of pity came over Rose, and he hoped that he would never be reduced to picking lice from his clothing for entertainment.

"Pick it up, nigger!" a voice cried out in the darkness, intruding on Rose's thoughts.

Rose turned in the direction of the voice, straining to determine its source.

"You lazy darkies are all alike," the disembodied voice continued. "Not a one of y'all is any good. Now pick it up!"

Through the shadows Rose could make out the form of a slightly built black man, picking up the pieces of firewood which he had apparently dropped. Beside him someone stood menacingly, his arm raised. Rose could barely make out the outline of the stick before it came crashing down across the black man's back.

"Jest like down on the plantation, ain't it, nigger?" the assailant mocked as his unfortunate victim scrambled to gather the wood.

"This is what y'all are sayin' we should let go free," he went on, facing the prisoners who were watching the scene unfold. "These dumb niggers wouldn't last a week if'n we let 'em go free. They's too dumb and too lazy to figger out how to even carry firewood without droppin' it."

By now the man had hastily retrieved the wood, and without a glance at either his antagonist or the prisoners, he resumed his journey to wherever he had been ordered to carry the wood. His guard followed closely behind, verbally abusing him with every step.

"Do they keep slaves in here, too?" Rose asked the prisoner standing beside him, still hearing the continuing harangue.

"No sir, Colonel," the man replied. "Most of the coloreds in here were cooks or servants of some of the officers who were captured. They keep 'em here to do some of the jobs nobody else wants to do, like cookin', sweepin' up, carryin' firewood..." The man's voice trailed off. "Shouldn't beat a man like that, though, no matter what his color," he mumbled.

"Nothin' we say's gonna stop it," another man said. "Happens every day, and we all know it. Turner'll beat that man tomorrow for somethin' else."

"Don't make it right," the first man countered.

"Turner? That can't be Major Turner, can it?" Rose exclaimed.

"No sir," the first man replied. "That there's Captain Turner. There's two Turners, yuh see, and each one of 'em tries to be worse'n the other."

"They related?" Rose asked.

"Only to the devil," came the answer. "I don't see how one family could have two like them in it. Captain Turner there, he doesn't even have reason to be escortin' that darkie. He just does it 'cause he likes to beat on people... 'specially black ones!"

Rose shook his head and squeezed through the crowd, leaving the two to continue their discussion. He wondered how the human race had reached this level, where men could be imprisoned and beaten, and friends could go to war against each other over a difference in philosophy. Although Rose had no strong feelings concerning slavery, he did know it was wrong to mistreat any human being.

Rose continued exploring his new home. The third floor room he was presently in appeared to be at least as large as the office area downstairs, and he remembered passing a similar room on the second floor. Reaching into his pocket he found the pencil which he had deftly picked up from the table downstairs while he gathered his belongings after being searched. Taking his diary from his breast pocket, he began making notes. "If I'm going to escape," he reasoned, "I might just as well get started with the planning."

For the next hour, Rose did nothing but wander around his confinement, pacing off distances and entering the results on the sketch which was slowly beginning to take shape. As large as the prison was, he quickly realized that it would take many explorations like this one to even come close to having a complete floor plan. Without knowing the layout, however, he knew his chances of escape were considerably reduced, and that realization spurred him on.

Reaching a window, he cautiously looked out, remembering the shooting incident of a few hours earlier. He could see the street below and was surprised to observe that many citizens were still milling about, gazing up at the barred windows in hopes of catching a glimpse of a Yankee. By now, the daylight was beginning to fade, and he felt reasonably safe, confident that the gathering dusk would make it difficult for any of the sentries to see him unless he stood directly in front of the window.

"I wouldn't stand there too long, Colonel. Remember what happened when they brought us in."

Rose turned to see a young lieutenant standing next to him. "Yeah, I remember," he answered.

"I thought I'd seen just about the worst the South had to offer, but none of it holds a candle to this place. You think we'll be here long?" asked the lieutenant.

"Not if I can help it, Lieutenant," said Rose, his eyes still lingering on the street below.

If the lieutenant caught the implication of Rose's comment, he allowed it to pass. "They got you at Chickamauga, too, didn't they?"

The mention of Rose's place of capture aroused his interest, and Rose turned his gaze away from the window and looked into the young lieutenant's face. "Too? You mean you were there, too?"

"Yep. As bad as it was, I wish I was still there. At least I was breathin' free air." He paused, then continued. "I saw you on the train on the way up here. I heard you got away once, but they brought you back. I was hopin' you'd make it."

"Not as much as I was, Lieutenant," Rose replied with a wry grin.

The lieutenant smiled at the irony of Rose's comment. "I'm sure that's a fact, sir," he answered.

After a short silence, Rose extended his hand and said, "Colonel Thomas Rose, 77th Pennsylvania."

"How do you do, sir?" answered the lieutenant, shaking Rose's hand. "Lieutenant James Gageby, Company A, 19th U.S. Regulars, and a fellow Pennsylvanian."

"It's always good to see someone from home, Lieutenant. Where in Pennsylvania do you hail from?"

"Johnstown," came the reply. "And you?"

"Bucks County," said Rose. "Do people from your end of the state know how to escape from Rebel prisons?"

"I can't say I've had much experience at it, sir, but I sure am willing to learn. Wouldn't mind havin' my first lesson right now, as a matter of fact."

Rose studied Gageby momentarily. He liked the young man's enthusiasm. And the lieutenant obviously didn't want to stay in Libby any longer than he had to, either. "Looks like we've got a lot in common, Lieutenant. Maybe we can learn together."

As the gaslights on Cary Street came on, Rose and Gageby stood near the window, discussing the war, how they were captured, and most importantly, how they could get out of Libby. By now it was completely dark outside, and the meager candle stubs scattered throughout the room glowed like so many stars. Around them, men were beginning to lie down on the damp floor, preparing to sleep.

As the two watched, prisoners took their places on the floor in an odd pattern: head to head and feet to feet. Nobody gave directions; everybody just seemed to know where and how to lie down. None had any bedding, simply stretching out on the damp wooden floor. Occasionally a burst of laughter would ring out, totally out of place in the gloomy atmosphere. Here and there, a voice could be heard bidding good night to nearby friends. Nearly everyone settling down for the night drew their shirts over their heads. Looking at each other curiously, Gageby said to Rose, "Certainly can't be doin' that to shut out the bright lights, can they?"

Smiling, Rose nodded agreement.

A scruffy looking man, even by Libby Prison standards, who had been seated near Rose and Gageby throughout their conversation stood and approached them. "Couldn't help overhearin' what you were talkin' about earlier, Colonel. If you don't mind my bein'a little forward, I'd like to give both of you some advice on your first night in Libby."

Rose and Gageby looked at the man. He was filthy, with open sores on his hands and face. He smelled as if he had been sleeping in the privy. "We're listening," said Rose, trying not to inhale too deeply in the man's presence.

"First off, you might want to forget about gettin' out of here for now. It used to be pretty easy, but after so many of our boys got away, the Turners decided nobody else was gonna leave without their blessin'. There's two Turners, y'know, and you don't want to cross either of 'em. Major Turner's in charge of the whole prison. Dick Turner seems to be in charge of all the guards. That was him that beat that darkie this afternoon. I hear they ain't relatives, but they may as well be. Neither one's any good. Anybody gets caught tryin' to get out now gets a beatin', then they throw 'im in one of them cells down in the basement. I hear tell those poor wretches don't even get food ever' day. When they come back out of them cells, they don't ever think about escapin' again. That Major Turner, I swear he's the devil hisself! And, by the way, don't make the mistake of thinkin' everyone in here is a Yankee. Major Turner's got some Rebs planted in here to listen in on conversations just like yours. I've known people to get thrown in the basement just for talkin' about escapin'. Turner's spies hear them, they run and tell him, and he takes it from there, so be careful who's around when you're talkin'."

"Thanks for the advice," replied Rose, embarrassed for not having thought of that possibility. "We'll keep that in mind."

"You do that, Colonel," said the man. "Second thing..." he continued, placing a filthy hand on Rose's arm before he could turn away, " ...you better be makin' plans on where you're gonna sleep. You don't want to be too near these windows 'cause the rain blows in. And you don't want to be too near the privy, either. I don't think I have to tell you why that's not a good spot." The man laughed at his own attempt at humor. "Other than that, one place is about as good as another."

Watching the men taking their positions on the floor in the peculiar pattern that was apparently followed by everyone, Rose asked, "What are they doing there? Is there some rule that we haven't been told?"

Looking in the direction of Rose's gaze, the man chuckled. "That's just the way we save space. You can see there isn't much room in here, so we sleep spoon fashion. Only thing bad about that is, when one person wants to roll over, everyone has to roll over. Bein' crowded ain't all that bad, though. Keeps you a little warmer, anyways. By the way, you should put all your clothes on for sleepin'. These floors get mighty cold by mornin' and you might as well be warm for at least part of the night."

Rose was about to thank the man for his advice when the man began again. "You prob'ly noticed that most of us pull our shirts up over our heads when we turn in. I'd suggest you do it, too. Keeps some of the stink out, and it makes it a little harder for the bugs to get in. You prob'ly won't sleep much for a few nights, anyway. The smell keeps most of the new prisoners awake, or wakes 'em up early if they do doze off. After a few nights you'll get used to it, though. Then you'll sleep like a baby."

Before the man could be thanked, he moved away to watch a card game. Rose mentally berated himself for not realizing that there would be spies in Libby. It only stood to reason. He could only hope that the stranger was really a Northerner, and not one of Turner's men playing mind games with him. Rose vowed not to trust anyone, including Gageby, until he could get to know them better. That mistake would not be made again.

"What do you think, Colonel? That spot good enough to bunk in?" asked Gageby, indicating a small open area nearby. "It doesn't look too wet."

"Should be fine," answered Rose absentmindedly, still disturbed about the warning he had just received.

Lying down in the prescribed spoon fashion, the two did their best to get comfortable. It was no easy task, lying on a wet floor with no mattress or blanket, with a sickening stench almost overwhelming them and the bugs crawling over them from all directions.

The sound of an open hand swatting the critters was followed by the lament, "I don't know what I hate the most, the Rebs or these vermin! I swat one and twenty more come to pay their last respects!"

Some of the men laughed at their friend's problem. "I can't understand why any self respectin' bug would come near you," one blurted out. "That's why I always bunk beside you. I figger you'll drive all the critters away and I'll get a good night's sleep."

Not to be outdone, the first man shot back, "Well, your snorin' brings 'em all back. They come flockin' in just to see what all the ruckus is about."

As the banter continued, the familiar strains of the Star Spangled Banner began to fill the room. Opening his eyes, Rose noticed that most of the prisoners were joining in. Before they had reached the midpoint of the first verse, several guards began shouting for the singing to stop.

"Y'all quit that singin' in there or we'll come in and make you stop, ourselves."

The singing continued, only louder, in response to the guard's threat.

"I mean it. If we have to come in there, we will."

"C'mon in, Reb. We're waitin' for you. We'll teach you the second verse!" came the rejoinder from a man near Rose.

"Y'all think I won't? Jest keep it up and we'll see who teaches who a second verse."

"This goes on every night," explained a tall prisoner standing beside Gageby, as the comments were shouted back and forth. The singing in the background only made the scene more bizarre, as each man appeared to try to outsing the person beside him. "We sing patriotic songs to make them mad, and it always works. Then they holler at us, and we holler back and sing louder. They get madder and madder, but they never come in. They know better. Oh, maybe once in a while they'll throw a bucket of canal water on whoever is closest, but that's as far as it goes. We'll keep singin' and they'll keep gettin' madder, 'till we get tired of singin'. Then things quiet down until the next night."

Rose smiled at the game. As the men moved into The Battle Hymn of the Republic, to the accompaniment of more shouts from the guards, he leaned back and closed his eyes. As long as there was a way to annoy the guards, life in Libby would be a little more tolerable.

Chapter Three

As the helpful prisoner had predicted, Rose had not slept well. The stench of his surroundings had kept him awake and semi-nauseous. The hard, cold floor left him feeling stiff, not to mention chilled to the bone. And the sensation of insects crawling over him, whether real or imagined, had him scratching and swatting for the better part of the night.

Apparently Gageby had even more difficulty, for he was already nowhere to be seen. Other prisoners were likewise awake and into their morning routines. Rose looked around and observed shadowy figures cutting wood, others exercising as best they could in the crowded quarters, and still others conversing in muted tones so as not to disturb those still sleeping.

Rose stood and stretched. He rubbed his broken foot, which was still quite sore, possibly even worse than yesterday because of the march from the train station. However, it would still bear his weight, so he wasn't overly concerned. Others around him showed worse signs of injury. Many wore blood-soaked bandages over wounds that were oozing and festering. Just a few feet away a young lieutenant sat, cradling the head of a wounded companion in his lap. The prone man had bandages around his head and eyes, and the bloody dressing on his hand was covered with flies. Infection had apparently set in, as he mumbled deliriously.

"How long's he been like this, Lieutenant?" asked Rose.

"He was wounded a couple of weeks ago, sir, but he's only been this bad the last few days. I'm afraid he's slippin' away."

"Why can't we get him some medical attention?" Rose asked incredulously.

"We tried, Colonel, but Dick Turner said the hospital room was too crowded, and only the worst could go down there."

"Well, he oughtta soon qualify," said Rose, his frustration showing. "Where is the hospital room?"

"First floor, sir. I've never seen it myself, but I hear that most of those that go in never come back out. I don't really think they get much medical help. It sounds like they just put them in there to die," said the lieutenant, his voice rising in anger. "I'd like to get those Turners in here for just a few minutes. I'd give 'em a chance to use their own hospital, and I'd hope they'd leave it the same way our boys do!"

Placing his hand on the young man's shoulder, Rose promised, "I'm going to try to get your friend some help. I'll be back as soon as I have an answer."

Rose saw a tear form in the young soldier's eye. "He's not just a friend, sir," the lieutenant said as the tear ran down his cheek and disappeared in the stubble on his chin. "He's my older brother, and I'd just as soon look after him myself, if it's all the same to you. If he's gonna die I want him to be in friendly arms, not in some Rebel hospital bed with nobody around."

The lieutenant's shoulders shook as he unsuccessfully tried to stifle a sob. Although he had seen death hundreds of times on the battlefield, it was something Rose had never gotten used to, and he was glad for that. He never wanted to be so callous that it didn't hurt when he saw a young soldier grieving for a lost friend or relative.

Unable to talk because of the lump which had formed in his throat, Rose simply patted the lieutenant on the shoulder a few times, then turned and strode away.

Rose could not get the two brothers out of his mind as he walked around the room. Although he quickly regained his composure, the image of the two men could not be obliterated from his thoughts, try as he might. "This war has changed so many lives," he mused. "Even those of us who survive will never be the same again. Maybe our country won't, either."

Speaking occasionally to other prisoners as he walked aimlessly toward the windows, his attention was drawn to a tall, thin man leaning against a post. The smoke from a pipe curled around his head, and now and then a spark would drift from the pipe's bowl as he exhaled. A small pile of chips had accumulated around his feet as he worked with his knife on a piece of wood no larger than a man's hand. Noticing that Rose was watching him, he smiled slightly and held out the carving for Rose to see. The intricate details of the carving fascinated Rose, as a bird in flight was being freed from the block of pine.

"That's quite a talent you have there," Rose commented appreciatively.

The woodcarver looked up, his pride apparent on his face. "Oh, I'm not really all that good, sir. I just do this to pass the time. We have some other fellas in here that are really talented. They can make anything you want. The real good carvers work with pieces of bone, but I can't do that, yet. There's some real good painters here, too. And singers, poets, preachers... you name it, there's probably somebody in here that's good at it."

"I guess there's a pretty diverse group in here, at that," Rose agreed.

The man nodded wordlessly, his fingers continuing to manipulate the carving knife.

Rose observed for several minutes, admiring the carver's ability and comparing it with his own lack of artistic talent. A low growl from the pit of his stomach reminded him that it had been more then twenty-four hours since he had last eaten. "Do they ever feed us in here?" he asked the carver sarcastically.

"Not very much, sir, or very often, for that matter," came the answer, a shower of sparks erupting from the pipe with each word. "They'll bring us something to eat, all right, but it will be when they get around to it. Could be anytime between now and noon. When you see what they bring, you'll ask yourself why you looked forward to it."

"What do we do in the meantime?" asked Rose.

"Well, sir," the carver answered, "Some folks buy from the sutler and cook their own meals. It's not a bad idea, if you can afford it. There's a lot of scurvy in here 'cause the Rebs don't bring us no vegetables. Trouble is, not many of us can afford to buy them from those robbers that call themselves sutlers. If you decide not to buy from the sutler, you'll get two meals a day, if you want to call them meals. We get water, too, but I don't suggest you drink it. They get it directly out of the canal and it usually sits in a bucket for a few days before they freshen it, so most likely it'll make you sick."

"Sounds like I don't have to worry about getting fat in here, then," Rose muttered softly.

"No, sir, you don't at that. Look around you and tell me how many fat prisoners you see in here," answered the man.

In spite of himself, Rose glanced around, knowing full well what he would see. As implied, none of the prisoners showed any signs of being overweight.

"Once all you fellas from Chickamauga get settled in they'll assign you to a mess. Colonel Tilden'll do that. Lieutenant Colonel Sanderson, he's in charge of the kitchen. Calls himself the culinary director. He sets up the eatin' schedules. Each mess has a mess sergeant who gets the rations from the Rebs. He'll assign a couple men to do the cookin' for the whole mess. Rations are pretty slim, so the cookin' part ain't too hard. It's the cleanin' up after that I can do without. Only have to do it once every few weeks, though, so it ain't too bad. Your turn'll come."

"I've never been much of a cook," replied Rose.

"Don't have to be, Colonel. You won't find too many in here that'll complain about the cookin'. It's what's cooked that they complain about."

"Thanks for the culinary information," said Rose. "I think I'll just stretch my legs a little until they bring something to eat."

"Suit yourself, Colonel," came the reply. "I'll still be here when you get back. One thing's sure, I don't have any place special to go today."

Rose smiled and gave the man a nod, then began working his way closer to the windows. Reaching them, he cautiously peeked out. The sun was beginning to come up, and it looked like it would be a beautiful Virginia day. Outside these walls, it would, anyway. Sunrise was Rose's favorite time of day, and he never got tired of seeing the world around him coming to life.

In the half light of dawn Rose watched the forms of Confederate guards carrying something out of the prison and throwing it onto a pile. Some of Richmond's early risers walked beneath his window, their voices unintelligible despite the quiet of the hour. Looking into the rising sun, the buildings of the city appeared as silhouettes, and from Rose's vantage point, Richmond appeared to have been spared the ravages of war thus far, appearing as normal as any city in the North.

As the morning light grew brighter, Rose watched the movements of the guards with greater interest. The forms which they had been carrying to the growing pile now took on a familiar shape. Despite the distance, Rose could now make out the stiffened limbs of human bodies jutting out from the pile at odd angles. He involuntarily clenched his fists, his fingernails digging into the flesh. Even to a man hardened by the sights of battle, this was a sickening sight. At least the bodies on the battlefield were treated with respect, even those of the enemy.

As he watched in anger, wanting to look away but being drawn back by a morbid curiosity, he felt the presence of someone else behind him. Turning to acknowledge his fellow observer's presence, his eyes were drawn to the colonel's insignia on the man's uniform.

The man smiled at Rose's look of surprise. "I'm Colonel Abel Streight," he said. "I've been here for five months now, so I guess you could say I'm one of the old timers in here. I try to meet as many of the new arrivals as I can. I must say, though, Chickamauga made my job as a greeter a lot busier."

"Nice to know you, Colonel," Rose replied, as he introduced himself.

Although Rose wanted to know more about the dead men he had seen being carried out, Streight was obviously interested in learning more about Chickamauga. The two men conversed about the battle for a few minutes, Rose filling the colonel in on the details. Then, in a brief lull in the conversation, Rose asked, "Where are all those bodies coming from out there?"

Streight glanced out the window, then somberly looked back to Rose. "The Rebs are cleaning out the dead room."

"What's the dead room?" Rose asked, half knowing the answer before he formed the question.

"Those are the poor wretches who died during the night," came the reply. "The guards take them all down to the dead room, then they haul them out to the street in the morning."

"Aren't they at least going to give them a decent burial?" Rose asked, with a hint of exasperation in his voice.

"Oh, they'll get buried eventually, Colonel. Later today some of the coloreds will be taken out on burial detail. It's not a job anyone wants, though, even if it means getting outside for a few hours. Those bodies will lie out in the sun for the better part of the day before they'll be buried, so it really isn't very pleasant work."

Rose could feel the anger rising within him again. These men had been soldiers, someone's sons or husbands, and they deserved better.

"As unpleasant as it is, sometimes I think those men lying out there to bloat up in the heat of the day are the lucky ones. They'll not have to spend another hour in this hole!" Streight said quietly.

"I'm beginning to see how Libby got its reputation," said Rose, "and I've been here less than a day."

Before Streight could say anything in reply, a guard on the street below shouted in a loud voice, "Sutler's here! Sutler's here!"

"Well, Colonel, I've got other prisoners to greet. It's been nice talking with you. I hope we can get to know each other better," said Streight, his hand outstretched.

"Thank you, Colonel," said Rose, grasping the extended hand. "I do as well."

Rose watched as the colonel walked away. Streight seemed like he would be a good man to get to know. Their common rank would allow them to talk freely, and if he indeed had been in Libby for five months, he would surely know the prison's layout. And its weaknesses. Weaknesses which could be exploited. Having been in Libby for a relatively long time he may also be someone who had the respect of the prison officials. That could be useful, as well. Rose had no way of knowing that Streight was the one prisoner the authorities hated more than any other, the one least likely to command their respect.

After the colonel disappeared into the crowd, Rose worked his way downstairs to another room which was new to him, and where the milling prisoners indicated the presence of the sutler in the doorway. Four guards surrounded the sutler's cart, preventing even the most foolhardy from attempting to get past the cart and break for freedom. As Rose neared the group he could hear a voice with a southern accent saying, "Union greenbacks! I only accept Union greenbacks!"

The sutler obviously recognized the value of federal dollars as opposed to those of the Confederacy. Peering over the heads of those in front of him, Rose was able to make out the small hand-printed prices. Even though he had been able to hide over a hundred dollars behind his belt buckle, he knew it wouldn't last long if he dealt with the sutler very often. Brown sugar was advertised at $12 per pound, butter at $11 per pound. A block of cheese, and a small block at that, sold for $10. "I've got fresh Chesapeake oysters at only $6 a quart," the sutler was telling one of the prisoners. "How many quarts do you want?"

The prisoner simply shook his head, then pushed his way back through the crowd in frustration, not saying a word.

Rose observed the bargaining for a few minutes, then bought a tooth-brush, for which he paid $3. "Looks like I'm going to have to depend on Libby's chefs for my meals," he mused to himself. "Only the rich, and I don't see many of them in here, will be able to afford these prices."

Promising himself he would return to this room to examine it better after the sutler left, he walked back upstairs and took a position beside the window on the east side of the building. Trying not to look at the pile of bodies he had observed earlier, Rose looked out over the city of Richmond. Under other circumstances, the view would have been enjoyable. To his left he could see the canal and the river, the city's buildings rising straight ahead. Then, he saw something which made his pulse quicken! There, out in the center of the street, several workmen were lowering themselves down into a hole. "That has to be the sewer," Rose thought. "They're going down to work in the sewer!"

Rose quickly looked around, not knowing whether he had spoken out loud in his excitement. None of the other prisoners looked his way, to his relief. Turning his attention back to the workers, who by now had disappeared under the street, Rose took out his diary and added the information to his drawing. A sewer would most likely lead to either the canal or the river, he deduced. If a man could find a way to get to that sewer he could follow it to its outlet. Wherever the outlet was, he was sure that it would lead to freedom.

Buoyed by his discovery, he spent the next few hours wandering from room to room, window to window. He took copious notes, and made meticulous sketches. As he learned more about the building he refined the sketches. Somewhere, on that floor plan, would be the clue that would tell him how he could get to that sewer.

He now knew that there was a third room on each level, with each room extending more than 100 feet, and being at least half that wide. On the top floor and the floor below, doorways had been cut into the stone walls, allowing free movement between rooms. He learned also that he was permitted to pass unhindered between the two floors. This gave him six large rooms to work with, plus the center room on the first floor, and surely there would be a way out of one of them.

The center room on the first floor, where he had visited the sutler's cart, was accessible to the prisoners during the daytime and was used as a cooking room. This room, situated between the office area and the hospital, was called the kitchen by the prisoners, and it contained two stoves. Behind each stove was a fireplace. The massive door leading out to the street, where the sutler had set up shop, was now barred and guarded. This room was the only room in the prison in which Rose had seen anything resembling furniture, other than the office. Several long pine tables gave the men a place to prepare their meals and eat. Permanent benches were affixed to each table. The floor was covered with water and human waste from broken water lines and waste troughs, and the stench was unlike anything he could recall ever smelling before, even upstairs.

A second cooking area had been established in the east basement, directly beneath the hospital. This area had a number of large cauldrons placed into a crudely built furnace. As nearly as Rose could determine from his conversations with other prisoners, the other two basement rooms were not used for anything, although someone had told him that part of the center basement room contained cells for unruly prisoners, or for those who had tried to escape. This information tallied with what the odorous prisoner had told Rose and Gageby last night. It had sent a chill up his spine, and he vowed that he would never verify this bit of information by personal experience.

Among other things, Rose observed that the Confederates had chosen their prison well. It was ideally suited for its present use. Standing completely detached from any other building and surrounded by a street on each side, it afforded relatively easy guarding with a limited number of sentries.

Consulting his sketch, Rose counted a total of twelve rooms in the prison. One of these was the office area, and another was the hospital. Obviously neither of these would afford much opportunity for access or escape. This left him with ten remaining rooms. Those on the upper floors would be of no use, nor would the first floor cooking area because of the guards' constant presence. His mind kept coming back to the basement. That would probably have to figure heavily in his escape plans.

As he studied his notes, a commotion at the door caught his attention. The guards were bringing in the food for those not yet assigned to a mess! Following the crowd, he eventually worked his way to the front. Soup had been brought in by the guards in huge wooden buckets. His excitement at finally getting something to eat was quickly tempered when he looked into the buckets. The gray concoction smelled almost as bad as it looked. Mostly water, small pieces of rancid bacon could be seen here and there, interspersed with what appeared to be small grains of rice and a few beans. As the guard scooped some into his bowl, Rose got a closer look. What he had thought to be rice wasn't rice at all. The white particles floating on top of the water were maggots that had boiled out of the bacon!

"Beans and bugs, Colonel, beans and bugs," chortled the guard, responding to the look of disgust that had involuntarily appeared on Rose's face. "Just drink it through yer clenched teeth and ya'll should be able to strain most of the white things out." The guard was obviously enjoying his job, as he continued to dish out the gruel.

Although he had often been hungry when on the march, he had always been able to forage something to eat. Never in his worst dreams did he ever imagine having to eat what had just been placed before him. Looking around the room, he noticed that everyone was eating the gruel despite its contents. "Judging from everything else I've seen so far in here, the next meal probably isn't going to be much better, either," he rationalized to himself. "I'll need my strength if I'm going to get out of here, and I am pretty hungry."

Picking the maggots out of the soup with his fingers, he steeled himself for what had never been an unpleasant task before. Closing his eyes, he raised the cup to his lips and drank it as quickly as he could. The prisoner beside him couldn't suppress a chuckle.

"You'll never get used to it, Colonel. I've been here since Gettysburg, and I'm here to tell ya that the only good thing about the meals the Rebs give us is that there's never enough for us to have seconds. Sometimes a man gets hungry enough he'll eat anything. Even two cups of this swill. I'm glad I don't have the choice."

Rose looked at the man as he wiped his mouth on the back of his hand. "I don't remember ever eatin' anything that was still movin' before," he said.

The prisoner, who had probably been considered handsome before entering Libby, smiled. "Every once in a while we all put our money together and buy a real meal from the sutler, complete with vegetables. Those days you forget all about meals like this, even if it's only for a few hours."

"If this is what the meals are like in here, you can count me in the next time you do that," said Rose.

"Be glad to," said the young man, extending his hand. "I'm Captain Starr, 104th New York."

Rose introduced himself. "The guards must not eat their own cookin'," he said.

"I don't imagine they do," replied Starr, "but I hear the Rebs don't have a whole lot either. Nothin's gettin' through since our boys have been tearin' up all their railroads. Colonel Streight and some others have been tryin' to get Washington to send some better food down, but we haven't seen any so far. Even if it gets here, Major Turner'll probably take what he wants first. Then Dick Turner'll take the leavin's."

"I'm going to have to meet these Turners," said Rose. "I keep hearin' about them. Are they really that bad?"

"Whatever you've heard, they're worse. I don't think you really want to meet them, sir. They're as vile as they come. Even their own guards hate them! I hear tell Major Turner got himself drummed out of West Point for forgery. That oughtta give you some idea of the type of man he is," Starr spat out with contempt. "And Dick Turner was a bootblack, I hear. Sounds about right. His heart's as black as any pair of boots he ever cleaned."

"Well," said Rose, standing up, "maybe we'll get to meet them under better circumstances some day, like on the end of a rope!"

"There's a thousand men in here that'll tie the knot, sir," came Starr's rejoinder.

"Sounds like you might be at the front of the line, Captain," said Rose, his eyes twinkling.

"That you can count on, sir," Starr said with a smile. "But I'll let you pull it tight."

"Fair enough," Rose laughed. Then, preparing to leave, he looked at Starr and, remembering what he had just eaten, said, "Maybe I'll see you at the next banquet!"

"I'll be here, sir," Starr replied as Rose worked his way toward the stairs

Later that afternoon, Rose visited the basement cook room. Only a few others were in the room, affording him the opportunity to do some more exploring without arousing suspicion.

Picking up a candle, he slowly worked his way toward the north end of the room, eventually blending into the shadows as the other men engaged in conversation. Once away from the cooking area, the room was unremarkable until he came to an area where the floor was covered with straw as deep as his knees. Raising his candle, he saw that the straw extended beyond the reaches of the light.

Taking a step into the straw, he felt a scurrying under his feet. Rats! There must have been hundreds of them! Everywhere he looked the straw seemed to be alive.

Another step, more scurrying. "Surely the Rebs didn't put this straw down here just to keep the rats happy," he thought. The straw did make an ideal place for the rodents, though, and he had no doubts that the rats were everywhere the straw was stored.

Grabbing a rake which was leaning against a nearby post, he smacked the straw ahead of him as he wandered through it, sending squealing rats in all directions. "As disgusting as this room is, it could have some advantages," he thought. "If I was a guard, I'd never come in here. This place could prove useful to me."

As he contemplated his surroundings, Rose became aware of a new sound. He quickly blew out his candle and stood motionless. The muffled but unmistakable disturbance of the tinder-dry straw continued. Different from the noise made by the scurrying rats, it grew louder. It seemed to be coming from the other side of a stack of barrels. Rose tensely listened, a cold sweat breaking out on his upper lip. Someone else was down here!

Slowly, a soft glow began to materialize to his right, the glow of a candle. Was the man friend or foe? Had he seen Rose? The scurrying of the rats continued as the man worked his way in Rose's direction. Rose grasped the rake handle tightly and drew it back. He wouldn't use it if the man didn't see him, but he would do whatever the situation called for.

The soft sound of footsteps in the straw grew louder as he drew closer. Soon, the glow of the candle emerged from behind the barrels, revealing a blue uniform. "At least he's a Yankee," thought Rose, still maintaining his grip on the rake handle.

After a few more stealthy steps the man stopped, apparently sensing Rose's presence. With the heightened awareness of a wild animal, he stood motionless, only his eyes moving back and forth as he tried to pick out Rose's form in the darkness. "Who's there?" he finally whispered loudly.

Rose, still not certain of the man's motives, remained silent.

"I know there's somebody here," the voice said apprehensively. "Who is it?"

Rose, choosing to believe the man actually was a Northern officer, whispered back, "Over here. I'm one of the prisoners."

The intruder looked in the direction of Rose's voice. Then, still unable to make out Rose's form in the shadows, he said, "Come toward the light so I can see you. It's all right, I'm a prisoner, too."

Slowly Rose made his way toward the glow of the candle, still clutching the rake and ready to use it as a weapon, if necessary.

The man gave out a mild oath when he saw Rose. "You might just as well shoot me as scare me to death," he said, visibly relaxing in the dim light. Then, spying the insignia on Rose's coat, he quickly said, "Oh, I'm sorry, sir. I didn't realize..."

"That's all right," said Rose. "You had no way of knowing. And by the way, you didn't do my heart any good, either."

"I'm sorry for that, sir. I just never expected to see anyone else down here and you took me by surprise."

"You come down here often, do you?"

"This is only the second time. I just came down to look around and see if I can find a way out," came the answer. "Haven't had much good fortune so far, though."

Placing the rake aside, Rose remembered the conversation he had with the man who had warned him of Turner's spies. He couldn't believe that this man was not who he said he was. Why would anyone come down here on the chance he would catch a prisoner trying to find a way out? He chose to trust him. Maybe they could work together toward their common goal of getting back to the North.

"What's your name, soldier?" Rose asked.

"Hamilton, sir. Andrew Hamilton. I'm a captain in the 12th Kentucky Cavalry, or at least I was until they put me in here. I've only been here about a week and I hate it already."

Rose introduced himself, saying, "I think we're both down here for the same reason. Maybe we can work together." Taking out his floor plan, he proceeded to show Hamilton the information he had accumulated.

Hamilton had his own information, which he was willing to share, and the two conversed excitedly about possible escape.

"From what I've found out so far," said Hamilton, "I think our best hope for getting out of here involves this part of the basement. Upstairs we call it Rat Hell, and I think you can see why."

"You've named it well, Captain," agreed Rose, as the movement continued under the straw.

"The fellows I've talked to have never known the guards to come in here," offered Hamilton. "They'll come into the other part of the room, but they don't like these rats. Can't say as I blame them."

"Why is all this straw here?" asked Rose. "If the straw wasn't here the rats probably wouldn't be either."

"The Rebs used it for bedding up in the hospital, for a while," came the answer. "They don't seem to use it any more, though, so nobody ever comes into this part of the building."

"That can help us. Is there any way out of this room that will get us to the street?" asked Rose.

"None that I know of," said Hamilton. "And even if there was, the sentries would almost be sure to see anyone who stepped outside."

Rose told Hamilton about the workers he had seen entering the sewer. "We've got to find a way to get to that sewer," he said. "If we can't get out a door, there's only one other way I can think of."

Hamilton looked puzzled in the dim light. "I've searched this cellar high and low and I haven't found a way. What's your idea?"

Rose looked at Hamilton for a moment, trying to gauge his determination. Satisfied that anyone who was willing to come down into a dark, foul-smelling cellar and walk around with rats, just to find a means of escape, had all the resolve he would need, Rose queried, "How do you feel about digging a tunnel, Captain?"

Chapter Four

Hamilton's enthusiasm for digging a tunnel matched that of Rose's, and the two immediately separated to forage around the rat-infested basement for any kind of tool that could be used in the process. After an hour long search, however, their combined efforts produced only a broken shovel.

"That'll have to do," said Rose, when Hamilton showed him the prize.

"How 'bout a case knife, Colonel?" queried Hamilton. "Mine's in pretty good shape, and it's better than nothin'."

"It's worth a try," answered Rose. "I never thought about a case knife. I have one, too. Maybe between the two knives and the shovel we'll have everything we need."

"I found something else, too, Colonel," Hamilton offered with a half grin. "There's an old room over that way, and unless I miss my guess it's on the side of the building we need to dig from. That'll give us a good place to work from, with a little privacy, to boot, if the Rebs come down here for any reason."

"Good job, Mr. Hamilton!" Rose said with mock formality.

"Thank you, Mr. Rose," Hamilton shot back in the same tone.

The two laughed and began to work their way toward the abandoned room which Hamilton had located. Blowing out his candle, Rose said, "No need for both of us to have a light. We may need this one later on."

"Sure," Hamilton said with a chuckle. "Let the lowly captain carry the candle for the Rebs to shoot at." He turned and smiled at Rose to let him know there was no malice in what he had said.

Rose grinned in the darkness. He liked this man already. Not only did he have the courage to attempt an escape, he also had a pleasant demeanor. That would make their ordeal more bearable.

"You know, Captain," said Rose, "We're going to be seeing a lot of each other over the course of getting out of here. If you aren't too uncomfortable with familiarity, and Lord knows you don't appear to be, why don't we drop the military titles and call each other by our given names?"

"You want me to call you Thomas?" asked Hamilton, incredulously, stopping in his tracks.

"Why not?" replied Rose. "My mother always did."

"Uh...I don't know about that, sir. That's going to take a little gettin' used to."

"It'll be fine...Andrew."

"Thomas," Hamilton repeated, getting used to calling a superior officer by his first name. "Thomas. Tom. Tommy. Tom, the Colonel."

"Just Thomas will do, Captain," said Rose, shaking his head and grinning.

"Thomas it will be, then," said Hamilton, leading the way into the abandoned room.

After looking around the small enclosure briefly, Rose knelt down at the wall and picked at the mortar between the stones with his knife. It flaked away easily. He looked up at Hamilton and grinned. "This is starting off on a good note," he said.

After only a few minutes of digging at the mortar, Rose had the first stone loose enough to pry out. Behind the stone lay another, which Rose had anticipated. "This wall's probably several rows thick, just like upstairs. We'll be able to get through it without too much trouble, though."

The two continued to work in the semi-darkness, speaking little, for several hours. Finally, as the pile of debris grew larger, the removal of yet another stone revealed nothing but dirt on the other side. They had broken through!

"If it's this easy the whole way, we should be able to dig through in just a few days," said Rose.

Hamilton agreed. "Not a bad first day's work, Thomas."

The two men looked at the pile of stones they had removed, then at each other. "We're on our way, Andrew," said Rose with a wide grin.

The two shook hands and decided to stop for the day. There would be time enough, and the soil did not appear to be formidable. The two worked their way back to the main basement and went upstairs.

"Have you seen the latest newspaper, Major Turner?" the Prison Commander queried as he tossed the newspaper across the table.

"No sir, I haven't," answered Turner. He picked the paper up with scarcely a glance at his superior officer, Brigadier General John H. Winder, head of the Virginia prison system.

"You will see that the story isn't very flattering, I'm afraid," said Winder, his eyes on Turner.

Turner read the first few paragraphs of the lead story, his jaw clenching in anger as he went along. "How can an editor get away with saying something like this?" his voice finally boomed. "Telling the people of Richmond that the Yankee prisoners are eating well while the citizens of this city can't get enough to eat is an outright lie!" Turner slammed the paper down onto the table.

Winder nonchalantly picked the paper up, then looked at Turner. "I agree with you, Major. Trouble is, this editor doesn't."

Turner's eyes flashed. Short tempered to begin with, he wasn't about to let this pass. "I say we go grab the idiot that wrote this and bring him over to Libby for about a month. Let him see for himself what the Yanks are eating. Let him eat with them. Then we'll see if he writes the same way when he gets out."

"You know we can't do that, Major. There has to be another way."

Turner didn't even let on that he had heard. "Those prisoners don't even have meat for days on end. They haven't had any meat since last week, matter of fact."

It was Winder's turn to take the offensive. "Are you telling me that we haven't given the prisoners any meat for over a week?" he exploded.

"That's the truth of the matter, sir," replied Turner, somewhat taken back by Winder's sudden change of emotion.

"This is the fourth time this has happened, Major. What is going on?"

"There isn't much I can do, General," answered Turner. "The railroads are all torn up and nothin's gettin' through. On top of that, all those new prisoners we got in from Chickamauga used up what we did have. All our supplies are short. If I give the meat to the prisoners, our own boys won't have enough."

"I'm very much aware of the railroad problem, Major," said the agitated Winder. "But you should be aware of the rules. Food is to be divided up evenly. Prisoners will get the same rations that the guards get. Only if we are in danger of running out completely do we treat the guards with preference. Those aren't my rules. They were set down by the Secretary of War, and we're going to go along with them until they are changed. I'm responsible for more than 14,000 prisoners here in Richmond, and if they decide to rise up I'm afraid there won't be much we can do to stop them."

"They won't be rising up, General. At least not in Libby. I'll see to that personally," said Turner with a menacing grin.

Winder looked at Turner with disgust. He knew how Turner would take care of such a situation. Winder and Turner had often disagreed on how to handle the prisoners. However, although Winder didn't care much for Turner as an individual, he had to admit that the major was a loyal soldier, and that he had kept a potentially explosive situation under control thus far.

"I'm not asking you to do any such thing. I just want you to understand that the situation is getting serious, and it will get worse now that the newspapers are spreading rumors such as this. My contacts in Washington tell me that some of the prisoners are smuggling letters out, complaining about the meals."

"I don't care what the prisoners are smuggling out, General," Turner spat out. "Those Yanks would complain about anything we fed them. Thing is, they wouldn't know a good meal anyway. Best Yankee meal I ever ate wasn't good enough to throw out to the hogs. You think the Yanks are giving our boys biscuits and gravy up at Point Lookout?"

Winder buried his face in his hands and rubbed his eyes. He instinctively knew Turner was right. He had talked to some of the prisoners who had been paroled from Point Lookout and other northern prisons, and all had said they had been poorly fed.

Turner saw that he had put Winder on the defensive. He continued to press, but with a little more finesse. "Tell the truth, General. You've ate a lot of Yankee cookin'. You ever eat anything up there that compared with a good Southern breakfast, or a plate full of ham and black-eyed peas and grits?"

"No, Major, I have to admit that the South has much better cooks," Winder said with a smile. "But that's all the more reason for us to feed the prisoners right."

"Well, General. You get Abe Lincoln to tell his troops to stop tearin' up our railroads and we'll have all the food we need to feed the prisoners AND the good people of Richmond, includin'a certain newspaper editor."

Winder looked at Turner. "I don't think Mr. Lincoln is in any mood to discuss railroads or supply distribution right now, seeing as how Ben Hardin Helm was killed down at Chickamauga a few weeks ago."

A confused look appeared on Turner's face. "Why would the President of the United States care about a Confederate general gettin' killed?" he asked.

"Didn't you know, Major? Ben was Old Abe's brother-in-law. I understand that Abe wasn't too happy that Ben threw in with the South in the first place. Now that Ben's dead, Lincoln is sure to be in a bad frame of mind." Winder shook his head slowly. The war had split so many families. Even the President's.

Turner just looked at Winder. He had heard of Helm's death, but had no idea that he had been related to Lincoln.

After a few moments of silence, Winder's eyes twinkled. "If you want to go up to Washington and ask Lincoln yourself why his troops won't let our supplies through, I'll be happy to provide you with a flag of truce to get you through the lines."

Turner knew Winder was being sarcastic. "I'll let that to the politicians," he countered. "If it was up to me, we wouldn't even have any prisoners to feed. Every time we capture a group of prisoners we have to assign a bunch of able-bodied fightin' men to look after them and escort them back to Richmond. If I had my way, we'd just shoot every last mother's son of them right out there on the battlefield."

Winder knew Turner was serious. The major had no compassion for his own men, let alone an enemy soldier. "Would you have the Yankees do the same to our men, Major?"

"That's not the point, General. The Yankees have the food. They just choose not to give it to their prisoners. We don't have the food and can't get it. That's the difference. We can't even feed our own men proper. Now because some snivelin' bluebelly writes a letter to his friends in Washington we're supposed to be able to pull food out of the air. They tear up our railroads and then complain when we can't get food through for the prisoners. It don't make no sense, General. It ain't right."

Despite their differences, Winder had to sympathize. "I realize you're doing the best you can with what you've been given to work with, Major. Just treat them fairly, that's all I'm asking."

"I treat them accordin' to Turner's General Orders for Prisoners, sir," said Turner with a smirk.

"Let's try Winder's General Orders for a change, Major," offered the General.

His tone left no doubt in Turner's mind that this was an order, not a request. Turner, if nothing else, was a good soldier. He obeyed orders, even those he didn't like. Unless he was sure he could get away with disobeying.

"Yes, sir," he responded.

"I'll see what I can do about getting a request to Washington to get them to send some rations down for their men. I can't say it will do much good, but maybe they'll agree." Winder's demeanor told Turner that the conversation was nearing an end. Turner took his cue and started for the door. Pausing with his hand on the latch, he turned to Winder.

"You do that, General. And I'll see to it that there won't be any uprising among the prisoners. At least not at my prison." He then saluted sharply, waited for Winder to return the salute, and left.

* * *

As Rose and Hamilton had expected, the soil offered little resistance to their daily digging. Within a week the tunnel had been extended well toward freedom.

"If we don't soon get out of here, we're going to starve to death, Thomas," said Hamilton.

"Or die of scurvy," added Rose.

The two had just returned from the cellar and had entered into the main topic of conversation among the prisoners—food.

"Washington sure did us a favor when they shipped all those rations down, didn't they?" Hamilton asked in a derisive tone.

"That's a fact," Rose answered with a wry chuckle. "Twenty-five hundred pounds of beef. That's a couple of cows, at least. And for only 14,000 prisoners. I hope nobody overate."

"Works out to less than three ounces of beef for each prisoner. What were they thinking of up there? I hear we wouldn't even have gotten that if Winder hadn't asked for it."

"I heard that, too. I also heard that the Rebs are afraid we're going to rise up if we don't get more to eat. I overheard some of the guards talking last night. They said some of their officials are even moving their families out of town for a while, until things quiet down a bit. Appears the newspaper is reporting that the reason the local citizens can't get any meat is that it's all being saved for us prisoners. Least, that's what I heard the guards saying."

"Well, if there's any good coming out of this at all, it's that. Keeping the Rebs uneasy is about all we've got on our side right now. Might as well enjoy it," Hamilton said, an uncharacteristic scowl on his face.

"What about all those rats in the cellar? Think you could bring yourself to eat one of 'em?" asked Rose.

A look of disgust crossed Hamilton's face as he considered Rose's question. Finally, he said, "I don't know if I'm that hungry yet. But I'm gettin' there!"

"You know, we wouldn't be the first ones in here to do that," offered Rose.

"Yeah, I know. And it'll probably come to that. But I'm gonna hold off as long as I can."

The conversation came to a temporary halt as Colonel Streight approached, with an older man immediately behind. The two men stood to greet them, noticing immediately that the old man was a general. They quickly saluted, a gesture returned by the general.

"This is Brigadier General Neal Dow," said Streight. "He's the ranking officer in here right now. I'm taking him around and introducing him to you newcomers."

Despite his rank, Dow did not cut an imposing figure. Wearing a red skull cap, he had a comedic appearance. He also seemed feeble, shuffling rather than walking. Rose immediately felt a sense of pity for the man, afraid that he would not be able to withstand the rigors of Libby for an extended period.

After all had been introduced, Rose felt compelled to ask, "Why haven't I seen you around the prison before this, General. Were you just captured?"

The old man chuckled. "Not exactly, Colonel. I was captured in July, but they only kept me here for a few weeks. Seems they got the idea that I had been stirring up some of the slaves, trying to get them to leave their masters and form their own military organizations. General Winder had me sent to Mobile, Alabama for investigation. They couldn't find any real evidence, so they sent me back. Just got back yesterday."

"Stirrin' up slaves," mused Rose. "How'd they come up with an idea like that?"

"I guess 'cause it was true," said the General, obviously enjoying the story. "I only said they couldn't find any real evidence, I didn't say there wasn't any. They just didn't look in the right places."

The four men laughed, a sound heard all too seldom inside Libby's walls.

"I know you two aren't getting enough to eat, just like everyone else," Dow said. "But are you getting by?"

"We'll be fine, General," answered Rose. "But I have to admit I do miss having a good meal now and again."

"Well, there isn't much we can do about additional food right now, other than what I understand Washington sent a few days ago, but I do have some good news about clothing and blankets."

Rose and Hamilton leaned forward almost imperceptibly. The nights were beginning to get cold and the need for warm clothing was talked about almost as much as the food shortage.

"Seems like some of our better writers..." said Dow, with a pointed glance at Streight, "...sent letters to General Meredith, telling him how some of our boys were dying of exposure over on Belle Isle and a few other places. Meredith's offering to send blankets, shoes, overcoats, and hats if the Confederates will let us have them. Major Turner told me when he signed me in yesterday that General Winder has ordered him to allow a board of prisoners to distribute them. Turner made it plain to me that he was following orders, and that it wasn't something he agreed with, but he's going to let us do it. If we can do it with no problems, they'll send some more later. The word I'm getting is they may also send some money so we can buy some decent food."

"That is good news, sir," Hamilton said with excitement.

"I thought you'd be glad to hear it," replied Dow. "I have to talk to a few others yet, but I think we'll distribute everything here at Libby on the first shipment. That way we'll be able to control the distribution better. I don't want to take a chance on something going wrong at one of the other prisons, something that we can't control, and then finding out that the government won't send anything more."

"That's probably the best way to do it," agreed Rose. "If you need some help with the distribution, you can count me in."

"Me, too," chimed in Hamilton.

"Thanks to both of you," said Dow, "But I think we have enough help. I just thought you should know what's happening."

"Appreciate it, General," said Rose.

"Well, just do the best you can. I can't promise you things are going to get any better anytime soon, so try to keep your spirits up," Dow said, obviously preparing to leave.

"We'll do that, sir. Everyone seems to be handling the situation pretty well, I'd say," said Rose.

"They are, indeed, Colonel. They are, indeed," was the reply. With that, Dow raised his hand in a slight wave and moved on to the next group to pass on the news.

Instinctively, both Rose and Hamilton saluted, even though Dow already had his back to them.

"Nice old man," said Hamilton.

"I couldn't agree more," answered Rose. "I just hope he makes it out of here alive."

"I have a feeling he's a lot tougher than he appears," Hamilton commented, continuing to watch the frail, old General as he talked to another group of prisoners.

"I hope you're right, Andrew. The world can't afford to lose good men."

The first drops of rain were beginning to fall as Rose stood and stretched. It was almost dusk and he had been sitting with his back to the wall, listening to the low rumble of thunder as it drew closer. The thunder reminded Rose of artillery, taking him momentarily back to the battlefields.

"I wonder what kind of battles I've missed by being in here?" he thought to himself. "I hope the 77th is all right. I know it's giving a good account of itself, wherever it may be."

Rose felt a pang of wistfulness, almost a need. A need to be a part of a military unit again. He missed the camaraderie, the decision making which could determine the outcome of even a small skirmish, and the fighting, although he had never gotten used to people shooting at him. Some treated it almost as if it were a game, but Rose couldn't. It was too important. Good men would live or die, based on his decisions. At the time he had hated it, he would have given anything to have the fighting end. Now he felt left out. "Maybe I'm more of a soldier than I thought I was," he mused.

It was almost time to meet Hamilton in the cook room for another night of digging, and Rose began working his way downstairs. The two had decided to dig at night, reasoning that the chances of being discovered were not as great. They didn't fear detection by the guards. Their biggest challenge came in keeping the other prisoners from realizing what they were doing.

"When the time comes, we can tell some of the others," Rose had said, "but the more men who know what we are doing, the better the chance that someone is going to let something slip in front of a guard."

Hamilton had not disagreed, and the two had become experts at slowly and inconspicuously working their way out of the center of activity in the basement cook room until they were swallowed up by the shadows.

Starting down the stairs, Rose was surprised to see Hamilton on his way up to meet him.

"We have a problem, Thomas," Hamilton said, trying to keep his voice down so the other prisoners couldn't hear.

"What's wrong," said Rose, fearing the worst.

"The Rebs are sealin' off the cellar. I don't know if they've found the tunnel or not, but they're sealin' off the cellar." Hamilton was showing his agitation.

"Calm down, Andrew. We don't want to let on that we're concerned. Even if they did find the tunnel, they don't know we're the ones doing the digging."

"How could they have found it?" Hamilton asked, almost to himself. "They never go down there with all those rats."

"We don't even know yet that they did find it," Rose countered. "Let's just see what is happening, then worry about whether or not they found it."

The two descended the stairs and made their way to the steps leading to the basement cook room, trying not to appear too eager. As they approached, the sound of hammering became louder. Nearing the doorway to the stairwell leading to the basement cook room, they observed two guards nailing heavy planks across the door.

"Why are you taking our kitchen away from us," Rose demanded of the guards. He hoped that he could convince the guards his anger came from losing the cook room privileges, rather than letting on he had other reasons for wanting to be in the cellar.

The taller of the two men turned. "Major Turner's orders, Yank. Guess he figgers since we ain't got no food to give y'all there ain't no need for a place to cook it no more."

The second guard laughed, a strange, high-pitched cackle. Bending down to pick up another plank, he offered his own theory. "Mebbe he thought too many of you Yanks wuz gettin' ideas about leavin' us."

Rose felt a cold sweat form on his brow as he glanced sidelong at Hamilton. Hamilton was looking away, not wishing to look at Rose. He feared that the guards may be smarter than they appeared.

"I haven't heard anything about anybody escaping," Rose said.

"Ain't happened yet," said the first guard, "And y'all can be sure it ain't gonna happen now."

"Now, Jacob," said the second man, "Y'all know we've had some Yanks get outta here."

"Not through the cellar, we didn't" answered Jacob. "And they ain't gonna get the chance."

"You have some reason to think someone is going to try to get out through the cellar?" Rose queried, trying not to be too obvious.

"None that I know of," said Jacob. Rose hoped the two Rebels didn't read the look of relief which he was sure was making its presence on his face. "All's I know is, Major Turner said we needed to make this place more secure, and that's what I'm doin'."

"Where are we supposed to cook now?" asked Rose, defiantly.

"Ain't none of my concern," said Jacob. "You want an answer to that, go see Major Turner."

"Maybe we'll just do that," answered Rose, knowing full well that neither he nor Hamilton had any intentions of drawing attention to themselves by protesting to Turner.

As Rose and Hamilton turned to leave and plan their next move, they heard the second guard comment as he returned to his hammering, "I swear I ain't never gonna understand these Yanks. First they complain about the stink and all the rats in the cellar, then they complain when we tell them they can't go down there no more!"

"Don't let 'em get you down, boy. As long as y'all are alive y'all got a chance. Never give up hope." The voice of the old man at the railroad stop rattled its way out of the recesses of Rose's mind as he shuffled back to the stairs. "Never give up hope," it kept repeating. "Never give up hope."

Rose could hear the rain coming down harder.

Chapter Five

Rose awoke with a start. The sounds of cheering and laughing confused him at first, and he thought he may be having a dream. Allowing a few moments to clear his head, he realized that the cheering was actually happening. He raised up on one elbow and tried to determine the source. It appeared to be coming from a group gathered around the window.

"Look at that big one go!"

"Keep runnin', boy."

"There goes another one!"

"C'mon, fella. You can make it."

"There must be hundreds of 'em."

Was an escape in progress? It sounded as if several prisoners must be making their way out of the prison. But why now, with dawn's light breaking? And why were no shots being fired by the guards?

Rose hobbled quickly to the window and tried to peer over the heads of those in front. All he could see was the rain coming down in torrents. Try as he would he could not get close enough to the window to see what was happening.

What's going on?" he asked a nearby prisoner who was sitting on the shoulders of a companion.

"Rats, Colonel. Rats everywhere!" he shouted above the din, never taking his eyes away from the street.

"What do you mean, rats?" Rose queried.

"Just what I said, sir, rats. The cellar must be floodin' out with all this rain, and the rats are just pourin' out of the windows and doors and out onto the street. They're all headin' for higher ground, I'd guess."

Rose looked around him. For the first time since he had arrived at Libby the men were excited about something! Most of them, those who could see the spectacle, at least, actually had smiles on their faces. Some were even laughing out loud.

Working his way around the perimeter of the crowd, he found a small pile of firewood near the window and climbed up on it. The unsteady foundation shifted under his weight, but held. He placed his hand on the shoulders of those in front of him to steady himself and leaned toward the window. He was now able to see a portion of the street, and, as the other prisoner had said, it was alive with rats!

"I got a watch here that I'm willing to bet that the guards are gonna start taking target practice on them rats pretty soon," shouted someone near the front. "Anyone interested?"

Immediately several of the others began to clamor for the opportunity to bet against him. Those who were unsuccessful began setting up bets of their own with others nearby.

"A good gambler can always find something to bet on," Rose thought to himself with amusement, "and someone to bet with, too."

The betting continued as Rose looked back to the strange sight outside. The two guards whose presence had unknowingly started the gambling could be seen on the opposite side of the street. They both were enjoying the show as much as the prisoners, and showed no inclination to shoot at the rats which were swarming all around them, much to the consternation of the losing bettors. And, for a change, they didn't seem to mind the prisoners who were milling around the windows.

"On a normal day they'd have shot at us a long time ago," thought Rose. "It's strange how everyone's mood can be changed with a little diversion in a place like this."

"I don't care much for rainstorms," said the light haired young captain with a wisp of a beard, on whose shoulders Rose was leaning. "And I like rats even less. But I wouldn't mind seeing something like this every few days just to break the boredom. What do you think, Colonel?"

Rose smiled as he looked at his questioner. "If that's all it takes to bring the morale up, I'm all in favor of it."

Several others nearby laughed in agreement.

"Wonder if we can get Major Turner to schedule rat races for us once a week," one of them said, to a chorus of laughter.

"Why not?" came the answer. "They're all his relatives!"

When the laughter died down a third voice chimed in. "Yeah, but the rats are better lookin', don't you think?"

By now some of the men were literally hanging onto their companions as they guffawed hysterically.

Just as the men were calming down, a voice on the other side of the crowd shouted out, "They're a lot friendlier, too!"

This touched off another round of convulsive laughter, as one after another insulted the commandant. The affronts to Turner's personality became more and more outrageous. Under normal circumstances none would have brought more than a smile, but here in Libby, under the control of the enemy, each one brought a new uproar.

"Only thing none of us thought of is, that there's good food runnin' away," said a voice near the front.

The laughter quickly drew silent, as each came to the sober realization that the speaker was right. "Rodent stew" was rapidly becoming a staple of many diets in Libby. Although Rose had not yet reached that stage, he feared it would be coming. Only his natural aversion to rats had kept him from it until now. Nor did he encourage the others to supplement their meals accordingly. He didn't really care what the rest ate; he just didn't want dozens of inmates scrambling around in the basement catching their supper while he and Hamilton were only a few feet away trying to clandestinely dig their way to freedom.

"They'll be back, soon as the water goes down," interjected General Dow.

With that simple statement, the mood was uplifted, and the insults immediately resumed.

Rose watched and listened for nearly an hour, joining in the levity and enjoying it to its fullest. Then, even watching the rats escape the rising water became mundane, and the crowd began to drift apart, the spectators going to their card games, reading, or whatever else they could find to pass the time.

"Care for some onions, Colonel?" said a familiar voice.
Rose turned to see Gageby holding a small bunch of onions at eye level.

"Where in the world did you find onions, Jim?" Rose asked incredulously. "Bought 'em from one of the guards," said Gageby with a grin. "Only two Secesh dollars for four of 'em."

"That's a bargain at Libby prices," agreed Rose.

"Thought I'd boil 'em and make a soup. What do you think?"
"Sounds delicious, Jim," said Rose, "but aren't you afraid you'll get bad breath?"

Gageby's face registered confusion at first, until he realized that Rose was not serious. "Been so long since I've had a real toothbrush in my mouth...," he said wistfully, not finishing his sentence. Then, smiling again, he said, "I don't reckon a cup of onion stew's going to make much difference at this point. Turner doesn't come in and kiss me good night, anyway."

The two laughed, then proceeded to the cook room to enjoy Gageby's onion stew.

* * *

"Come here, Thomas. I'd like you to meet someone," called General Dow, reflecting his informality with military protocol as he waved his hand in Rose's direction.

Rose worked his way toward Dow. As he approached, Rose was surprised to see a woman seated next to Dow. In her mid-forties, she was plain looking, with short, dark, curly hair. Many prisoners had acquaintances in Richmond, so visitors were not an uncommon sight in Libby. Few visitors, however, were women.

"This is Elizabeth Van Lew, Thomas. Elizabeth, Colonel Thomas Rose," said Dow, gesturing to Rose to sit down.

Rose and the woman exchanged pleasantries, followed by a quizzical look from Rose to Dow.

"Miss Van Lew's a regular visitor here, Thomas," said Dow in response to Rose's apparent confusion at seeing a woman inside the confines of Libby. "Isn't that right, Elizabeth?"

"Why, I certainly am, General," Elizabeth answered in a soft southern drawl.

"Elizabeth's a citizen of Richmond," Dow went on, his voice lowering to where Rose almost had to strain to hear him, "but she's very helpful to us Northerners, if you know what I mean. She's only here today as a visitor, but she does bring some...oh, shall we say, interesting information from time to time. Takes some away with her on occasion, too, I dare say. In fact, General Meade values her information better than he does that of Pinkerton's."

The visitor smiled coyly.

"Well, I don't know how good your information is, ma'am, but I would certainly hope it's more accurate than Pinkerton's. Sometimes I think that man's spying for the Rebs instead of us." Rose had long ago disavowed anything he heard from anyone in the Pinkerton organization.

"He is a bit cautious, Colonel, I must agree," said Elizabeth.

"Cautious? He can look at a company of Rebs and see a battalion. I don't know how many opportunities we missed because we thought we were outnumbered."

The three traded stories about the Pinkerton spy network, none of them complimentary.

Then, Rose changed the topic of conversation. "May I ask why you are more loyal to Washington than to the glorious state of Virginia, Miss Van Lew?"

"Certainly, Colonel. I make it no secret, even though my neighbors despise me for it. You see, my father was northern born and was very wealthy. We live in a handsome house up on Grace Street, with beautiful terraced gardens, lots of tall oaks, everything you could ever want in a home. My father was a hardware merchant, and he owned slaves right up until the day he died, almost two years ago." Elizabeth paused, thinking about her late father.

"When he died," she finally went on, "my mother and I let all the slaves go free. We just never felt comfortable owning another human being. We still have some servants, but they aren't slaves. They come and go as they please. Our friends and neighbors never understood that. Then, we refused to sew uniforms for the war effort. I couldn't in good conscience. I didn't support the Confederacy's ideas, and I couldn't bring myself to make uniforms for the men to fight in. Even the newspaper criticized mother and me for that. Of course, we weren't mentioned by name, but the paper made it plain enough. Why, we even received death threats after the story was printed."

"So you became a spy?"

"In a sense. I probably would have, anyway. I always felt Virginia was wrong in siding with the Confederacy, although it never surprised me when it happened. At any rate, now everyone in Richmond calls me Crazy Bet because I don't support the Confederacy."

"You mean everyone else down here does?" asked Rose.

"Oh, no, Colonel," Elizabeth replied with a smile. "They're just not as vocal about it as I am."

"I see," said Rose. "And now you visit prisoners in your spare time."

"That's right. Among my other traitorous avocations, according to my former friends."

"She even has a direct line to Jeff Davis's mansion, Thomas," Dow injected admiringly.

"Really?" Rose exclaimed in surprise.

"I'm very fortunate to have a former slave working for President Davis," explained Elizabeth. "In fact, her name is Elizabeth, too. Mary Elizabeth, that is. Mary Elizabeth Bowser. I had sent her to Pennsylvania before the war began, to be educated. Now she repays me by keeping her eyes and ears open around the Executive Mansion. She has proved very helpful, I might add."

"What happens if she's caught, Miss Van Lew. What happens if you are caught. Is it really worth it?" Rose asked.

Elizabeth thought for a moment before answering. "Sometimes I'm not sure, to be honest. I don't know what they will do if they catch us. Hang us, most likely. I try not to think about that. I do know I miss the way things used to be. I miss my friends. I miss my former lifestyle. But I think it has been worth it. We'll know for sure when the war is over. I'm just glad I can make a small contribution."

"You've made more than a small contribution, Elizabeth," interrupted Dow. Turning to Rose he said, "Sometimes she even brings us food or writing paper. I got these shoes from you, remember, Elizabeth?"

Elizabeth nodded with a smile. "It was my pleasure, General," she said. "But everything depends on who the guards are when I get here. Some I can bribe to let me bring things in, some I can't."

"I know that," said Dow, "But my point is, we owe a lot to you and your mother."

"Not at all, General. We're proud to do our part."

An awkward silence followed, ended when Elizabeth noticed a tear in the knee of Rose's trousers. "Do you have nothing to mend with, Colonel?" she asked.

Rose looked down at his exposed knee and said with a grin, "My good trousers are at the tailor shop to be altered. I just wear these until they are returned."

"Well, until you get them back, why don't you accept this as a gift?" she said, holding out her hand.

Taking the offered object from her, Rose saw that he had been given a small mending kit. Smiling, he said, "I appreciate this ma'am. I really do. I traded my housewife to one of the guards for a compass, and up till now I didn't have anything to work with."

"Well, now you do, Colonel," answered Elizabeth. With a knowing twinkle in her eye she continued, "And why on earth do you feel a need for a compass in here?"

"It's a big building, ma'am," said Rose, smiling.

"It's a big state, too, Colonel. If you or any of your friends should ever happen to find yourselves outside these walls, you're going to need more than a compass. I can get you a guide to lead you to the nearest Federal pickets. Remember that."

"I will, ma'am. And thanks for the housewife. I do appreciate it," said Rose, rising to leave.

"You're welcome."

"She means that, Thomas," said Dow, quietly. "Everyone in here should know that. I don't know if I'll ever get out of here, but you're still young enough and strong enough. You can do what you want. But if I were in your place, I know what I'd be thinking about. I'd be planning my escape right this minute. And if you do get out, you try to get to Elizabeth's?"

"Yes, sir," answered Rose. "I surely will."

"There's always a candle in the window, Colonel. When you get to Grace Street, just look for it," said Elizabeth as Rose shook her hand and bowed slightly.

"We'll meet again, ma'am," said Rose, making his leave.

"I'm sure we will, Colonel," she answered. "I'm sure we will."

* * *

The lightning flashed as Rose stealthily crept along the upstairs wall. Somewhere up here there should be a trapdoor to the roof, he reasoned, and he was determined to find it.

The thunder seemed to present one continuous rumble as he inched along, feeling for any kind of an opening. If he could just find the trapdoor he would at least be able to explore the roof and try to set up a plan for some later date. Of course, if the opportunity presented itself...

A flash of lightning lit up the corner of the room. In the brief moment that he had enough light to see, Rose thought he had seen someone else. Was it another prisoner, or was it one of Turner's guards looking for anyone who may have been trying to make an escape during the storm?

Several more flashes of lightning revealed nothing, and Rose was beginning to feel foolish for being so apprehensive. Then, another flash. There he is again!

Rose instinctively reached for the sidearm which had been taken from him when he was captured. Realizing it wasn't there, his mind raced. Should he run and hope that the guard, if the man really was a guard, wouldn't see him? Or if he saw him, hope that he couldn't see his face? Maybe a story about why he was up here where he had no reason to be. That may be better, but what could he say that would be believable? Trying to figure his next move, he saw the figure again in the next flash of lightning.

"Thomas? Is that you?" Rose heard a familiar voice ask hesitantly.

"Andrew?"

"Yeah, it's me," the voice whispered. "I thought that was you. Or maybe I should say, I hoped that was you."

"We're going to have to quit meeting like this, Andrew. My heart won't take it," said Rose.

"I agree, Thomas. I never expected to see anyone up here, though. In fact, I wasn't even sure what I'd find when I got here. I was just sort of lookin' and hopin', you might say."

"Me, too," answered Rose. "You find anything?"

"Maybe," came the unexpected reply. "There's a platform of some kind that runs along the outside wall on the end of the building. I was thinking that maybe a man could get out on that platform and climb down to the ground. On a night like this the sentries will probably be huddled in some doorway tryin' to keep dry. With a little luck we might be able to do it without bein' seen."

"It might work," answered Rose. "Let's take a look."

Working their way toward the end of the room, Rose could feel his heart begin to pound harder with excitement. This could be the opportunity he had been looking for.

The lightning continued to flash, accompanied almost instantly by the crash of thunder. Gaining even more intensity, the storm appeared to be inside the prison with them. It seemed that the room would darken after one flash of lightning, only to immediately light up again from the next.

"Hope you don't mind gettin'a little wet, Thomas," said Hamilton.

"Andrew," Rose answered, "If you've found us a way out of here I don't care if I never dry out. It'll be worth it."

"This here's a good ole fashioned Kentucky gully washer, this is," Hamilton went on. "Never thought I'd look forward to bein' out in weather like this."

"Me either," answered Rose, "But I have a feeling we won't mind it a bit."

"I reckon you're right. Which way do we go once we're out, though?" queried Hamilton.

Rose immediately remembered the conversation he had with Elizabeth Van Lew, and proceeded to tell Hamilton about what she had said.

"You think you can find her house?" Hamilton asked.

"I don't know, but it's worth trying. She described it pretty well, and General Dow gave me a pretty good idea of how to get there. If we can find her, she should be able to get us back to Union lines."

"Sounds pretty good to me," answered Hamilton. "Only thing is, we're wearin' blue and everyone else is gonna be wearing gray or butternut. How will we get past the Rebs that we run into?"

"I don't think we have to worry, Andrew," Rose replied. "I've been noticing that a lot of the Rebs are wearing Union uniforms. Probably stole them from supply trains in some of their raids. I think we can blend in, especially in the dark."

"I hope you're right, Thomas. I hope you're right."

Andrew carefully positioned himself near the window and cautiously peered out. As he had hoped, no sentries were in view. Motioning for Rose to approach the window, he looked out again.

"What do you think?" Hamilton asked. "Think we can make it?"

Rose peered down at the platform, ignoring the rain as it pelted his face.

"It's a pretty good drop," he said. "I think we can do it, though."

"What if the guards are standing under it? They'll probably hear us when we land," Hamilton said, his voice barely audible over the clap of the thunder.

"Maybe we could climb down by hanging on to the window ledges," said Rose, looking from one end of the platform to the other. "We wouldn't have too much of a drop, that way."

By now Hamilton was nearly hanging out the window, planning his route. The rain soaked him mercilessly. He appeared not to notice.

Pulling back inside, he turned to Rose. "We better just stand watch here for a while before we do anything, don't you think? I'd feel a lot better about this if I knew exactly where those guards are sittin'."

"Not a bad idea, Andrew," Rose agreed. "I learned a long time ago that the chance for success goes up if the plan gets thought through."

The two watched in silence as the rain seemed to be almost horizontal at times. The gas lights flickered, their brightness alternately ebbing and brightening as the wind and rain dictated. Still no sentries could be seen anywhere.

"You think they're out there?" Hamilton asked, as the lightning flashed again.

"You can depend on it," said Rose. "They might be ducked in under a doorway, but they're out there."

"Maybe they won't figure anybody's daft enough to venture out on a night like this," Hamilton offered hopefully.

"Maybe," said Rose. "Or maybe they'll be extra vigilant because it's a perfect night for two idiots like us to try to break out."

"I vote for my idea, Thomas," countered Hamilton.

"I don't think our vote counts for much, Andrew," Rose said with a chuckle.

The two fell silent again, watching for any sign that the sentries were present. The lightning continued to flash.

After a few minutes of observation, Rose broke the silence.

"I hate to say this, Andrew, but there's something else that bothers me about this."

Hamilton turned toward Rose. They were so close to getting out. What was Rose afraid of?

"What's that, Thomas," he asked, not really wanting to hear what Rose was going to say.

"This lightning," Rose answered. "If the guards are watching at all, there's no way we'll be able to get away from the building without being seen. Just count the time between flashes."

Hamilton watched for a short time, the lightning flashing brightly all the while. Each bolt lit the street enough that he realized Rose was right.

"You're right," he said, disappointment obvious in his tone. "We'd never make it. Not tonight, anyway."

"My mind's set on getting out tonight, though," Rose said after a brief silence. "I don't want to have to wait until another night."

"I don't either, Thomas, but we're right in the middle here. If it's stormy enough to come up here without anyone seein' us, it's probably going to be too stormy to get out without the lightning giving us away."

"I know you're right, Andrew," said Rose. "But we're so close. So close."

The two continued to watch, hoping against the odds that the lightning would cease, providing them with the darkness they needed to make their way away from the prison. But the elements refused to relinquish their grip. If anything, the rain came down harder, the lightning flashed more frequently, and the chances of success were slipping away with each rivulet of water running down the wall and into the street.

"I don't like this at all," said Rose.

"The more I think about it, I have to agree," Hamilton said. "What do you think? Do you have any other ideas?"

"I might," answered Rose. "I just might."

Chapter Six

"Well, let's hear it," said Hamilton. "I don't want to spend one more day in here if I don't have to."

"I have to agree," answered Rose. "Anyway, I'm not sure, but this might be worth looking at."

He pulled away from the window and sat with his back against the wall, his soaked beard plastered against his face.

"Remember me tellin' you about seein' workmen goin' in and out of the basement over on the south side of the building?"

"Yeah, but what good's that going to do us?" asked Hamilton, unsure of what Rose was leading up to.

"Maybe nothing," answered Rose. "But I was thinkin'. If we could get back down to the basement, maybe we could go out that same door they're usin'. We're already pretty sure the guards are huddled in some doorway tonight. If we can just get outside without them seeing us, we might be able to just walk away like we're local citizens hurryin' home to get out of the rain."

"It's worth lookin' at," said Hamilton, his hopes rising again. "Let's go see if we can figure a way down to the basement. Maybe we can pry those planks off the door or something."

The two departed for the kitchen on the first floor, passing other prisoners on the way. It was not uncommon to encounter other men in the various rooms, whatever the hour. Some were looking for a way out, just as Rose and Hamilton were doing. Others, in various stages of mental illness, wandered for no particular reason. Still others, with the onset of cooler weather, found it too cold to sleep and spent the night walking to keep warm, trying to sleep during the warmer daylight hours.

Upon reaching the kitchen the two went directly to the door leading to the basement cook room. Trying to pull the planks off the doorway, they quickly realized that it would take more than two men, no matter how determined, using just their bare hands.

"The war will be over before we get the last plank off here," complained Hamilton. "If those Rebs can't do anything else, they sure are good at nailin' planks."

Rose didn't answer. There had to be some way into that basement.

As the lightning continued to flash, Rose picked a piece of pinewood out of the wood pile. About a foot long, it would serve his purpose well.

"See if you can find a loose floorboard while I shape this," he directed Hamilton.

Taking out his pocket knife he began to whittle the pinewood into a wedge.

"Looks like all of them have a peg or two out," said Hamilton, checking the floorboards. "This one right here only has a couple holdin' it."

When Rose had completed carving the wedge, he knelt at the end of the board which Hamilton had indicated. Hamilton dropped to his knees beside him, anticipating what Rose was about to do.

Fitting the narrow end of the wedge into the crack between the boards, Rose pried up on the loose board which Hamilton had found. At first, it refused to yield, its fibers swollen by the constant presence of water and human waste. Finally, the two men were able to get it to move just a little.

"One more push should do it," said Rose, his voice straining with the effort.

As Rose knelt on the wedge, using his weight for leverage, Hamilton was finally able to get his fingers under the edge of the floorboard.

"Now it oughtta go," he said.

The two repositioned their hands under the edge of the board and lifted. Suddenly it released, and they had found their access to the basement!

Lifting the end of the board high enough to allow him to get his upper body through, Rose peered down into the darkened basement. He had never been in this part of the prison, and he wasn't sure what to expect. Leaning in further, he tried to see what the basement offered, but it was too dark to make out anything other than a few indiscernible shapes when the lightning flashed. Hearing nothing, he eased his way back into the cook room.

"See anything?" asked Hamilton.

"No," answered Rose. "It's too dark. But I couldn't hear anything. I don't think anyone's down there. I'm all for goin' down and seein' what's there."

"Let's do it," Hamilton agreed. "We came this far, maybe we can get out of here tonight after all."

Rose removed one of the long bench seats from a nearby table. Sliding it into the opening in the floor, he found that it reached the floor below and still had at least a foot extending above the kitchen floor.

"I'll go down and see if there's a way out," he said to Hamilton as he prepared to slide down the plank. "You stay up here and keep watch."

With the storm still raging, Rose quickly slid down the bench to the room below, ignoring the splinters which penetrated the flesh of his hands. The faint beams of a street lamp cast strange shadows into the room. Pausing for a few minutes to gather his thoughts, he heard the muffled steps of a guard pacing outside. Against the subdued light of the street lamp the lonely sentinel came into view as a silhouette, his shoulders hunched against the driving rain. When the sentinel passed, Rose cautiously crept toward the window.

Softly placing one foot in front of the other, he was able to reach the window with only one minor stumble, tripping over some unknown object hidden in the darkness. Looking out the window, he was able to see the sentinel who had just passed. No others were visible.

Groping his way along the wall he slowly worked toward where he believed the door to be. Within minutes, the glow of streetlights revealed its presence. Even more, the light allowed him to see that there was no door in the opening, and that the doorway led directly out onto the street. Catlike, he moved toward the opening.

Standing just outside the faint beam of light reaching into the cellar from the street, he watched and waited. Still no signs of another sentry. Patiently, he crouched against the wall, trying to determine the extent of activity outside, much as he had often attempted to ascertain the strength of enemy forces in the field. The sentinel's soft steps, each foot making a muffled sucking sound as it pulled out of the mud, could be heard as he slowly drew nearer. Soon, the guard walked past the opening, still hunched over, cradling his musket in his arms. He passed so close to the door that Rose could have reached through the opening and touched him. Rose feared that the thumping of his heart would draw the Rebel's attention.

Waiting until the guard had proceeded down the street, Rose finally moved. Standing painfully, his legs and feet tingled from the cramped position in which he had been crouching. His injured foot throbbed as the circulation returned. Already wet and cold, the protestations of his body were only a minor inconvenience.

When the feeling had totally returned to his limbs he moved away from the doorway. Feeling his way around the room rather than seeing, he located an area which seemed to be a carpenter's shop. Heavy tables, an anvil, and what felt like large trunks used for storing tools were easily identified. He groped in the darkness for the presence of a hammer or some other tool that could be used as a weapon, but found nothing. Other than a few irregularly shaped boards, he felt nothing on the table tops.

"Neat workmen," he thought as the guard passed once again through the frame of light that indicated the presence of the now distant doorway.

Continuing his exploration, he eventually reached a door. Softly trying the latch, he found it to be locked. Feeling his way along the wall he almost immediately located another door, also locked. When he reached a third door within a few feet of the second, the realization struck him. The cells! These had to be the cells he had been hearing about!

Running his hands over the door, he located a small opening at about eye level. The darkness on the other side of the door refused to give way to his gaze through the opening. He softly tapped on the door, then waited for an answer. None came.

Moving from door to door, he tapped at each one, waiting for anyone inside to reveal their presence with an answering tap, before moving on. Reaching the last door, he was relieved to find that nobody was confined in any of the cells.

"That's good news," he thought. "It also means that there won't be any guards down here to watch for."

Pausing to gather his bearings, he realized that the better part of the night had passed by. It would be too late to try to escape any more tonight, but the last few hours had definitely not been wasted. He slowly worked his way back to the bench he had used to gain access into the cellar.

Laboriously he worked his way up the plank until he felt Hamilton's hands grasping his arm. Their combined efforts soon had him back in the kitchen.

"We can do it, Andrew!" Rose whispered loudly. "We can get out of here!"

As the two maneuvered the floorboard back into position, Rose excitedly told Hamilton about the opening to the street, the lone sentinel, and the cells.

"Anybody in the cells?" Hamilton asked.

"Not as close as I could tell," came Rose's answer.

"If this doesn't work, two of them are going to be occupied real soon," Hamilton offered.

"It'll work," said Rose. "I'm sure of it!"

"Then let's mark this floorboard so's we can find it again," said Hamilton, taking out his pocket knife. As Rose watched his friend, Hamilton opened the knife and got down on his knees. Quickly, he began digging into the sodden plank.

When he had carved his initials in the board he looked up at Rose as the first light of dawn peeked through the window. Grinning, he extended his hand. Rose shook it excitedly.

"We'd best be getting back upstairs," Rose said. "First mess'll be coming down soon to get breakfast started."

Looking at the floorboard and the freshly carved AH, Hamilton joked, "We'll be back. Don't you let none of them Rebel guards pry you up and figure out what we're doin'."

Rose looked at his friend incredulously. "I don't know if I want to leave this place with someone who talks to the floor."

"I'd a heap rather talk to that floor than to either of the Turners," Hamilton replied as the two climbed the stairs.

Reaching the top step, Rose turned to Hamilton. "We'll be out of here before we ever have to talk to the Turners," he whispered with a grin.

Hamilton grinned back and nodded. The two then split up to go to their respective quarters.

So many prisoners had been brought in from Chickamauga that the two rooms housing them had been dubbed Upper Chickamauga and Lower Chickamauga. Rose was staying in Upper Chickamauga, the center room on the top floor. Hamilton, although he had not been captured at Chickamauga, had come in with many of the Chickamauga prisoners and was assigned to Lower Chickamauga. In similar fashion there were Upper and Lower Gettysburg rooms.

Rose settled down onto a relatively dry place near the window, leaning against the wall. He stretched his legs in front of him and folded his arms, placing his hands into his armpits for warmth. Closing his eyes he felt the delicious feeling of sleep overtake his body. Sleep. One of the few pleasures he had found in Libby.

When he awoke the sun was high in the sky. The storm had finally passed and, although the day was clear, it was also cold. A brisk wind blew through the glassless windows. Winter would be here soon. He feared that many of his fellow prisoners would succumb within the next few months. He prayed that he would not be among them.

Rose had dreamed of Lydia, as he often did. He cursed the war, the Turners, the Confederacy, and everything else that was keeping them apart.

Shifting his position, he took out a sheet of paper which General Dow had given him yesterday. Elizabeth Van Lew had brought several sheets for the men to write letters home. Rose had seen her several times since their first meeting, but had not had the opportunity to talk to her again. If nothing else, he wanted to thank her for the little things, things as simple as a piece of writing paper, that helped make the days in Libby more bearable.

"My dearest Lydia...," he wrote, then stopped. Rose never knew just what to say in his letters home, not because he didn't have anything to say, but because he knew that his letter would be read by the Rebels before it was approved for forwarding. Certainly he couldn't tell Lydia that he was planning to escape, even though he wanted to tell her that more than anything. He had already described the prison, not in glowing terms but muted enough that she would not worry for his health. He could use some money but feared that his request would be censored or, perhaps worse, permitted to pass through but noted as a warning to thoroughly search any packages coming in his name. Packages were usually rummaged through before they got to the prisoners, even now. No reason to give the Rebels an excuse to look even closer.

After several minutes of thought, Rose told Lydia that he was in generally good health. He refrained from telling her about the prisoner who had died next to him since his last letter. The poor soul had been so close that Rose had been wakened by the man's death rattle. Rose also asked about news of the war, and of the fate of the 77th, hoping that her answer would be allowed through. He hoped that Lydia would realize why his letters contained little of a personal nature. Some things were private, not for the eyes of others to read, especially the enemy. He would personally tell her of his love for her and the children as soon as he fled this God-forsaken place.

Rose's writing was interrupted by the presence of General Dow.

"Good news, Thomas," said the old man. "The government has sent us 500 blankets to distribute. God knows we could use double that, but I guess we should be thankful for anything the Rebs let us have."

"Especially with the weather turning, General," answered Rose. "How are they going to be handed out?"

"The only fair way I can think of is to give out one to every two prisoners," said the General. "That should just about work out for now. If we're still short, we'll just have to triple up where we have to. At least for a while, until Washington sends some more."

"Think they will?" asked Rose, maneuvering his injured foot so that he could stand with a minimum of pain.

"Who knows?" responded Dow. "I'm as loyal as any man in here, but sometimes I have to question some of the things the government does. I just can't understand why more isn't being done to set up some exchanges. I know what the President is saying, about recognizing the Confederacy and all, but it seems like nobody up there realizes just what we're going through down here."

"I get thinkin' that way too, sometimes. But it doesn't help to fret about it, does it?" commented Rose.

"I guess not. I just get a little down in the mouth once in a while. Guess this is one of those days. At any rate, to answer your question, Washington is still promising us more blankets and warm clothes if this distribution goes smooth. Guess they don't want any trouble over a few blankets."

"Well," said Rose, "It looks like we'll have to make sure there are no hitches then, won't we? At least, none that they have to hear about."

Nearby, a scruffy looking Rebel guard lurked in the shadows, appearing to watch over the prisoners but obviously taking in the conversation.

"Something you want to know about, Reb?" asked Rose, his voice dripping with sarcasm.

Somewhat sheepishly, the guard shuffled closer.

"Couldn't help overhearin' yer conversation, Yank," he said with a grin.

"I don't guess you could, seein' as how your ears were cocked our way," said Rose.

Dow placed a hand on Rose's arm, a cautioning gesture to warn Rose not to let his emotions control the situation.

"Jest doin' my job, Colonel," said the man.

Rose looked him over with a steely glare, seemingly staring clear through the guard as his eyes swept from his head to his feet and back again. Rose's contempt didn't seem to faze the Rebel, a tall, thinly built man with a Satan-like mustache and goatee. Gently rubbing his hand over his own full beard, Rose finally spoke.

"Your job is what, Private? To listen in to our conversations? Then what? Run to Turner? Must get pretty dull, eavesdropping on a conversation about blankets." Rose could feel General Dow's grip tighten as the older officer tried to keep him calm.

"Passes the time, Colonel," the guard said with a smirk. "Passes the time."

Rose clenched and unclenched his fists, wishing he could physically attack him. He knew he couldn't, however much he wanted to. To do so would mean certain banishment to the cells.

"Not the way I want to get to the cellar," thought Rose.

Looking at General Dow, the guard spat a stream of tobacco juice onto the floor. Wiping his mouth on a grimy sleeve, he grinned and said to Dow, "Y'know, General, y'all oughtta train yer officers to be a little more polite. Might jest make things a whole lot better fer y'all. Y'unnerstan' what I'm sayin'?"

"That goes two ways, Private," shot back Dow. "If any of my men offend you with their attitude, it doesn't bother me one bit. This place isn't exactly Heaven on earth, in the event you haven't noticed."

"Well now, General, I reckon y'all jest might about as well git used to it. With Abe sendin' y'all blankets, looks like he's fixin' to let y'all stay here all winter, don't it?"

"I wouldn't count on that, Private," said Dow. "Richmond's going to belong to us shortly, anyway, and when it does, we'll have all the blan-

kets we're going to need. And hogslop like you won't have anything to say about it."

Rose simply stared at the guard with scorn. The General obviously wasn't going to need his help. From all appearances, the old man was going to be able to hold his own.

"Now that's where you're wrong, General," countered the Rebel. "The Stars 'n' Bars will be flyin' over Richmond long after both of y'all are dead and gone. Over Washington, too, fer that matter. And hogslop like me'll be what makes it possible. I'll be marchin' up the streets of Washington 'fore you see the light of a free day again."

Rose had heard enough. Arguing with the likes of this man would serve no purpose. It would only lead to trouble. Trouble that could interfere with any escape attempt.

"Let 'im go, General. He's not worth arguin' with," said Rose.

The Rebel's eyes flashed. Hatred seemed to ooze from every pore as he spat again, this time onto Rose's boot.

"Don't matter none to me, Yank. Y'all don't have to like me. Yuh jest have to do as I say, and y'all both know that's a fact. Now...seein' as how Washington don't seem to care about exchangin' fer yuh, I reckon we'll have a chance to have lots of these little talks, don't y'all agree?" His mouth turned upward in an evil grin as he taunted the two officers.

Rose stared in disgust at the tobacco juice on his boot, then turned away, pulling his arm out of Dow's grasp. As the two moved away from the guard, his mocking voice trailed after them.

"Don't get them blankets dirty now, Yanks. Y'all ain't gonna be gittin' any more fer a while," the Rebel said with a jeering laugh. "Abe figgers he done about enough fer now, givin' y'all half a blanket each."

Rose and Dow worked their way through the crowd, trying to silence the guard by getting out of his sight.

When the mocking remarks no longer fell on their ears, Rose stopped and turned to Dow. "You should have grabbed your own arm, General, instead of mine. I thought you were goin' to go after him there, for a while. Wouldn't have blamed you if you did."

Dow looked at Rose for a few seconds, then burst into laughter. "Wouldn't that have been a sight, Thomas? An old man like me trying to teach a young pup like that some manners. Thirty years ago, maybe, but no more. He wouldn't even have broken a sweat takin' care of the likes of me."

Rose laughed along with Dow. Looking at him admiringly, he said, "You have enough friends in here, General. We wouldn't have let that happen. Anyway, I have a feeling you would have held your own, for a while at least."

"A real short while, Thomas," Dow said, still chuckling. "Maybe I should have turned him over my knee, though. They wouldn't throw me in the cells for that, would they?"

Rose laughed again. "Not a chance, sir. Not a chance."

The two continued talking, changing the subject from time to time as their moods dictated. Rose always enjoyed his talks with Dow. He had found him to be a very intelligent man, although his opinions didn't always dovetail with Rose's. Still, the two got along well, and the differences of opinion merely served to break the monotony of prison life.

Suddenly, the conversation was interrupted by angry shouts.

"What in tarnation's wrong with you, man?" shouted a young captain, his face red with anger.

"Ain't nothin' wrong with me," came the answer from the lieutenant, his relatively clean appearance indicating his recent arrival at Libby.

"Well, there must be, for you to throw away a good piece of meat like that," the captain shot back.

"Good piece of meat? Good piece of meat?" the lieutenant repeated incredulously. "That there hunk of ham was rotten clean into the bone. Ain't no way on God's earth I'm gonna stick a piece of green meat in my mouth that smells like that did."

The captain cautiously peered out the window at the piece of ham that had started the argument, now lying innocently on the street below.

"Days gonna come, Lieutenant, that you're gonna wish you had that piece of rotten ham back. Don't you ever throw away good food like that again. If you don't want it, I'll eat it. God knows I've eaten worse than that in here."

Murmurs of agreement went up from the men who had gathered around the window to gaze wistfully at the discarded meat.

The lieutenant looked around the group, then back at the captain, who by now was standing directly in front of him.

"All due respect, Captain, but if I want to throw away a piece of rancid meat, there ain't nothin' you can do about it."

"We'll see, Lieutenant. Throw another piece out that window and you'll find out what I can do."

"I don't have another piece to throw out, but if I did, I'd do it right now just to give you your comeuppance," said the lieutenant, his voice rising for the first time.

"You don't have to wait until you get another piece of meat to throw out the window, Lieutenant. Why don't you give me my comeuppance right now?" the captain challenged.

The lieutenant's eyes narrowed to a squint, as if he wanted to get a better look at his opponent. Then, without warning, he lunged at the captain, his left shoulder thrusting into the captain's chest. The charge caused both men to fall onto the filthy floor.

The two combatants fought fiercely, rolling back and forth through the muck. Their oaths filled the air as the other prisoners cheered them on. Most of the shouting observers sided with the captain, and cheered wildly with each blow that he landed on the newcomer.

Then, as quickly as it had started, the fight was ended when a guard rushed over to determine the source of the shouting. Seeing the two men flailing about on the floor, he grabbed a nearby water bucket, dumping its contents over the fighters.

The two stopped fighting immediately, stunned by the shock of the icy water. Gasping for breath, partly from the exertion and partly from the sudden dousing, they looked up at the guard.

A look of amusement crossed the Rebel's face.

"Yanks, it don't make a bit a' difference to me if'n y'all want to tear each other apart over a piece of rancid meat. Fact is, I'd kinda like to see it. But I got my orders to keep y'all under control, and that's jest what I'm gonna do. Now, if'n y'all keep it up, we're gonna have to separate yuh fer a spell. Mebbe a few days in a private cell downstairs'll git y'all to likin' each other a little better. What's it gonna be?"

The two simply stared at the guard. Before either could reply, a voice in the back of the crowd shouted out, "If you Rebs would just give us enough to eat there'd be no fights."

The guard whirled in the direction of the voice. "I ain't even got enough to eat, myself," he shouted back, "And I'll be hanged if'n I'm gonna share any of it with the likes of y'all."

Another voice rang out. "You stinkin' Seceshes wouldn't share it even if you had it!"

"Not with y'all, I wouldn't," said the guard, a sinister grin appearing on his face. "I'd just as soon throw it out myself, as give it to a Yank."

An angry murmur rose from the prisoners, causing the guard to edge toward the door. Although he wasn't the brightest the South had to offer, he was smart enough to realize that even an armed guard wouldn't last long against a room full of desperate prisoners.

"Y'all jest remember what I said. Any more fightin' and y'all can count on spendin' some time down in the cellar."

As he left the room, those closest to the window turned and looked longingly again at the tainted meat. As the captain had said, they all had eaten far worse. And even rotten meat was better than nothing, to a starving man.

"Git back in there," came the shout from the street, followed by a blast from the sentry's musket toward the men in the window.

The prisoners cursed at the guard as he hurriedly reloaded. One of the men pulled a loose brick from the wall and hurled it at the shooter. The guard looked up nervously as the brick passed within a few feet of his head. Pulling the ramrod out of the muzzle, he raised his gun again. His targets had prudently pulled back from the window, however, and his chance was gone.

As angry voices continued to rain their invectives onto the guard, Dow turned to Rose.

"They're turning us into animals, Thomas."

"We agree on that, sir," answered Rose. "Outside, I wouldn't even consider eating a piece of meat like that. But in here, I'd fight for it, too. You never know. That might be the last piece of ham we'll see for some time."

"If President Lincoln could just see the way men are risking their lives fighting for a piece of meat they don't really want in the first instance, there'd be no more delays in getting the exchanges going again," Dow said, almost to himself as he watched the two drenched prisoners wringing out their clothing. "We've got to find a way to convince Washington to get us out of here."

"Or do it ourselves," thought Rose.

Chapter Seven

The distribution of the blankets had gone surprisingly well. With few exceptions, the prisoners understood that the shipment was all that would be forthcoming for the time being. Although each would have preferred to have his own blanket, even sharing with another prisoner was a luxury compared to what they had become used to.

Of course, there were those who felt that their government had forgotten them. The guards did their best to reinforce this feeling, constantly reminding the prisoners that they were suffering for a government which had chosen to ignore them. Those who were gullible enough to believe the guards became more sullen and bitter. This, in turn, gave the guards new avenues to explore.

"Jest heard about some new exchange talks, Yank," a guard would typically say to one of those giving vent to his bitterness.

The desperate prisoner would often rise to the bait. "What are they saying? Is it soon?"

"Yep. Too bad it won't help y'all none," would come the answer.

"Why not?"

The guard would then say with amusement, knowing full well what the reaction would be, "Yer government says they want the men who were captured most recent to be exchanged first."

While most of the prisoners would recognize the cruel hoax for what it was, some would not. At that point the guards' enjoyment would truly begin, as a tirade would flow from the unsuspecting prisoner.

"How do yuh like that?" the man would typically say. "I was one of the first in line to serve my country, and now the government shows its appreciation by exchangin' for every other prisoner 'cept me. It ain't fair!"

61

As the man would get more vocal, other prisoners would try to convince him that the guards were simply agitating. After some time, the victim of the taunting would recognize what had happened, and become even more despondent for having been taken in.

With more than 1,000 prisoners in Libby, the guards were never lacking for unsuspecting prisoners to mock in this manner, and the constant reminder to the prisoners of their plight was the guards' primary source of amusement.

Meanwhile, the prisoners were getting weaker by the day, either from hunger or illness, or both. For some, the only things that kept them alive were the shipments from family and friends in the North. Although the Rebels searched the packages and kept the best items for themselves, enough food and clothing were allowed through that many were able to stay alive, to wait for the next package. The boxes and crates in which the packages arrived were salvaged by the prisoners and used to build tables and benches. Gradually, furniture was appearing throughout the prison.

Rose, leaning against a post, watched wordlessly as two men dismantled a large packing crate. These two prisoners had already gained a well-deserved reputation as master carpenters, and Rose was anxious to observe their skills first hand. The men expertly disassembled the box with loving care, making sure they did not splinter any of the precious wood.

"What's it going to be?" Rose finally asked.

"Not sure yet, Colonel," the taller of the two answered. His hands, gnarled and strong, gave away the fact that in his civilian life the man had made his living through some type of physical effort. A blacksmith, Rose had heard. "Thinkin' about makin' a chair or two, but it all depends on how much wood we get from this ole crate."

The second man, a young lieutenant whose face bore the scars of more than one battle, looked up with a smile.

"One thing's sure, Colonel. Whatever we end up buildin', I'm sure we ain't got one a'ready."

Rose laughed. "That's a pretty safe statement, Lieutenant. This place isn't exactly overcrowded with furniture, is it?"

Both men grinned, then returned to their task. A brick from the wall served as their hammer, while a knife performed double duty, being used to pry out nails one minute, then to cut and shape the boards the next. Seeing the taller man struggling with a piece of the framework for the crate, Rose stepped in to help. After several minutes of wrestling with the stubborn section of crate, it gave way. The wood, so thick that Rose could barely get both hands completely around it, seemed too large to serve much purpose for chair building.

"What will you use this for?" Rose asked.

"Oh, we'll cut that up and use it for the legs, Colonel. Should give us a good sturdy base." The man seemed pleased that Rose had asked. Many higher ranking officers didn't seem all that interested in what the younger men were building, at least not until they saw the finished product. Then, however, they were quick to put the new piece of furniture to use.

"You'll cut it up," Rose repeated. Looking around, he then asked the next obvious question. "You'll cut it up with what?"

Both carpenters looked at Rose and grinned. Then they looked at each other, then back at Rose. Their countenances told Rose that they knew something he didn't.

"We got us a saw, Colonel. Just don't leave it out where the guards'll see it, that's all," the younger man finally said. "Daniel here found a saw blade down in the kitchen a few days ago."

The taller man, Daniel, interjected, "Well, I guess I didn't exactly find it. One of them Rebel carpenters they got in here puttin' bars on the windows just happened to lay it down when I was walkin' past. Must've stuck to my hand, cause when I got back up here I looked up my sleeve and there it was. Yuh think I should take it back down and try to find the owner?"

The two men laughed, and Rose joined in.

"No, I guess not," said Rose. "Not until you've got all your furniture made, at any rate."

The three laughed again. Suddenly, Daniel stopped laughing, a serious look coming over his face.

"Here comes trouble," he said, looking over Rose's shoulder.

Rose turned and spied two guards being led by a thin wiry man, their gait obviously hastened by anger. The leader, a black haired man with a beard, appeared to be in his forties, with dark eyes and a sinister appearance.

"Outta my way, Yank," the leader snarled, shoving a prisoner aside as he strode toward the doorway leading to the next room.

The prisoners were silent to a man, which intensified the staccato clicks of the leader's boots on the damp floor.

"Captain Turner," said Daniel, his voice dripping with contempt. "Looks like he's mad about somethin'. Then again, he's always mad about somethin', ain't he, John?"

"That he is. But he looks madder'n usual this time."

The three watched as Turner and the two guards walked briskly past, stopping at the doorway. The next room, known among the prisoners as Colonel Streight's room out of respect for the Indiana officer, had been designated off limits to the men of Upper Chickamauga by prison officials. Likewise, the men of Streight's room were not to wander into Upper Chickamauga. The liberal policies of the first few days of Rose's stay had been tightened up, at least in theory. Most of the guards had long ago given up on trying to enforce the new rules, outnumbered as they were by the prisoners who ignored the orders.

"Y'all don't want to do what we tell yuh?" said Turner. "Then we'll fix it so y'all don't have any choice."

The two guards began closing the door between the two rooms.

"What's the problem here?" said Streight, his presence in the doorway preventing the guards from closing it completely. The tone of his voice made it apparent that he was not asking a question; he was questioning Turner's actions.

"Well now, Colonel Streight. It appears as though you Yanks either ain't smart enough to follow simple orders, or y'all ain't showin' no respect to those of us who are lookin' out fer yer well bein'. Which is it?" Turner said with more than a hint of sarcasm.

"I'm not sure I understand," replied Streight.

"Y'all don't understand," repeated Turner.

"He don't understand," Turner then said to his guards, somewhat louder. The two guards grinned as they continued to hold onto the door.

"Fer yer information, Colonel Streight, and fer the rest a' y'all, too, y'all have been told not to go from one room to the other. But fer some reason, y'all don't want to follow those orders. We can't tell who's who up here, and we're tired of tryin'. It's got so bad that the Clerk is complainin' that he can't even get an accurate count up here no more." Turner's voice was rising in anger, and saliva shot out of his mouth as he nearly shouted at the men gathered around.

"Y'all might think it's funny to sneak over to the next room and get counted, then sneak back to yer own room and get counted again. But this here's serious business. We have to know who's here and who ain't. Fer all we know, some of y'all might decide to wander off, and we wouldn't know about it. Y'all might get outside where we can't take care of yuh, and how would we explain it to Washington if'n y'all were to get hurt?" Turner said, the sarcasm returning to his voice.

Streight, presenting an imposing figure, refused to move out of the doorway. By now, Rose had learned that Streight was despised by the prison officials for the letters he was constantly sending to Washington, and Streight's feelings toward his captors were mutual. Streight had done nothing to endear himself to his captors since his arrival, showing his disrespect at every opportunity. The Confederates also had heard rumors, all untrue, that Streight had commanded a regiment of black soldiers. This, in the eyes of the Confederates, made Streight a figure of contempt.

"Y'all better move back into yer own room, Colonel, so's we can nail this here door shut," said Turner. "Otherwise we'll have to move y'all down to the cellar."

Turner's tone told Streight that it would be futile to protest further. He reluctantly retreated into his own room, allowing the guards to close the door. They immediately began nailing it so that it could not be reopened. Turner gazed at the throng of prisoners around him with an evil smirk.

"Yuh see?" he said, to nobody in particular. "If'n y'all would jest cooperate a little, we wouldn't have to go to these extremes. But y'all have to resist ever'thing we ask y'all to do. Then General Winder hears about it and gets mad. And when he gets mad, I get mad. And when I get mad... well, most of y'all know what happens when I get mad." He chuckled at his attempt at humor. No one else acknowledged it.

"Thing is, yer General Dow's downstairs talkin' to General Winder right now. Washington sent some more blankets and clothes, and Dow wants to take them over to Belle Isle. The way y'all are actin' I've got half a mind to go down there and tell General Winder not to let none of the shipment through."

"You've got half a mind, that's a fact!" a voice shouted from the middle of the crowd.

Turner turned in the direction of the insult, his eyes blazing with anger.

"Who said that?" he shouted, the tendons on the sides of his neck distending with rage.

"Who said that?" he repeated after no answer was forthcoming. Again, there was no reply.

"Well, now. Reckon I'll just have to go downstairs and tell General Winder to send them blankets back."

"Wrap yourself up in one of them before he does," another voice called out.

"Y'all think this is a joke, do yuh? Well, we'll see who's laughin' after a few of yer enlisted men freeze to death over on Belle Isle." Turner gave one last hateful look at the group, then turned on his heel and stormed toward the stairs, the guards trailing closely behind.

"Don't forget your puppy dogs. They're havin' a tough time keepin up with you," an unknown voice shouted from the midst of the group.

One of the guards stopped and glared back, not happy at being called one of Dick Turner's puppy dogs.

From the back of the group came a "Woof! Woof!"

Immediately others in the group took up the cry, barking like dogs at the guards. The guard, realizing the futility of trying to stop the group of barking prisoners, turned and followed the others down the stairs.

When the barking had subsided, Rose, Daniel, and John looked at one another. Rose spoke first.

"Looks like we've seen the last of Colonel Streight for a while." The two colonels had become friends in the short time Rose had been in Libby, and he would miss their many discussions.

"Not necessarily, Colonel," came an unexpected answer from Daniel.

Enjoying the puzzled look on Rose's face, Daniel turned to John and said, "John, fetch that bench we made yesterday and bring it over to the door."

John hastened to comply with his friend's request. When he had done so, Daniel pulled the bench into a position directly across the doorway, then knelt so that his eyes were level with the bench.

Rose continued to watch, still having no idea how a bench was going to have anything to do with opening the door. Daniel took a pencil and drew a line on the door, level with the top of the bench. Standing, he turned to Rose and proudly declared, "We'll be talkin' to Colonel Streight inside the hour, sir."

Daniel then walked away, leaving Rose and the others who had gathered to guess what was going to happen next. Even John wasn't sure what to expect.

In less than a minute Daniel returned, now carrying the saw that he had liberated from the Rebel carpenters. Without a word, he knelt and began digging into the door with a penknife, just below the line he had drawn. Within a half hour he had worked a hole completely through the door, and Rose finally realized what Daniel was up to. As he watched, Daniel worked the saw blade into the hole he had just made, then began working the saw back and forth. In a short time he had the door cut the entire width, and he opened the bottom two feet of the door with a flourishing gesture.

"Anybody want to see Colonel Streight?" he asked, with a grin.

Several men dropped to their knees and crawled through the opening, after which Daniel again closed the door. He then pulled the bench in front of the doorway. Rose was impressed when he realized that the bench now hid the crack between the two sections of door, and unless someone moved the bench, it was impossible to know that the door had ever been cut.

Rose grinned at Daniel, then shook his head.

"Yankee ingenuity, Colonel. Never underestimate it," Daniel said with a smile.

"I won't, Daniel. But l hope the Rebs continue to."

"They always do, sir," said John. After a short pause, he stated matter of factly, "Well, time to get back to work. You coming, Colonel?"

Daniel and John then started back to their crate, to build whatever furniture the salvaged lumber would yield. Rose followed.

Over the next several hours Rose was fascinated by the display of craftsmanship exhibited by the two men. Each seemed to know what the other was going to do, even before he did it. They worked together like a team that had been together for years, and the end result was two chairs

which, except for a few details which could not be incorporated because of the lack of tools, could have come from any factory. The two pieces of furniture were more than functional.

John stepped back to admire his handiwork. "They keep us here long enough, we'll have this place decorated pretty good, don't you think, sir?"

Rose chuckled. "I don't doubt that you could, John. I just hope you don't have the chance."

"I'd like to see you get your wish, Colonel. I can make furniture like this at home in Ohio just as easy as I can in here."

Putting his hand on John's shoulder, Rose said, "You'll get that chance again, John. We won't be here forever."

The three men took turns sitting in the new chairs, after which they all agreed that the chairs were a vast improvement over sitting on the wet floor.

By now darkness had fallen, and after what passed for a meal in Libby, Rose decided to get some sleep before he met Hamilton for their nightly exploration.

"Colonel Rose, Colonel White's looking for you," said Gageby, tapping Rose on the shoulder.

"Thanks, Jim. I'll go see him shortly."

Rose was not in a particularly good mood. He and Hamilton had gone to the cellar again last night, intent on escaping through the doorway, only to find a sentry standing beside the opening. Nothing seemed to be going in their favor. Now Colonel White wanted to see him about something. Rose was seated in one of the many classes which the prisoners often conducted. This one, being taught by a Lieutenant Colonel who had been a Professor of History in his civilian life, had something to do with medieval Europe. Rose wasn't sure exactly what it was about because he really had very little interest in it. His attendance was merely a means of fighting the mind-numbing boredom which made every day seem endless. A man could only sleep so much, so Rose did what most of the others also did. He sat in on lectures and classes, attended debates by prisoners who considered themselves great orators, and even decided to try his hand at carving. He quickly learned that it was not one of his talents.

Whatever Colonel White wanted, it would probably be more interesting than listening to a lecture on medieval Europe. Rose quietly slipped away from the assembled prisoners and made his way to where he thought the colonel would be.

"There you are, Thomas. I see Gageby found you," Colonel White's voice boomed from behind Rose.

Rose had known White for some time before they had met again in Libby, and the two, although not close friends, got along well.

"Hello, Harry. How'd the distribution go?" Rose asked.

White had been among the delegation from Libby which had been authorized by prison officials to take the second distribution of blankets and clothes to Belle Isle, the prison for the enlisted men. Despite Dick Turner's protests, General Winder had not stopped the shipment. White, along with General Dow, Colonel Alexander von Schrader, and Lieutenant Colonel Joseph Boyd, had spent the better part of the previous day passing out the badly needed supplies to the enlisted men, many of whom were sleeping on the open ground with no blankets or tents. Several had already frozen to death.

"That's what I wanted to speak to you about, Thomas," said White. "Let's go for a walk."

The two strolled through the throng nonchalantly, White describing the conditions the men on Belle Isle were experiencing.

"It's inhumane, Thomas, it really is. At least we have a roof over our heads here. It might leak a little, but it keeps most of the bad weather out. But over there, those poor devils have nothing. Nothing! No food, only a few tents, no coats. Some of them are walking around with no shirts. Can you imagine that? And in this weather? I'm glad we were able to get the blankets and clothes to them. We might save a few lives, anyway."

"How much did we end up getting from Washington?" Rose asked.

"They sent fifteen hundred blankets and about a thousand suits of clothing. Not enough for everyone, but it's better than nothing," answered White. "But...I really wanted to talk to you about something else."

By now they had reached the outside wall, and White looked around the room like a man who had something to hide. He knelt beside a blanket which appeared to be covering something, motioning Rose to join him near the floor. Satisfied that nobody was paying them any attention, White drew back the corner of the blanket to reveal a nearly new coil of rope.

"What do you think, Thomas. Can you use it?" he asked.

"For what?" Rose returned.

"Thomas, Thomas, Thomas. We know each other better than that. I'm not asking you for details, but I've heard about your nightly forays downstairs. I don't know exactly what you're planning, but I suspect a rope may come in handy when you do it."

Still not wishing to divulge any unnecessary information, Rose asked, "Where did you get it?"

"It was used to tie some of the bales of blankets up. I just confiscated it."

"Well, yes. It could come in very handy," Rose stated somewhat sheepishly, after a long pause. "What made you think of me, though."

"You do have something planned, don't you, you old devil!" White exclaimed in a stage whisper.

"Nothing definite, Harry. Honest. But the rope may prove useful," Rose remarked, unable to conceal a wry grin.

"Nothing definite, but something, right?"

"Something, Harry, but even I don't know what it is, for sure," Rose admitted. "I just know I don't want to stay in here any longer than I have to."

"Nobody does, Thomas," said White. "You just happen to be doing more about it than most of us. I would ask one thing of you, though. Let me know before you leave, if you can. You don't have to tell me any details. Just let me know. And take me with you, if that's possible."

Rose looked into White's eyes. He thought he could see a tear forming before White looked away.

"I'll try, Harry. I really will. And thanks for thinking of me. I'll put the rope to good use."

"You're welcome, Thomas. And good luck."

The two shook hands, Rose wishing he could tell White his plans but still afraid of letting too many know.

"Can I leave the rope here until tonight?" Rose asked. "Carrying a bundle of this size around in the light of day is bound to raise a lot of questions I'd rather not have to answer."

"By all means. Just remember who got it for you when the time comes."

"I won't forget, Harry. And thanks again."

Rose shook White's hand one more time, then left. Walking back to his own area, he could hardly contain his excitement. A rope could open up a realm of new possibilities, and he could scarcely wait to let Hamilton know of their good fortune. Maybe things were beginning to turn their way, finally.

The day dragged on interminably. Would darkness never get here? Rose tried to occupy his time by reading a well worn book which had been passed from prisoner to prisoner, but had difficulty concentrating. He watched Daniel and John build a small table, thankful more for the time that was occupied than for the table itself.

Finally, nightfall arrived. The men began to settle for the night, and the familiar routine of singing and arguing with the guards began. "This might be the one thing I'll miss about this place," he thought, listening to the patriotic songs interspersed with curses from the guards.

At long last, the men were settled enough for Rose to make his way to the kitchen. Detouring to pick up the rope, he reached the room to find Hamilton pacing.

"Sorry I'm late, Andrew," Rose offered.

"That's all right. I was just wondering what became of you. For a minute I thought maybe you left without me," Hamilton said, the look of concern disappearing from his face when he saw his friend. Then, spying the rope slung over Rose's shoulder he exclaimed, "What've you got there?"

"This's why I'm late. Colonel White got it for us," answered Rose, with a smile.

"We sure could've used that a few nights ago when we were trying to get down to that roof in the rainstorm, couldn't we?" Hamilton asked.

"Sure could've," Rose agreed. "But I think the cellar door is a better way, now."

"I do, too. But, if nothin' else, that rope'll make it a whole lot easier to get down there."

"How did Colonel White ever get this," Hamilton asked, running his fingers over the inch-thick hemp.

"He never said, exactly. Just said he confiscated it. We probably don't want to know the rest," said Rose.

"Yeah, you're prob'ly right," Hamilton commented, still admiring the rope. After a short pause, he went on, "Well, might just as well start to use it, don't you think?"

Rose agreed and the two quickly tied the rope to one of the support posts, carrying the loose end to the initialed floorboard. Raising the plank, Rose tossed the end of the rope into the inky darkness below. Looking up at Hamilton as he squeezed through the opening, he replied, "Maybe tonight's our lucky night."

"Let's hope so, Thomas," came the reply.

The two quickly lowered themselves to the basement and stealthily traveled the now familiar route through the darkness to the doorway. As was their custom, they stopped some distance from the opening to allow themselves the opportunity to observe the sentry's movements.

Standing quietly in the shadows, the sentry came by the doorway within a few minutes. As they awaited his return, they were surprised to see another pass shortly later.

"What's he doin' here?" Hamilton expostulated, almost to himself.

"I don't know," Rose answered. Two sentries on this side of the building was something they had not seen before. "Maybe he's just here to relieve the other one."

The two stood without talking, watching the guards' routine. After some time, it became apparent that the second man was not there as relief. For some reason there were now two sentries patrolling where one had always been before.

"This is going to make things a little harder, Andrew."

"No doubt," answered Hamilton. "You just can't trust the Johnnies, Thomas. About the time you think you've figured them out, they do something like this. Why would they ever decide to put two guards here, now?"

"It doesn't matter why, Andrew. They're here, and we'd be wise to forget about getting out tonight and just spend a few nights watching and learning."

"I guess you're right. I'm just gettin'a little tired of all these setbacks, that's all."

"I understand. I feel the same way, but this'll just make us appreciate freedom a little more when we get it," Rose commented philosophically.

The rest of the night was spent in watchful silence, each man lost in his own thoughts as he observed the movements of the two sentries. They spoke only when necessary, and then only in curt whispers. Both were impressed with the conscientious performances of both guards. Neither sentry appeared to be anything but vigilant.

Finally, after several hours, Rose signaled to Hamilton that it was time to go back upstairs.

Reaching the kitchen, Hamilton began gathering the rope. "General Bobby Lee'd be right proud of them two, wouldn't he, Thomas?" said Hamilton.

"He surely would. And he should be. They did a good job, unfortunate as it was for us," agreed Rose.

Hamilton hid the rope behind a pile of straw in the corner, still muttering about the efficiency of the guards. "Many's the time I wished my pickets did that good a job," he said loud enough for Rose to hear.

"They're well drilled, I'll give you that. But I think I spotted something," said Rose. "I noticed that they pass each other going in opposite directions. After they pass, they're walking with their backs to each other. And they're looking away from the door. We'd only have a few seconds, but I think if we time it right, we can get out and into the shadows before they turn around."

"You really think we can?" asked Hamilton, as the two started up the stairs.

"Yeah, I do," answered Rose. "And I'm willing to give it a go tomorrow night."

Hamilton's hopes rose. "I'm all for it," he said.

Rose refrained from saying anything further, as another prisoner started down the stairs toward them. The young man stopped in front of Rose, even though there was plenty of room on the stair to pass.

"How's everything in the basement this fine evening, Colonel?" he queried.

Rose could feel his heart race, and his palms began to sweat despite the chill of the air. How much did this man know, and who is he?

"Don't worry, Colonel. I don't know anything about what you're doing. And I'm a legitimate Yankee, honest I am." Holding out his hand, he introduced himself. "Lieutenant James Wells, sir. Eighth Michigan Cavalry. Cavalry, just like you, Captain," he said, turning his head toward Hamilton.

Shaking his hand, Rose glanced at Hamilton, who also appeared puzzled about what was going on.

Squinting in the dim candlelight, Rose finally asked, "What are you going downstairs for, Lieutenant, and what do you know about our visits to the basement?"

"I go down every night, sir. A few weeks ago, when I was on mess, I saw that they soak the kettles overnight to loosen up the burned rice. I come down each night and scrape it off the bottom of the pot. It's burnt, and a mite soggy, but it's edible. Just about doubles what we get to eat in a day." Wells seemed willing to discuss his reasons for venturing to the kitchen. "As for your visits to the cellar, I don't know much. I happened to see the two of you go down a couple of times. And once I saw you puttin' the floorboard back in place when you came back up. Other'n that, I don't know anything."

Rose and Hamilton exchanged glances again. For once, Hamilton was silent, letting Rose handle the talking.

"You tell anyone?" Rose asked.

"Tell anyone what?" answered Wells. "That you're lookin' for a way out? Colonel, half the men in here have the same thing in mind. Some of their ideas sound pretty good, others I don't want any part of. But tell someone? No, sir. That's up to you if you want the rest to know how your leavin'."

"We're not really planning anything," Rose protested. "Just lookin' around."

Wells was unconvinced. "Like I say, Colonel. None of my business. But I sure wish you'd keep me in mind when the time comes. I can be of good use to you, I really can."

"If I decide to leave, I'll let you know, Lieutenant," said Rose. "But for right now, I don't have any strong plans to put Libby behind me."

"That's fine, Colonel. I just don't happen to believe you, but I'm sure not going to tell anyone. I'm down here 'most every night. When you're ready to go, just give me a whistle," said Wells, starting down the steps.

Rose gave an uneasy glance at Hamilton. Hamilton's eyes were boring into the back of Wells as the latter continued down the steps.

Finally, Hamilton broke the silence. "Think he's a real Yankee, Thomas?"

"I'm not sure," came the answer. "But if he knows we're goin' into the basement every night, you can bet a whole lot of others do, too."

"Well, long as everyone that knows is a Yankee we'll be all right, won't we?" Hamilton asked.

"Maybe," said Rose. "But when people know about something like this, sooner or later they talk about it. And when people talk, other people hear things, if you know what I mean."

"Rebs?" asked Hamilton.

"Yep," answered Rose. "And I don't like this one bit."

"You think they know?" asked Hamilton, a worried look on his face.

"No way of tellin' for sure," Rose shot back, looking more than a little concerned himself. "We're just gonna have to be careful, and that's a fact. And I think we should figure on takin' our little walk tomorrow night, if we can. Every night we wait is a night that someone else might find out what we're up to."

The two talked briefly at the top of the stairs, outlining plans to meet the following evening after dark. If all went well, they would only be going to the basement one more time. The time for action was here, before the Confederates learned anything about their plan. If their daring plan to walk out through the basement doorway did not work...well, that was something Rose didn't even want to think about. It had to work. It just had to.

The appointed hour arrived. Although it was something both men had long anticipated, they were very nervous nonetheless.

"You think we're ready for this, Thomas?" asked Hamilton, a hollow feeling in the pit of his stomach.

"I sure hope so," answered Rose. "If we aren't, may God help us."

The two were huddled in the darkness of the basement. They had remained hidden in the shadows of the kitchen for nearly an hour before sliding down the rope to the basement, just to see if Wells or any other prisoner had entered. Nobody had made an appearance.

Watching the two sentries walking their appointed routes, Rose noticed that they did not pass each other directly in front of the doorway. That would make it even more difficult, because each sentry would have his back to the doorway only after passing it. If one passed while the other was still approaching, several valuable seconds would be lost until the second guard passed and faced away from the portal.

After observing several cycles, Rose whispered to Hamilton, "The fat one passes the door first. As soon as he goes past, we'll get ready. The other one will be along in about eight seconds. As soon as he goes past, I'll run across the street and duck into the shadows. You do the same on the next pass."

Hamilton nodded that he understood, wiping the perspiration from his brow despite the cold temperature in the basement.

The two stealthily crept closer to the opening, taking care to remain out of the dim glow cast into the cellar from the streetlight.

After what seemed like hours, the first guard could be heard approaching. Rose looked at Hamilton and nodded. Hamilton patted him on the back. "Good luck, Thomas. See you on the other side."

"You, too, Andrew."

The first guard passed the opening. Rose began to mentally count the seconds. Exactly as the two would-be escapees had observed, the second sentry passed on the count of eight. Allowing the guard a few additional seconds to get away from the doorway, Rose took a deep breath and slipped out into the street.

After only a few steps away from the building he heard one of the guards shout, "Halt!"

Rose froze in mid stride. Was the guard shouting at him, or was there someone else out in the street?

"You, there," shouted the guard. "Who are you and where are you going?"

Rose turned and saw that the guard was, indeed, shouting at him. For whatever the reason, the guard had turned sooner than anticipated and had seen Rose before he had even reached the middle of the street.

Instinctively, Rose reacted. Turning back toward Libby, he made a mad dash for the doorway, hoping that the guard would not shoot. Fortunately, the second guard had heard the other's shouts and had come running, thus putting himself into the line of fire. The first guard cursed as Rose reached the doorway.

"Let's go, Andrew!" he whispered loudly at Hamilton as he ran past.

Hamilton, who had observed everything, was ready. He joined Rose in the dash for the rope, just as the first guard reached the doorway.

"Yuh see anythin'?" the second guard queried as he also reached the opening.

"Nope, but I'm sure he came in here. Get the corporal," he commanded.

"Don't yuh think we should go in after 'im?" asked the second guard, a relative newcomer to guard duty at Libby.

"Y'all wanna go in with them rats, go ahead. As fer me, I'm gonna wait 'til the corporal gits here and foller him in."

The delay was all that Rose and Hamilton needed. They raced for the rope which would take them back to safety. Behind them, the sentries waited for their superior officer to lead them into the rat-infested gloom.

Scrambling up the rope, Rose and Hamilton could hear the Rebels filing into the basement. As they replaced the plank, the two could see the glow of a lantern approaching below.

Quickly hurling the rope into the straw in the corner, they scurried up the steps, not waiting to listen to the guards below. Reaching the top, the two raced to their respective sleeping areas without so much as a word to one another. Deftly trying to step over prone bodies, Rose found little room to place his feet. More than one prisoner cursed at the unknown man running through their midst, giving little regard to those who were trying to sleep. Reaching his sleeping area, he quickly dropped to the floor and hoped his heaving chest would not give him away if the guards came in.

Downstairs, the sentries angrily searched the basement, unaware that they were looking for two prisoners, and that they had made their way to the floor above.

"How could y'all let them get away when they wuz right under yer nose?" the corporal of the guard angrily demanded.

"We follered them in as soon as we seen 'em, Corporal. They wuz jest too quick, is all."

"Too quick," the corporal spat out with disdain. "Y'all wuz just too slow. I better not find out y'all wuz standin' around chewin' the fat when y'all wuz supposed to be on watch!"

"No sir, Corporal. We wuz doin' our duty," said the guard in an apprehensive tone.

The corporal of the guard tossed a nail keg aside and peered into a darkened corner. As he did so, a man raised up to a sitting position, rubbing his eyes, at the outer perimeter of the lantern's beam.

With an oath, the corporal pointed his pistol at the man.

"Don't shoot! Don't shoot!" the man shouted in fear as he raised his hands in surrender.

At the outburst, a second man also raised up just a few feet away.

"Who are you, and what are y'all doin' down here?" shouted the corporal.

By now, several others had stood up, all looking bewildered and wondering what it was that had caused the guards to come into their sleeping quarters so abruptly.

One of the first men to arise finally stammered, "We're...we're... we're jest sleepin' here. We're all loyal Virginians, sir. We work here durin' the day, fixin' the windows 'n' such. We ain't doin' nothin' wrong. Honest, we ain't."

The guard knew that workers had been adding bars to the windows and strengthening the doors, and the men did appear to belong in the basement.

Looking around at the group, the Corporal held the lantern as high as he could and fairly shouted at the men, "Y'all are lucky we didn't shoot yuh. Which one of yuh wuz jest out in the street?"

The men looked around at one another, puzzled. Why would one of their number have a reason to go out into the street, they wondered?

"We know one of yuh wuz out there. One of these here guards seen yuh. Ain't nobody in trouble. We jest want to know what's goin' on, is all." The corporal was calming down now, and was speaking in a more reasonable tone.

"Weren't one of us, sir. It sure weren't. Night's too short, now. Ain't no way any one of us is gonna be out wanderin' around and losin' more sleep."

The guards looked around the group, some of them still not appearing to be fully awake.

"Hadda be one of them, Corporal. Ain't nobody else down here, y'all can see that fer yerself," one of the guards offered, hoping that the corporal would agree. After all, there was no possible way for any of the prisoners to get down here at night, let alone get back inside and hide. The guards' search of the basement had been too thorough for anyone to still be down here without being seen.

"Maybe," said the corporal. "I still ain't sure."

The corporal looked at each man directly, then glanced around the basement. Lowering the lantern, he rubbed his chin thoughtfully. Finally, he spat into the straw and said, "Whoever yuh wuz out there in the street, y'all better jest stay back inside from now on. Yuh never know, we jest might take y'all fer a Yankee tryin' to get back up North, and I'd surely hate to see one of y'all get shot fer a bluebelly. Y'all say yer loyal Virginians, and fer now I'll believe yuh. But there ain't no worse way fer a Virginian to die than to have someone think he's a Yank, and that's a fact!"

 *Chapter Eight*

The Confederate officers stood up as Dow entered the room, showing their respect for a general officer, even one who served under the enemy flag.

"Thank you for coming, General," spoke the first. "You know Major Turner, I trust?"

"General Winder, I am very familiar with Major Turner. Every time my stomach growls I remember him," said Dow.

Ignoring Dow's comment, Turner greeted the Northern General with a curt nod.

Winder walked around his desk and sat on its front. "The reason I've asked you to visit today, General, is to let you know that your government has approached us with an interesting offer. A very interesting offer. We thought you may want to hear about it."

"Any offer from Washington is of interest to me, General," said Dow.

"I thought as much, General Dow," countered Winder.

Winder shifted positions on the desk, now half leaning, half sitting on the edge. He seemed in no particular rush to let Dow know what was going on. In fact, he seemed to enjoy the suspense he was creating, and carefully watched Dow's face to gauge the reaction. Dow, recognizing Winder's motives, remained expressionless, not wishing to let the Confederate general know that he was, in fact, quite anxious to hear what kind of offer Washington had made.

Finally, Winder began. "First off, y'all may be interested to know that your friend, General Meredith, has sent us 24,000 rations to distribute to the prisoners held here in Richmond. They'll be distributed here at Libby, Belle Isle, Castle Thunder,...everywhere. Each prison will get some.

Now, I realize that 24,000 rations won't stretch all that far, but y'all are going to have to take that up with your people in Washington. All I'm doing is passing out what they send."

"Every little bit helps, General," said Dow, agreeing in his mind that 24,000 rations would hardly make a dent in the food shortage. "By the way, is that 24,000 rations before or after your men have helped themselves?"

"Why, General," said Winder, with a slight smile, "I do believe you're a bit out of sorts today. What do you think, Major."

"Tell yuh the truth, General, I think he's downright insultin'. Ain't no call to make accusations like that," said Turner, his face showing anger. Turning to Dow, he spoke in clipped tones, "Y'all are lucky we're lettin y'all have any of it. We could claim it as spoils of war, yuh know."

Dow's eyebrows rose. "Oh, yes, Major. We do consider ourselves among the more fortunate here in Libby. We get fresh meat every time we're quick enough to catch a rat, another suit of clothes or a blanket every time a man dies, and the opportunity to converse with such pleasant personalities as yourself. I must apologize for my men if we've given you the impression that we aren't most gracious for your hospitality."

Turner took a step toward Dow, but was stopped by the restraining hand of Winder on his chest.

"General, there's no need to be sarcastic," said Winder. "We are fully aware of the shortages. But you must understand, we wouldn't be short of food or clothing if your government would cooperate. We sympathize, really we do. But your anger is directed toward the wrong people. You should be taking that up with Mr. Lincoln."

Dow remained silent. He had already said more than he should have, and he knew it. He just couldn't help himself when he got around Turner, and General Winder, although not all that unpleasant, was feeling the effects of Dow's hatred toward Turner.

Seeing that Dow was not going to respond, Winder continued. "You see, General Dow, your attitude toward us is cause for concern. For that reason, I've decided to let the distribution of these rations be handled by your own Lieutenant Colonel Sanderson, rather than yourself."

Try as he might, Dow could not contain himself after hearing this. He hated Lieutenant Colonel James M. Sanderson as much or more than he hated Turner, despite the fact that Sanderson was on the same side as Dow, or was supposed to be. In fact, most of Libby's prisoners disliked Sanderson to some degree. Many merely didn't like him for the zeal with which he handled his position as head of the cooking details, giving choice assignments and eating schedules to his friends. Others disliked him for his stern demeanor and insistence on military obedience, even in the dismal confines of Libby, where any relaxation of military rules was welcomed enthusiastically as a diversion from the daily routine.

Most of the prisoners who had been in Libby for any length of time, however, had their own reason for hating Sanderson. Several months earlier, an elaborate escape plan had been devised. Using local spies to spread the word among other prisons, the plan had called for the prisoners of Libby and Castle Thunder to rise up on a prearranged signal and overpower the guards at their respective prisons. The mass escape was then to be extended to other prisons within Richmond. The daring plan had been carefully thought out and rehearsed in great detail at both prisons, and those responsible envisioned thousands of federal prisoners making their escapes. Just before it was to have taken place, however, Confederate authorities learned of the scheme from one of the prisoners, and the plan was thwarted. Most of the men believed that it had been Sanderson who had leaked word to the Rebels. This line of thought was even substantiated by some of the Richmond newspapers.

"You can't be serious, General," Dow literally shouted in anger. "I'm the senior officer here and I deserve more respect than this."

"Respect, General?" offered Winder. "I didn't know you were aware of the word. You certainly haven't shown any toward us."

"My respect must be earned, General," Dow said indignantly. "You have yet to do that, and your lackey here will never be able to earn it, no matter what he does."

Turner, bristling at Dow's reference to him as a lackey, leaned forward menacingly. "Now that's just what we mean, General. Y'all are disrespectful, y'all are rude, and y'all are just flat out hard to like. That's why Sanderson is going to handle the distribution."

Turning away, Turner mumbled to himself, but still loud enough for the other two to hear, "I swear I don't know how y'all ever got to be a general. If y'all was in our army you'd be a corporal at best."

"That's enough, Major," interjected Winder. "Let's not make a bad situation worse. It doesn't really matter what General Dow thinks of my choice, the decision is made. Lieutenant Colonel Sanderson will distribute the rations. And before you say anything more, General Dow, you may want to hear about the rest of Washington's offer."

"I can hardly wait," said Dow. "Have they offered to give you Sanderson to serve as Bobby Lee's aide?"

"No, but that doesn't sound like a bad idea," said Winder. "Sanderson appears to be quite efficient."

"Indeed, General," said Dow, regaining his composure. "And he's more a Southerner than a loyal Northerner, too. But I don't have to tell you that, do I?"

"You really aren't helping yourself, here, General," said Winder.

"I don't expect I am," answered Dow, "But I've got to tell the truth as I see it."

"Be that as it may, General, I prefer not to get into a discussion with you concerning your personal feelings toward Mr. Sanderson," Winder said haughtily. "If you wish to hear the rest of Washington's offer, such as it is, I am prepared to discuss that."

Dow could see that nothing was to be gained by arguing any further. "I'm waiting, General," he finally said.

Winder looked at Turner, then back to Dow. "Washington has offered to take all the Federal prisoners off our hands and keep them on parole," he said. "They say that this will guarantee that you prisoners will be living in better conditions, and that we won't have to worry about feeding and guarding y'all any longer."

"In other words, we can all go home?" queried Dow.

"That's what they're offerin', General."

"And your decision?"

"Not mine to make, General. That decision comes from Commissioner Ould. Interestingly enough, though, Washington is also telling us that our boys are gettin' three servings of meat every day and sleepin' in beds in comfortable quarters. Unfortunately, we know that to be a lie, and if they're willin' to lie about that, then we must assume they are lyin' about keepin' y'all on parole. I personally would be most disappointed if I would send you home on parole and later find out that you were still here in Virginia somewhere, fighting' us."

Turner gave a short snicker, knowing that Dow could see that his chances for going home were not very good.

Dow stroked his chin thoughtfully, then spoke in a soft tone. "Sounds to me as though the decision has already been made."

"Oh, it has, General, it has," Winder answered. "In the words of the Commissioner of Exchange, 'You can't trust any Yankee, whether he's a private or a President.' Every one of y'all lies, and Mr. Ould isn't about to be taken in by an offer to keep y'all on parole when he knows it ain't goin' to happen."

"I didn't know you to be a cynical man, General," said Dow, trying to mask his disappointment.

"You Yankees have made me this way, General. I've heard too many of your lies, and so has Commissioner Ould. In fact, he's already prepared his reply to the offer."

"Can you tell me what that reply is?" asked Dow, knowing that Winder was going to tell him whether he asked or not.

"Certainly, General. Mr. Ould has decided to give you Yanks a taste of your own medicine. He's tellin' Washington that not only are we refusin' their offer, but y'all are eatin' real good down here, yourselves. His report on the conditions of our prisons sounds so good that I'm thinkin' of goin' out and gettin' myself captured by some Virginia cavalry regiment, just so's I can stay here, too."

Dow was not amused by Winder's answer, but Turner apparently found it hilarious. He laughed out loud, one of the few times Dow had ever seen him respond to anything in a positive fashion.

"You don't expect Washington to believe a report like that, do you?" Dow asked incredulously. "Especially after sending all those blankets, and now 24,000 rations?"

"Don't matter none to me, General," said Winder, still enjoying the specter of getting captured by one of his own regiments. "Reckon your people will get the message, though. The first liar's gonna get topped by a better liar every time. You can count on that!"

Turner laughed again. He really appeared to be enjoying himself.

By now, Dow had heard enough. He realized that nothing constructive was going to come from additional conversation. He had been summoned to talk to the two merely so they could emphasize his plight. They had control over his destiny for the present, and they were doing a fine job of reminding him of that.

"Well, gentlemen," he said as he stood. "Unless there's something else you wish to add, I think I'll be returning to my quarters now. I'm sure you want me to spread this wonderful news among the other men. Or has Sanderson already been given that opportunity?"

"No, General," said Winder. "You may have that pleasure."

Dow knew that ordinarily, military protocol would have called for him to salute before he departed. However, under the circumstances, he was in no mood to acknowledge either man, despite their ranks. Wordlessly, he turned and made his way to the door.

As he exited the room and made his way back upstairs, he could hear Winder and Turner laughing. Although not normally given to paranoia, he was sure that the laughter was at his expense.

The prisoners were animated in their discussions. An exchange was finally to take place. Most had heard rumors of an exchange for some time, but only the most desperate chose to believe. Their hopes had been dashed too many times. Guards had often spoken of the boat that was coming to take the sick and wounded back to the North. However, the boat had never come. This time, though, it really seemed to be happening. Several prisoners had officially been told to be prepared to leave, and the men hoped that this was not another cruel hoax.

Those selected for the exchange were all ill, most from typhoid, chronic diarrhea, or scurvy. They would have little chance at survival if they were to remain in Libby, and even those who would be left behind were genuinely happy for those going home.

Throughout the prison, men hastily scribbled letters to loved ones, to be given to those who were leaving. The men selected for exchange would normally be searched when they left, but the prisoners were gambling that the guards would not want to get too close to the sick prisoners. Even if they were searched, by then the letters would have been sewn inside the linings of caps and coats, or secreted into hollow boot heels or belt buckles. Prisoners called this practice "rat-hole telegraph" and it represented a way to get letters past the ever watchful censors.

Those who were leaving gave their blankets and extra clothing to those who were being left behind. Rose bade his companions farewell, and watched as others hugged friends and shook their hands. It was a joyous day, to be sure!

A major, looking old beyond his years, approached Rose. The man's body showed the signs of advanced scurvy, with so many open sores that several had blended together to form larger ones. His teeth had long since dropped out from the effects of the disease, and his mouth was so sore he had difficulty speaking.

"I just want to say goodbye, Colonel," he said laboriously.

Rose shook the man's hand. "You be sure to take care of yourself, Major. I'm sure you'll be as good as new after a few months at home."

"I hope so, Colonel. And you take care, as well. I'll be thinkin' of you back here."

"I appreciate that," said Rose. "You won't be forgotten either."

The man winced slightly as he shuffled closer. "I know about your plans to get out of here, Colonel," he said in a lowered voice.

Rose felt the same sinking feeling he had experienced the night he had been confronted on the stairs by Wells, as he and Hamilton had returned from the basement.

"What do you know?" Rose asked in a worried tone.

"Oh, I don't know any details, but I do know that you are working on a way to get out."

"How did you find out?" Rose asked, again fearful that others may also be aware of his activities.

"People talk, Colonel. It's no secret. I don't think the Johnnies are suspicious, though, so you don't have to worry about that. Just make sure Sanderson doesn't get wind of it."

"That much you can be sure of, my friend," replied Rose. He had heard the story about Sanderson several times. Although he still wasn't sure as to its authenticity, he would take no chances.

"I just wanted to wish you luck, sir," the major continued. "Maybe after you get out we can celebrate somewhere."

"I'd like that," said Rose. "Nothing would please me more than for everyone in here to be able to lift a toast to a successful departure from Libby."

"Maybe we could get General Dow to join us," said the major, trying to smile, although the sores on his lips and mouth made it difficult. "Think he'd join us in tippin' a glass or two?"

Rose laughed at the reference to Dow's well-known aversion to any form of alcohol. "For that, he just might."

The two chuckled at the thought, then grew silent. Finally, the major drew himself up and spoke. "I'm real glad I got to know you, Colonel, even though I never had the chance to serve with you. You take care of yourself, and keep those Seceshes wonderin' what you're up to. Good luck."

Rose returned the man's salute. "Thanks, Major," he said. "The same to you."

As he watched his ill friend shuffle off, Rose began to worry again. This escape was taking entirely too long. And the longer it took, the more people who would hear of it. Apparently, several already were aware of the escape plans. Sooner or later, the prison officials were going to know about it, too, and that would spell disaster.

Rose made a mental note to discuss this with Hamilton tonight. They may have to take some daring chances to get out, as undesirable as that may be. They had almost been discovered once, despite their planning. Maybe an impulsive action would have be necessary.

When Rose told Hamilton of his discussion with the departing prisoner, Hamilton showed no surprise.

"I've been gettin' a lot of questions, myself," he said. "A lot of people see us prowlin' around at night and they're startin' to figure out what we're up to. I've talked to Wells several times, and he said he's even taken to walkin' around the room for several hours at a time, just to build himself up for the day when he can escape. And he's not the only one."

"If that many of our own boys know, then the Rebs could, too," reasoned Rose.

"That's the way I see it, too," said Hamilton. "But if the Rebs knew, don't you think they'd have done somethin' about it by now?"

"Maybe," answered Rose. "Or, they might just be waitin' to see exactly what we have planned."

"That should keep them busy," offered Hamilton. "We don't even know what we have planned."

"Y'know, that could be to our advantage," Rose said, stroking his beard. "Maybe we should just make a dash for it and take our chances. No special plan, no advance studyin'. Just go."

"You really think that would work?" queried Hamilton.

Rose sat thoughtfully. "Probably not," he finally conceded. "I guess I'm just gettin' a little jumpy. And desperate."

"Just take a deep breath and relax, Thomas," said Hamilton. Then, almost as an afterthought, he remembered the reeking air. "On second thought, you might want to skip the deep breath and go right to the relaxin' part."

Rose could not suppress a grin. Hamilton always found a way to raise his spirits.

Lowering the rope through the kitchen floor, Rose looked up at Hamilton and said, "Let's go. We can relax when we're out of here. And I have a feelin' tonight will be our night."

The two slid down the rope and picked up the broadaxes they had found on a previous excursion. They wouldn't help much against a well-aimed musket, but just to feel the weight of the implement in their hands was reassuring. The two wended their way over the now familiar route to the doorway.

Then, Rose saw movement in the shadows! At about the same time, the intruder noticed Rose. Both stopped and stood peering at the other.

"Don't hurt me, mister," said the intruder finally, in a quivering voice. "I mean you no harm."

"Who are you, and why are you down here?" shot Rose, tightening his grip on the broadax.

"I'm just one of the workers," came the answer. "I couldn't sleep, so I thought I'd just stretch my legs a little." He held his hands out to his side to indicate he had no weapon.

Rose had hoped that this was another prisoner, even though he still didn't feel comfortable joining forces with anyone else. But this man presented an entirely different set of problems. He obviously was a Southerner, or he wouldn't be working in the prison. Would he go to the authorities? Or worse, would he sound the alarm right now, calling for the guards?

Rose took an uneasy step toward the man, prepared to attack with the broadax at the first sign of trouble. He could hear Hamilton working around to the man's side. "A classic flanking movement," Rose thought, admiringly.

Recovering his composure, the worker spoke again. "That was you two that was down here a few nights ago, weren't it?"

Neither Hamilton nor Rose answered, choosing to let the worker do the talking for the time being.

"For God's sake, man, don't come back down here at night," the man pleaded. "It's too dangerous for everybody. If y'all want to escape, that's yer own concern. I ain't goin' to tell nobody. But when the guards come runnin' in here, anything can happen. Some of them boys shoot at anything they see. I don't want to be their target, yuh hear what I'm sayin'?"

"We understand," Rose answered softly. "We aren't here to cause you trouble, either."

"I'm much obliged to y'all," said the worker. "And I'd appreciate it if'n y'all would just go back upstairs, however you do it, and let us workers alone down here. I surely would!"

Taking a chance, Rose asked hopefully, "Do you think you could help us?"

"Not a chance, Yank," said the man. "I said I wouldn't tell nobody, and I won't. But I'm still a Virginian, even if'n I don't agree with everything that's goin' on. I won't go back on my home state."

Rose looked at him for a moment. In the dark, he could not make out his features. He knew the man could not see him, either, and would not be able to identify him even if he did change his mind and tell the guards.

"I respect loyalty," Rose finally said. "You seem like an honorable man, and we won't be botherin' you. We'll just be goin' back upstairs for now."

"I'd surely appreciate that," the worker countered. "And please, don't be comin' back down here."

Rose and Hamilton wordlessly slipped back into the shadows, dejectedly walking toward the rope that would take them back upstairs, back to the stench, the deprivation, the hopelessness.

Reaching the kitchen, Rose assisted Hamilton through the opening in the floor and began to reposition the floorboard. While he did that, Hamilton wound the rope into a coil and returned it to its hiding place. Neither had spoken a word since leaving the workman.

Finally, Rose spoke. "Y'know, Andrew, we're going to have a lot of trouble getting out that doorway, no matter how well we plan it. There are just too many things we can't control."

"You may be right, Thomas," replied Hamilton. "We've had nothing but bad luck since we started this plan."

The two sat wordlessly for some time, each feeling sorry for himself and the misfortune they had encountered.

"We could jump those two guards," said Hamilton hopefully.

"First we'd have to get passed those workers," said Rose. "Then, if we would be able to jump the guards, we'd have to do it so fast that they wouldn't be able to warn each other. I don't know about that."

"We can do it, Thomas," Hamilton interjected excitedly. "They'd never know what hit them!"

"But, if we didn't silence them immediately, they'd be able to make enough noise that the guards on the other sides of the building would come running before we could get across the street," Rose protested.

"What kind of noise could they make?" asked Hamilton, rhetorically. "We just hit them over the head with those broadaxes, they'll stay quiet for quite a while."

"They could still squeeze the triggers of those muskets," said Rose. "A musket goin' off in the dead of night makes an awful lot of noise."

Hamilton did not answer. Instinctively he knew Rose was right. Everything would have to fall perfectly into place for the plan to be successful, and that had not been happening.

"There might be a way," he finally offered, cautiously. "I'm not sure you want to hear it, though."

Rose looked at him quizzically. "What's your idea?" he asked.

Hamilton looked down at his boots, then back at Rose. "More help," he said.

Chapter Nine

"Help?" exclaimed Rose. "What kind of help are you talking about?"

"Men, Thomas," Hamilton answered hesitantly. "We need more men to help us."

"I don't know, Andrew. You know my feelings about letting too many people know what we're doing," said Rose.

"I know that," said Hamilton. "And under ordinary circumstances I'd agree with you. In fact, I have agreed with you on that from the very beginning. But now it's obvious that the two of us are not going to be able to do this. Already, there are several, maybe dozens, who already suspect what we have in mind. The longer we wait, the better the chance that one of them is going to be overheard talking about it, and then we're done. Not only that, we have already lost precious time. The Seceshes have already sealed the cellar off once, and we know what that did to us. They could do it again, especially if they start to suspect that there's a plot to escape."

Rose remained silent. As much as he hated to admit it, Hamilton was right. The time had come to include others in on the plan. To wait any longer would invite failure.

Rose sighed deeply. "You're probably right, Andrew," he said reluctantly.

"I know I am, Thomas," said Hamilton. "With a little help we can get out of here, but alone, I'm not so sure."

"If we do include others, who do we include, and how do we decide who they will be?" Rose asked.

"I think the best way is to find out how many know. We know who's been asking all the questions, so we go to them first. Wells would be one, and that colonel that got us the rope, what was his name?"

"White. Colonel White," answered Rose.

"Yeah. Colonel White. You said he suspected something, so he would be another. I have a few others in mind who I think have an idea something's going on. And I'm sure you can think of some." Hamilton was becoming more enthusiastic again.

"Gageby, Lucas, McDonald, Randall, Garbett...they'd all be good to have along. We should probably tell General Dow, too. I guess we should be able to come up with enough," Rose said after a short pause. "We should have some kind of plan, though, before we go recruitin' people."

"What's wrong with just stormin' the sentries and knockin' 'em out?" offered Hamilton. "That's what we talked about with just the two of us. It should be easy to do with more people."

"Yeah," said Rose, "I guess that would work. Why don't we go back up and get some sleep? We can start talkin' to some of the others in the morning. Then we'll meet tomorrow night and compare names and see how many we have. If we have enough, we'll set up a plan and proceed from there."

"Sounds good, Thomas. I think this is the one that's going to work," said Hamilton.

"We've both said that more than once, haven't we?" said Rose. "Maybe this time, we'll be right."

Morning's light found Rose already awake and compiling a list in his mind of those he would recruit. The people he wanted would have to be brave and loyal. And they couldn't be friendly with Sanderson.

After limbering his sore foot, Rose began searching for Gageby. His fellow Pennsylvanian should have the chance to go, and he gave every appearance of being just the kind of soldier who would do whatever he had to do to make sure a plan succeeded. He found him watching a card game.

"Morning, Jim," Rose said cheerfully.

"Mornin', Colonel," Gageby answered. "How's the foot today?"

"Not too bad," said Rose. "Each day it gets a little better. Do you have a minute we can talk?"

Gageby looked at Rose and grinned. "Well, Colonel, as you can see, I'm pretty busy right now. I guess I can break away for a few minutes, though."

Rose watched as one of the men bet a pinch of salt, hoping his two aces would be good enough to win the pot. With no money available, the men bet whatever they could gather. Some bet salt, others a pinch of pepper. Those who had recently received a package from home bet the heaviest, at least until a better card player took their booty from them.

Taking Gageby by the elbow, Rose guided him away from the group. Stopping where the two could talk and not easily be overheard, Rose sat down. Gageby joined him on the reeking floor.

Rose looked around, making sure that unfriendly ears could not overhear what he was about to say. "I'm going to try to get out of here, Jim," he whispered.

Gageby also looked around, then turned back to Rose. In the same whispering tone, he said, "Yeah, I know."

Hoping the look of surprise that crossed his face would not make others curious as to the content of their conversation, Rose quickly asked, "What do you mean, you know? How do you know?"

Gageby shrugged his shoulders. "I just know, that's all. Lots of people do."

Rose stared at Gageby. Shaking his head in wonder, he said, "And you never said anything. Why didn't you ask me about it?"

Gageby smiled and said, "You wouldn't have told me anything, anyway. I just figured you'd tell me when the time was right." Seeing Rose smile in return, he went on, "Guess the time is right."

"I believe it is," said Rose, "And I want you to go along."

"Yes, sir!" Gageby said emphatically. "When?"

"Don't you even want to know how we're going to do it?" asked Rose.

"Doesn't matter none. I'm still goin'." said Gageby. "When do we leave? And who else will be with us?"

"I can't answer either question yet. As soon as I know, you'll know. But I still think you should know the plan before you commit yourself. You may want to change your mind."

"I doubt it," said Gageby, "But go ahead."

"We're going to have to storm the guards," said Rose. "It could be dangerous."

"How dangerous?" Gageby asked.

"Some or all of us could be killed. I think you should be aware of that. I don't think that's going to happen, but it could," answered Rose.

"I'm not real thrilled about that part," said Gageby, soberly, "But you can still count on me. If we wait much longer, we're all going to be so weak from hunger or disease that none of us will be able to get out."

"You're right about that, Jim. There's one other thing, too."

"And that is what?"

"We may have to kill the guards to keep them from sounding an alarm."

Gageby's face lit up. "You mean we may have to kill one of Turner's killers? One of those devils that shoots at us every time we look out the window? This gets better all the time!"

"We'll only do that if we have to," said Rose, chuckling at Gageby's outburst. "If you don't have the stomach for it, I'll understand. But somehow, I don't think that's going to be a problem."

"Not with me, sir," said Gageby. "I'm not one for killin' innocent people, and God knows I've never got used to killin', even in battle. But this is different. Those guards are evil, just like Turner. If we're forced into something, I'll have no problem doin' it."

"I'll be countin' on you, then," said Rose. "I'll let you know more in a day or two."

"Thank you, Colonel," said Gageby. "I've been waitin' for this chance for a long time."

"We all have, Jim," said Rose, rising. "And one more thing. Don't breathe a word of this to anyone. I'll do the recruitin'. Do you understand?"

"Perfectly, Colonel," said Gageby. "Just don't forget me."

The two parted, Gageby going back to watch the card game, Rose to find some of the others he had in mind as fellow escapees. Both could feel the adrenaline flowing, even though the actual time for escape had not yet arrived.

The next person Rose talked to was not as enthusiastic as Gageby. A major, he was interested initially but his excitement diminished when he learned that he could possibly die in the attempt.

"I've got a wife and four children at home, Colonel," he said. "God knows I want to see them again more than anything in the world. But I'm not gonna do them any good if I get killed tryin' to get back to them. I'd really like to join you, but I think I'll just wait for the next exchange. I hope you understand."

"I do," Rose answered sympathetically. "I really do. I have a wife and children, too. But I'm willin' to take the risk. That doesn't make either of us right or wrong. We each have to do what we think is right. I'm not interested in makin' anyone do something he doesn't feel good about."

"I appreciate your understanding, Colonel. I'd really like to go, but... well, I just think it's better for me if I wait."

"I hope the exchange comes soon, Major," said Rose. "And I'd really be grateful if you didn't say anything to anyone about this."

"You can trust me, sir. No one will ever know. Not from me, anyway. Godspeed, Colonel."

"Thanks," said Rose. "Godspeed to you, too."

Rose then left the major, still wondering how he had been mistaken about his desire to get out of Libby. Rose would have never guessed that he would refuse to join in, but everybody is different. There were more than one thousand men in Libby. It would not be hard to find someone willing to take the chance.

Rose didn't have to wait long. His next candidate, Colonel Kendrick of the Third West Tennessee Cavalry, jumped at the opportunity.

"I've been thinkin' about how I was gonna do it, myself," he said. "This is like Christmas for me!"

Even after Rose had explained the plan and its dangers, Kendrick was willing.

"Look here," he said, reaching into his coat. Pulling out a wrinkled piece of paper, he laid it on his thigh and smoothed it out as best he could. It appeared to Rose to be a map of some sort.

Kendrick held the map out proudly for Rose to see. "This'll get us to Fortress Monroe," he said.

"Where did you get this?" Rose asked as he followed the markings on the paper.

"Made it myself," Kendrick said, his pride obvious.

"But how did you know these routes?" asked Rose. "You fellows didn't do much fightin' around these parts, did you?"

"Nope. But a lot of other fellows did. I just asked a few questions now and then, not enough to make it obvious. Some of the guards even contributed. They just don't know it."

"Are you sure it's accurate?" asked Rose, not wishing to appear too skeptical but recognizing that there was a great chance for error in such a map.

"As accurate as it can be, I reckon," said the optimistic Kendrick, taking the map. "Look. We all know how to get to the York River railroad. That's where this starts."

His finger traced the route. "We just keep the railroad on our left, see? We'll move toward the Chickahominy. We'll have to pass through Boar Swamp, but that shouldn't be too big a problem. Then we'll cross the road leading to Bottom's Bridge, keeping the road on our left."

"That looks like a good plan, Colonel," interrupted Rose. "But we can't all take the same route or we'll be too easy to follow. Maybe you can take a few men with you, but the rest of us should find some other way to the Union lines."

"Yeah, I reckon you're right," said Kendrick. "A mob of blue coats walkin' through Boar Swamp might be a little obvious."

"Just a little," said Rose with a grin. He patted Kendrick on his shoulder. "But a few blue coats should be able to do it, with a little help from some of the local people."

"We'll make it. You just watch," said Kendrick, his voice showing his excitement.

Rose had known all along he could count on Kendrick. The two had often talked about what they'd do if they escaped, but neither had ever let on to the other that he had any serious plans. And that map! The more

Rose looked at it, the better it looked. Kendrick had done a painstaking job. If everyone in the escape party did the same, the whole group would fare well!

"We've got to have absolute secrecy. No exceptions. And I will be the only recognized leader," Rose announced to those who had assembled in the kitchen. The group was a little larger than Rose had anticipated, but it should not present a problem. "If anything happens to me, Captain Hamilton will take over. I realize that some of you outrank him, but he has been in on this plan from the beginning and is the only one who knows it as well as I do. If any man here doesn't like that, I have to know about it now."

The men all looked around the group. Nobody dissented.

"I think we all just want to get out of here," spoke up Kendrick. "Nobody cares who takes the lead."

"I'm glad to hear that, Colonel," said Rose. "Does everyone else agree?"

Murmurs of consent rippled through the assemblage.

"Alright, then. Over the next few nights, Captain Hamilton and I will be taking you down to Rat Hell in small groups, to get you familiar with the area. Anybody here afraid of rats?" said Rose.

"Two legged or four legged?" one of the men asked.

The rest of the group chuckled appreciatively.

"We may see both," said Rose, his face crinkling into a smile.

"No problem either way, sir," said the man, as the rest of the group laughed and commented among themselves.

"For tonight, we'll take you men down," said Rose, pointing to a man directly in front of him and swinging his arm in an arc until he reached a captain near the end of the front row. "The rest of you go back upstairs and get some rest. Tomorrow night, this group will go down with us." He indicated another section of the crowd. He continued grouping small segments of the party until all had been assigned a night for visiting Rat Hell.

As the group prepared to disband, Rose gave them one last reminder. "Remember, nobody talks about this upstairs. Even among yourselves. We'll let you know more after everyone has had a chance to see what we're going to do and where we're going to be leavin' from."

The men began filing back up the stairs, those who were about to enter the cellar remaining behind. Rose and Hamilton looked at each other and grinned.

"Let's do it," said Hamilton, walking to where the rope was hidden. The men watched with fascination as Rose and Hamilton raised the floorboard and attached the rope. None had even suspected that the board was loose, despite their being in the room on a daily basis.

"I've stood on that board," said one, shaking his head in amazement. The others murmured in agreement.

"Gentlemen," said Hamilton, starting down the rope. "Follow me to the North!"

After each group had been given the opportunity to visit Rat Hell and become familiar with the plan, the entire party reassembled in the kitchen area. The night had finally arrived.

Each man was absorbed in his own thoughts. All had been given an assigned task, and each mentally reviewed his job, not wanting to be the cause of a failed attempt. Nobody spoke, but the nervous energy that was present could be felt by all.

Rose moved to the front of the group, standing by the opening in the floor. "We have to have complete silence from this point on," he said. "You all know what you are to do and where you are to be positioned. I have confidence in every one of you. Are there any last questions?"

The men all looked around at one another, but no one spoke.

"Alright, then. Let's all take a deep breath and try to get our hearts to slow down a little. I'll see you all in Washington!"

The men shook hands with one another, then took their places at the entrance to the basement.

Rose slid down the rope to the familiar darkness of Rat Hell. He could hardly believe the moment was finally here. Wordlessly, he made his way to the doorway, knowing that Hamilton was right behind him and that the others were already going to their appointed stations. For the first time, he carried the loose end of the rope with him. It would serve as a communication link with the last man in line, who would serve as a lookout. The others would hold the rope loosely, so they could feel any pull from either end, a sign of a problem.

Seated at the doorway, he looked around as well as he could in the darkness. He could see some of the men in the shadows. Everyone appeared to be where he was supposed to be. Watching for the sentry, Rose could feel his heart pounding. The excitement of the moment was almost overpowering. The rope in his hand felt strange, awkward.

In a short time, the first sentry approached. As the footfalls neared the doorway, Rose instinctively pulled back deeper into the shadow, even though he knew the sentry could not see him unless he came inside. Then, the sentry passed. Rose had watched these men so many times that he almost felt that he knew them. This one he had observed many times in the past. He did his job well, as Rose recalled.

In a few seconds, the second sentry approached from the opposite direction. Rose recognized him, as well. After he had passed, Rose shifted his position and looked around at the others. The plan called for them to observe several cycles of the guards' passing, to be sure they were following their normal patterns.

The guards passed through their second cycle, then the third.

Suddenly, Rose felt a tug on the rope. Looking around he could see that the others had felt it, too. The signal from the lookout that something was amiss! Rose could only hope that each man remembered his instructions on what to do in the event of such a signal. All had been warned and drilled countless times on the need to get back upstairs as quickly and quietly as possible, and that even a small noise, or the panic of one man, could be enough to cause the effort to fail.

Being closest to the door, Rose was the last to reach the entry to the kitchen above. As he watched proudly, each man noiselessly climbed rapidly to the kitchen, those still waiting to climb giving a boost to the others as they pulled themselves up the rope. Above, friendly hands reached down through the opening to assist the climbers. From below, Rose could see the faces of some of the men already upstairs, helping the others and occasionally glancing nervously over their shoulders.

Finally, it was Rose's turn. Reaching the top, he could see several of his accomplices quietly dashing across the room to ascend the stairs. Pulling himself through the opening, he quickly began replacing the floorboard as Hamilton gathered the rope and threw it into its hiding place behind a barrel. Having done so, he ran for the stairs.

Across the room, Rose heard the outside door being flung open, light from the street pouring in. He could see several guards outlined in the doorway, the leader carrying a lantern. To dash across the room to the stairs now would take him directly across their paths.

Fighting panic, Rose stepped backwards into the shadows. Looking quickly at the floorboard, he was relieved that it had fallen into its proper place and looked like all the others. At least that much was going well.

As he backed up, still watching the approaching Confederate guards, Rose felt the edge of a table. Without taking his eyes off the lantern carried by the leader, he felt for the bench. Touching it, he quickly sat down, seeing a pipe lying on the table as he did. Sticking the pipe in his mouth, he hoped he looked nonchalant, despite his pounding heart and shortness of breath.

As the guard's lantern beam soon revealed Rose's presence, the men abruptly stopped. They had not expected to see a Yankee prisoner seated alone in the kitchen at this hour. Rose looked up at the group, feeling a sense of relief that none of them had gone near the stairs. Apparently, everyone else had been able to reach the safety of the upstairs rooms.

Coolly, Rose played with the pipe between his teeth, hoping that nobody would notice that it wasn't lit. The guards were still eerily silent.

The leader raised his lantern slightly, to extend the beam into the room a little further. After peering around as far as the lantern's beam would allow, he walked toward Rose, still not saying anything.

Reaching the table, he looked at Rose, then looked around the room again. Rose could feel a trickle of nervous sweat run down his back as he looked into the man's face. The guard swung the lantern closer to Rose, almost into his face, as if to get a better look at this prisoner who had, for some reason, felt compelled to come to the kitchen for a late-night smoke. Staring into Rose's face for several seconds, he finally withdrew the lantern and proceeded back to the stairs, followed closely by the other guards.

As the sentries climbed the stairs, Rose felt his legs quiver. The ruse had apparently worked, but now the greater danger was to those who had gone back to their sleeping quarters. Rose felt reasonably sure that they had been given ample time to reach safety, but there was always that slim thread of pessimism that told him that someone may get caught.

For what seemed like ages, Rose sat at the table, still 'smoking' his pipe. After several minutes, he heard the boots of the guards clomping back down the stairs. Appearing unfazed by their presence, he did not turn to look at them as they approached.

The lantern's beam grew brighter as they got nearer, then the leader was standing beside him once more. Again, he stopped and looked directly into Rose's face. This time the look was much more sinister, a look which seemed to say, "I know you're up to something, but I can't figure out what it is. I know you aren't down here to smoke your pipe." The words remained unspoken, however, and the guards soon walked away.

Reaching the door to Cary Street, the men paused and looked back one last time, although Rose was sure they could no longer see far enough into the room to see him. Then the door slammed shut and Rose was alone in the room once more.

What had roused the guards' suspicions? What had caused them to burst into the room? Rose's mind raced in several directions at once. Then, the realization came to him that, in fact, the plan had worked to perfection. Despite the fact that nobody had been able to escape tonight, nobody had been caught, either. And even though the Confederates were now suspicious, there would be another night to do this again!

Chapter Ten

The following morning found knots of prisoners discussing the aborted breakout of the night before. Miraculously, the word had already spread like wildfire among even those who had been asleep at the time of the incident. Both Hamilton and Rose were besieged by questioners, giving the two no small amount of concern.

"This is almost out of control, Andrew," said Rose, after fending off another batch of questions. "It's just a matter of time 'til Turner and Winder hear about it."

"Yeah, I'm afraid you're right," agreed Hamilton. "But what can we do about it?"

"Not much, I'm afraid," Rose stated. "Unless..."

"You've got that look, Thomas," noted Hamilton. "Unless what?"

"Well, I was thinkin'. What if we include everyone in the escape plan who knows anything? That way, we swear them all to secrecy, and the talk dies down. What do you think?"

Hamilton pondered the idea. "It might work. At least it's worth tryin'. You want me to check around and find out how many we'd have to include?

"Why don't you?" asked Rose. "We can get together again this evening to see just what size of a group we have."

Hamilton spent the rest of the day trying inconspicuously to learn who knew anything at all about the plan to overpower the guards. Those who had somehow become aware were asked to refrain from discussing it, with their reward being inclusion in the next attempt. All agreed that it was a good arrangement for everyone concerned, and everyone was eager to comply.

At dusk, Rose sought out Hamilton, anxious to determine what the Kentuckian had learned and how many men had been included. Hamilton appeared uncharacteristically somber.

"What'd you find out, Andrew," Rose inquired after the two had walked to a corner of the room.

Hesitating, Hamilton finally said softly, "Well, Thomas, quite a few fellows know what we're up to. Most of 'em have known for some time, as a matter of fact. I had to expand the list a little."

"That's fine," said Rose. "We figured there'd be some new faces. How many did you have to add?"

Still hesitating, Hamilton stared at the floor for a few moments. "I, uh...well, I had to include more than I thought I'd have to."

Becoming suspicious, Rose asked, "What do you mean by 'more'? We already had seventy. There can't be that many more. What do we have now, a hundred?"

"Uh...more than that, I'm afraid."

"More than one hundred? How many more? We can't have two hundred, surely," Rose said with exasperation.

"More than two hundred, Thomas," Hamilton answered. Looking back at the floor, he muttered to himself, "A lot more than two hundred."

Rose took a deep breath. He hadn't counted on a crowd like this. "Give me a real number, Andrew. 'More than two hundred' still doesn't tell me much."

Hamilton looked at his friend seriously. Following a long pause, he said, "I've come up with about four hundred and twenty, Thomas."

"**FOUR HUN**..." Rose fairly shouted, catching himself before finishing. Looking around the room, he lowered his voice. "Four hundred and twenty? Four hundred and twenty? You can't be serious. You mean four hundred and twenty men in here know what we plan to do?"

"Near as I can tell," answered Hamilton, looking relieved that he had finally told Rose what he knew his companion would not want to hear.

"What does that mean, as near as you can tell?"

"Well, it's possible I might have missed a few," offered Hamilton.

Rose's shoulders sagged. He never anticipated leading more than four hundred men in an escape attempt. He wasn't even sure if such an undertaking could be achieved. "Four hundred and twenty," he said softly, almost to himself, as he still tried to absorb the shock of Hamilton's news. "Four hundred and twenty. That's almost half the prison, Andrew. You mean every second man in here knows?"

Slowly looking around at the men in the room, Hamilton opined, "That would be about right, Thomas."

Rose also surveyed the room. Many of the men were looking in his direction, some with knowing smiles. Rose looked into the sea of faces for several minutes before speaking again. "Well, Andrew. Four hundred and twenty men ought to be enough to overpower two guards, don't you think?"

"I'd expect so, Thomas. Might even have a few extra," Hamilton deadpanned.

Rose stared at Hamilton. Always eager, Hamilton had outdone himself this time. Finally, the absurdity of the situation hit Rose, and he burst into laughter. "Four hundred and twenty men, Andrew. Why don't you invite the Turners along, too?"

"I thought about it, Thomas. I truly did. But I was afraid two more would make the group too big," said Hamilton, joining in the levity.

After a few light moments, Rose finally became serious again. "You know we can't go out with that many people, Andrew. A crowd like that could never blend in. The alarm would go out in minutes. Not only that, we don't even know for sure where our nearest troops are, and the Rebs would be able to round us all back up within a few hours, at most."

"I been thinkin' about that, Thomas. What if we had a column of Federal cavalry alerted that we were gonna do this? They could be ready to give us a hand. We'd just have to find a way to get the word to them."

"Outside help," Rose mused. He mulled the idea over. "That's a possibility, maybe. I'm sure Elizabeth Van Lew would help get the word to the troops."

"You think that would work?" asked Hamilton, appearing surprised that Rose would even consider the idea.

"I don't know. Let's think about it a little. Four hundred and twenty men is still a pretty big group to take out of here, even with outside help."

The two men discussed the pros and cons of the idea for more than an hour. The cumbersome size of the group kept coming into the conversation, as it became more apparent that such an undertaking was not practical. After much discussion, both agreed that, even with the help of Federal cavalry, help which could not be guaranteed, it would be foolhardy to take the chance.

"As much as I hate to say it, Andrew, I think we should abandon the idea," Rose concluded.

"I've got to agree," said Hamilton. "We take a chance like that, it either has to succeed completely or we'll not get a second try."

"Spread the word that we just can't do it, not with a group of that size," Rose suggested.

"Gonna be a lot of disappointed men, Thomas," Hamilton said dejectedly, "But I guess there's no other way."

"I don't see any," countered Rose.

After a few minutes of silence, during which each gave second thoughts to the decision they had reached, Hamilton stood and stretched. "Reckon I might as well get started," he said. "Got a lot of people to talk to."

"Yeah," said Rose to himself. "Four hundred and twenty, to be exact."

With the word passed through the population that an escape was no longer being considered, the questions ceased. The prisoners, as Hamilton had predicted, were extremely disappointed. Depression set in, and the daily routine of prison life again took over. Abraham Lincoln became as much an object of the prisoners' bitterness as Jefferson Davis, for not pressing harder for their release. Visiting preachers, who called at regular intervals to spread the Gospel and pass out religious publications, found themselves spending greater periods of their time counseling men who were losing hope.

This proved to be a blessing in disguise for Rose and Hamilton, who once again found themselves free to plot an escape, no longer burdened by the questions of other prisoners. The two sat at one of the tables in the vile smelling kitchen, staring at the far wall. Dozens of other prisoners milled about, allowing the two conspirators to blend in without arousing any suspicion.

Their discussions always centered on escape.

"Rat Hell, Andrew," Rose commented. "I'm convinced that's the only way we're gonna get out of here. And we're probably gonna have to tunnel."

"A tunnel's our best option, I'll agree to that," said Hamilton. "I can't figure out a way to get down there, though. The Rebs have the entrances to the cook room sealed off. Unless we can get there from the middle cellar somehow."

"I've been thinkin' about that," countered Rose, "And I don't think that's the answer. Those carpenters are in and out of there all day long, and so are the guards. Anything we do down there is going to be too easy to discover. And that wall between the two cellars is so thick that we'd make a lot of noise breaking through. There has to be a way into Rat Hell that we aren't seeing."

"The hospital's right above it," Hamilton suggested. "Maybe we could get in there and go down through the floor again."

"Too public, I'm afraid," rebutted Rose. "There's no way we could do it without some of the patients wanting to be included. And the doctors would surely see something and pass the word on to the Turners."

The two discussed various possibilities, none practical.

"What about dyin', Thomas?" Hamilton asked. "I mean, we don't really die. We just get into the hospital, then fake it. We let them carry us down to the dead room and when we're not bein' watched, we walk out. It's been done, y' know."

"I know it has. That's why it won't work. The Rebs are wise to it."

"Well, we know bribin' the guard doesn't work. You can't trust 'im to stay bribed. I've heard of some fellows who bribed a guard, then he grabbed 'em as soon as they got outside. He got himself praised by Turner, and kept the bribe, to boot."

"Yeah, I heard that, too," Rose said in a dejected tone.

"You hear the story about that major?" asked Hamilton after a short silence. "Halstead, I think his name was. He was a tailor before the war. Offering to repair the prison surgeon's coat, he worked on it a couple days, then put it on and pretended he was the good doctor. Walked right out past the guard and kept on goin', I hear. Took a friend with 'im, too. Told the guards he was a hospital steward or somethin', I reckon."

"No, I never heard that," said Rose. "You make that story up?"

"No, sir," answered Hamilton, defensively. "Heard it more than once, too."

Out of ideas, the conversation came to a halt. The two simply sat, each trying to think of something they had overlooked. Then, as he sat gazing at one of the kitchen's fireplaces, an idea came to Hamilton.

"Thomas," he said tentatively, "Do you mind if I take another look at those sketches you made?"

Rose looked at his friend. "Sure," he said, reaching into his coat and retrieving the drawings. "You have an idea?"

Hamilton remained silent as he smoothed the paper out on the table. Looking at the sketch of the kitchen, then back to the fireplace, then to the sketch again, he finally said softly, "I think I've got it, Thomas. Our way to Rat Hell."

Rose looked at the drawing, but nothing stood out. "Where?" he asked.

"Right over there," answered Hamilton, indicating the fireplace with his eyes. "Look at this."

He pointed to the fireplace on the sketch. "We go through the back of the fireplace."

Looking at the drawing, Rose was still puzzled. "That puts us into the hospital. We've already ruled that out."

"Not if we don't go clean through the wall," countered Hamilton. "We can cut into the wall behind the fireplace, but not through it. Then we dig down to where we're below the floor of the hospital, then we dig through the rest of the way. We'll come into Rat Hell below the ceiling, or the floor of the hospital if you want to call it that."

Turning the sketch over, he pulled the stub of a pencil from his pocket and drew a side view of the rooms, with the wall between. When done, the hole through the wall resembled a reversed letter 'S' and immediately became obvious to Rose.

"That's it!" he exclaimed softly. "You've got it. We'll just have to be careful not to break through either wall after we get in behind the fireplace. If we knocked those stones out on the carpenter's shop side we'd be in just as much trouble as if we broke through to the hospital. But, if we're careful, we can do it!"

"We can make it just big enough for a man to fit through," suggested Hamilton. "The less dirt we have to hide, the better."

"We better think about this a little more, Andrew," said Rose cautiously. "I'm not so sure it's gonna be that easy."

"What do you mean," Hamilton asked. "I know it won't be as easy as goin' straight through the wall like we did down in Rat Hell, but I don't see why we can't do it."

"Think about it a minute," Rose commented. "The guards are pacin' back and forth out there on the sidewalk, not ten feet from the fireplace. They look in the window at the wrong time and we're gonna find ourselves down in the cells for a few weeks. There are men in this room all day long, startin' long before dawn and goin' on till dark. We'd never be able to do it while they're in here. Then, there's no place to hide the dirt. And all we have to dig with is our two knives and that old chisel I found down in the carpenter's shop. How many reasons is that so far? Four? And I haven't even thought hard about it yet."

Hamilton sat silently, still thinking. "You got a better idea?" he finally said.

"Nope. I just don't want us rushin' into somethin' before we think it through, is all," answered Rose.

The two men sat without further discussion for several minutes. Then, Hamilton broke the silence. "This room empties out around ten at night. The first risers don't come down till about four in the mornin'. That gives us a good five or six hours every night to work. We just don't work durin' the day. And the dirt and stones we can take down into the middle cellar through the floorboard. What were them other two objections you had?"

Seeing that Hamilton was determined, Rose said simply, "The guards, and not much to dig with."

"Right," said Hamilton, duly reminded. "There's only gonna be room inside the wall for one of us, anyway. The other can stand picket. Anybody comes down the steps, the picket warns the digger. And if we just move one of them slop barrels between the fireplace and the window the guard won't see what we're up to even if he does look in." A smug look crossed Hamilton's face, feeling satisfied that he had countered Rose's objections. "And the diggin' tools...?" Rose threw out again.

"Not the best," Hamilton admitted, "But we work with what we got. Besides, we didn't even have that chisel the first time, so we're better off already."

Seeing that Hamilton would not be deterred, Rose said nothing. Hamilton allowed him a few minutes to absorb all that had been said.

"What do ya think?" Hamilton finally asked.

"I can't come up with a better plan," said Rose. "And it sure beats sittin' around waitin' for an exchange."

"You agree, then?" queried Hamilton.

"Yep," said Rose. "I don't think we're ready to start tonight, but tomorrow night should be good. Think you can find somethin' to hold the dirt in?"

"I'll try," answered Hamilton. Then, he continued, "One other thing, Thomas."

"What's that?" Rose answered cautiously, his suspicions aroused.

"I want one other man to help me," was the answer.

"Why do you need more help?" asked Rose. "Don't you think the two of us can handle this?"

"No offense, Thomas," said Hamilton, "But unless we get them stones back into the fireplace each morning just right, the Rebs'll be on to our plan before we know it. I have experience in stone work, but you don't. I'd like to have Capt. Gallagher help me. I think he was a stone mason or something like that, back in Ohio, and he can make those stones set in there like they've never been out."

Rose thought about Hamilton's suggestion, then asked, "Can he be trusted?"

"I'm pretty sure," answered Hamilton, "And he wants outta here worse'n us, if that's possible."

"You're probably right about getting those stones back in place just right," said Rose after several minutes of deliberation. "If you think you need the help, and if you're sure Gallagher can be trusted, talk to him. But make sure he doesn't say a word to anyone."

"I'll do that," responded Hamilton. "He'll be a big help, Thomas. You'll see."

"Well," Rose said as he stood up, "I sure hope so. Tell him to get plenty of sleep tomorrow, 'cause we're gonna spend as much time down here every night for as long as it takes."

Hamilton rose with Rose. "I'm almost afraid to get my hopes up, you know what I mean, Thomas? We've been so close and been knocked back down every time. It just gets old, real fast."

"I agree, Andrew," Rose commiserated. "But the good news is we haven't been caught, yet. Came close a couple times, maybe, but they haven't caught us so far. An old man told me on the way here that as long as I was alive I shouldn't give up hope. And I'm tryin' real hard to follow that advice."

"I hear what you're sayin', Thomas, and I agree with it. But it doesn't make it any easier, sometimes."

Placing his hand on his friend's shoulder, Rose said, "I know it doesn't, Andrew. Just don't quit hopin', you hear me? We'll make it one of these days. Just keep thinkin' how much fun you'll have wavin' goodbye to Major Turner."

The two men walked across the room to the stairs, their shoes making splashing sounds in the water on the floor. They climbed the stairs wordlessly, stopping at the top.

Turning to Hamilton, Rose said, "See you about nine tomorrow night, Andrew. Down at the table. And don't give up hope."

Hamilton smiled. "I'll be there. You can count on it. And I'm feelin' better already."

When Rose got to the kitchen the next night, Hamilton and Gallagher were already seated at the table. Hamilton made the introductions.

"Get lots of sleep?" Rose asked.

"Most of the day, Thomas," said Hamilton, as Gallagher merely nodded. "Just had enough awake time to get somethin' you might be interested in."

"What is it?" asked Rose, his curiosity piqued.

"Rubber blanket from the hospital," Hamilton answered matter of factly, as if everyone had such an item in his possession. Opening the top two buttons on his coat, he showed a portion of the blanket, shielding it so that others could not see. "Thought we could use it to haul dirt."

"How did you come by a rubber blanket?" Rose asked, incredulously.

"Swapped for it," Hamilton answered. "Gave one of the guards some buttons off an old coat. Told 'im I needed the rubber blanket to lay down on, cause the floor's too wet. You ever know how much the guards like those buttons?"

"These things?" Rose asked, fingering the buttons on his coat.

"Yep. They like that eagle on 'em. They poke fun at 'em, callin' 'em buttons with chickens on, but they really do like 'em. They can call that there eagle a chicken all day long if they want to, as long as they're willin' to swap somethin' for 'em."

The men discussed their plans again, waiting for the room to empty. Once they were sure they all knew what had to be done, they turned to small talk.

"Where do you think we should head for, once we're out, Thomas?" asked Hamilton.

"I guess Elizabeth Van Lew's," answered Rose. "She said she could find someone to get us to the nearest Federal lines."

"Where you reckon' that may be?"

"I'm not sure," said Rose. "I guess we'd have to trust her on that."

Hamilton placed his chin on his hand. "I was thinkin', maybe we should head for the mountains. When I was still out there, we was always runnin' into bands of deserters and bushwackers from both sides. They didn't want nothin' to do with us, then, but I've heard they're always takin' in boys who have escaped from one side or the other. They don't seem to mind which side they're on, either, as long as they've escaped from someone."

"Yeah," said Rose, rubbing his sore foot, "We ran into them a lot, too. Might be a thought."

"Last I heard, we still controlled East Tennessee. Should be some friendly faces around there, don't you think?" Gallagher offered.

"May be. As long as they have food, they'll be friendly enough to suit me," said Rose, a wistful look coming over his face. "Even if we have to travel at night, at least we can dig up some sweet potatoes or somethin'. I just want to eat normal again."

"Been a long time, hasn't it?" agreed Hamilton.

The men got quiet, each lost in his own thoughts about food and home.

"If I had some food and you didn't, you think you could bring your-self to steal some from me?" Hamilton asked Rose pointedly.

Surprised by the question, Rose thought for a while. "I don't know. What kind of question is that? We're friends. I don't think I could ever steal anything from you, no matter how hungry I was."

Then, after a few moments, Rose continued. "You could offer me some of it, though. I wouldn't refuse it, you know."

"Oh, I would, Thomas, you know that. I was just wonderin' about it, is all," Hamilton interjected quickly. "I don't reckon I'd ever steal any-thing from you, either. Wouldn't be right."

The men sat silently for a few minutes. Then, when Rose had almost forgotten the conversation, Hamilton spoke up. "A'course, if you had a nice apple pie and I thought you wouldn't miss a piece or two..."

Rose and Gallagher couldn't suppress a laugh. Putting his arm around his hungry friend's shoulder, Rose said, "It'd be yours, Andrew. No question."

By now, the last of the prisoners was filtering out of the room. As the final stragglers made their way to the stairs, Rose nonchalantly sauntered to the window looking out onto Cary Street. The sentinels could be seen walking their appointed routes.

Meanwhile, Hamilton and Gallagher moved one of the slop barrels to the street side of the fireplace. Satisfied that it would block the view of any guard looking in the window, Hamilton pulled the rubber blanket from inside his coat. Surveying the fireplace, he tried to visualize the best way to approach the task.

As Rose stood watch, Hamilton spread the rubber blanket in front of the hearth. He and Gallagher then placed the ashes and soot from the fire-place onto the blanket and pulled the blanket aside to allow room to work.

Using his knife, Hamilton began digging the mortar from between the bricks at the back of the fireplace. Gallagher followed suit. As each brick was freed, they carefully placed it to the side, taking the utmost care not to break any of them. They would have to be placed back in position in the morning.

The digging went according to plan, but was painfully slow. Periodically, Rose would take the extra bricks to the basement and stack them neatly along a wall. If anyone should come into the area during the day, the presence of the bricks would appear innocent enough, stacked neatly out of the way.

At the sentinel's call of three o'clock each morning, the digging would be halted and the front row of bricks placed back into position. That done, the ashes and soot which were placed on the rubber blanket at the beginning of each night's digging would be dragged back to the hearth. The three men would then fling the ashes against the newly replaced bricks, filling the cracks and creating the illusion that the bricks had never been removed. They would then stealthily creep up the stairs to their sleeping areas, quickly falling into a fitful sleep. They would sleep nearly all day, usually rising only for meals and meeting again in the evening to begin another night's work.

Night after night the routine was followed. Hamilton and Gallagher did most of the digging, with Rose removing the extra bricks and mortar. Rose's primary purpose, however, was to stand guard, diverting the attention of anyone coming down to the kitchen. While the sentries were a constant threat, other prisoners presented the greater danger. Well meaning, they often approached Rose to engage in casual conversation, not realizing that Hamilton was in the process of tunneling to freedom, only a few feet away.

Finally, after several nights of digging, the goal was attained. The last row of bricks was breached, and the opening into Rat Hell was a reality. Hamilton crawled out of the hole to tell Rose and Gallagher the good news.

As they replaced the front row of bricks and prepared to return the fireplace to its normal appearance, the men talked excitedly.

"We can hang the rope down through the hole real easy, Thomas," whispered Hamilton. "It's plenty long enough to reach the floor down in Rat Hell."

Rose scratched his nose on his sleeve, not wishing to smear ashes onto his face. "Tomorrow night we'll go down and check out that old room we were in before. We might as well use the old tunnel, even though it's not that far along."

"Every little bit helps, Thomas," said Hamilton, his spirits obviously buoyed by their progress. "At least all the bricks are out of the wall down there, and I've dug out all the bricks I hope to ever dig out, between that wall and this fireplace."

The three cleaned the area and returned it to normal, then proceeded up the stairs one more time. They reached the top just as a naked man jumped onto a bench and began shouting as loud as he could.

"Only prayer will save you," he shouted to the throng of prisoners, most of them still either asleep or in the early stages of waking.

"You will never leave this prison unless you repent!" he continued. "You must follow the way of the Lord! You are all sinners, gambling all day long, playing cards, stealing food from one another. You must turn to prayer or you will be doomed to spending eternity in Hell!"

"Someone shut him up!" came the shout from a sleepy prisoner.

"You're daft, old man!" shouted another, throwing an old shoe at the preacher. Two of his friends sympathetically helped him down from the bench and covered his naked body with a blanket. Still shouting, he offered no resistance as his friends led him away. As his rantings faded into the distance, Rose turned to Hamilton.

"Think you'll miss all this?" he asked rhetorically.

"About as much as you will, Thomas," came the answer.

Chapter Eleven

"You go first, Thomas. I've already seen what it looks like down there," said Hamilton.

The two men had come to the kitchen to make good on their plan to enter Rat Hell through the familiar fireplace. Gallagher, all had agreed, would not be needed for the initial exploration. He remained upstairs, asleep. While both Rose and Hamilton knew that this was only the first step, they were nonetheless excited. With any kind of good fortune, they would soon be digging their way under the street, on the first leg of their journey toward Federal lines.

Rose threw the rope down through the opening after fastening the other end to a post. With one last look at Hamilton, and a hard tug on the rope to make sure it would support his weight, he entered the opening feet first.

From the beginning Rose noticed that he had very little room to maneuver. While the opening had been large enough for Hamilton, the larger Rose found it much tighter than he had expected it to be. Still, he was able to get through the first horizontal portion of the opening and make the turn into the vertical section.

"If my bearings are right, I should be down to the bottom part soon," he thought. Even though he could see nothing in the inky darkness, he believed he must be below the hospital's floor by now. Then his feet touched bottom. That would be the second turn. In a matter of seconds he would be in Rat Hell!

Suddenly, his feet no longer supporting him as he reached around the turn to get additional leverage, he felt his body slide. Almost instantly he was pinned in the narrow opening. As he tried to withdraw his outstretched arms, he found he had no room to bend his elbows. Stretching them out further in an effort to acquire a better handhold, he felt himself sliding further in, pinning him still tighter.

With his feet and part of his legs having already made the turn into the bottom horizontal section, his neck and back were arched abnormally, making it extremely difficult to breathe. The rest of his body was wedged in the vertical portion of the wall. Only his hands and wrists were visible to Hamilton upstairs, and he waved them frantically to get the Kentuckian's attention.

Each effort seemed to push him deeper into the hole, and Rose could breathe only minimally. Afraid to cry out, although desperately wanting to do so, he squirmed even more vigorously to attract Hamilton's attention. Finally, after what seemed an eternity, he felt Hamilton grab his wrists and pull.

Unable to garner any leverage in the small opening, Hamilton could not begin to free Rose. Pulling desperately, he quickly realized that the opening was too small for Rose's legs to be pulled up high enough to allow him to bend his knees. Rose's thrashing became more and more frantic, and Hamilton feared for his friend's life.

Rose began feeling faint as he gasped for air, gulping rather than breathing. His weight forced him against the walls of the opening in an agonizing position, his body forming the same reverse 'S' that the hole formed. With his neck and back bent unnaturally backward, he feared he would suffocate. Still, he refused to cry out, afraid of alerting the nearby guards.

After several painful pulls it became apparent that Hamilton was not going to free Rose alone. Difficult as it was to leave him, Hamilton decided to run for help.

As he dashed frantically across the room and up the steps, his mind raced. "Where does Gallagher sleep? Will he be there?"

Gallagher, who was already showing himself to be dependable, would know what to do. Hamilton stumbled his way through the darkened room, stepping on sleeping men. As he trampled on arms and legs, angry shouts followed his desperate path.

Reaching what he thought to be Gallagher's sleeping place, Hamilton was frustrated to see that he was not there!

"Get off my leg, whoever you are!" shouted an angry voice, just one of many reverberating throughout the room.

Hamilton almost fell as the furious man yanked his own leg back. Reaching down to steady himself, he placed his hand directly over the face of another man, to the accompaniment of more angry shouts.

"Who are you, man?" a rudely awakened prisoner burst out.

"What's going on? Get out of here!" shouted another.

Pandemonium reigned, and Hamilton felt a strong hand grab his coat just below the neck.

"You better have the devil behind you, soldier," the man said. "Other than that, you have no excuses."

"Major Fitzsimmons? Is that you?" Hamilton cried out frantically at the sound of the familiar voice.

"Yeah, it is. Who's this?" came the answer.

"It's me. Hamilton. Don't waste time asking me questions. I need help."

Breaking free of Fitzsimmons's grasp, Hamilton began to retrace his steps. The major leaped up and followed. The two stomped their way across many of the same prone bodies that Hamilton had run across on his first trip through the room. The curses began anew. Both fell several times, receiving more punches than they would later care to remember. The clamor was almost deafening, as loud as either man had ever heard in combat, except for the obvious lack of gunfire.

Half running, half falling down the stairs, Major George W. Fitzsimmons of the 30th Indiana Infantry wondered what he was being drawn into. This behavior was outrageous even for Hamilton.

Reaching the fireplace, both men could make out the dim form of Rose's hands, now waving only feebly as the smothering man was nearly out of strength. Still not knowing whose wrists he was pulling, Fitzsimmons joined Hamilton in a desperate race against time. As each man pulled almost violently, Hamilton feared Rose's back would break as it contorted unnaturally. "Better a broken back than to suffocate inside a wall of Libby Prison," thought Hamilton.

Finally, after several intense tugs, Hamilton felt his friend's body move slightly higher into the hole. Spurred on by even this small sign of success, Hamilton and Fitzsimmons pulled even harder. Slowly, Rose's nearly lifeless body came to the surface.

Rose could feel his body being pulled up, but was too weak to help his rescuers. Fighting with all his strength to keep from losing consciousness, he was only slightly aware of the fresh air on his face.

"That's Colonel Rose!" exclaimed Fitzsimmons, recognizing the nearly lifeless face in the dim glow of a candle.

"Thomas! Thomas! Can you hear me?" Hamilton whispered loudly. Grappling at the buttons on Rose's coat, Hamilton literally tore the garment open to give his friend more air.

Fitzsimmons removed his cap and began rapidly fanning air into Rose's face as Hamilton slapped the colonel's cheeks gently.

"C'mon, Thomas! C'mon! You can do it!" Hamilton whispered as loudly as he dared.

"You call him Thomas?" the bewildered Fitzsimmons asked, as he continued to fan.

Hamilton didn't answer, instead shaking Rose by the shoulders as he continued to call out his name. Finally, Rose's eyelids fluttered. His mouth gaped open as he gulped for air.

Slowly, he felt himself returning to the living. He soon struggled to a sitting position with the assistance of Fitzsimmons and Hamilton.

Seeing that his friend was out of danger, Hamilton asked, "Are you all right, Thomas?"

Rose, still shaken, could only nod.

"I was afraid we lost you there for a while, Thomas," Hamilton said softly, as the reality of the situation began to settle in. Feeling his knees buckling, Hamilton sat on the floor beside his now reviving friend.

Taking a deep breath, Rose looked at Hamilton, then at Fitzsimmons. "Thanks," he managed to whisper. "I was sure I was about to cross to the other side. I was squeezed so tight in there I couldn't even pant, to get my breath. It felt like a vise was tightening on my chest."

The still confused Fitzsimmons remained silent. Hamilton rubbed Rose's neck and upper back, as Rose flexed and rolled his shoulders.

As Rose slowly regained his senses, he rubbed his limbs. "Who's this?" he asked, looking up at Fitzsimmons, seemingly seeing him for the first time.

Hamilton quickly introduced Fitzsimmons, explaining why he had been forced to bring a new man into the growing group.

Rose shook Fitzsimmons's hand, his face breaking into a smile.

Hamilton's worried look slowly vanished, as he realized Rose was going to be all right. Even Fitzsimmons looked relieved, although he was still reluctant to ask what Rose was doing inside the wall in the first place.

After several minutes of conversation, Rose finally struggled to his feet. Turning to Fitzsimmons, he said, "I'll let Andrew explain what's going on here. I've got to walk around a little and get the feeling back in my legs." After a short pause, he said, "Thanks again, Major. I do appreciate your help."

"Any time, Colonel," said Fitzsimmons as he shook Rose's hand.

"Thomas," corrected Rose. "The name's Thomas. You just helped save my life. I'm not going to hold you to a little thing like respect for rank. I certainly don't get any from him," he said, winking at Hamilton.

"Yes, sir, and I'm George," answered Fitzsimmons, as Hamilton slapped Rose on the back.

While Rose limped around the room he could occasionally hear Hamilton explaining in detail the series of events which had led to the nearly fatal incident. Rose's mind raced as he gave more thought to his brush with death. The pain in his broken foot was nearly forgotten as he contemplated what almost had happened. The faces of his wife, Lydia, and their children passed into view as he thought intently about his real reasons for wanting to escape. Somehow, he knew that his life had been spared for a reason, and that, while he was again unsuccessful in his attempt, the day would come.

Returning to his rescuers as they stood in front of the fireplace discussing the planned escape, Rose felt emotionally drained.

"How ya feel, Thomas?" Hamilton asked sympathetically.

"I'll be fine, but I think I'm done for the night," answered Rose. "Why don't we forget about doing any more for now and go back upstairs and gather our thoughts? I don't think I'm gonna be worth much right now."

"Understandable, sir," said Fitzsimmons. "Why don't you go on up? I'll give Captain Hamilton a hand here with whatever has to be done."

"Thanks, George. I appreciate it," said Rose. "And by the way, George, I think you can understand the need for absolute secrecy in this matter. I'd be much obliged if you didn't say anything to anyone about this."

"Oh, certainly, sir!" Fitzsimmons replied enthusiastically. "You didn't even have to mention that. Nobody's gonna hear a word about anything you're doin', I promise you."

"It may not be that simple, though," said Hamilton, his brow wrinkling thoughtfully.

"What do you mean?" asked Fitzsimmons.

"Well, right now there's a whole bunch of real mad people upstairs who're just waitin' for you and me to come back upstairs so's they can let us know how they feel about us," answered Hamilton. "They're gonna want to know what's goin' on, don't you think?"

"What's this all about?" asked Rose, who was still unaware of the wild scene that had taken place as Hamilton had frantically searched for help.

Hamilton quickly informed Rose of the havoc he had wrought while Rose struggled inside the wall. When he finished, Rose could not suppress a laugh, despite his still throbbing foot and aching back.

"I wish I could have seen that, Andrew. I really do," Rose said, still laughing. "And I hope I can get to see how you explain to everybody why you were trampling on everyone while they slept."

"Well, no disrespect meant, Thomas, but you can laugh all you want. I'm the one they're all waitin' for, and I'm gonna have to come up with a real good story," Hamilton said, half in anger. "And you're not gonna get away easy, either," he said, looking at Fitzsimmons.

"Me?" asked the major, incredulously. "I was just followin' you. Everybody knows that. You stepped all over me, too, don't forget."

"Why don't you just tell everybody you lost your mind, Andrew? said Rose, still enjoying Hamilton's obvious consternation. "Anyone'd believe that with no trouble."

"I'm not so sure he didn't," said Fitzsimmons, recalling the scene.

"This's what I get for savin' your life, is it?" said Hamilton to Rose. "If you wouldn't have been pluggin' up the hole I'd been just as well off to leave you in there. I just didn't wanna have to dig another one, and I could see I wasn't gonna get by ya down there."

Rose began moving toward the stairs. "I'll talk to you tomorrow when you're in a better frame of mind," he said, still laughing. "I'm sure you'll be able to come up with a story that everyone'll believe. George'll help you, won't you, George?"

"Yes, sir," said the major, pulling the rope from the hole. "Don't you worry none. We'll have a story cooked up before we start back upstairs."

Turning serious, Rose looked at the two men. "Thanks again, both of you. I really mean that," he said softly.

"My pleasure, sir," said Fitzsimmons.

"I guess I was glad to do it, Thomas," Hamilton mumbled.

"You guess you were?" asked Rose.

"Yeah," said Hamilton reluctantly. "I mean...well, you know what I mean. Sorry I got a little testy."

"It's alright," replied Rose. "We're all a little tense right now."

Hamilton nodded. "We'll get everything cleaned up, Thomas. Get some sleep."

Rose gave a slight wave of his hand and walked painfully up the steps.

Rose awoke the next morning and stretched his stiffened muscles. His foot hurt more than it usually did, and his neck and back were sore, but otherwise he suffered no ill effects from his ordeal. He spent most of the day dozing off and on. He had not realized how much sleep he was losing by spending each night in the kitchen. After several naps, he felt refreshed.

As he wrote a brief letter to Lydia, he looked up to see a familiar face walking briskly past. It was Wells. Rose had not seen him since the night the group had almost been discovered, the night Rose referred to as the night he smoked a pipe.

"How are ya, Colonel?" Wells said cheerfully, stopping in front of Rose.

"Good, Lieutenant," Rose answered. "How 'bout yourself?"

"Doin' real good, Colonel," came the answer.

"Still goin' down at night and eatin' that soggy burned rice, are you?" Rose asked, as he folded the letter and placed it inside his coat.

"Now and again, sir," said Wells. "Haven't seen you down there, though. You give up your explorin' for a while?"

"Yeah," Rose lied. "Didn't see anything down there I thought was worth gettin' shot over."

"I never got to tell you, Colonel, but that was some night, wasn't it?" said Wells. "I hate to admit it, but I kinda enjoyed it. Even the part where we almost got caught. Sure broke the monotony, wouldn't you say?"

"It did do that, Lieutenant," Rose admitted. Then, after a brief pause, he asked, "What are you doin' now, walkin' so fast?"

Wells looked around to see if anyone was listening. "Well, sir, truth be told, I'm still thinkin' of gettin' out of here. Not sure how yet, but somethin'll come up. And when it does, I'm gonna be ready. I walk around the room every day, sometimes for hours at a time. I figure it's gonna be a long walk to Union lines, and if I'm gonna get caught I don't want it to be because I wasn't strong enough to make the hike."

"That's not a bad idea, Lieutenant," said Rose, admiringly. He liked the optimism and enthusiasm Wells showed.

"Passes the time, too," Wells went on. "I was doin' some figurin' while I was walkin' yesterday, and close as I can tell, I think I put in about twenty miles."

"Twenty miles?" Rose said in honest amazement.

"Yep," replied Wells. "Walked for almost six straight hours at a real steady pace. I know your foot's hurt and all, but you might want to think about startin' to walk some every day, yourself. Never know when the opportunity to leave might come along."

"I'll give it some thought," said Rose, grudgingly admitting to himself that it probably wasn't a bad idea. Not today, though. His body was still a little too sore for that.

"Well, I'm gonna be on my way, Colonel," said Wells. "You think about what I said. You'll have to be strong to walk any distance. And we're gonna get out of here. I don't know why I feel that way, but I just have a feelin' that we're gonna get another chance. I hope we can go out together, sir."

"Thanks, Lieutenant," said Rose. "I hope you're right. And good luck!"

"Same to you, sir," said Wells, moving away from Rose. "See you outside the walls."

"Lookin' forward to it," replied Rose.

Wells walked briskly away, and Rose took out his letter to Lydia to read it once more, making sure it sounded right. As he read slowly, a shadow crossed the paper. Looking up, he was surprised to see Hamilton.

"Hello, Andrew," he said. "What brings you up to Upper Chickamauga?"

"Just wanted to see how you were feelin' today," came the answer.

"Like I been run over by a team of horses, to tell the truth," said Rose. "Mostly my neck and back, and my foot's pretty sore. I'm ready to go back down and try again, though."

"I thought as much," Hamilton said with a smile. "Figured you'd stiffen up by today."

"Well, it would've been a lot worse except for you and George," Rose said appreciatively.

"Don't mention it, Thomas. You woulda done it for me. Anyway, c'mere a minute," Hamilton went on. "I want you to see something."

Rose followed Hamilton to a nearby window. "Don't get too close, Andrew," he warned.

"That's not a problem today," said Hamilton. "The Johnnies want us to watch this."

Rose peered out the opening at a sight he never expected to see. Several of the prisoners had been taken outside, where they were taking the oath of allegiance to the Confederacy.

"What's goin' on here?" he asked angrily.

Colonel Streight, standing on the opposite side of the group which was now gathering at the window heard Rose's question.

"Galvanized Yankees selling their souls, Thomas," he said with contempt. "After they take the oath, the Rebs will give them a job in some factory, or let 'em join their army. Back in the Spring, over two hundred men took the oath. Rebs gave a bunch of 'em jobs at the Tredegar Iron Works makin' ammunition. The traitors never thought about what that ammunition was gonna be used for, or who it was gonna be used against. All they thought about was the two dollars a day they were gonna get."

"That ain't true, Streight," shouted a nearby guard who was listening in on the conversation. "Them fellas just see that they're on the wrong side, that's all. They's seen the light, and decided to come over to our side."

"They didn't see any light," spat out Streight. "They know you'll take care of 'em if they tell you what you want to hear. Just like Sanderson and Tilden, when they signed those statements sayin' how well they were bein' treated in here. Everyone knows they get extra food and special privileges for that."

"Just ain't true, Colonel," retorted the guard. "Colonel Tilden and Lieutenant Colonel Sanderson signed those statements voluntarily. They just happen to be gentlemen, is all, and we appreciate that."

"Gentlemen?" said Streight. "Traitors is more like it. And they aren't the only ones. I got no time for men like that. Turned their backs on their country, if you ask me."

"Now, I gotta disagree with y'all again, Colonel," the guard shot back argumentatively. "Seems to me that your country's turned it's back on y'all, not the other way around."

"I don't see it that way, Johnny Reb," said Streight. "Those men took an oath of allegiance to the United States, and they should be willin' to honor it."

The guard removed a plug of tobacco from his mouth and tossed it out the window. Wiping his hand on his pant leg, he resumed his argument. "Way I see it, Colonel, any man fool enough to leave his family and take up arms against the South is dishonorable enough to violate any oath he mighta took."

Streight could feel his composure slipping away. The rest of the prisoners could see it, too, and feared he may do something foolish. As much as the prison administration hated Streight, he didn't have to do much to provoke some form of retaliation.

"Leave 'im be, Colonel," said one.

"Yeah," said another. "He ain't one to be talkin' about honor, anyway. Not the way they treat us in here."

"That's fer sure," said a third. "You make him mad enough and they'll cut our rations even more."

"He's got a point, Colonel," interjected Rose, agreeing with the third man. "These guards don't care a hoot about us. If they starve a few of us to death, there's more food for them. Just ignore him."

Streight looked at Rose. The two shared a mutual respect, and Streight valued Rose's advice as much as any man's, including General Dow's. Reluctantly, he nodded wordlessly. He wasn't even supposed to be in this room in the first place, and he didn't want the guard to punish any of the men just because he had ignored the rules again. Pushing this guard too far could prove disastrous. He turned back to the window.

"That's good advice there, Streight," said the guard. "Y'all say too much and Cap'n Turner's gonna hear 'bout it."

Streight ignored the guard's comment. "Thanks, Thomas," he said to Rose. "Sometimes these guards get me goin' to where I just don't think straight anymore."

"That's alright," answered Rose. "You were right in what you were sayin'. I just didn't want to see any unnecessary punishment bein' handed out. It's rough enough in here as it is."

"You're right about that," agreed Streight, watching the activity in the street. "I'm sorry I put you men in that position. It won't happen again."

Immediately the others showed their disagreement.

"Don't worry about it, Colonel. We can take anything they can do to us."

"You don't have to apologize, Colonel. You were right in what you said."

"We're all in this together, Colonel. Anything they do to you they'll have to do to us, too."

The voices of the prisoners indicated their support for Streight. He smiled in appreciation.

"I wouldn't trade one person in here for ten of those traitors out there, Thomas," he said to Rose.

"You're right about that," agreed Rose. "When those men out there jump sides they're just doin' the North a favor."

Streight watched for a few more minutes, then shook his head in disgust. Turning from the window he said to nobody in particular, "That's all I can watch. I've no time for a man who deserts his friends."

With that, he nodded to Rose and strode away.

"Honorable man," said Hamilton, watching Streight disappear into the crowd.

"That he is," agreed Rose. "And I think I've seen enough, too."

As the pair shouldered their way through the crowd, they could hear the prisoners who remained at the window shouting insults at those who had taken the oath. Just a short time before, many had been friends. This, however, was unforgivable.

"I think I got more respect for the Seceshes than I do for those men out there, Thomas," said Hamilton. "At least the Rebs are fightin' for what they believe in. Those men are just switchin' sides 'cause they got somethin' in return."

"Yeah," said Rose. "We'll be out of here soon ourselves, though, and we'll do it with honor."

That night, Rose casually worked his way through the throng of prisoners to the kitchen. Hamilton and Gallagher were already there. Rose, who had never thought it necessary to tell Gallagher about Wells, now proceeded to talk to the men about the miles Wells was accumulating.

"That's a good idea, Thomas," Hamilton agreed. "But we could never walk all day and dig all night. There'd be no time to sleep. And I think we need that more."

Gallagher agreed.

"I guess you're right," said Rose. "It does seem like a good idea, though. It shows the men are still anxious to get out of here, too. That's a good sign."

"That it is," replied Gallagher. "Even when I didn't know what you two were up to, I know all of us upstairs were talkin' all the time about how we could escape. If the time comes, I know there won't be any shortage of help."

"That's good to hear," said Rose, "But for now I think the three of us can handle everything. And our first job is making that hole bigger!"

"I been thinkin', Thomas," said Hamilton, "I'm not too sure we can do that. We're takin' the chance of poppin' some of those bricks out and findin' out we've broke through the other side. I'd feel a whole lot better knowin' how thick that wall is, so we'd know how far we can dig."

"Yeah," agreed Rose. "I feel the same, but we don't have any way of findin' that out. We're just gonna have to be careful."

"It's gotta be about the same as it is upstairs, don't you think?" asked Gallagher. "Even the Rebs wouldn't make the walls different thicknesses from floor to floor, would they? We can count the bricks in the doorway."

"That's a good point, John," said Rose. "If we know the wall thickness upstairs we can come mighty close to knowin' what we have to work with down here. What do you think, Andrew?"

"Makes sense to me," said Hamilton. "Want me to go up and check it out?"

"Go ahead," said Rose. "We'll start openin' things up down here till you get back."

While Hamilton went upstairs to check the rows of bricks in the doorway on the second floor, the others began pulling the bricks out of the fireplace wall. By the time they were done, Hamilton had returned.

"Close as I can tell, we can take about two more rows out," he said.

"Well, let's get started, then," said Gallagher, leaning into the hole to begin digging.

They alternated digging at the mortar between the bricks, enlarging the hole its entire length in just two nights of digging. Although it was only marginally wider, it was now sufficient to allow Rose through with no problems. The completion of the hole now allowed them free access to Rat Hell, and the digging of the old tunnel was resumed.

"You've been busier than I realized," commented Gallagher when he first was introduced to the tunnel. "When did you do this?"

"Right after we got here," explained Rose. "Only trouble was, the Rebs boarded up the entry to the cellar cook room. Took us this long to figure out how to get back down here."

"They know you was diggin'?" Gallagher asked.

"We don't think so," Hamilton replied. "Made us a little jumpy at the time, though, didn't it, Thomas?"

"Not me," lied Rose, grinning. "You were a mite put out, though, as I recall."

"You weren't, I guess," said Hamilton derisively. "You shoulda seen him. I thought he was gonna pop that Reb when he saw him hammerin' those boards up."

Gallagher laughed at the thought.

"We'd probably be gettin out of those cells just about now if I'd done that, don't you think, Andrew?" said Rose.

"You, maybe," answered Hamilton. "I woulda charmed my way out long before this."

Rose left out a snort.

"I'd like to see that," he said. "You, charmin' the Turners. Now that would be worth stayin' in here a little longer, just to see that."

Using knives and clam shells, the digging continued, the dirt being scattered under the straw to keep anyone venturing into the bowels of Rat Hell from getting suspicious. As dawn approached, the three rolled a barrel in front of the opening and returned upstairs to return the fireplace to its normal appearance.

The next night, on their return to Rat Hell, the men brought with them a spittoon from the kitchen, to be used for hauling dirt. The spittoon, a wooden box about eight inches square and five inches deep, didn't hold much dirt, but it was much easier than transporting the dirt by hand.

As the tunnel grew in length, two problems became apparent. The first, the digging time lost while carrying the spittoon in and out of the excavation, was easily resolved by attaching a piece of clothesline to each end. The rope, one of the few amenities allowed by the prison authorities, was appropriated from its original use and vastly increased the speed with which dirt could be removed. When the spittoon was full, the digger would tug on the rope as a signal for the man at the tunnel mouth to pull it out. When it reached the opening, it would be passed to the next person, who would scatter the contents and return it. The rope was then tugged again to signal the digger, who would pull it back in for refilling. The routine became monotonous in its efficiency, but nobody complained.

The other problem, however, was unanticipated, and more difficult to neutralize. As the tunnel had been extended, the candle often flickered, and would occasionally extinguish. The men attributed it to air currents, and would relight it. It became most apparent one night with Rose in the tunnel, when the candle would extinguish with greater frequency. Finally, Rose was unable to keep the match lit long enough to light the candle.

Backing out of the tunnel, Rose confronted the rest of the group. "Our problem isn't too much air," he said, "It's not enough air. The candle won't stay lit any more."

The three resolutely continued their task, one man digging, another fanning air into the tunnel with his cap, and the third depositing the dirt. This system, however, made it difficult to maintain a watch.

"It's only a matter of time till someone comes in here and catches us," said Rose one night, while they were preparing to go back upstairs. "We just can't keep vigil the way we should."

"You're right about keepin' watch," agreed Gallagher. "There's just too many things to be doin' to keep a lookout the way we should."

"What's the answer?" asked Hamilton. "Slow the diggin'?"

"I don't think we want to do that," answered Rose after a pause. "I think the time is here that we're gonna need some more help."

Chapter Twelve

A small group of trusted prisoners was chosen to assist with the tunneling effort. Sworn to absolute secrecy, as before, all were required to agree that Rose would act as leader. The little band included, in addition to Rose, Hamilton, and Gallagher, the following: Captain Terrence Clark and Second Lieutenant John Mitchell of the 79th Illinois Infantry; First Lieutenant John C. Fislar of the Indiana Light Artillery; Major George W. Fitzsimmons of the 30th Indiana Infantry; Captain William Wallick of the 51st Indiana Infantry; Second Lieutenant David Garbet of Rose's 77th Pennsylvania Infantry; Captain I. N. Johnston of the 6th Kentucky Infantry; Captain John Lucas of the 5th Kentucky Infantry; Major Bedan B. McDonald of the 101st Ohio Infantry; Lieutenant J. Ludlow of the 5th United States Artillery; Lieutenant Walter Clifford of the 16th United States Infantry; and Lieutenant M. C. Causton of the 19th United States Infantry. The size of this crew had not come about by accident. It was chosen to allow each man two nights off after each night of digging. This, Rose believed, would keep everyone relatively fresh. He and Hamilton, on the other hand, chose to be present nearly every night.

The chosen prisoners were called together in the kitchen, where Rose began explaining just what was expected of each of them. Barely into the instructions, the gathering was interrupted by the sharp crack of a musket from the street just outside the window.

"Hope that wasn't meant for anyone in particular," said McDonald.

Almost immediately, as if in answer to McDonald's observation, angry shouts could be heard from one of the upstairs rooms.

"Sounds like somethin's goin' on," said Rose. "Someone go and find out what happened."

119

Garbet dashed for the steps, returning within a matter of minutes. "Dirty Rebs shot someone," he cried out.

"Who was it?" shouted Rose, as the clamor from upstairs continued.

"I couldn't get close enough to tell," answered Garbet. "He must've got too close to the window."

The men clambered rapidly up the steps, the meeting over for now. Reaching the top of the stairs, they could see the others milling about at the stairs to Upper Chickamauga on the third floor. Try as they would, the throng was in no mood to allow them to pass. Everyone was determined to get up the steps himself, to see just what had happened, and nobody was about to step aside to permit someone else to go ahead.

By pushing and shoving, Rose was able to reach the foot of the stairs but could go no further. Two armed guards stood about halfway up the stairs, letting nobody pass.

"Anyone know what happened?" he asked a captain next to him.

"All's I know, somebody upstairs got shot," the captain answered, his anger apparent in his voice.

Another prisoner interjected, "I didn't hear who it was, sir, but from what I've been told he was up in Upper Chickamauga mindin' his own business. Weren't near a window or nothin'. Just standin' and talkin' to some of the others. Then one of those stinkin' Seceshes decides to shoot at someone on the second floor in Lower Chickamauga. He missed the man in Lower Chickamauga and the ball went clean up through the ceilin' and hits the feller in Upper Chickamauga."

"Yeah, that's what I heard, too," said one of the others standing nearby.

Much of the anger in the crowd was being directed toward the two guards on the stairs, even though nobody knew exactly what had happened. The two Rebels were all the prisoners could see that represented the Confederacy, and it was they who bore the brunt of the men's outrage.

"You'll not live a day after we get out of here, Reb," shouted someone to the pair on the stairs. "We'll never forget your faces, and we'll come lookin' for you, count on it."

"Don't bother me none," retorted one of the guards with an air of bravado. "Y'all ain't gonna git out, so I ain't worried."

"Oh, we'll get out, all right," yelled a prisoner, angrily. "And if that man dies up there, you'll pay the price."

"By the time y'all git out, Yank, y'all gonna be trippin' over your beard," mocked the guard. His bitterness toward his captives was apparent, as his lip curled in scorn as he talked. The second guard, a young man of about seventeen, appeared cowed by the prisoners, and he tried to stay behind the first man at all times.

"Why don't you put that musket down and come on down here so's we can chat a little?" asked another prisoner.

Before the Confederate could answer, Major Turner appeared at the top of the stairs, followed by two men carrying the limp body of the shooting victim.

"Move outta the way if y'all want this man to have a chance to live," shouted Turner to the throng.

At the sight of Turner the mob grew angrier, the din increasing. The crowd parted, however, allowing the guards to pass, followed by Turner and the two men bearing the victim. As they hurried through on their way to the hospital room, those near the front could see the victim's pale face, his eyes half open and his face contorted in pain. A bright red blotch covered the upper right portion of his chest, the blood leaving a trail of droplets on the filthy floor.

With the guards having followed the victim to the hospital room, there was nobody left behind to receive the angry shouts of the prisoners, and gradually the noise level returned to normal. Still, the men talked angrily among themselves. While they didn't happen every day, shootings took place on a fairly routine basis, and they only served to make the prisoners more determined to escape.

After several minutes, the crowd began to slowly disperse, gathering into small knots to discuss the incident further. Hamilton and Rose retired to the kitchen, where they met with the others in the digging party. None was in the mood to discuss the tunnel, so Rose reluctantly dismissed them with orders to return the following night.

"I think I'm gonna come back down tonight, Thomas," said Hamilton.

"For what?" queried Rose. "Nobody else will be here, so we can't do much."

"Well, I been thinkin' about that rope of ours," said Hamilton. "What would you say if I was to make it into a ladder? Be a lot easier to go up and down that way, wouldn't it?"

"Might be," agreed Rose, "But it's also gonna be tougher to hide. It'll be a lot bulkier."

"Yeah, I know," said Hamilton. "But what if we leave it inside the wall? We'd just have to pull it up out of Rat Hell when we come up in the mornin', and slip the other end inside the fireplace walls when we close up."

Rose contemplated Hamilton's plan for a minute or two. "Go ahead, if you think you can do it," he finally said.

"I can do it, Thomas. I know I can," Hamilton said with excitement. "Fact is, I wish it was dark now, so's I could get started."

The two ascended the stairs, still shaken by the shooting incident.

"I think we need this break, Andrew," Rose said. "I keep thinkin' about that poor soul that got shot."

"Me, too," agreed Hamilton. "I probably wouldn't be good for much tonight except makin' a ladder, anyways. That'll keep my mind occupied."

The two split up, each with his own thoughts. One more day would have little effect on their escape plan. But they would be sure to stay near the center of the room, where stray shots would not penetrate.

The tiny band gathered again the next evening. As Hamilton had promised, he had fashioned a ladder from the rope. The diggers gathered around and admired his handiwork, all the while discussing the previous day's shooting incident. Major Turner, with his inimitable talent for taking a bad situation and making it worse, had tried to convince the prisoners that the guard's musket had gone off accidentally. Those who had seen the sentry aiming at the second floor window had vehemently disputed this, the result being a prolonging of the prisoners' anger. The topic had been on every prisoner's lips throughout the day.

Rose raised his hand to get the attention of his followers. "All right, boys. Let's settle down and get to work," he said with authority. "I know we all feel pretty bad right now about the shooting, but there isn't anything we can do about it. Let's try to keep our minds on what we have to do."

The group grew quiet, all anxious to hear Rose's plan.

"Now, here's my idea," he said. "When we get down to Rat Hell we're gonna dig down along the east wall. We'll split up into teams to do that. Some of you will dig, some will haul dirt, others will stand watch. You can spell each other off if you want, but I think we'll do better if everybody sticks with the thing he does best."

The men glanced around, nodding agreement.

Rose continued. "Then, once we get through the wall, we're gonna take the tunnel toward the sewer. After we get into the sewer we can just follow it to wherever it comes out." Rose then proceeded to explain how he had seen the workers entering the sewer, and offered his theory that it would lead to either the canal or the river, either of which would allow their passage to freedom.

Once the plan had been laid out, it was discussed excitedly. All agreed that it was an ingenious plan, and that they would be long gone before the rebels ever missed them.

After splitting into groups, the first began to dig. The others went back upstairs to await their shift of tunneling.

Using penknives and clam shells, the diggers attacked their work feverishly. However, at the end of the first night's work, little progress had been made.

"We ain't gonna dig through that, Colonel," said Clark. "That's solid timbers."

"We've got to," answered Rose. "It's the only way to get to the sewer."

The digging began anew, each driven by the thought of going home. The timbers proved to be much stronger than they could hope to penetrate with their almost primitive digging equipment, but they pressed on. Slowly, almost imperceptibly, the wood gave way.

A few nights after the digging had begun, Rose and the rest of his team gathered to begin another night's work. The men were uncharacteristically quiet, almost somber.

"What's the problem?" asked Rose.

"Ah, we just feel a little down tonight, is all," answered Garbet. "One of the new boys got some real bad news today. We were all there with 'im at the time."

Rose's curiosity was aroused. "What kind of bad news?"

"Seems his sister died the day after he was captured. Poor fella got his first letter since he was captured, and that was the news. Took it kinda hard, he did. All of us feel bad fer 'im."

"That is too bad," agreed Rose. "A lotta lives bein' affected by this war. He'd been with her if it weren't for the fightin', that's a fact. No wonder yer all feelin' down."

His thoughts immediately went to Lydia. What would he do if he received a letter like that? If he lost Lydia? He didn't even want to think about it, and he forced the thought from his mind.

Changing the subject, Rose tried to appear upbeat. "I heard some better news today, myself."

The men, anxious to hear something positive, looked at him with anticipation.

"Can't vouch fer it," he said, "But I heard our boys did real good over in Tennessee a few weeks ago. Took a place called Lookout Mountain. Drove the Rebs right off it, I hear."

"That would be good news," said Garbet. "Hope it's right. We'll never know the truth in here, though. Those guards'll be tellin' us that they took that mountain, and we won't have any way of knowin'."

"We'll know," said Rose. "Elizabeth Van Lew will tell us, next time she's in."

"That the lady what comes in to talk to General Dow and Colonel Streight?" asked Garbet.

"That's her," said Rose, who proceeded to tell the men about Van Lew's offer to help any prisoner who was able to escape.

"You get to her place," he concluded. "She'll get you to the closest Union pickets. And General Dow says she's not just talkin', either. She can do it."

The men discussed their hopes for escape, their plans after getting out.

Finally, Rose interrupted the discussion. "If we just sit here talkin' about it, it's never gonna happen. Let's get to work."

With that, the thoughts of escape were turned to action, all pitching in to carve their way through the huge timbers which had thus far proven so formidable. Well after midnight, their efforts were rewarded.

"I've got dirt here, Colonel," cried out Clark.

Rose, who had been taking a short rest while Clark worked, rushed over, as did the others. He signaled to Clark to come back out of the short tunnel. As Clark stood up, a bright smile appeared.

"We got it, Colonel," he said, his excitement showing.

Rose crawled into the tunnel on his belly, pushing the candle stub ahead of him. Clark had indeed struck dirt on the opposite side of the timbers. The men had finally hacked their way through! "Now the real diggin' can start," thought Rose.

He began digging at the dirt in earnest, filling up the spittoon in a matter of seconds. Pulling on the rope to signal those outside the tunnel that he had dirt to be dumped, Rose breathed a short prayer of thanks.

Rose was by far the most proficient digger of the entire group, and would, therefore, be in the tunnel more than most. Never letting his goal get far from his thoughts, he had no problem motivating himself to get to work. By the end of the night's digging he had personally advanced the tunnel more than two feet.

"A good night's work, gentlemen," he commented to the others as they stole up the stairs. "A good night's work."

The men murmured their agreements, fatigue preventing further conversation. Sleep would again come easy to the men, despite the colder temperatures.

"Too bad the Johnnies can't put some glass in those windows, instead of bars," was a common complaint.

Nevertheless, Rose barely remembered settling down before he was in a deep slumber. That was one benefit of the hard night of digging; he was rarely kept awake by the cold.

Rose awoke several hours later when one of the other prisoners shook him.

"Chow time, Colonel," said the man. "Don't want to miss it, do you?"

Rubbing his face to break through the haze of sleep, Rose looked up. "I could probably miss it and my stomach wouldn't see the difference," he said.

"Now, there's the truth, sir," his friend said with a laugh.

By the time Rose reached the kitchen area he was completely awake. As usual, the area teemed with prisoners. Some, like Rose, were there to eat. Others spent the day there, huddled around one of the fireplaces, seeking what warmth they could find wherever they could find it. Across the room he spied Hamilton, who waved a greeting. The two spent little time together during the daylight hours, not wishing to arouse anyone's suspicion.

Often, prisoners used the gathering as a sounding board. Political debates took place almost daily, and Lincoln was cursed almost as often as the Confederate government, for his failure to gain the prisoners' release.

Today, General Dow took his turn. Climbing onto one of the tables, he surveyed the throng. Seeing him taking his place, many let out a groan.

"Here we go again," said someone seated near Rose.

Rose did not acknowledge the comment, although he knew what the general's forum would be. Dow had been an ardent prohibitionist in Maine prior to the war, and never failed to pass an opportunity to warn others of the evils of demon rum.

"We ain't got no food and he's gonna tell us we shouldn't drink no whiskey," another went on. "Don't make no sense to me."

Only the respect for Dow's rank protected him from overt verbal abuse. Most of the men either pretended to listen or ignored him completely. Only a few, the disgruntled minority present in every large group, found it necessary to retort.

"I promise you, General," shouted a captain from New Jersey, "I won't touch a drop of the hard stuff the whole time I'm in here."

A smattering of laughs greeted the comment, but Dow ignored it, choosing instead to continue his lecture. Rose looked at Dow attentively, but his mind was on the tunnel.

"Don't forget me, Colonel," said a familiar voice. "I'm still exercisin' and ready to go when you are."

"Wells," said Rose. "How are you doin'?"

"Good, sir. A little hungry, maybe, but otherwise fit as a fiddle."

"I guess we're all a little hungry," said Rose, welcoming the diversion. He didn't feel like listening to General Dow's views on temperance today, even though he liked the old man.

"I hear you're diggin' a tunnel, Colonel. That true?" asked Wells in a whisper.

"A tunnel?" Rose asked incredulously. "Where'd you ever hear a thing like that?"

"I got my contacts, sir," answered Wells. "What about it? Are you?"

"Do you really think, if there was a tunnel out of here, that I'd be sittin' at this table listenin' to General Dow go on about the evils of corn squeezin's?" countered Rose.

"Not if it was finished," said Wells. "But, if it was still bein' dug, you wouldn't have much choice now, would you?"

"I guess I wouldn't," agreed Rose, innocently. "But, there's no tunnel that I know about."

"No tunnel," said Wells, obviously not believing what Rose was telling him.

"Nope. No tunnel," lied Rose.

Wells drew silent. Then, a mischievous grin crossed his face. "I believe you if you say so, Colonel. If you tell me there's no tunnel, then there's no tunnel. Only thing I ask is, be sure to take me with you when you get it finished." He patted Rose on the shoulder as he stood to leave.

Rose smiled in spite of himself. "I'll be sure to do that, Wells," he said. "That is, if I ever find out there really is a tunnel."

Wells winked at him, then turned and walked away. "How does he always know what we're doin'?" Rose thought, shaking his head slightly. "Gageby, too. He always seems to know. I hope we don't have a spy in the group."

Rose made a mental note to ask the others if they were getting questioned by the other prisoners. It was inevitable that a few people would guess what was going on. There were more than twelve hundred in here, after all, and there wasn't much to do but talk. It only stood to reason that a few outsiders would know, or at least suspect, that something was going on. But if too many knew, it could mean someone inside the group was talking, and that would be dangerous.

That night, the discussion centered on these concerns. None of the others had been hearing any of the prisoners discuss the tunnel. Rose's mind was eased somewhat, but he warned the rest about the danger of talking about it with anyone not already in the group. All agreed on the need for secrecy, then turned to their appointed tasks.

Following their usual work assignments, Rose found himself inside the tight confines of the tunnel. Something seemed different in the dim light of the candle. At first it was not apparent, and Rose busied himself with digging. Then, while waiting for the spittoon to be emptied and returned, he realized just what had changed. The texture of the dirt was different. On previous nights, the dirt had felt loose, almost sandy. Tonight it stuck together in clumps. Not really wet, but at least damp. It made the digging slightly more difficult, and the tunnel's progress slowed in proportion.

Over the next few hours, the soil became wetter. The changing conditions had Rose confused, almost troubled. "What could be causing this?" he thought. He considered discussing it with the others, but he didn't want to stop digging. Even a few minutes spent talking about escape were precious minutes that were not being used to extend the tunnel.

He pressed on. The tunnel was so small that he barely had room to maneuver. His body served as a block against any fresh air the men back in Rat Hell were able to fan in to him, and the candle often extinguished for lack of oxygen. At best, it flickered feebly, as if it were desperately trying to stay alive.

By now, each spittoon full of earth was wetter than the previous. In the dim glow of the candle, Rose thought he could see the water forming a small pool on the tunnel floor. Touching it, his fingers came back wet. Mystified, Rose held the candle closer to the face of the tunnel. Then, even with the minimal light given off by the oxygen-starved candle, he saw it!

At first, he didn't even notice. Then, passing the candle in front of his face again, the light picked up the unmistakable sheen of the water.

Only a trickle, it nonetheless was flowing. For several moments he watched it, still not sure what to make of this new problem.

Feeling a cold sensation on his arm, he touched his sleeve. It, too, was wet. He was now lying in water, and he could see several small rivulets coming through the tunnel walls.

"Please, God, no," he prayed. "We couldn't have misjudged that badly. Please don't let us be below the canal."

But they were. The recent heavy rains had raised the level of the canal to a point where the tunnel was lower than the surface of the water. The contents of the canal were now finding their way into the small hole in which every one of the diggers had placed their last measure of hope.

As Rose contemplated the situation, the water flowed more heavily. He no longer needed the glow of the candle to see the many streams which were now entering through the walls. He began to slowly back out of the tunnel to discuss this new dilemma. Placing his hands on the tunnel floor, he found himself lying in mud. Although he had not broken through, the water was pushing against the other side of the tunnel wall with such force that his clothes were now soaked.

Scrambling by now to get out of the tunnel, Rose raced the water. No matter how much closer he got to Rat Hell, he could not get away from the flow! The walls would not be able to hold the force back much longer!

Finally he felt his feet strike the straw of Rat Hell. Quickly, he stood and looked at the others. "We've got to plug this fast!" he said as loudly as he dared.

The men looked at each other in disbelief. Unable to fathom what Rose was telling them, nobody moved.

"Come on!" Rose exhorted them. "There's no time to waste. We've broken through to the canal!"

Rose grabbed dirt, straw, anything he could grasp, shoving it into the mouth of the opening in desperation. By now, water was flowing out of the tunnel into Rat Hell.

Almost to a man, the realization struck at once. Each dropped to his knees and began the task of closing the only means of escape they had. Their dreams of freedom were slowly snuffed out with each handful of dirt they threw into the opening.

Finally, the flow of canal water was stopped. The men tamped the earth to solidify the barrier. Dejected, Rose returned to the kitchen and slumped to the floor. The exhausted men joined him, asking what had happened.

As Rose explained what had taken place inside the tunnel, he occupied his hands by replacing the bricks. Hamilton joined him, and soon the others were passing the bricks from man to man, just to have something to do.

"Who's gonna tell the others?" asked a downtrodden Hobart.

"I will," said Rose, trying to wipe some of the mud from his coat. "They need to know as soon as possible. It's only right."

"You want me to go fetch them, Colonel?" asked Hobart.

"No," said Rose, after contemplating Hobart's suggestion. "That would be too risky. Someone's bound to wonder why you're getting them up in the middle of the night. I'll talk to each one in the morning."

They sat silently for several minutes, each with his own thoughts. The feeling of disappointment was oppressive, and each man had to come to terms with it in his own way.

Hamilton, remembering their earlier failings, broke the silence. "Y'know, Thomas," he said. "This gettin' away business is sure hard on a man's mind. Just about the time you think things are finally goin' right, everything comes down around yer ears."

Understanding his friend's pain, Rose felt no need to answer.

Chapter Thirteen

The dejected group of would-be escapees, although not totally disbanded, became inactive for several days. There was no longer a need to meet clandestinely in the kitchen after hours, no longer a need to crawl down through a wall to a rat-infested cellar, and no longer a need to slither through a narrow opening to dig a tunnel in air that was so foul that it could not support the flame of a candle. There was no longer a tunnel to be dug.

Several days after their ill-fated effort, Rose had spied Hamilton in the kitchen.

"Gather everyone for a meeting tonight," he had said tersely.

"For what," Hamilton had asked.

"We're gonna dig again," was the answer.

And so it was that the men who were so determined to breach Libby's walls had again assembled before their leader on a night in which the wind howled through the cracks of the walls and the snow filtered in through the open windows.

Rose had explained to his friends that he wanted to begin another tunnel, this one from the southeast corner of the basement. This plan had called for the tunnel to extend to a small sewer, a sewer which would lead them to the main sewer which had been their original target.

All had listened as Rose had outlined the new plan, and the role each would play in its implementation. The vote to resume digging had been unanimous, and the first bricks had been removed that very night. Digging had been in progress for several nights when the word reached Rose that he had better come to the window at the east end of the building.

Reaching the window, Rose sidled up to it cautiously. Garbet had warned him that he thought there was a problem with the tunnel, that it may have been discovered. Peering cautiously around the edge of the window, Rose was not prepared for what he saw. A large brick furnace leaned at an odd angle. He immediately realized that the tunnel had inadvertently been dug directly beneath the furnace, with the weight of the furnace causing the ceiling of the tunnel to cave in.

He looked at Garbet, who returned his glance with an apprehensive look. Listening anxiously next to the window, being sure to stay safely back from the vision of anyone on the street, Rose was relieved to hear that the presence of a tunnel was not suspected.

"What's going on here,"a voice thundered. Rose recognized the voice as Major Turner's.

"Rats, sir," answered a guard nervously, apparently intimidated by Turner's presence.

"Rats?" questioned Turner.

"Yes, sir. Rats. They's all over the place here. Everything's undercut," the guard answered.

"You mean there's so many rat holes and tunnels under us that this furnace just fell through the street?" Turner asked in amazement.

"Yes, sir. Happens all the time. Why, jest last week one of them supply wagons broke through jest like this. Wheel dropped clean through the street, right over there," the guard offered, pointing with his musket to a spot not twenty yards away. "Funniest thing. That ole darkie was whippin' them horses, tryin' to get that wagon out before the whole thing got swallered up. I like to popped my buttons laughin', sir."

Turner looked at the furnace, shaking his head. He walked over and surveyed it more closely. Rose held his breath, hoping that Turner would not look too closely at the hole. Finally, Turner turned back to the guard. "Get some help and get this mess straightened up," he directed.

"Yes, sir," the man responded, still smiling as he recalled the sight of the wagon's driver attempting to extricate the wheel.

Watching Turner walk away, Rose felt a new wave of frustration overcome him.

"Another setback!" he said to nobody in particular.

With a heavy sigh, Rose turned to Garbet. "Go get Andrew. Then, the two of you get the word to all the men about what's happened. I'm gonna go down to Rat Hell tonight and see if there's any sign that the Rebs suspect that anything aside from rats caused that furnace to sink. I'll let everyone know what I find out."

Alone, Rose entered Rat Hell after the prisoners settled in for the night. After his initial inspection revealed nothing to indicate that the guards had been in the basement, he settled into a corner to watch. Throughout the cold night he fought off the urge to sleep. There was too much at stake, too many were dependent on him to find out just how much the Confederates knew.

The hours dragged on. Still no sign of anyone showing an interest in entering Rat Hell. Finally, he heard the sentry call out, "Five o'clock, and all's well at Post Six!"

As the time was echoed from post to post, Rose felt his apprehension disappearing. "If anything was suspected, someone would have been in here before this," he reasoned.

Satisfied that the tunnel had not been discovered, Rose went back upstairs. Even though that tunnel could no longer be used, the plan itself was still safe. Rose spread the word to the group of diggers throughout the day. Each had been told of the problem by either Garbet or Hamilton and, to a man, they were excited about the prospects of starting a third tunnel.

"What else can go wrong now?" Captain Lucas had said. "The next one should make it with no trouble."

Rose and Hamilton met later that afternoon to discuss the next step. Seated with their backs against a post, each sipped coffee from a dirty cup. Lydia had sent a package to Rose, a package which had obviously been rummaged through before it had been released. The coffee had not been stolen, although it appeared that someone had sifted through it. Rose assumed that prison officials had been attempting to uncover contraband. As did most of the other prisoners, Rose shared his booty.

Taking another sip of coffee, Rose looked into the cup. "This stuff isn't the best I've ever had," he said to Hamilton, "But it kills the taste of the canal water."

Hamilton nodded in agreement.

The two sat in silence. Neither had a plan at this point. Nobody had anticipated the intrusion of the furnace into the tunnel. However, there was no doubt in the minds of the tunnel party that another attempt would be made.

As they contemplated their next effort, General Dow joined them.

"You boys hear about the escape?" he asked excitedly.

Rose and Hamilton instantly looked at one another. Had the Confederates learned of the tunnel after all?

"What escape is that, General?" Rose asked apprehensively, trying to keep his voice calm.

"Captains Anderson and Skelton," answered Dow, to the relief of his listeners. "Bribed one of the guards and just walked away."

"Is that a fact?" exclaimed Rose. "Good for them. I hope they make it."

"We all do," said Dow. "Of course, the best part is that they did it. But the next best part is that Turner and Winder are really upset! I just left them and Turner's so hot you could light a cigar on his forehead."

"I'd like to see that," said Hamilton.

Dow could hardly contain himself. "One of the best day's I've had since I've been in Libby," he exclaimed gleefully.

"Did you know they were gonna do that?" asked Rose, wondering how extensively the two captains had planned their escape.

"Not for sure, I didn't," answered Dow. "Probably just saw their chance and took it. Didn't surprise me none, though. Just about every man in here has thoughts of escaping. I'm sure it's crossed your mind more than once."

"It has at that, sir," confessed Rose. "Maybe one of these days..."

Dow rose to leave. "Maybe one of these days we'll all be out of here," he said, finishing Rose's sentence.

Hamilton and Rose watched the old man shuffle his way to the fireplace to warm his hands.

"At least someone's having a good run of luck," exclaimed Hamilton.

"Sorta makes you want to try again, doesn't it?" mused Rose.

"I'm ready when you are, Thomas," declared Hamilton.

"I'm ready to get out just so I can get a decent meal again," complained Rose.

"Yeah. Me, too," agreed Hamilton.

"Colonel Streight was telling me that he wrote a letter to General Meredith a few months ago, complainin' about the food," said Rose.

"Is that so?" responded Hamilton. "I didn't know about that."

"Nor did I," answered Rose, finishing the last bit of coffee. "Guess it happened before we got here. At any rate, he said he told Meredith about the poor food, as well as the lack of it. Even told him that the only thing keepin' the prisoners alive was the fact that they were poolin' their money and usin' it to buy vegetables. Only thing was, they were spendin' over a thousand dollars a day, and they were about out of money. Colonel Streight said he asked that the government take whatever measures they had to in order to secure proper treatment for the prisoners."

"Didn't seem to do much good, did it?" said Hamilton, cynically.

"Nope," answered Rose. "Leastways, not yet. Said he never got an answer from General Meredith, but General Winder called him downstairs to the office and told him that we were bein' treated no worse than the Rebel prisoners bein' held at Point Lookout and Fort Delaware."

"Winder said that?" Hamilton asked, raising his eyebrows in surprise.

"So Colonel Streight says. I guess Winder was pretty mad about that letter, but he finally agreed to find out if any rations were bein' held back. Colonel Streight says he figured that alone was worth sendin' the letter for. That letter raised a lot of hackles, though."

"I reckon it would," said Hamilton. "Guess it ain't too hard to figure out why the Rebs hate Colonel Streight so much, is it?"

"Guess not," agreed Rose. "Doesn't seem to bother 'im much though, does it?"

"Would it bother you if a Secesh didn't like you?" Hamilton asked sarcastically.

"Not much," Rose said with a grin. "There's been a lot of times they didn't seem to find me in their favor. Like at Chickamauga, for instance. I try not to take it too personal, though."

"Well, now," responded Hamilton, "I'm sure they appreciate that."

A guard interrupted the conversation. "Y'all wanna see some of yer boys, they's comin' up the street right now."

The men dashed to the windows. Each strained to peer out around the corners of the openings, hoping to see the latest batch of prisoners being brought in. Soon, several companies of well-dressed Confederate soldiers came into view, followed by a motley looking group of half-dressed Union prisoners.

The approaching prisoners looked like walking skeletons. All were filthy. Some limped badly, others draped the arms of companions over their shoulders to keep them from collapsing onto the muddy street. Many of the men were shoeless, despite the cold temperatures, and several wore no coats. Not a hat or cap was to be seen.

"Glory be," said one of the men gathered at the window. "Did ya ever see such a sight?"

The others inside Libby said nothing in response. They were having difficulty believing what they were seeing. These men were more dead than alive, and many looked as if each step may be their last. The Confederate soldiers accompanying them, however, were uncharacteristically well uniformed.

"Where you boys from?" shouted one of the Libby inhabitants to the Northerners marching past.

A chorus of regiment numbers immediately rang out: "Fifteenth Regulars! Twentieth Wisconsin! USS Rattler! Fifty-fourth Pennsylvania," came the cry.

"Eighty-ninth Ohio," the nearest passing prisoner answered feebly, his voice barely audible. "We're goin' home."

"You bein' exchanged?" the Libby prisoner shouted back.

"Yep," the man answered in a hollow tone. "We're all from Belle Isle. Hope they take you fellas next."

By now the man had passed from voice range. His voice range, at least. General Dow shouted to another, a young man looking far older than his years.

"How are the men on Belle Isle getting along, son?"

The youth looked toward the window, attempting to focus on the face which accompanied the voice.

"None too good, sir," he said haltingly. "We're among the healthiest of the lot, so that should give you an idea. A lot of the men there can't even stand up no more. Some of them are comin' on behind, in ambulances. Any left behind'll be dead by warm weather, no doubt."

Someone from one of the lower floors tossed a scrap of corn bread to the passing prisoners. Several of the marching men broke rank and dove into the mud to retrieve it. The lucky one quickly stuffed the soggy morsel into his mouth before it could be stolen from him. The scene was heartbreaking, even to the men inside the walls of Libby who had little to eat, themselves.

"Good luck," shouted someone from another window. "Be sure to tell the government what's happenin' down here!"

The officers in Libby watched in near silence as the last row of prisoners from Belle Isle marched by. Soon, a string of ambulance wagons rumbled past the windows. Inside the wagons could be seen the prone figures of those too sick to walk. Many already appeared to be dead.

The faces peering from Libby's windows were sullen. Many of the Libby prisoners had recognized faces from their own regiments. Many other faces, no doubt, would have been familiar were it not for the layers of filth, the sores and scabs, and the emaciated appearances.

As the last ambulance rolled by, another company of well-dressed, heavily-armed Confederates brought up the rear. Still shaken by the appearances of many of those who were on their way to exchange, the men of Libby said little.

"Do we look that bad?" one asked.

"We ain't gonna win no prizes fer looks, that's fer sure," answered another. "But I think those boys looked a lot worse'n us, by a long shot."

"Well," responded a third man, "It ain't no wonder. They's sleepin' in tents over there, even in this cold weather. The lucky ones, that is. There ain't enough tents fer the number of prisoners, so lots of 'em sleep out on the bare ground, I hear."

"You see them Rebs, though?" the first prisoner asked. "Ain't they the fancy ones?"

"Bet they ain't seen the elephant, lookin' like that," commented a man standing beside him, in reference to the Confederate soldiers' apparent lack of battle experience.

"Don't be too certain," answered General Dow.

"Those boys?" the man queried. "Ain't no way on God's earth those men've been shot at yet. They probably ain't even spent their first night out in the field."

Several of the prisoners laughed in agreement.

"Those uniforms were all a part of the show they were putting on for us," said Dow, softly.

"What do ya mean by show?" several asked.

"Didn't it seem strange to you that the guards didn't mind that we were at the windows?" asked Dow. "In fact, one of 'em even told us that the boys from Belle Isle would be along shortly."

The men looked around at one another. That had not yet sunk in. Murmurs passed through the throng.

"Those new uniforms you just saw will be back in the warehouse by nightfall," said Dow. "Right alongside those shiny new muskets."

"What makes you think that, General?" someone asked.

"Rebs'll do that," said Dow. "They'll let us see those well-dressed soldiers, all carryin' fancy new weapons, just to make us think they're well equipped. They're hopin' those boys bein' exchanged will tell everyone up north that the South is sendin' all these well-armed men to the war."

"Not only that," chimed in a young captain, "them mules you saw pullin' the ambulance wagons ain't long fer this world, neither."

"What do you mean by that?" asked another prisoner.

"Well, ain't it easy to see?" the captain answered. "The Rebs ain't got no beef to give us. Where do you think that meat you ate yesterday came from?"

"Mules?" was the query.

"O'course, mules. We been eatin' mule meat all along, I'll bet."

"You really think we been gettin' mule meat?" someone asked.

"I surely do," the captain shot back. "At first I thought it tasted funny 'cause it was boiled in canal water. But then I started noticin', there ain't no mules out in the streets no more. What do you think happened to 'em? We're eatin' 'em, that's what happened to 'em!"

"Can't be!" another prisoner countered, refusing to believe he had been eating mule meat rather than beef.

"'Tis so," said the captain. "I can guarantee it. I've ate horse meat before, and them mules tasted just the same!"

Turning to a nearby guard, the captain called to him. "How 'bout it, Johnny Reb? We eatin' mule meat?"

Taken by surprise, the guard appeared flustered. Barely out of his teens, he groped for a good comeback. Then, regaining his composure, he answered, "Don't know fer sure, Yank. But I surely hope not. I'd hate to think the CSA is wastin' good mules on the likes of y'all!"

"You wouldn't tell us, anyway," said the captain, derisively.

"Well, now, I surely would," the guard protested. "I jest said I hope we ain't killin' valuable mules jest to keep y'all from goin' hungry. Fact is, a good Missouri mule is worth a hundred Yankees, and mebbe more."

"Well," said the captain good-naturedly, "Whatever that stuff is, we ain't gettin' enough of it. Even if it's mule meat, we could use some more. Think you can help us out, Johnny?"

The guard laughed, then answered, "I don't think I kin do that, Yank. Why, if'n I was to get you more meat, next thing you'd say is y'all only want the meat off'n the hind quarters. How'm I gonna tell Major Turner that?"

"You ain't such a bad Reb," the captain said. "He'll listen to you. You know yourself, a good steak now and again tastes pretty good, don't it? Even if it's mule steak!"

The guard laughed again, obviously enjoying a friendly conversation for a change. "Well, now. If y'all jest joined the right army, y'all could have steak any time y'all wanted it."

"Like you do, Johnny?" laughed the captain. "When's the last time you had a good steak? And don't be tellin' us you get 'em all the time when you're out on the march. We know better!

"We do, Yank. We do. Reckon' mebbe it's 'cause the folks down here in Virginia like us boys a mite more'n they like y'all. They's always makin' us eat good when we pass their farms."

"Is that a fact?" the captain said, as his friends chuckled at the banter.

"It's the gospel, Captain," answered the guard. "If'n y'all ain't gettin 'nuff to eat when y'all are marchin', it's gotta be the color of your uniform."

"I'm not thinkin' about what I eat when I'm marchin'," the captain burst out. "I'm more concerned with what I ain't eatin' while I'm in here."

"Reckon I can understand that," laughed the guard. Then, turning more serious he said, "Truth be told, we don't eat all that good, either."

"They ain't gonna let you starve, though, Johnny, and that's a fact. Us poor Yanks, though, that's another story," disagreed the captain.

"Yeah," answered the young guard. "Reckon that's the truth. Y'all kin starve to death in here, and won't nobody say nothin'."

"We all know that," the captain said, to the agreeing murmurs of the others. "Leastways, your government could let us have the supplies our families send us."

The guard became defensive. "Now, y'all know them supplies are given out, sooner or later."

A mocking laugh arose from the group. "More later than sooner," said a voice with a New England accent.

"That's jest 'cause your government's spreadin' so many lies," the guard said testily. "Meredith keeps on tellin' ever'one that y'all ain't gettin' nothin that's bein' sent, and y'all know that ain't so. He's sayin' we're keepin' what's bein' sent, 'stead of lettin y'all have it."

"We might get 'em, but it sure takes a long time," a tall major interjected. Gesturing toward the window he went on, "You keep 'em stored in that warehouse over yonder for weeks before we can go claim 'em. Then, when we do, someone's already gone through everything."

"Well, that ain't gonna get no better," said the guard. "I hear tell that Colonel Ould's done gone and told your government he ain't even gonna accept no more supplies from your families or your government, on 'count 'a all them lies. Said when that warehouse is empty, they ain't gonna be no more."

"That's petty revenge!" shouted the captain. "Even you Rebs wouldn't be that cruel. You know yourself, those supplies are all that's keepin' us alive."

"I ain't got no say in it, Yank. I jest do like I'm told, jest like you do," retorted the guard.

"You think that's right?" asked the major.

"Don't matter what I think," the youthful guard answered. Then, realizing that the conversation was becoming more heated than he cared for it to be, he started toward the stairs. "Y'all kin complain to someone else. I ain't gonna talk about it no more!"

Angry comments followed the guard as he worked his way through the crowd. Once he disappeared, the men discussed the startling turn of events. The prisoners could not bring themselves to believe that future packages would be refused. Most agreed that the young guard was merely spouting off a rumor, or that he had misunderstood something. Or perhaps it was wishful thinking on the part of those incarcerated in Libby. Without packages from home, whether food or clothing, they all knew that many of them would not be able to survive the winter.

"We'll look a heap worse'n any of those boys we seen bein' exchanged today," one of the prisoners offered, to the agreement of all.

The discussion continued long past the point at which it would have died if it were taking place outside the walls of Libby. Boredom has a way of prolonging even the mundane.

As the last glimmer of outside light faded, overtaken by the December night, Dick Turner appeared at the top of the stairs. Behind him, three soldiers struggled with large buckets of water.

"Scrub squad!" shouted Turner. "Stand back."

As the men watched, the soldiers dumped the contents of their buckets over the floor. Those unfortunate prisoners closest to the flow found themselves drenched from the knees down.

"What's the meaning of this?" shouted General Dow angrily.

"Jest scrubbin yer floors, is all, General," Turner said mockingly.

"At this hour?" demanded Dow. "You know this floor won't be dry when the men turn in for the night!"

"Yeah, I know," Turner replied, an evil grin appearing on his face. "I figgered y'all would rather sleep in a puddle of canal water than in the overflow from the privy, though. Which would you prefer, General?"

"I would prefer that it be done in the morning, just like you would if you were forced to sleep on the floor," Dow shot back.

Feigning surprise, Turner raised his eyebrows. "Y'know, that jest might not be a bad idea, General. I'll try to remember that next year when we scrub again."

Dow stared at Turner, not trusting himself to reply. He knew to do so would be playing into Turner's hands.

"The day will come," he thought, "that you will be called to answer for this kind of treatment. I just hope I'm around to see the results."

Seeing that Dow would respond no further, Turner turned and motioned for his guards to follow.

"Sorry 'bout the mess, gentlemen," he said to the angry throng. "It should freeze pretty soon, though. Then you won't have to sleep in the puddles."

With a sneer, Turner strode to the stairs. "Now they'll have something to talk about aside from the meals," he muttered to no one in particular.

Chapter Fourteen

What the prisoners had hoped was only a rumor turned out to be all too true. Keeping their word, the Confederates informed the Union that no more supplies would be accepted on behalf of the prisoners. Upon hearing this, the diggers knew that escape was now even more important than before. Many truly believed that to remain in Libby meant certain death by starvation or disease.

"We have little choice," Rose told the digging party now assembled before him. "If anybody wants to be relieved of his duties, I need to know about it now. Otherwise, I'll be counting on your help."

The men who had gathered in the darkened kitchen looked around at one another. Nobody spoke. Nor did anyone expect otherwise. All knew that their hope lie in escape, by whatever means possible.

Greeted by the silence of consent, Rose smiled. "Good. I'm glad to have everyone back on the job. Now, here's the plan."

As the men listened intently, Rose outlined his latest idea. He still believed that the sewer held the key to escape. His new plan, however, called for the tunnel to intercept a smaller sewer leading out of the prison, then use it as a tunnel to get to the main sewer. The main sewer would be followed to the canal, as the plan before had called for. As the idea unfolded, murmurs of agreement went up. It was a good plan.

Access to Rat Hell remained through the fireplace. That was the easiest and most direct route, and there had been no reason to change it. The digging resumed in earnest. The tunnel was progressing according to plan.

"Did you hear about Colonel Streight?" Gageby asked Rose excitedly as they sat down to eat.

"No. What about him?" Rose responded.

139

"The Rebs threw him down in one of the cells," Gageby said, looking around to see if any of the guards were listening. "Seems he bribed one of the guards with a gold watch and the Reb grabbed him as soon as he got outside."

"Really?" Rose reacted, too stunned to say more. He had not seen Streight for a day or two, but that was not unusual. With more than twelve hundred in the prison, the crowded conditions did not lend themselves to wandering around. Besides, Rose was now spending most of his days sleeping, to allow him to work on the tunnel every night.

"Just like so many others," Gageby went on. "Bribing a guard is no guarantee, is it?"

"No, it isn't," Rose agreed. "In fact, I wouldn't be surprised if there were more unsuccessful bribes than successful. Seems like every time we hear about someone bribing a guard, we find out the man who did the bribin' is in the cells."

"You're right about that, Colonel," said Gageby. "I can only remember a few that made it."

"Not a real good way to try to get out, I guess," Rose opined.

"That's a fact," agreed Gageby.

They continued their meal in silence. Both were thinking of Streight. Suddenly, the thought struck Rose. If Streight is in the basement, there would be guards there, too. Rose immediately felt guilty for thinking of how Streight's predicament would affect the escape attempt.

"I'm sure he didn't get caught just so we would be inconvenienced," Rose berated himself.

Still, this new turn of events had to be considered, and the tunnel would be temporarily halted if need be. They had come too far to risk discovery by one of Streight's guards.

However, when it was discussed by the group that night, they strongly believed that the digging should continue, even though it would require extra vigilance. All agreed that absolute silence while in the basement would also have to be in effect, so as not to alert enemy ears. Under these guidelines the digging continued.

As the tunnel progressed underground, the unrest continued at its own rapid pace on the streets of Richmond. Shortages were causing escalating prices in the city, prompting prison officials to voice their concern to their superiors that, if the prisoners were to rise up, many citizens of Richmond may be moved to join them in their rebellion.

Many prisoners favored such an uprising, and the prison officials knew it. As a result, many of the restrictions became even more rigidly enforced. Coupled with the food shortages, conditions were rapidly becoming unbearable.

The mood of the tunnel party became even more grim when the word came back late one night that the first sewer had been reached and that it was too small for a man to enter! This latest failure took its toll. Digging in the foul air was bad enough, but at least the diggers had consoled themselves with the thought that escape would make it all worthwhile. Now, however, physical exhaustion and empty stomachs left the tunnelers vulnerable, and dejection set in.

"We can't quit now," Hamilton exhorted them.

"Why not?" said McDonald, obviously depressed by the latest setback.

"'Cause it's almost Christmas," said Hamilton.

The men, totally confused, merely looked at him. Finally, Lucas spoke for all of them. "What's that have to do with diggin a tunnel?"

Rose looked at Hamilton strangely. Although he agreed with Hamilton that the work should continue, he too was confused by Hamilton's logic.

"I guess it don't have nothin' to do with diggin'a tunnel," Hamilton replied in a subdued tone. "I'm not even sure why I said it. I just don't want to give up, is all."

"Andrew's right," interjected Rose. "We can tear out the wood planks that line that sewer. That'll give us more room. Maybe it won't be easy to get through, but it will be passable."

"I don't know, Colonel," said McDonald, his doubts showing. "We're tired, we're sick from the bad air, we have to beat off the rats with a shovel, and we aren't makin' much progress. Not only that, those guards down at the cells get bored and start wanderin' around...who knows when one of 'em is gonna show up?"

"You're right about all of that. But that doesn't mean we have to quit. We've been through setbacks before. And we've bounced back, right? What if Lincoln felt that way after Bull Run? We wouldn't even have a Union today!" lectured Rose, his exasperation beginning to show.

Rose looked at his companions. None gave any indication that Rose's words had raised any pangs of guilt, nor did any appear converted. McDonald nonchalantly picked at a callous on his hand. Lucas stared blankly into the distance. Others sat with their eyes turned toward the floor, their elbows resting on their knees or their hands clasped together.

After several minutes of silence, Rose spoke again. "You can do what you want. You can quit or you can stay. But if you quit, all I ask is that you don't breathe a word about the tunnel to anyone, 'cause I'm gonna stick with it. I'll dig by myself if I have to." Saying that, he turned and walked to the fireplace, where he was immediately joined by Hamilton.

"Good speech, Thomas," said Hamilton. "Think they'll stay?"

Rose looked back at the group, who were talking among themselves. "I hope so, Andrew. But I meant what I said. If they quit, I'll either get new helpers or dig alone."

"You won't dig alone, Thomas," said Hamilton resolutely.

"I guess I knew all along you'd stay," said Rose gratefully, "'I was talkin' to the others, not you."

"Just so's you know, Thomas. I'm in this until we either get out or we join Colonel Streight down in the cells. Besides, it's almost Christmas. We can't quit now," responded Hamilton, his eyes twinkling.

Rose grinned. "Yeah, I meant to ask you about that. Where did that come from?"

Hamilton laughed. "I don't know. Just seemed like somethin' to say at the time."

"Well, it's something to think about, anyway. We won't be out by Christmas, but maybe it won't be much longer than that," Rose said optimistically.

"I hope you're right, Thomas," responded Hamilton. He started to say more but was interrupted by Gallagher, who was now at their side.

"They've have decided to keep at it, sir," he said.

"Good!" exclaimed Rose. "I was hopin' they'd decide that way. Let's go talk to 'em."

Their momentary dejection now behind them, the men seemed eager as ever to get back to work. A plan for removing the plank lining of the sewer was devised, and the work was begun.

"Merry Christmas, Colonel," said Gageby.

"Merry Christmas to you, Jim," Rose responded.

The men were huddled around the fireplace, where the last of the firewood was being burned. Several of the prisoners were in the process of breaking up benches and tables to be thrown into the fire after the firewood was gone. Although this meant they would be sitting on the floors again, just as they had a few months before, there was little choice. As one of the men had put it somewhat less eloquently, "I ain't gonna freeze to death just so's I can have a place to sit while I ain't got nothin' to eat!"

"You ever think you'd spend a Christmas with nothin' to eat, Jim?" Rose asked.

"No sir, I didn't. Then again, I never thought I'd be spendin' a Christmas in a place like this, either," answered Gageby, shaking his head.

"This is inhumane, though," said Hamilton. "Back home we wouldn't even treat an animal like this. You have to feed people, and give them firewood in weather like this. I ain't askin' for a fancy meal. Even some of the gruel that passes for food in here would be alright."

"Maybe they'll find some, since it's Christmas," offered Dow, who had been offered a place near the fire in deference to his rank.

"Not likely, sir," said Gageby. "I heard some of the guards sayin' there'd be no food at all today."

"Of all the days not to have anything to eat, you'd think they'd find something," said Dow, his eyes blazing. "And our own government is not blameless in this, either. I've written to Washington several times, telling them about conditions here. I never hear another word from anyone up there."

"I won't be here next Christmas, that you can count on!" said Rose angrily, giving a clue to his intentions for the first time. By now, however, all the prisoners had thoughts of escape, and his remark went unnoticed.

The group returned to silence, each occupied by his own thoughts. Thoughts of food, thoughts of home, thoughts of loved ones. Rose's mind drifted to Lydia and the children. They would be celebrating Christmas right about now, at least as much as they could knowing that the head of the family was present only in their hearts.

Rose felt a lump form in his throat, and his eyes became misty. He missed them more than he realized! Finally, to avoid having the others see his reaction to his thoughts, he walked away from the fireplace. Had he bothered to look, he would have noticed that many other eyes around the fireplace were just as misty.

As he approached the doorway which led out to Cary Street he spied a guard with whom he had spent many an evening talking. The man had been born in the North, somewhere in New England, Rose thought, but had been working in Richmond when the war broke out. He had been conscripted into the Confederate army, and although he was a loyal soldier, he still retained his Northern roots.

"I see you're lucky enough to pull guard duty on Christmas, Jedediah," Rose said in greeting.

"Yeah," said the man. "Reckon war don't take no holiday, not even Christmas."

"I guess you're right," agreed Rose. "You hear anything about us gettin' any food today?"

"Nope," said Jedediah. "Can't say as I did. But if you do, I'll be surprised. I don't know of nothin' in the warehouse."

"That's what I was afraid you'd say," said Rose dejectedly.

"Pretty hungry are you, Colonel?" the man asked in a friendly fashion.

"I passed hungry a long time ago," said Rose. "What comes about two stages after hungry?"

The man grinned, revealing a large gap where two teeth had been knocked out by a Union soldier's musket. The teeth were probably still lying in the woods where the hand-to-hand combat had taken place. Somewhere near Winchester, Virginia, as Jedediah remembered, but he could never recall the exact name of the place.

"Don't know what that stage is called, Colonel, but I got a piece of hardtack here, if y'all want it."

"Thanks, but no," Rose refused. "Wouldn't be right. Not with everyone else in here just as hungry as I am."

"Suit yerself, Colonel. It's yours if y'all want it."

"I know it is," said Rose, "And I appreciate it. I just wouldn't feel right about it."

The two men fell silent, the guard's eyes continually sweeping around the room, looking for anything out of the ordinary.

"What made you want to fight for the South, Jedediah?" Rose finally asked, breaking the silence. "I mean, I know you were drafted and all that, but why did you stay?"

The guard's eyes turned toward Rose. "I ain't no trouble maker, Colonel. I surely ain't. I'd just as soon be with my kin up North. But there ain't no way what the government is doin' is right. I guess I feel strong enough about it to take up a weapon and fight alongside the others that think like I do."

"What do you mean, what the government is doin' isn't right?" Rose asked, genuinely not sure.

"Well, Colonel," Jedediah said after a long pause, "I ain't never owned no slaves, and that's a fact. Don't expect to, neither. So I don't care much whether slavery lives or dies. I ain't fightin' fer that. But I don't think the government has the right to tell a man how to live. If a man wants to have slaves, that ain't none of the government's business."

"You really think it's right for one man to own another?" asked Rose.

"I don't know one way or the other," came the answer, "But I do know that my great-grandfather fought under General Washington just so's this country could be free from that kinda thinkin'. I remember, when I was just a little feller, how he would sit and rock in that old rockin' chair and tell us about how he fought the Redcoats. Mostly lies, probably, but we all believed 'em. He'd show us where one of the King's men had shot him in the arm, then go on about how we had to fight to show England we meant business about bein' our own country. His mind wasn't as sharp as it used to be, by then, but it was clear enough that he hadn't forgot why he'd fought. That ain't changed, Colonel. Oh, I know we ain't got no trouble with the King no more, but only the names are different. It ain't the colonies against England no more. It's us against Washington, don't y'all see? The United States was born 'cause of people like my great-grandfather, and mebbe yours, too. They didn't want the King of England tellin' them how to live, and we don't want the President of the United States tellin' us how to live. It's as simple as that."

Rose shook his head. "If only it was as simple as that," he said. "But what it all comes down to is breakin' up the Union. And that's not right. I don't care about the slaves themselves, either. Don't know any of 'em. But I do know a few darkies back home, and they aren't too bad. A lot like you and me, I guess, least in some ways."

"Don't matter, Colonel," the guard insisted. "You say it ain't right for the Union to break up. I say it ain't right for the government to tell us how to live. Guess neither one of us is gonna change the other's mind."

"Probably not," Rose chuckled. "But I can try. Maybe someday you'll see the light and come over to the right side."

Jedediah laughed. "I am on the right side, Colonel. Leastways in here, I am. You can tell just by lookin' at the two of us. I'm the one carryin' the musket."

Rose laughed with the man. Although he represented the enemy, the guard was a good man, himself. He always showed a genuine compassion for the prisoners, and there was no animosity between him and Rose. Jedediah obviously felt just as strongly about the Confederacy's cause as Rose felt about preserving the Union. Guarding the prisoners just happened to be his job right now, and Rose knew there was nothing personal in it as far as Jedediah was concerned.

"Just find us somethin' to eat, Jedediah," said Rose, good naturedly as he turned to go back to the fireplace. He knew the food shortage wasn't the fault of Jedediah, or the other guards for that matter. Even though some of those same guards would have probably withheld food from the prisoners if it was in their power, he knew that such was not the case in this instance. But it still would be nice to have something to eat on Christmas!

Rose and the others spent the better part of the day huddled around the fireplaces, each taking his turn at breaking up benches to feed into the fire. Variety in the conversation was almost nonexistent, simply consisting of discussions of home, food, and various means of escape. Rose was relieved to note that nobody suggested a tunnel.

By removing the planks which lined the small sewer, the would-be escapees found that they were progressing well toward the main sewer which, they hoped, would finally lead them to freedom. The tunnel which they had dug left little room for maneuvering, but it seemed palatial compared to the confines of the small sewer line. To remove the planks it was necessary for the man in the sewer to manipulate the planks apart one at a time, then slide the plank between his body and the wall until it was behind him. Then, he would slide his body back out of the sewer and push the plank with his feet until it reached the opening. There, another would reach in and remove the plank, allowing the man in the line to return to bring out the next plank in the same manner.

All agreed that the shortage of food had benefited them in one respect: they were now thin enough that entry into the small sewer, while difficult, was not impossible. Food had become available the day after Christmas, but nobody was in danger of gaining weight.

Needless to say, the stench in the sewer line was sickening, and no-body, including Rose, was able to stay inside for any length of time. As Garbet had put it, though, referring to the odor each man carried with him at all times, "For the first time since I been in Libby nobody crowds up against me while I sleep."

On New Year's Eve the prisoners took it upon themselves to cel-ebrate. Several weeks earlier they had pooled what little cash they had left and bought a fiddle and a banjo from the sutler. Despite the obvious lack of feminine companionship, they decided to hold a dance in the kitchen. Temporarily putting the tunnel out of their minds, Rose, Hamilton, and the others happily joined in. Even the guards appeared to be in a festive frame of mind.

Finally, only a few days later, those in the small sewer could see the main sewer ahead of them, in the glow of the candle. Once there, it would be a simple matter of breaking out the planks at the entrance to the main line and following the line to the canal.

The time had come. The group stood nervously at the entrance to the fireplace, awaiting the word that the planks had been removed, that the way was now clear. Tension mounted. Nobody spoke. Each was lost in his thoughts.

Every man reviewed in his mind the route he would take to reach Federal lines. Some carried homemade maps. Others merely had a rough idea of the route they planned to take, simply following the stars until they reached friendly pickets.

Rose was brought back to reality by a soft whisper. "Bad news, Colo-nel! Bad news!"

"What could have gone wrong?" Rose thought, as he stuck his head into the fireplace opening to talk to the digger who had just returned from the sewer.

"What happened?" asked Rose, as the others anxiously crowded around behind him, hoping to catch bits and pieces of the conversation.

"We can't get into the main line, sir," came the answer. "Those planks are seasoned oak, and they're about three inches thick. Hard as bone, they are. We can't even scratch 'em with these knives and clam shells we got."

"Maybe we can get in some other way," suggested Rose, desperately.

"Not a chance, sir," was the reply. "We looked everywhere we could think of. There's nothin' else we can do. We broke two knives on those planks, already, and the shells just crumble. Believe me, Colonel, we did everything we could think of."

Rose slumped against the wall, totally dejected. "I know you did," was all he could say. "Come on up and we'll tell the others."

Breaking the news was not easy. All had worked so hard and en-dured almost impossible conditions. They were sick from the air, nearly always wet and cold, and the primitive tools they had been using were no longer up to the task. Now, this bit of news was the final blow. They sat in stunned silence. This couldn't be happening!

Finally, a voice spoke up in the darkness. "I don't think I can do no more, Colonel. I'm plumb wore out."

Another voice agreed. Slowly, the chorus grew until nearly everyone stated his intent to drop out. Only Hamilton indicated a willingness to stay on.

After much discussion, Rose finally accepted the inevitable. "I guess I can understand how all of you feel," he said. "Just like before, though, I have to ask you not to talk about this. Andrew and I are gonna keep on goin', so we'd appreciate it if you'd not put us in danger. Once we're out of here, you can talk about it all you want. You can even follow us if you want. Just don't say anything, fer now."

They agreed, then slowly filed back upstairs to curse their bad luck and try to sleep. Disappointed and unsure of their next move, Hamilton and Rose followed.

Rose did not sleep well that night. Upon awaking he sought out Hamilton, who likewise had tossed and turned all night. The two talked briefly, then walked through the crowd toward the windows, where several had gathered to watch a chess game. The two, still dejected, watched in comparative silence.

"Watcha lookin' at, Yank?" a voice from the street shouted.

No answer was given. Again the voice sounded out. "Aintcha never seen no coffins before?"

Rose and Hamilton looked at each other, then edged their ways toward the open window. Down on the street a wagon load of coffins was being unloaded. The soldiers who were unloading the wagon were engaged in a shouting match with some of the more vocal prisoners.

"This one here looks like it oughtta be about yer size," shouted a burly Confederate at one particularly loud antagonist.

"Don't you worry 'bout me," the Union officer, a lieutenant from Maine, shouted back. "Just make sure you save one for yourself. And maybe the Turners, too, while yer at it!"

"Major Turner's the one that said to set one aside fer y'all," the man at the back of the wagon fired back.

"I'll see him as food fer the worms before I'm put in one a' those," said the defiant lieutenant.

"I reckon he'd see it a little different," was the retort. "Specially seein' as how y'all are where y'all are and he's where he is. And y'all don't have to worry 'bout us runnin' out of these things. One thing we got lots of, and that's pinewood. We fill these up, we just go and get another load!"

"Put those muskets down and let us out there with yuh for a few minutes," said a captain who had been silent up until now. "We'll show you how to fill them up in a hurry!"

One of the guards raised his musket in the direction of the window, causing the men to withdraw quickly. Outside, the laughter of the guards rang in the prisoners' ears. "We could fill this load with one pull of these triggers," one of them shouted up at the quickly vacated window.

The two Union officers continued to trade insults with those out in the street, albeit from a position out of the line of sight of the guards' gun muzzles. As the shouting match continued, Hamilton tugged on Rose's sleeve, indicating he wanted to talk to him away from the others.

Reaching a place of relative seclusion, Hamilton spoke excitedly. "I got an idea, Thomas. I think I see a way out of here."

"Great," said Rose in an unenthusiastic manner, still not over the setback of the previous evening. "Let's hear it."

"Those coffins," said Hamilton, animatedly. "Don't ya see? Those coffins are our way out. All we gotta do is get into one of them coffins down in the dead house and let the Rebs carry us out. When we get away from Libby, we climb out first chance we get and sneak away. We can do it, Thomas! I know we can!"

"We've talked about gettin' carried out of here with the dead before, Andrew," said Rose. "We already ruled it out."

"This is different, don't ya see?" persisted Hamilton. "Before, we just talked about fakin' our deaths and lettin' the Rebs throw us on the dead pile. This way, though, we just sneak down to the dead room and crawl into a coffin. Let the Johnnies carry us out fer burial, then jump out and run."

"Settle down, Andrew," said Rose. "You aren't even makin' sense. I want outta here as much as you do, maybe more. But I'm not gonna let the Rebs nail a lid over me and hope I can find a way to get out before I run out of air."

"Wait, Thomas," said Hamilton, not wanting to give up on his idea so quickly. "There has to be a way we can use them coffins. Let's think about it."

"I don't have to think about it," answered Rose. "I'm only gonna get in one of those things once, and when I do I'm not gonna worry about gettin' back out."

"You have a better idea," Hamilton asked in an irritated tone.

"Not yet," was the answer. "But I will. And soon."

Chapter Fifteen

Hamilton and Rose now busied themselves with finding a new location from which to tunnel. Recalling the tunnel which had flooded out when it had been dug below the canal level, they concluded that their only hope would be to dig the next tunnel from the upper side of the prison, the side away from the canal.

Having tentatively selected the new location for the tunnel, they took positions on either side of the window on the second floor at the east end of the building. They had come to see what was on the opposite side of the street, the side where the tunnel would eventually come to the surface. They did not like what they were seeing.

Taking particular care not to get so close to the window that the guards might be tempted to shoot at them, they gazed across the street, beyond which an open lot ended at a board fence.

"Pretty long way to tunnel," said Hamilton.

Rose agreed. "Not impossible, though. The thing that bothers me more than anything is that the only way out of the tunnel is through that gate that leads out onto Cary Street. Any man sneakin' out that way has to come out into the light from that street lamp, right where the guards are gonna see 'im."

The two friends watched, carefully studying the terrain.

"How 'bout if we..." started Hamilton, before being cut off by a wave of Rose's hand. Hamilton looked out onto the street to see what had caused Rose to cut him off so abruptly, then realized that he was counting something.

When Rose had finished his count of whatever it was that had drawn his attention, Hamilton asked, "What's that all about?"

Rose looked at the Kentuckian and smiled broadly. "Andrew," he said. "I think there's a way we can do it. Watch that sentinel coming toward us."

Hamilton watched the guard until he stopped near the corner of the building and turned to return in the direction of the gate which they had been discussing.

"If we go out the gate when the sentinel is walking toward the prison, we have about twenty seconds to get out before he turns around, by my count. And look how far he's gonna be from that gate. Even if he does turn around too soon and see someone, he isn't gonna be able to see the color of our uniforms from that distance, especially if we get into the shadows right away."

"Yeah," agreed Hamilton. "I see what you mean. And even then, unless they're sure they're lookin at Yankee prisoners, these guards aren't gonna want to be bothered with stoppin' private citizens. They'll probably just ignore 'em and let the provost guards check 'em if they see 'em."

"We'll just have to make sure the provost guards don't see us then, won't we?" said Rose with a wink.

That night, the men began digging what they hoped would be their last tunnel. Problems arose almost immediately, as the wall had to be broken through in three different places before they found soil strong enough to keep the tunnel from caving in.

Then, it soon became apparent that the man outside the tunnel could not fan air into the tunnel, haul dirt out, dispose of it, and keep watch properly. As soon as the outside man stopped fanning, the air would become so foul that the candle would extinguish.

"And we're still only a few feet into the tunnel," complained Rose. "It's only gonna get worse."

The two were assessing the situation, trying to come up with a solution, when Hamilton said, "Thomas, you think we oughtta talk to the others again?"

Rose looked at him with a steady gaze. "I don't think we have any other choice," he finally answered after much deliberation.

It was decided to gather the original tunnel group again, to determine the interest level in digging a new tunnel. As expected, the disappointments of past failures had already faded with time. Still, four of the original diggers chose to drop out. Ludlow, Clifford, Causton, and Wallick were replaced by Captain W. S. B. Randall of the 2nd Ohio Infantry, 1st Lieutenant John Simpson of the 10th Indiana Infantry, 1st Lieutenant Nineoch McKean of the 21st Illinois Infantry, and 2nd Lieutenant Eli Foster of the 31st Indiana Infantry. A meeting was convened in the kitchen, where Rose explained the new plan.

"We're gonna work from a new area," Rose explained. "We've found some abutments that extend out from the wall. Andrew and I have already started another tunnel just next to one of those abutments. The abutment blocks the view from just about everywhere, even during the day, so it should give us a little more protection. You almost have to be standing right in front of the hole to see it."

The same plan for digging was used that had worked so well in the past, using the spittoon to haul the dirt. One improvement on the old system, however, made the digging much more bearable. Hamilton had rigged up his faithful rubber blanket to a wooden frame, and the apparatus now functioned as a huge bellows. Getting air into the tunnel was now much easier, and, although it didn't solve the problem of foul air, it did make it easier to keep the candle lit.

Although it was possible for the men to estimate the distance which they would have to dig, fate intervened and allowed for a far more accurate measurement than could be made by peering out the windows.

Having made his point, Commissioner Ould announced to Washington that the Confederacy would once again allow packages to be sent to the prisoners in Richmond. Those packages were stored in a warehouse across the street from Libby, presumably to be checked in. The prisoners chose to believe that the warehouse was used to facilitate the confiscation of the more choice items by some of the less reputable guards.

"I'm pretty certain I have a package over there in the warehouse," said Gallagher to one of the unsuspecting guards. "I'd like to go over and get it."

The guard did not appear to suspect anything. Escorting prisoners to obtain packages was not at all unusual, and both parties looked forward to the break from the normal routine. "Well," he said, "We can't go over right now. Soon's I get someone to relieve me, I'll take y'all over."

When the relief arrived, Gallagher was escorted to the warehouse by the guard, who had recruited a friend to go along. The two walked behind Gallagher, chatting between themselves while keeping watchful eyes on Gallagher. Some prisoners had been foolish enough to try to escape while walking across the street, none successfully. However, the two were aware that Gallagher could also be desperate enough to make an attempt, and remained attentive. They could not, however, know what he was really doing.

As Rose and several of the other men watched from a safe angle at the upper window, the trio crossed the street. As they crossed, Gallagher made a conscious effort to keep his steps all the same length. Prior to initiating the request to go to the warehouse, Gallagher had walked a short distance along the wall while the tunnelers observed. After several trials, they had counted the number of bricks between steps and calculated his stride length.

This information was now being put to use as Gallagher slowly traversed the distance from the prison to the warehouse. As the guards talked, Gallagher counted his steps. Those watching intently from the window saw him reach the warehouse and go inside, reappearing a short time later with his package.

Recrossing the street, he counted his steps once more. Upon reaching the door to Libby once again, the guards made certain he was securely inside, then took their leave.

Gallagher made his way to the top floor and quickly sought out Colonel Rose and the others.

"Close as I can figure, Colonel," he said excitedly, "I think it's about fifty to fifty-five feet from the wall to where we'll come out on the other side of that fence."

"Good job, John," said Rose. The original estimate of sixty-five feet had been as accurate as it could have been, under the circumstances, but now that an even shorter distance had been confirmed, spirits rose still higher. "We'll get Andrew to fix us up a piece of clothesline about that long so we'll know when we're about there. That way we'll know when to turn the tunnel upward."

This information gave them new hope. Although it was longer than they had ever dug before, they now felt confident that things were going better than they had in the past. They knew what they had to do, and how far they had to dig.

The location of the new tunnel, concealed as it was, now allowed them to dig during the day, as well. This, however, meant that the diggers had to enter the fireplace before anyone entered the kitchen in the morning, then stay until everyone left at night. At that time, a new digging crew would enter, with the first crew coming out and concealing the opening. It required them to work long hours, but it also permitted the tunnel to be dug much faster than before.

"Guards coming!" whispered the watcher. He had seen the lantern of a contingent of guards approaching from the opposite side of the prison. The men were learning to be constantly on the alert, Major Turner having given strict orders to his staff that every area of the prison must be inspected daily. Fortunately, the guards were reluctant to walk among the rats any more than was necessary, and usually gave only a perfunctory examination. Their goal was simply to satisfy Turner's instructions. The odds were slim that they would find anything out of the ordinary, they reasoned, so why go to the trouble of wandering around in the dark in a basement full of rats?

The man doing the fanning alerted the digger, who stopped his digging immediately. Those outside the tunnel hid themselves in the deepest shadows of the abutment. All watched the bobbing light as it approached, still a considerable distance away.

As before, the guards made a superficial glance around the area covered by the glow of the lantern, not even near enough for the conspirators

to make out what was being said. Then, having satisfied their orders, they left, allowing the would-be escapees to return to their arduous task.

Despite the apparent lack of concern on the part of the guards, the men still were wary. Absolute silence had to be maintained, a rule that was never violated. This rule, coupled with the pitch darkness, made it difficult to keep the group constantly together. Often, the person who was assigned the task of dumping the dirt would lose his bearings in the darkness and have difficulty finding his way back. This would delay the digging until the spittoon was finally returned. Because it was dangerous to call out for directions, this sometimes took an agonizingly long time. Often, those waiting back at the tunnel would disperse to look for their lost compatriot, in an effort to return him so the digging could resume. As expected, this would often result in not one, but two people being lost in the blackest reaches of Rat Hell. Despite these nagging delays, the tunnel progressed well.

Rose, Hamilton, Lucas, Randall, and Garbet had seated themselves at a table in the cook room, waiting for the room to empty out so they could take their turn in the tunnel.

"You ever get scared down there, Colonel?" asked Garbet.

"Scared?" said Rose. "No, not really. I mean, I get a little worried sometimes. That tunnel could fall in on us, or we could be discovered. But I can't say that I get scared."

"It's just that so many things have gone wrong, already," said Garbet. "I sometimes get scared that maybe those were warnings. That maybe we aren't supposed to get out of here. Know what I mean?"

"Yeah, I think that way sometimes, too," said Lucas. "But there's nothing like crawling on your belly in an eighteen inch diameter hole to get the blood flowin'. That keeps me goin'."

"I think doin' somethin' like this tells a man a little about himself," interjected Randall. "I hate rats...just seein' one gives me the chills. And I ain't never been one fer crawlin' into tight places, neither. But this is somethin' I don't mind doin', fer some reason. I can't understand it altogether, myself. It's just somethin' I need to be doin'."

"Well," said Hamilton, stretching as if he had just awakened, "I think just bein' in prison tells a man what he's really like. Brings out his worst or his best, dependin' on who he is."

"How do you mean?" queried Randall.

"Well, take us, fer instance," answered Hamilton. "I'm not sayin' we're something special, or anything, but we're down here tryin' to do our soldierly duties by escapin'. Just like we're supposed to. None of us likes bein' down in this hole, right? Some of us are even scared of rats, but you're down here doin' what has to be done, just to escape if yuh can. Now that's what I mean by bringin' out the best in a man. On the other hand, we all know some aren't to be trusted. Not just with information about the tunnel, but with anything. Some of the people in here'll steal yer eyes out if you ain't careful."

Hamilton paused to allow his words to sink in. Garbet was already nodding in agreement.

Hamilton continued. "Anybody here think Samuelson and Tilden are to be trusted? They're two that have had their worst brought out. I didn't know either one before I came here, but maybe they weren't too bad. Since they've been in Libby, though, they've turned their backs on the rest of us. They cozy up to Turner and Winder, just to get special privileges. Maybe they wouldn't be that way if they'd never been put in prison."

"Prison didn't make 'em that way, though," disagreed Rose. "That was always in 'em. Libby just happened to bring it out, that's all."

"That's what I'm sayin'," said Hamilton. "Prison brings out a man's real personality. When things get tough, a man goes one of two ways. They went the wrong way."

"Yeah," said Lucas. "I reckon I'd have to agree with yuh. Those two are good examples of how prison brings out the worst in a man, like Andrew's sayin'."

The rest nodded agreement.

"You boys been able to get things lined up to help yourselves after you get outside?" asked Rose, changing the subject.

"I bought me a piece of soap off one of the guards," said Lucas. "Might not help much when I get out, but it'll make things a little better in here."

"For the rest of us, too," said Randall, wrinkling his face as he pretended to sniff around Lucas. The others laughed, including Lucas.

Lucas then reigned indignation. "Well, then, what did you get?" he inquired of Randall.

Randall looked at Lucas. Then, not wishing to drop the subject of Lucas's soap, he said, "I got a copy of McClellan's war map of Virginia, and if you promise to use that soap I'll let you look at it."

"I think he's tryin' to tell you somethin', John," said Rose with a laugh. The others joined in the laughter.

Then Garbet, still chuckling, said, "Well, I got me a compass yesterday. Bought it from one of the guards for seven Federal dollars. Probably worth about fifty cents back home, but if it gets me back up North it'll be worth a whole lot more'n seven dollars. Also got some stuff to put on our boots so's the dogs can't track us. I made that myself."

Interested, Lucas asked, "What's in it? Can we make up some more to make sure we have enough?"

"It's not hard to make," answered Garbet. "Mostly red pepper. Messes up the dogs' noses real good. They do more sneezin' than barkin'. Only trouble is, I don't have any more red pepper."

"We should be able to get some," said Rose. "Anybody else get anything new?"

Met with silence, Rose remained cheerful. "Those things are all good. Some of the others have told me they've been doin' the same thing. We should have a pretty good collection by the time we get out."

"Most important thing is John's soap," said Garbet, as the others laughed again.

The mood was uplifted. The digging had been going reasonably well, and there had been nothing to even resemble a close brush with the guards in the basement. Each day brought them closer to their goal.

"I guess we'll all appreciate little things like a bar of soap more after this, won't we," offered Hamilton.

Everyone agreed.

"I don't think I'll complain about my wife's cookin' no more, either," said Lucas, to more affirmative nods. The group drew silent for a few moments.

Garbet broke the silence by saying, "I'm lookin' forward to a few luxuries again, though. Haven't had any such thing in a long time. My brother's been to Europe, and he told me everyone over there wears silk shirts. Wouldn't mind havin' a couple of fancy shirts, myself."

"I wouldn't mind havin' a couple of clean shirts even if they was made outta some old flour sack," said Hamilton.

"Yeah," agreed Garbet, "But silk would be a whole lot nicer. We'll all be able to get silk shirts once we're outta here."

"Sounds good to me," said Hamilton, to a chorus of agreement.

They said good night to a group starting up the stairs, then resumed their conversation. There were still several small knots of prisoners milling about the room, making it impossible to enter the fireplace at this time. The conspirators nonchalantly sat and talked, as many prisoners were doing, and attracted no suspicion from the others. They were, to all appearances, just five friends passing the evening hours in the cook room as so many others did each night.

Looking around at the other four, Randall chuckled. "Think we'll be able to blend in with the good citizens of Richmond?" he asked.

The others glanced around the small circle, then suddenly realized what Randall was saying. A bedraggled looking group they were, to say the least. Randall wore a cap whose brim had fallen off a long time ago. Lucas had been wearing a pair of mismatched shoes since his arrival. One was a cavalry boot, the other a shoe of a different size. Hamilton's shirt had no sleeves, and one of Garbet's pant legs was torn off at the knee. Only Rose wore a complete uniform and it, along with everyone else's, was filthy and odorous from the many hours spent crawling on his belly in the tunnel and sewer lines of Libby Prison.

"We are a real attractive group, aren't we," said Lucas with a laugh.

"I haven't seen that bar of soap you bought, John," said Rose, "But I'm willing to bet it isn't big enough to clean all of us up to the point where we're presentable."

The laughter rang out again. It was good to hear, in such dismal confines.

"We're all kinda funny lookin', I'll give you that much," said Garbet. Turning to Rose, he asked, "Any ideas, Colonel?"

"Well, we've all seen the Rebels wearin' Federal uniforms that they've intercepted," said Rose. "So the people of Richmond are used to seein' soldiers walkin' around in blue coats. There isn't much we can do about the conditions of our clothes. We'll just have to stay away from other people as much as we can. If anyone asks, we'll just have to tell them we're Rebel soldiers who've been out in the field for quite a while. Just make sure you all know the names of some Confederate regiments that might be around the area, so you don't make anyone suspicious. I wish we could look a little better, too, but we can't do much about that. Maybe by the time we're ready to go, we'll all have better clothes from our packages."

"If the Seceshes don't steal them first," said Hamilton.

Another group of men rose to go upstairs. The crowd in the room was slowly beginning to thin out.

The conversation among the five continued for another hour, as the other prisoners slowly drifted out of the cook room. Finally, the five were alone in the room. They used a piece of firewood to pull the remaining hot coals from the hearth. After allowing the bricks to cool, Rose stood up.

"Well," he said. "I think we've pretty well beat this conversation to death, don't you think? Let's go dig ourselves a tunnel!"

Chapter Sixteen

To maintain control over the prisoners, prison authorities called for periodic counts of the men. These were usually conducted at least twice each day, most often in the morning and again late in the afternoon. The count was conducted by the clerk of the prison, a short, pleasant man named Erastus Ross. Ross was well-liked by the prisoners, partly for his sense of humor and partly because he showed compassion to the plight of the officers incarcerated in Libby. A Virginian, he nonetheless showed little passion for the Southern cause. He appeared to the prisoners to be a Rebel only because Virginians were expected to be. His stature gave rise to the nickname bestowed upon him by the prisoners—Little Ross.

"Fall in, Yanks, in four rows," Ross shouted in his customary greeting on this particularly cold morning.

The men obeyed, albeit slowly and with much grumbling. Ross waited patiently for the din to die down.

When the men had fallen into rank, Ross looked across the group. "Mornin' men," he said loudly enough for the men in the back row to hear. "We're gonna take our little census again this mornin'. Jest makin' sure none of y'all got a little rabbit in yuh overnight and decided to run."

Ross fidgeted with a sheaf of papers in his hands before continuing. Glancing to a guard on his right, Ross said, "This here's Adjutant Latouche. That there's Sergeant Stansil of the 18th Georgia over yonder. They'll be helpin' with the count today."

The tunnel was progressing well under the twenty-four hour digging schedule which had been established. This schedule, however, was disrupted by the daily roll calls. To maintain continuity, yet minimize the chance for discovery, Rose had devised a scheme which allowed the digging to continue while still accounting for everyone.

This plan called for all but one or two men to return to their rooms for the count, then return to the tunnel as soon as it could be done with any degree of practicality. Because the entry to the fireplace was so public, this required the men to get downstairs as quickly as possible, before the kitchen became occupied. To account for those missing, the prisoners developed great skill at a practice known as "repeating."

This process, ingenious as it was, created a great deal of anxiety among those who were in on the plot. The risk of detection was omnipresent, and they were unsure of their punishment should they be caught, having never had that happen.

To accomplish the scheme, the tunnel party always tried to position themselves near the right side of either the second or third row. The count invariably was made from right to left. This allowed anyone on the right side, those who had already been counted, to crouch low and run behind the rank to the left end of the line. They would then take the places of those in the tunnel, getting counted twice in the process and allowing the count to come out correctly. This had been working well. On those rare instances in which the count did not agree with the books, Ross would order a second count. To date, the second count had always been correct.

That was not to be the case on this particular day, however. For some reason, several of the prisoners were in a playful mood. Seeing Rose's men performing the repeating process, they decided to join in the fun. As Rose and the others looked on helplessly, they observed the unauthorized repeaters crouching down and running to the far reaches of the line.

"What are they doing?" Rose whispered in exasperation to Hamilton, who had taken a position next to his friend.

"I don't know," Hamilton answered, cursing them under his breath.

The counting of more than twelve hundred men, especially when they were not of a mind to cooperate, was no easy task. It was not all that unusual for the count to be incorrect on the first try, even without the repeating. When the count on this occasion was wrong, Ross merely ordered it to take place again.

The guards counted a second time, getting a different number, as more of the prisoners joined in the repeating. The results were the same on the third and fourth counts. The most frustrating part of the count was that the total was different every time. On one count it would appear that several were missing. On the next there would be more than would be expected. The prisoners who were in position to see what was happening had difficulty hiding their enjoyment. After several unsuccessful counts, many were openly snickering. Those in on the escape plot, however, were fearful that discovery was imminent.

After another count in which the prison population had mysteriously grown by twenty over the previous count, Ross could no longer control himself. He could see the prisoners giggling, and suspected that some of the guards were doing the same behind his back. His anger boiled over.

"Now looka here, gentlemen!" he shouted. "I ain't no dummy! I kin count to a hundred as good as any man. But fer some reason I ain't able to count you Yankees this mornin'."

Ross's eyes looked as if they were about to pop completely out of his head as he stomped back and forth in front of his grinning audience. "Gentlemen," he went on. "There's one thing fer certain. There's about eight or ten of y'all here that ain't here!"

For a moment the room was silent as Ross's words were absorbed. Everyone had heard what he had said, but nobody was sure he had heard it correctly. Finally, someone in the back row could conceal his delight no longer, letting out with a loud snort as he tried not to laugh out loud.

The snort served as a signal to the others and soon every prisoner was convulsed with laughter. Even the guards became caught up in the moment, laughing uproariously.

Confused, Ross thought about what he had said to bring on this outburst. As the absurdity of his logic finally struck home, he grinned, then chuckled, then became as much a part of the laughter as any man present. Had any citizen of Richmond been passing by that morning, he would have been convinced that the prison authorities had thrown a party for the prisoners.

As the uproar slowly calmed down, Ross conferred with his guards. They agreed to continue counting until the number matched the books. Finally, somehow, the numbers agreed, much to Ross's relief. The prisoners, on the other hand, welcomed this diversion to their boring routine, many of them already looking forward to the next roll call.

Their enjoyment was short lived, however. For the next count, Ross brought a large contingent of guards. These men stationed themselves throughout the room in such positions that repeating was nearly impossible.

Rose immediately saw the situation for the disaster it was. Two of the diggers, Johnston and McDonald, were still in the tunnel. Their absence would surely be discovered if there could be no repeating.

With no reference to the previous roll call, Ross and Latouche began the count. In spite of the overwhelming odds, two of the tunnelers attempted to repeat. With the guards watching the ranks closely, they tried to force their way into the ranks somewhere near the center, where the guards would have difficulty seeing what was happening.

Their efforts were unsuccessful, as those already in the ranks resisted their entry. They pushed their way in, but the commotion attracted the attention of the guards.

"What are y'all tryin' to do here?" one shouted out as he rushed to the center of the row. He was quickly joined by two more guards, as the count was momentarily suspended.

"I don't know what's goin' on here," he said, "But I ain't gonna stand fer y'all jumpin' around to change the count. If you two don't git back where y'all belong I'm gonna take both of y'all down to Major Turner's office myself!"

Realizing resistance would be futile, the dejected repeaters returned to their respective positions. The count continued.

As expected, the count was short by two. A second count resulted in the same shortage.

"Well, now," said Ross. "Looks like mebbe we got ourselves some deserters, don't it?" He thought for a moment, then dispatched Sergeant Stansil to the office. Upon his return the prisoners could see that he carried the prison's register with him. This could only mean one thing, and Rose and the other conspirators groaned inwardly. The roll call was about to be taken by name!

"Mister Latouche here is gonna read off yer names," Ross explained, as if no one had any idea what was to take place. Most of the prisoners did not object to the individual roll call. It would take a long time, but it would break up the day. The tunnelers, however, dreaded what was about to take place. And there was nothing they could do to stop it.

"When y'all hear yer name," Ross droned on, "I want y'all to let me know if'n yer here or not. You two men that ain't here don't have to answer."

Several of the prisoners giggled at Ross's last statement, but immediately stifled their merriment when he shot them a stern look that told them this was not the day to be doing that.

The roll call began.

"Adams!"

"Here!"

"Alwine!"

"Present!"

As each acknowledged his presence, he was ushered out of the room, passing through a gauntlet of guards.

The recitation dragged on. The crowd was growing smaller as those whose names had been called were taken from the room. Those whose names came near the end of the alphabet shifted their weight from one foot to the other as they waited patiently for their names to be called.

Rose and Hamilton, as well as the other conspirators, glanced nervously at one another, knowing it would only be a matter of time until Ross reached the J's.

Laboriously, the names were called. Finally, the dreaded moment was at hand.

"Johnson!" came the call.

The lieutenant colonel from the Fifteenth Wisconsin Infantry answered to his name.

"Johnston, with a "t", Sixth Kentucky," shouted Ross.

This time there was no response. Ross repeated the call, with the same result.

A confused murmur slowly rippled through the crowd.

Ross continued on, appearing unperturbed by Johnston's unexplained absence.

After several more names were called, Ross stopped momentarily. Looking across the ranks, he smiled and said, "I do believe my voice is beginnin' to fail me."

Handing the register to Latouche, he said, "Mr. Latouche, would you be so kind as to take over?"

Taking the register, Latouche continued the process as Ross paced around the perimeter of the group of fidgeting prisoners, his hands clasped behind his back.

Latouche's voice droned on, the size of the group slowly dwindling as man after man exited the room after responding to his name.

"Mayhew!" Latouche read from the register.

"I'm here," the Lieutenant Colonel responded, relieved that his name had finally been called and he could now go sit down.

"McDonald!" came the call.

Latouche was greeted with silence. He looked up and scanned the room, then repeated his call. "McDonald!" he said, more loudly this time.

Again, Bedan McDonald of the One Hundred First Ohio Infantry failed to respond. Once more a soft murmur rippled through the crowd of prisoners.

"Where's the major?" whispered one of the men to a companion.

"Don't know," came the confused answer.

"He was here yesterday."

When the call was greeted with silence, a knowing smile crossed Ross's face. "Any more of y'all that ain't here?" he asked. Nobody answered him. "Go on, Mr. Latouche," he said.

"Miles!" Latouche shouted out, moving to the next name on his register.

"Present!"

The roll call proceeded to the end, with each remaining name producing a positive response. The diminutive Ross looked pleased. He had reconciled his count while identifying the two missing prisoners. The fact that he had no idea where they may be did not matter at this point.

Having achieved his count, Ross and the guards made their exit. Immediately the prisoners gathered in small groups and talked about their missing comrades.

"Where do you think they are?" asked a tall man whose rank was not apparent by his uniform. In actuality, he was a major, but in Libby, few cared.

"McDonald stood right beside me at roll call a couple days ago," answered a young captain with a ruddy complexion.

"He's in my mess," stated another, "And I'm sure he ain't been missin' before this."

"I'll bet you even money they're on their way home right now!" said the major, excitedly.

"You think they escaped?" said another of the group.

"Had to," said the major. "Otherwise they'd answer their names, don't you think?"

"I know that," came the answer in a disgusted tone. "I just don't know how they could a' got out without someone knowin' about it."

"I agree," said the ruddy faced captain. "There ain't no way to keep somethin' like that a secret from everybody in the whole prison. Someone would know about it."

"Maybe someone does and just ain't sayin'," the major responded.

The conversations continued long after the roll call was completed. Rose, however, knew he had to get word to the two who were believed missing. He was finally able to discuss the problem with them that evening upon their exit from the fireplace.

"What'll we do now?" asked McDonald.

"I'm not sure yet," answered Rose. "But we're gonna have to come up with somethin', and that's a fact!"

They discussed their options.

"I reckon the best thing to do is show up tomorrow and give Ross some kind of tale," McDonald said softly, staring at the floor.

"Not me," said Johnston. "Ain't no way I'm gonna go back up there and tell Ross I just forgot to answer. I never was a very good liar. He'll catch me sure's I'm standin' here."

"Where are you gonna go?" asked Rose.

"I'll jest stay down in Rat Hell," replied Johnston.

McDonald's head quickly rose. He looked at Johnston in amazement. "You can't stay down in Rat Hell till the tunnel's finished!" he exclaimed.

"Who says I can't?" Johnston shot back.

"Why would you want to? asked Rose.

"Don't have no other choice, Colonel," answered Johnston. "As much as I'd like to go upstairs tomorrow and answer my name at roll call, I jest can't do it. Ross'll want to know where I was today, and I'll stutter and stammer somethin' stupid, and he'll know right away I ain't tellin' him the truth. I'd end up down in Turner's office, which don't bother me none, but I'm afraid they'd work the truth out of me. If that happens, all the work we've done'll be wasted. Like I said, I jest can't tell a good lie without givin' myself away. Never could."

"I don't know," Rose said softly. "Rat Hell's no place to be if you don't have to."

"That's jest it, Colonel," said Johnston. "I do have to, don't yuh see?"

"That's just gonna keep the excitement up, though," suggested Rose. "Ross isn't just gonna pass over the fact that you're missin'. Those guards'll tear this place apart tryin' to find you. Not to mention the fact that you'll have to stay down here breathin' this foul air and fightin' off rats."

"I can put up with the stink and the rats, sir," Johnston replied. "And once Ross is convinced I've escaped, he'll quit lookin' fer me."

"I don't know if that's gonna work," said McDonald.

Rose shook his head. "It just might, Bedan. If the Rebs are convinced he's escaped. They won't be lookin' for 'im any longer."

Turning back to Johnston, Rose said, "Maybe we could keep you down in the tunnel during the day and bring you up to sleep. We'll smuggle food down to you as best we can. What do you think?"

Johnston was agreeable. "I guess that means I won't have to see Turner again," he reasoned. "I will miss Little Ross, though. He ain't a bad Reb."

The plan in place, they talked for a short time, then returned to their respective rooms. After the prison settled down for the night, Johnston stealthily did the same.

The next morning the men assembled for roll call as usual. This time McDonald took his customary place in the ranks, much to the surprise of those around him.

To Ross's amazement, the count was only short by one, rather than by two. A confused look crossed his face.

"Mr. McDonald, are you here today?" he called out.

McDonald answered in the affirmative, causing Ross to quickly look up from his papers in surprise.

"Where are y'all, Mr. McDonald?" Ross asked pleasantly, as if he were addressing an old friend.

"Right here," came McDonald's answer.

"Well, now," said Ross, his demeanor still friendly. "It's right nice of y'all to come to our little gatherin' here today. We missed y'all yesterday."

McDonald refrained from commenting, reasoning that he was in enough trouble already. "Maybe Ross won't push the issue," hoped McDonald. He was wrong.

"Is your friend, Mr. Johnston also with you, by any chance?" Ross continued.

Receiving no answer, Ross scanned the crowded room.

"No matter," he exclaimed sarcastically. "At least one of our Prodigal Sons has returned."

Raising his right hand, he motioned for McDonald to come to the front of the room, which he reluctantly did. Immediately he was joined by two guards, one on either side.

"Now that y'all have decided to join us," Ross explained, "I do believe that Major Turner has a few things he'd like to discuss with yuh. Why don't y'all accompany these gentlemen downstairs so we can get this little matter settled?"

With that, the guards each took an arm and led McDonald to Turner's office. Once there, the Rebels retreated to a far corner of the room in silence.

Turner, seated at his desk, pretended to be busy with some papers. He continued shuffling them while McDonald stood stoically in front of him. After what he considered the proper amount of time, he addressed the prisoner.

"I understand y'all weren't present for roll call yesterday. Would y'all care to explain how yuh happened to be absent? I'd be especially interested in hearin' where y'all may have been, and how it was that we never found yuh."

McDonald decided to get it over with as quickly as possible. He took a deep breath, then began. "Well, Major Turner, I guess I just plain missed it. No excuses. I wasn't feelin' well the past few days, and I wrapped up in my blanket and fell asleep. Guess I must have been sleepin' better than I thought I was. Next thing I know, a bunch of the others is askin' me where I was durin' roll call. That's the first I noticed how late it was."

"You're tellin' me you were sick and fell asleep?" Turner asked suspiciously.

"That's the gospel, sir," lied McDonald.

Turner studied him for what seemed like forever. McDonald fought the urge to look away. Instead, he fixed his gaze on Turner's face. Turner finally looked away, himself.

"Y'all wouldn't lie to me, now, would yuh?" asked Turner, turning back to McDonald.

"Oh, no, sir!" declared McDonald. "I wouldn't lie to you."

"How are you feelin' today?" Turner asked, still believing that McDonald was lying but not knowing how to prove it.

"Much better, sir," answered McDonald. "Thank you for askin'."

Turner was now faced with the unusual dilemma of what to do about McDonald. No missing prisoner had ever returned before, not willingly, at least.

"Where were y'all sleepin', Mr. McDonald?" he asked. "In one of our fine hotels here in Richmond?"

"No, sir," said McDonald, ignoring Turner's sarcasm. "I was in Colonel Streight's room."

"How did you get in there?" Turner asked. "We sealed that door off some time ago."

McDonald had rehearsed his story well. He told how the men had cut through the door, knowing that he was giving away a secret. However, he and the others had reasoned that such a story might play to Turner's ego, giving him the idea that he had uncovered something. McDonald, trying to appear as contrite as possible, apologized profusely for any problems he may have inadvertently caused by falling asleep in an area which was off limits to him.

The ruse seemed to be working, as Turner showed pleasure in learning about the door. Turner was also pleased to see that McDonald was admitting his error. Perhaps this man wasn't so bad after all. He had no way of knowing that McDonald was secretly wishing he could get his hands around Turner's throat.

"I'm glad to see that y'all realize y'all were wrong," said Turner. "Mebbe we'll even let that door open, now that we know about it. Since y'all been so honest about this little incident, I reckon I'm gonna let it pass. Just fer this time, though, mind yuh. If I catch y'all in the wrong room again, or if y'all miss another roll call, I won't be so generous. Is that understood?"

"Perfectly, sir," said the humble McDonald.

"Well, then, get on back upstairs. And don't think y'all can get away with breakin' our rules fer very long. Y'all can see we learn about them sooner or later," said Turner, fully satisfied that he had uncovered a Yankee conspiracy.

"I'll remember that, sir," replied McDonald, quickly leaving the room before he said something that would change Turner's mind. As would be expected, he went straight to Rose to tell him how he had fared. All the men were pleased that the incident had turned out so well.

Next morning at roll call one of the men, thinking he was helping the still missing Johnston, excitedly told Ross that he had seen Johnston the previous night in his customary sleeping place. Johnston apparently was still inside Libby.

Hearing that, Ross again ordered a name by name roll call. With Johnston still unaccounted for, the prison was searched again while everyone stood in rank. Several who were not in on the escape plot believed that Johnston was still in the prison, somehow eluding the searchers. Agitated after being forced to stand in line while the search progressed, they began to curse Johnston for putting them through this harassment.

"Come on out, Johnston," one of them finally shouted. "This ain't fair to the rest of us."

"Yeah, Johnston," another chimed in. "We're all bein' punished 'cause the Rebs think you escaped. Show yerself so we can go sit down."

Fearing the men would stir others up needlessly, Rose immediately confronted the clerk. "He's not gonna come out, Ross, 'cause he's not here. I don't know who that man saw last night, but it couldn't have been Johnston. Your men have turned this place over from one end to the other. If he was here, they woulda found him. Let us go back to our quarters."

"I don't know..." Ross said in a hesitating voice.

Seeing that Rose had laid the groundwork, Fislar entered the conversation. The young lieutenant from the Indiana Light Artillery was quick to agree with Rose. "He's right, Mr. Ross. There ain't no way on God's green earth that he could still be in here, or anywhere else in the prison, not the way your men have checked everywhere."

Ross looked puzzled. "I ain't sure. I don't completely trust you Yanks. Wouldn't surprise me none if he poked his head out from 'round the corner right now. No, sirree. Y'all are gonna stay right here until we know fer sure!"

Fislar could see that Ross was not going to be easily swayed. "Well, sir," said Fislar softly, "I wasn't gonna say nothin' fer a while, but it ain't right that everybody has to suffer fer Johnston. He's gone."

Ross looked at Fislar intently. "What do y'all mean, he's gone?"

"Just what I said," Fislar replied. "He's gone. Escaped. Headed North. He and I are mess mates, and we sleep right next to each other. He ain't been around fer two or three nights."

"You tellin' me the truth?" queried Ross.

Yes, sir," Fislar replied, looking directly into Ross's eyes as convincingly as he could. The young Hoosier was not used to telling lies, and he wasn't sure he was any good at it. "Johnston told me a few days ago that he had a couple cousins who are guards. They got him a Reb uniform and helped him escape. I ain't sure how they did it, but the next thing I know, Johnston ain't around no more."

Hamilton could see that Ross was taking in the story. "I heard that, too," he said, reinforcing Fislar's lie. "I thought he was just talkin', though. You know how some of us boys from Kentucky like to tell a story."

Ross looked at the men, then in the direction of the searchers. He was still unsure, but the story sounded so plausible, and Ross himself couldn't understand how his men were missing Johnston if he really was there. Several others from the tunnel party contributed their versions of Johnston's escape, all building convincingly on previous lies. Finally, Ross relented.

"I figgered that all along," he said, allowing them to disperse. "I told myself that boy had to've escaped. When my boys start lookin' fer a prisoner, they always find 'im, whether he's inside the prison or outside. We'll sound the alarm. Mr. Johnston'll be back with us shortly."

Ross grinned at the departing prisoners self assuredly. "No, sirree," he said smugly. "They don't hide from Erastus Ross very long. I knowed he couldn't be in here."

Rose, Hamilton, and the rest casually ambled away. Once out of Ross's sight, however, they worked their way back to Rose's sleeping area, where a meeting was hastily held. All agreed that no more roll calls could be missed, and that the digging schedule would have to be adjusted accordingly. What to do about Johnston, however, presented a dilemma. The men all decided that Johnston should stay in Rat Hell around the clock.

Rose presented this unpleasant solution to Johnston that night. As would be expected, Johnston was not immediately agreeable.

"I don't know, Colonel," he said. "It's bad enough bein' down there with all them rats fer most of the day, not to mention the stink, the cold, and the dark. I don't know if I can do it fer twenty-four hours at a time."

"You have to," explained Rose. "If Ross gets word again that you're still here he won't rest until he finds out what's goin' on. There's no way we can keep him from findin' out about the tunnel. And if he finds you, you'll never get out of the cells."

Johnston, dejected, tried to come up with other alternatives. Finally, he suggested that he come back upstairs with a blanket wrapped around him in such a way as to hide his face. "I'll pretend I'm cold and sick. Nobody'll think nothin' of it."

"Well, it might work if you're real careful," agreed Rose reluctantly. "We're gonna have to be real careful doin' that, though. You got spotted the first time we tried that."

"Yeah, I know," admitted Johnston. "I'm real sorry 'bout that."

"That's alright," said Rose. "I didn't say it to make you feel bad. I just want you to know the risk you're takin' by comin' upstairs. Can't say as I blame you for not wantin' to stay down in Rat Hell until we get the tunnel done, though."

The decision having been made, Johnston made his way back to his new home in Rat Hell. Later that night he made his way stealthily back upstairs, wrapping a blanket around himself and pulling it up over his head so nobody would see his face. Most of the men were asleep already anyway. He settled down to sleep.

Some of his neighbors were still awake and, to his dismay, discussing him.

"How do you think he did it?" came a voice through the darkness.

"Wish I knew, I'd do it myself," came the answer.

The first voice went on, "That sly ole Johnston. Never said a word to me 'bout escapin'. I thought I'd be gone 'fore he was. I sat right next to him a few days ago at mess and we talked 'bout some tunnel I heard someone was diggin'. He said he didn't think anybody could dig a tunnel outta here, but there might be other ways to get out."

"He said that, did he?" the second voice asked.

"Yep," said the first. "Musta been thinkin' 'bout it right then. I didn't think much of it at the time. Everyone in here talks 'bout escapin'. Who'da known that he was gonna really do it?"

"Well," said the second man, "However he did it, I hope he's back in Union lines right now."

"Me, too," the first prisoner agreed.

The conversation fell silent. As Johnston listened to the sounds of men breathing heavily all around him, he smiled to himself. At least they hadn't said anything bad about him.

Chapter Seventeen

Rose and Hamilton stopped on the stairs, their way to the kitchen blocked by a guard. Below, near the fireplace, they could see a group of about sixty prisoners standing at attention. In front of them, Captain Turner paced angrily.

Recognizing the guard as one of those who had shown sympathy to the plight of the prisoners, Rose asked him, "What's goin' on, Private?"

The guard looked nervously at Turner before speaking to Rose. He did so without looking at him, to avoid drawing the ire of Turner for fraternizing with a prisoner.

"These men were down here marchin' around the kitchen at a double quick pace, gettin' some exercise," said the man. "They wouldn't have got in no trouble if'n they'da kept quiet, but they started singin' patriotic songs while they was marchin'. Cap'n Turner heard 'em and got a bunch of us guards to come in here and stop 'em."

"Why's that bother Turner," asked Rose.

"Oh, you know Turner," whispered the Rebel. "He don't want no patriotic singin' of any kind in here. Says it takes away our control or somethin'."

As Rose and Hamilton watched, Turner continued his harassment of the prisoners who had been marching and singing.

"Y'all know we have a rule against those kind of songs," he said loudly. "That rule will always be enforced as long as I'm in charge here."

Turner took out his watch and examined it. "It's about nine o'clock right now. I think a fair punishment will be for y'all to just stand here until...oh, say 'bout midnight. While y'all are standin' here y'all can think about rules, and why we have 'em in the first place."

169

Turning to the guards, Turner continued, speaking loud enough for the prisoners to hear. "Any of these men talks or sits down, or even so much as moves, I want y'all to shoot 'im. Do y'all understand?"

The guards nodded affirmatively.

Turning back to the prisoners, he said, "And do y'all understand? No singin', no talkin', no sittin' down, no movin', no nothin'. We'll see how good you Yanks are at standin' at attention."

The scene was too much for Rose. "You can't make those men stand at attention for three hours just for singin'," he shouted.

Turner whirled to face Rose, who had now started down the stairs and was being stopped by the guard, who had placed his musket across Rose's chest to hold him back.

"Oh, but I can, Colonel," said Turner. "And I'm going to. Would you like to join them?"

Rose felt Hamilton's restraining hand on his shoulder.

"Don't do it, Colonel," whispered the guard. "He'll make me shoot y'all, and I don't want to do that."

Rose refrained from answering, already regretting his outburst. He stared at Turner with contempt

Turner returned the stare, the corners of his mouth pulled back in a sneer. "I thought so," he said, after a short pause. He wheeled and started toward the door.

Stopping with his hand on the latch, he looked at the guards. "Y'all understand your orders?" he queried.

"Yes, sir," came the mumbled replies.

"I mean it. Any man so much as moves, y'all better shoot 'im. If I find out my orders ain't carried out, y'all will be shot, yerself."

Then, looking pointedly at Rose and the others who had gathered on the stairs to witness the scene, he said, "That goes fer them, too. They cause any kind of trouble, y'all shoot them, too." With that, he left, slamming the door.

For a moment, there was silence. Then, one of the guards looked at the door, then at the prisoners. "Y'all heard the man," he said. "Now, we don't want to shoot anyone. I mean that. But we don't want to get shot, neither. So y'all better mind what the Captain said. If y'all force us to shoot, we will."

"You wouldn't really shoot any of those men, would you?" Rose asked the guard who had stopped him on the stairs.

"What do you think?" said the man. Not getting an answer from Rose, he went on, "'Course I won't. Not unless I'm forced into it to keep from gettin' shot myself."

"What about the others?" Rose asked.

"Can't say," the guard answered honestly. "Most of 'em prob'ly won't. But that real tall feller over there...him, I don't know fer sure."

Rose looked at the man the guard had pointed out. He was sitting on one of the benches in front of the fireplace, staring at the men with an expression of hate.

"He don't like Yanks," the guard was saying, "And that's a fact. Told me once he's had two brothers killed in the war. Said he blames ever' one of y'all fer it. I don't know if he's tellin' the truth or not, but he told me he sliced a Yank's throat once in a skirmish over in Tennessee, then spit on the man while he was bleedin' to death."

"You believe him?" asked the astonished Hamilton.

"Don't have no way of knowin'. But I do know he ain't afraid to shoot any of yer friends if he thinks he has a reason."

"What about the others?" continued Rose. "Any other Yankee haters down there?"

"None that I know of that flat out hates y'all," was the answer. "But I can't say fer sure. That feller over there in the slouch hat, he ain't been here long enough fer me to git to know. Mebbe he would, mebbe he wouldn't. If I was y'all, I wouldn't give him no reason to shoot. That way, it don't matter none whether he likes Yanks or hates 'em."

"Well," said Rose, "I hope nobody moves to scratch his nose. I don't want anybody hurt over this, just for singin' a couple songs."

"Ain't nobody gonna get shot fer scratchin', Colonel," responded the guard. "I give y'all my word on that. I'll make sure none of our boys gits too anxious. Fact is, I think I'll go down there right now and talk to 'em. That is, if y'all promise to behave yerselves here till I git back."

"You have our word, Private," said Rose. "I'd appreciate anything you can do to keep your men under control."

The guard nodded, then proceeded to the kitchen to confer with the other guards. Rose and Hamilton sat down on the step to watch. The man spoke with the tall guard first, then to each of the others. Nobody in the ranks moved. Finally, after talking to the last guard, he walked among the prisoners, talking softly to them as he walked.

As the guard talked to the men in the kitchen, the men on the stairs, unable to hear what was being said, amused themselves as best they could.

"You wanna play odd or even?" a lieutenant with a thin mustache asked his companion as the two sat down directly behind Rose and Hamilton.

The second man, a captain, was wearing a pair of eyeglasses with one lens missing. He looked at the lieutenant for a brief moment, then said, "Yeah, I'll play. I'll take odds."

As the two reached into the deep recesses of their shirts, Hamilton turned and said angrily, "You two better throw them things away from me. I got enough of 'em now, and I don't want no more."

The men looked at Hamilton and laughed, still fumbling around inside their shirts.

"I ain't funnin'," said Hamilton. "I mean it. Throw 'em some other direction."

"We will, Andrew," said the lieutenant. "Don't get yourself all hepped up." With that, he withdrew his hand from inside his shirt and opened it slowly, counting the lice that he had pulled out. The captain did the same.

"I got nine," said the lieutenant. "How 'bout you?"

"Seven," came the dejected answer.

"That's sixteen!" hooted the lieutenant. "I win! Now, what was it we bet?"

"We didn't bet nothin' and you know it," said the captain, tossing his handful of lice over the side of the stairs as Hamilton watched him closely.

"C'mon," said the lieutenant. "Let's go again. You want to bet somethin' this time?"

"What are you talkin' about?" the captain replied. "Neither one of us owns nothin' to bet with. Let's just do it."

The men reached inside the shirts again. "I wonder if there's any nourishment from these little fellers?" said the captain. "Maybe I'll boil 'em and make a soup out of 'em. What do you think?"

Before the lieutenant could respond the guard returned. "I talked to all the boys," he said. "Won't nobody gonna do no shootin' as long as all yer men stays in rank. We don't care none if they don't stand at attention, long as they don't talk or git to movin' around."

"I really appreciate that, Private," said Rose, sincerely. "What about your tall friend over there?"

"He'll be all right," the guard answered. "He said he still don't like Yanks, but he doesn't want to shoot nobody that ain't got no chance to fight back."

"What if we was trying to escape," Rose asked, as Hamilton sucked in his breath in shock.

"Well, now," said the guard. "That there's a little different. We still got our duty to do, y'know." Then, squinting at Rose, he said, "Y'all ain't thinkin' of runnin', are yuh, Colonel? If'n yuh did, I would have to shoot then. Y'all know that, don't yuh?"

"Me?" asked Rose innocently. "Nah. I'm not gonna run. How could I? My shoes don't have any soles left to speak of, I don't have a coat or hat. I'd freeze to death in a matter of minutes out there."

"Well, that's good," said the guard, as he nodded his approval. I'd hate to have to shoot y'all. But I would if'n y'all tried to run. I just want y'all to understand that."

"Well," said Rose, "You won't have to worry about that. You won't see me runnin' away from Libby."

The guard drew silent. Hamilton nudged Rose with his elbow as if to say, "What are you doing?" Rose looked at him and grinned.

Then, changing the subject, he asked the guard, "When are you Rebs gonna get us some meat? We haven't had any goin' on eleven days, now."

"Yeah, I know," the guard answered sympathetically. "I wish I could help y'all there, but I can't. Ain't no meat to be had."

"No meat, no vegetables. How long do you Rebs think we can survive like this?" asked Hamilton.

"Ain't my fault, Cap'n," the guard apologized. "There just ain't any meat around. Even the people of Richmond are complainin'. They ain't eatin' none too good right now, either, y'know."

"It would sure be a shame if the prisoners rose up, wouldn't it?" said Hamilton. "More'n likely the people of Richmond would throw in with us. Then what would you do?"

"Don't rightly know," answered the guard. "I surely don't. But most likely the City Battalion would be called in to take care of any mobs out in the street. We'd have to take care of things in here, if'n you know what I mean."

"That sounds like a threat, Private," said Rose.

"Don't mean it to be, Colonel," said the guard. "I just want y'all to know that I understand how y'all feel, and I'll do what I can to help, but I still have a job to do."

"I guess I can understand that," said Rose. "Just don't do it too good."

The guard chuckled. "That there's just the way I do it, accordin' to Cap'n Turner...not too good!"

"Well, we think you do it just fine, and we appreciate it," said Hamilton.

"Thanks," responded the guard, starting back down the stairs. "But fer now, I reckon I better get down there with the rest 'fore someone complains to the cap'n. He ain't too mad at me right now, and I'd like to keep it that way."

"Thanks again," Rose and Hamilton said as one voice.

The guard responded with a wave of his hand, without looking back. He took a position near the ranks of prisoners still standing in the kitchen, looked at his pocket watch, and settled down to wait for midnight.

On the stairs the game of odd or even continued, with other prisoners swapping stories to pass the time. Nobody wanted to leave, not knowing what was going to happen, if anything. At midnight, the guards dismissed the men with little fanfare, however, and Rose and Hamilton made their way upstairs to get some much needed rest.

Rose had only been asleep for about an hour when he felt someone shaking him. It was McDonald.

"Colonel! Wake up. We got problems!" McDonald was whispering excitedly.

Rose tried to clear his head so he could grasp what McDonald was saying. "What happened?" he asked.

McDonald quickly explained. "I thought we were clean across, Colonel. I started diggin' up, but when I broke through I was short. Came up in the middle of the street. Right at the feet of the guards! One of the guards heard the noise. He was so close I could hear 'im talkin', Colonel. He asked the other guard if he heard somethin', and he said he did but he thought it was rats. I'm afraid they may have discovered the tunnel, Colonel! If they haven't already, they will by daylight."

"Let's not panic," cautioned Rose. "We don't know for sure that they've found it yet. Let's wait an hour or so, then go down and look around and see if there's any reason for alarm. Is the hole in the fireplace closed up?"

"No, sir," said McDonald. "We just moved the slop barrel in front of it so nobody could see it."

"Good," replied Rose. "We'll go down and make an inspection in a while. If they haven't found it, we'll keep going. We can use the hole for a vent. It might be a good thing. Give us a little better air for a while. Let's go find Andrew and let him know what's happened."

The two stealthily stepped over the sleeping bodies. Although it was difficult to avoid stepping on the prone men in the darkness, they eventually were able to successfully negotiate their path down the stairs and across the room below, where they woke Hamilton. Rose told him as much as he knew, himself.

Nobody spoke for several minutes. Then, McDonald said, "What about Johnston? If the Rebs did find the tunnel they're gonna follow it and come right out to 'im."

Hamilton, now fully awake, was still trying to absorb the enormity of the problem. The mention of Johnston's name seemed to drive it home. "And if they do find it, they're gonna know Johnston didn't do all that diggin' himself. Let me go down there now, and if they find us we'll say it was just the two of us."

Before Rose could respond, McDonald said, "I'll go with you. They'll believe I was in on it, since I missed roll call."

"No need for that," said Rose. "Any man caught down there is gonna be severely punished. You know that, don't you?"

"If they find Johnston by hisself, he'll be punished so bad that the Rebs'll find out about all of us," reasoned McDonald. "This way, only three of us'll get it."

Rose pondered the idea, then said reluctantly, "Alright. But don't take any chances. Tell Johnston what we're doin'. Keep me posted on what you find, if you can. If the Rebs haven't found the tunnel, we'll take a look and see how we can fix it so they don't."

The three wound their way to the cook room. With no hesitation, Hamilton and McDonald disappeared into the wall, leaving Rose to hide the opening.

An hour passed, then two. Finally, Rose heard someone clearing the hole in the wall. It was McDonald.

"What did you find, Bedan?" Rose asked anxiously.

"Andrew's stayin' down there with Johnston," said McDonald. "No sign of the Rebs yet. Maybe they really did think it was rats. They should have found us by now if they was gonna."

"You're probably right," agreed Rose "Let's go back down and look."

Upon reaching Rat Hell, the men found Hamilton and Johnston hidden deeply in the shadows of the abutment adjacent to the tunnel opening. After talking briefly, Rose entered the tunnel to see firsthand what McDonald had told him. As he crawled he tried to estimate the length of the tunnel. At about fifty feet he felt the tunnel slope upward. They couldn't be in the middle of the street! Gallagher had paced it off and the tunnel had turned upward exactly when it should have!

Above, the steps of the pacing guards could be heard. Where they had always been muffled before, they now sounded much louder, the hole allowing the sound to filter down into the tunnel much more readily.

At the end of the tunnel Rose could see a small opening about the size of his fist. The glare of a street lamp penetrated the darkness. McDonald was right. Somehow they had come up in the middle of the street. As Rose lay on his back studying the hole and trying to decide what had happened, and how it could be corrected, he could hear the voices of the sentries overhead. He couldn't see them, but they had to be near.

Rose backed out of the tunnel, slowly at first so the guards wouldn't hear, then faster when he got away from the opening. Reaching Rat Hell, he felt someone grasping his legs and helping him out of the tunnel. It was Hamilton.

"What's it look like, Thomas?" he said. "They find it?"

"I don't think so," Rose replied. "I couldn't make out what they were sayin' but I was close enough to hear them. They don't seem suspicious, though."

"What do we do?" asked Johnston.

"Well," said Rose. "We can't risk diggin' any more tonight. It'll be daybreak soon. I suggest we take a look out the window as soon as it's light and see just where the hole is. Then maybe we can figure out our next move."

"Sounds good to me," agreed Hamilton.

After discussing the situation for several minutes, they agreed to meet at the window on the end of the building as soon as it was light enough to see. Bidding Johnston good-night, they made their way back upstairs.

At dawn, the group was gathered around the appointed window. Rose peered out cautiously. Everything looked normal. The guards were walking their respective routes as if nothing had happened.

"You see anything, Colonel?' someone asked.

"No," he answered. "I can't even see the hole."

He backed away from the window and allowed the others to take a turn. Nobody could spot the opening.

"We need some kind of a marker," said Hamilton. "Something that's big enough to let us see, but not so big that it attracts attention."

"How 'bout this?" suggested Lucas, holding up an old shoe that he had spied sitting on a ledge.

"That oughtta do it," said Rose. "I'll take it down there tonight and stick it out the opening. We can push some dirt up in the hole and then stuff it up with an old pair of britches I have. Tomorrow, we can take another look."

The plan was agreeable to everyone, and the group dispersed. Hamilton remained behind for a while to talk with Rose, then he also left. Rose sat with his back against a post, holding the old shoe, and thought about the tunnel and how it could have come up so short. Surely, Gallagher couldn't have miscounted his steps by that much!

"How ya doin', Colonel? How's the foot?" asked Gageby.

"Good, Jim. And the foot's comin' along. How are you?" responded Rose.

"Tolerable, sir," was the answer. Gageby sat down beside Rose. "Colonel," he continued, "You hear anything about a tunnel bein' dug? I been hearin' some stories, and I thought you might know something."

Rose tried not to sound too defensive. "Why would I know anything about a tunnel, Jim?"

"Oh, I don't know," Gageby answered. "Just thought maybe you heard something, is all."

Rose studied Gageby's face. Did he know more than he was letting on? Rose decided to go along with Gageby's line of questioning.

"No, I haven't heard anything," said Rose. "Apparently you know more about it than I do. What are you hearing?"

"Not much," was the reply. "Just bits and pieces, really. Probably none of it reliable. I don't repeat none of it, except to you. I still ain't sure who to trust."

Rose nodded in agreement. He, too, had his doubts about some of the men. "I know exactly what you mean, Jim," he said. "There's quite a few in here that I think would be more comfortable wearin' gray."

Gageby brushed a louse from Rose's shoulder. "These things are just one reason I want to get out of here," he said, squashing the bug with his foot. "I'd sure like to find out that there really is a tunnel. I hate this place like a Baptist hates sin."

Rose debated mentally on the merits of telling Gageby the truth. He was a good man, and could be of help. On the other hand, the digging was nearly complete, and another participant would just mean one more possible source of a leak. Besides, it was still possible that the guards had discovered the tunnel, although that possibility was becoming more and more remote. Rose finally decided against telling Gageby the whole story, at least for now. However, a few clues wouldn't hurt.

"Jim, I'm not saying there is a tunnel, but with all the men in here that want out as bad as you do, it is a possibility." Gageby nodded quietly as Rose continued. "My suggestion to you would be to get ready to go. You never know when an opportunity might come up. Someone could be diggin' a tunnel right now, and when it's finished, maybe you could go out with the diggers. You hear what I'm sayin'?"

Gageby looked at Rose, then nodded again in comprehension. "I hear you, Colonel. I'll be ready. You can count on it. Thanks a lot."

"Don't mention it, Jim. Just be ready," said Rose.

"I will, Colonel," said Gageby.

The men grew silent. Then, Gageby spoke.

"You ever think you could hate a place as much as Libby, Colonel?"

Rose thought for a moment, then answered, "No, I don't think so. This war has made me think a lot of things I never woulda thought before, I guess."

"That's the truth there," agreed Gageby. "Like Rebs, fer instance. I never gave them a thought one way or another before the war. Oh, I heard about the Southern states and how they wanted to break away from the North, but I never paid it much mind. I never knew anyone from the South, but I figured they must be pretty much the same as us. Then, when they fired on Fort Sumter, I guess my opinion changed."

Rose listened thoughtfully as Gageby offered his philosophy.

"Soon as I heard about them firin' on the flag I started to hate 'em. Without no good reason, I guess. Just 'cause they did what they did. That's why I joined up...so's I could fight 'em and help preserve the Union."

Rose agreed. "I knew a few from fightin' in Mexico, though," he said, "And they were some fine men. Still, I know how you felt. I'da felt the same way if I didn't know some Southerners."

Gageby appeared thoughtful. "Then, I seen my first Reb up close. I still have nightmares about it." Gageby's eyes told Rose that his friend was no longer in Libby, but had been transported back two years to some unknown battlefield.

"I remember it like it was yesterday," Gageby went on. "We got in a skirmish with the Rebs. Didn't last long...probably no more'n a few minutes, although it seemed longer at the time, like everybody's first fight does. We got them on the run. We started chasin' them through the woods ...why we did, I'm still not sure. We didn't want to fight them again any more than they wanted to fight with us. I heard someone yell, 'Help me, Yank.' I looked over behind some bushes and seen this Reb sittin' on the ground, leanin' against a big rock. First thing I noticed about 'im was the big hole in his chest. I knew right away he wasn't gonna make it. He wanted some water, so I got my canteen out. While I'm holdin 'im with one arm around his back so he can raise up enough to swallow, I get a good look at his face. Couldn't been no older than sixteen. Probably didn't even shave regular, yet. I couldn't believe it! He was just a boy, Colonel! Just a boy. Probably had a ma and pa back home somewhere, just hopin' he'd get back home safe. Right then I saw the Rebs a little different. Have ever since. Even now, when some of these guards get to tormentin' us, I see that boy, and I can put up with it a little easier. He died in my arms, Colonel. Wasn't nothin' I could do to help 'im."

Gageby's eyes had misted, and a tear formed at the corner of one. The battle-hardened soldier was still feeling the pain of another human being. He sighed and wiped at the corner of his eye with a grimy hand.

"I've killed Rebs since then," he went on, "But not in hate. More out of duty, I guess. All the hate fer the Rebs drained out of me that day, right along with that boy's blood. I can still hate Libby Prison, but not the people that run it. They're just like us, Colonel. They're fightin' fer what they believe, just like us."

"I reckon you're right, Jim," said Rose thoughtfully. "I don't remember ever hatin' them. Not as a group, leastways. Some of them, like the Turners, I don't care much for, though. I don't know if it's hate, but it's a strong dislike."

"I know," said Gageby. "I don't care much for the Turners, either, but I've never looked at a Reb the same since I held that dyin' boy in my arms. That's what I meant about thinkin' of things different because of the war. Once this is over, if we live through it, we might all be friends again."

"I can't imagine ever bein' friends with either of the Turners," said Rose, "But I think I know what you mean."

"Don't get me wrong, Colonel," Gageby said quickly. "If we get out of here I'll still fight and do my sworn duty. All I'm sayin' is I can't see me ever hatin' another man again. And it's all 'cause of that boy. I've often thought how I wish I knew his name and where he was from. I'd look up his family and tell them how brave he was in his last minutes. Don't guess I'll ever be able to do that, though."

"Reckon not," said Rose softly.

The two sat in silence for a long time. Finally, Gageby stood up. "Sorry I went on like that, Colonel. I just felt like I wanted to talk about it," he said.

"That's alright, Jim," comforted Rose. "Sometimes that helps."

Gageby nodded. "Anyway, thanks fer listenin'. And thanks fer the advice about bein' ready to leave. I'll be sure to keep it to myself."

Rose gave Gageby a pat on the shoulder. "I'd appreciate that, Jim. I'll keep you informed as much as I can."

Gageby smiled as he walked away. Rose, watching him, wondered if he had told him too much. Or if he should have told him more.

Chapter Eighteen

That night, Rose and Hamilton took the discarded shoe and made their way to Rat Hell. Upon reaching the tunnel entrance they found Johnston eagerly awaiting their arrival.

"Any word, Colonel?" he asked. "Do they know about the tunnel?"

"I don't think so," Rose was happy to inform him. "There hasn't been any indication that they know anything. Has anyone been down here?"

"Not yet," said Johnston. "They come in, like they always do, but they only glance around and then leave. Anybody figure out how we happened to come up in the street instead of over in the vacant lot?"

"Not yet," replied Rose. He then proceeded to explain the plan for using the shoe as a marker. He withdrew the old pair of pantaloons from inside his coat. "We'll patch the hole with these," he said.

After discussing the plan in detail, Rose entered the tunnel while Hamilton and Johnston operated the ventilation system. It took but a few minutes to reach the end of the tunnel and place the shoe outside the opening. Rose then pushed dirt up into the hole and backed it up with the pantaloons. Having patched the hole he backed out of the tunnel and met again with Hamilton and Johnston.

"We'll take another look at daylight and see where the shoe is, so we can figure out exactly where we are," he explained to Johnston.

Rose and Hamilton decided to remain in the basement with Johnston for the night, to keep him company. They passed the time by talking and making plans for life after Libby. At about four o'clock in the morning Rose and Hamilton bade Johnston good night and returned upstairs.

Daybreak found them, along with several other anxious members of the tunnel party, assembled again at the window. Looking outside, Rose could not see the shoe. Finally, after scanning the area several times, he spied it, but it was several yards from where he had expected to see it. It immediately became clear how the tunnel had come up in the street. With no means of maintaining their direction in the dark confines of the tunnel, the diggers had gradually veered to the right. They were well off course!

"You see it, Thomas?" eagerly asked Hamilton.

"Yeah," said Rose. "We're nowhere near where we thought we were, though." He stepped back from the window to allow the others to look.

"How'd we get up there?" asked McKean, when he finally located the old shoe.

"Good thing we did come up in the street," said Hamilton. "If we'd kept on diggin' we would've circled clean around and come back into the prison."

Despite the seriousness of the situation, they laughed at the thought of reentering Libby by exiting the tunnel a few feet from where they had entered.

"Tell McDonald he ain't much of a navigator, but he sure saved us a lot of diggin'," said Gallagher with a laugh.

"Well, I think we know what we gotta do, don't we?" said Rose. The shoe had told them what they had set out to learn. Now the lesson had to be applied.

When digging resumed that night, adjustments in direction were made. Consulting his compass before entering the mouth of the tunnel, Rose was able to determine where the tunnel's direction had to be revised. Having made the adjustment, they dug at a faster pace without realizing it, as if to make up for the time lost by digging in the wrong direction.

The extra effort, combined with the constant stench, made every man extremely ill. Each had been giving everything he had, whether digging, fanning air, or dumping dirt. Now, there was little left to give. Still, they continued on, and slowly, inexorably, the tunnel inched its way toward the vacant lot.

"Colonel! I'm really glad you're here!" whispered Johnston excitedly. "I think the Johnnies are suspicious."

Rose had just arrived to begin another night of exhaustive digging, and was mentally unprepared for Johnston's news. Rose had thought the chances that the Confederates had learned of the tunnel had diminished to the point where they would no longer be of concern. Apparently he had guessed wrong.

"What's happened?" asked Rose incredulously.

"The guards came in this morning, just like they always do," began Johnston. "Only this time they didn't stop where they usually do. I was just hunkerin' down in the shadows, expectin' them to stop and pretend they were lookin' around. You know how they do it. Before I knew it, though, they were almost in here with me! I dug my way under the straw so they wouldn't see me and hoped I wouldn't sneeze!"

Johnston was showing Rose where he had burrowed under the straw. In his fatigued state, Rose was having trouble fully grasping what Johnston was telling him. The tunnel was within a few days of completion. It couldn't be discovered now!

"They stood right here and talked in real low tones," Johnston continued. "I couldn't make out everything they were sayin', but I did hear them say somethin' about an escape. One of them even scuffed around with his foot in the straw, just a few feet away from me!"

"How could they have found out?" Rose muttered to himself.

"When they left, I poked my head up out of the straw," said Johnston. "They were takin' their good ole time leavin', lookin' in corners, stoppin' to check things. Seemed to me like they were lookin' things over pretty good."

"Do you think they saw the tunnel?" queried Rose.

"No," answered Johnston, to Rose's relief. "I don't think so. But it looked like they might've been lookin' for it."

"I think I'm gonna go back upstairs and let the rest know about this," said Rose. "You be alright down here by yourself for a while?"

"Been alone down here for a couple weeks, Colonel," answered Johnston, cheerful despite the situation. "Few more hours won't matter."

Retreating to the kitchen, Rose gathered his partners around him and told them of the latest development. Predictably, their mood was crestfallen.

"It's not the end of the line," Rose said, trying to encourage them. "The Rebs are suspicious, but that's all. If they knew about the tunnel for sure, they would've done somethin' about it. I think we can still get out if we put a push on to finish the tunnel. We only have a little ways to go."

"What made them suspicious, Thomas?" asked Hamilton. "Any ideas?"

"None," replied Rose. "It doesn't really matter, I guess. We'll just have to make sure we aren't seen actin' suspicious. That means no gatherin' around and whisperin' in little groups like we've been doin', no gettin' real quiet anytime one of the guards walks past...nothin' that will make them wonder what we're up to."

"Tomorrow's Sunday," Hamilton reminded the group. "The Rebs don't usually go down in Rat Hell on Sundays. What about diggin' all day tomorrow, instead of just at night like we been doin'?"

"Good idea," agreed Rose. "Anyone have a problem with that?"

Anxious to finish the project, all agreed that around the clock digging should resume.

"We might about as well get started, then," suggested McDonald, proceeding toward the fireplace. The rest of the crew for the night followed him, the others returning upstairs to rest up for the final push.

Spurred on by the realization that every minute was now more important than ever, they dug furiously. Fighting fatigue, nausea, and muscle cramps, they extended the tunnel as they had never done before. The digging continued without ceasing through the night and all day Sunday. By Monday morning all believed they were within one day, or two at the most, of completing their tunnel to freedom.

The work crews pushed on. Scrape the dirt with a chisel, fill the loose dirt into the spittoon. When the spittoon is full, pull on the rope and let those outside pull it out and dump it. If the candle goes out, relight it. Ignore your nausea, stretch out the cramps. Fatigue? You can sleep after you escape. When the rope is jerked, retrieve the spittoon and start over. The routine never varied. Scrape, fill, pull, retrieve...scrape, fill, pull, retrieve....

Those who were not downstairs taking part in the digging were upstairs resting up for their own shift. Everyone did his part. This was not a job, nor a time, for shirkers. As the tunnel edged its way toward the vacant lot, the air became increasingly foul. Despite the efforts of the ventilation crew, the face of the tunnel was now too far away for the air to reach. What little air did reach the digger was almost totally blocked by his body, which nearly filled the small opening. There was barely room for the digger to move his arms to dig, let alone allow air to pass. Keeping the candle lit was now more trouble than it was worth, and most of the final digging was being performed in total darkness.

At the end of his shift, Rose dragged his exhausted body backwards out of the tunnel. Reaching Rat Hell, he felt friendly hands pulling him the last few feet, another digger prepared to immediately enter and take his place.

Rose rolled onto his back, completely spent. Almost immediately, the effects of the foul air took their toll. He quickly rolled back over to vomit. This was not at all unusual, with each man emptying the contents of his stomach at least once during every working shift. Still, they refused to slow their pace. The guards could enter the basement at any time now, and too much effort had been expended for the tunnel to be discovered at this stage.

It took all Rose's strength to climb the stairs. Reaching his sleeping area, he rarely remembered lying down, waking several hours later wondering how he had gotten back upstairs.

Today, he awoke to the sounds of another argument. Arguments were common occurrences in Libby, but this one included a familiar voice. Gageby!

"C'mon, Reb," Gageby was saying to a guard posted outside the door. "Let me see your newspaper. I haven't read a paper in weeks."

The guard was adamant about keeping his newspaper. "Ain't nothin' in here that y'all need to read about, Billy Yank," he said. "We're still winnin' battle after battle, and the war's almost over. Our boys'll be in Washington soon!"

"Is that a fact, now?" shouted Gageby. "If that's true, let me see it."

"Y'all don't need to see anything. Take my word fer it," the guard answered.

"You Rebs are always lyin' to us about somethin'," Gageby shot back. "If you aren't lyin' about an exchange, it's about breakin' into our packages from home. No reason I should believe you when you say you're winnin' the war."

"Well, I ain't lyin' now," said the guard, "And y'all ain't readin' my paper, neither. And when I'm done with it, I'm gonna start a fire with it."

"The only way I'll believe you is if I see it for myself," Gageby taunted the man. "If you was really winnin', you wouldn't mind showin' me the paper. And if you won't show me the paper, I have to believe you're lyin'."

"Suit yerself, Yank," the man said, refusing to rise to the challenge. "Y'all can believe anything y'all want to believe. Fact is, I say we're winnin', and you don't know nothin' different."

Gageby refused to give up. "That's probably a Richmond paper, anyway," he said. "It's full of Rebel lies, too."

The guard was becoming irritated. "Y'all best be mindin' yer manners, Yank. I can't read while y'all are chatterin'."

The guard's last statement was too much for Gageby to pass up. "I don't think you can read anyway. It don't make a heap of difference whether I'm chatterin' or not."

The guard threw his newspaper down and picked up his gun. "Well, Yank," he shouted at Gageby, "Mebbe I don't know how to read too good, but I am pretty fair at shootin' Yankees!"

Seeing the guard turn his gun toward the door, Gageby and those around him immediately retreated, out of the guard's range. His mocking laughter rang in their ears.

"What's wrong, Yank?" he shouted. "Y'all decide y'all don't want to read my paper after all?"

"The next paper I read is going to be tellin' about the Stars and Stripes flyin' over Richmond," shouted Gageby from a safe position behind a large post.

"Yer wrong about that, Yank," the guard shouted back as he laughed mockingly. "Next paper y'all read is gonna be tellin' how y'all died and rotted in Libby Prison!"

Gageby could see that there was no way he was going to read the guard's newspaper today. Maybe one of the other guards would have one, even if it was out of date. At least it would tell him if the North was winning any battles.

Shaking his head in resignation, he abandoned the game and walked back to his sleeping space. Passing Rose, he saw the colonel rubbing his eyes and trying to shake off the bone numbing fatigue that had overtaken him.

"Mornin', Colonel," said Gageby, quickly forgetting the encounter with the guard. "Sleepin' kinda late this mornin', are you?"

"Well, I was," responded Rose. "That is, until a certain lieutenant from Pennsylvania decided he had to read his mornin' newspaper."

"That?" said Gageby. "Oh, I'm real sorry about that. Didn't mean to wake yuh. I just wanted to find out how our boys are doin'."

"I'm sure they're doin' just fine, Jim," was Rose's retort.

"I hope so, Colonel," Gageby replied. "I surely hope so."

Rose was now fully awake. "If it means anything to you, Jim," he said, "I'm sure you were closer to bein' right about what's in that paper than the guard was."

"I figured I was," said Gageby. "I just didn't know he was gonna take it so serious. You see how fast he got that musket up?"

"You must have inspired him," Rose answered wryly.

Gageby laughed. "I have a way of doin' that with the Rebs."

"I think any one of us with a blue uniform has that knack," Rose said with a grin. "At least, in here we do."

"Reckon you're right, Colonel," replied Gageby. Then, lowering his voice, he continued, "Say, Colonel. I took your advice about bein' ready to go when the time comes. I'm ready to leave anytime."

Rose looked around him before answering. "Soon, Jim," he said. "Soon."

"Can't be too much further now, Colonel," said Gallagher as he handed the chisel to Rose. "Maybe you'll have the honors."

"I don't care who has the honors as long as we finish this thing up soon, John," Rose answered.

"Tonight, sir," said Gallagher, wiping the sweat from his brow. "I have a feelin' it's gonna be tonight."

"If you counted right, it could be," Rose said.

"Oh, I counted right," countered Gallagher. "You can be sure of that."

"Well, then," said Rose, "Maybe I'll wake you with good news in the mornin'."

"I'm lookin' forward to it, Colonel," responded Gallagher.

As Gallagher made his way to the rope ladder, Rose entered the hole in the wall. As he squirmed toward the face of the tunnel his thoughts turned to Lydia. What a story he would have to tell her!

Feeling his way along, he finally reached the end of the tunnel. He could feel the spittoon, its long trailing rope leading back to the basement. The familiar feel of the chisel in his hand gave him comfort. He would much rather be digging than resting upstairs. He would dig around the clock himself if his body would let him.

Pausing to regain his breath after his arduous crawl through the confined space, he thought about the past several months. The friends he had made here in Libby, the deprivations he and the others had experienced, the failed attempts at escape. With any kind of luck, that would soon be over.

He struck the dirt with the chisel, a tool which was now becoming quite worn but which had served the men well. As the dirt loosened and fell, he scooped it into the spittoon. Once full, he jerked the line to tell those in the cellar to haul it out. Rose was surprised at how tired he was already, and he had only filled the spittoon once. The many long hours in the tunnel, the lack of decent food, and especially the poor air, all were now banding together to create one last obstacle. He refused to succumb now. He would leave the tunnel head first tonight, into the cold night air of Virginia. That much he promised himself.

Hour after hour he dug, refusing to leave the tunnel and relinquish the chisel to the next digger. His muscles quivered with fatigue, but this had been his idea, and nobody was going to deprive him of the pleasure of breaking through the surface. He turned the tunnel upward, hoping his calculations were correct. He didn't want to come up into the street again!

Violent muscle spasms wracked his back, his legs, and his arms. They came with no warning, excruciating, almost paralyzing. Still, he forced his hands to scratch away at the dirt, his lungs to fill with still more foul air. Several times, he nearly fainted. Sweat ran into his eyes, its salty contents burning clear into his brain, he thought.

Thunk! The chisel struck something. Was it a rock? Shaking his head to clear his senses, Rose tried to figure out what he had hit. It didn't seem hard enough to be a rock, and the soil had shown little tendency to contain stones of this size. Feeling the offending object, he finally recognized it. It appeared to his touch to be a fence post. He was at the fence line of the vacant lot!

Immediately he forgot about his nausea and fatigue. The surface was near! "Dig, Thomas," he told himself. "Dig!"

His back bowed as he directed the tunnel upward. The memories of being caught in the wall flooded over him. If he were to get trapped in here, they would never be able to get to him in time to save him. They wouldn't even know he was trapped. Rose rolled over on his back to relieve the pressure on his back, relief which came immediately with the changed position.

The dirt now fell directly into his face and eyes as he scraped away. No matter. He could clear his eyes once he was outside.

Back in Rat Hell Hamilton and Johnston frantically tried to pump air into the opening. They knew that there was little chance that much was reaching Rose, if any, but still they labored. The rubber blanket had served its purpose well, as had the chisel.

Fighting another wave of nausea, Rose desperately scraped at the dirt with the chisel. The lack of oxygen was taking its toll. He felt as if someone had climbed upon his chest. Every breath was an effort. His head felt as if it were spinning. He no longer had strength to back out of the tunnel even if he had wanted to. There would be no turning back now.

Frustrated, he hacked at the dirt above him. "Break through!" he shouted at the chisel. "Break through!"

He fought like a man possessed. This tunnel would not defeat him. The Confederacy would not defeat him. Libby Prison would not defeat him. He would break through. He would. He would....

The resistance to his chisel suddenly was gone. He pulled it back, feeling a slight draft across his face. He reached up with his hand, poking his finger through the small hole the chisel had made. It felt cold! He clawed at the small hole, not even noticing the dirt falling into his face in large clumps.

As the hole grew larger, the air rushed in. No spring flowers ever smelled sweeter. It was the smell of free air. The first free air he had smelled in nearly nine months.

Then, prophetically, he heard it. The sentry, walking his post outside the fence, dutifully called out, "Half past one, and all's well!"

Fighting back emotion, Rose thought to himself, "All's well, indeed!"

Chapter Nineteen

Rose lay in the hole for several minutes, luxuriating in the fresh air that washed over his body. Lying on his back, the entire universe was spread out in front of him. The stars never looked brighter, the sky never more clear.

The fresh air quickly revived him. It seemed so perfect to just lie in the hole and enjoy the exhilaration of freedom, but he knew he would soon have to be back inside to report to the others. He decided that he would first reconnoiter the area, so that he could report something more meaningful.

Cautiously, he crawled out of the hole and brushed himself off. He checked his surroundings and was pleased to notice that this time, the tunnel's direction had been perfect. He had come up under a shed, on the far side of the fence. The sentries would be unlikely to see any activity in here if quiet could be maintained.

Above the top of the fence he could make out the towering form of Libby in the darkness. The blackened windows hid the misery that was a way of life behind those walls, a misery which Rose hoped would soon be behind him.

Crouching low out of instinct, even though the fence stood between him and the vision of the guards, he made his way to the gate, a massive swinging door nearly eight feet tall. A large bar served as a lock, to keep unauthorized wagons from entering the lot. Holding his breath, he slowly raised the bar and moved it aside. Although it took some effort to lift, Rose was able to achieve it with little noise.

Slowly he opened the gate and peered out through the crack. He could view the entire street without being detected. Everything was as it should be: the sentinels walking their beats, the street deserted. Only the glow of the street lamp caused him any concern, but it was nothing that hadn't been anticipated.

When the nearest guard turned his back and paced toward Libby, Rose, hoping he looked nonchalant, opened the gate and stepped out onto the street. He closed the gate behind him and casually strolled down the street, away from Libby.

Turning at the corner, he walked slowly down the street toward the canal, giving the appearance of a citizen of Richmond returning home. Staying on the opposite side of the street from the prison, he slowly walked around its entire perimeter, noting the presence of the sentries, the locations of street lamps, and anything else which he felt could be of use in making the escape. His inspection satisfied him that the hardest part of the escape was already accomplished, and that they could walk away unchallenged if the proper caution were taken.

Returning to his starting point, he reentered through the gate and closed it behind him. Picking up a piece of wood that he judged to be of sufficient size to hide the opening of the tunnel, he crawled back into the hole. He pulled the plank over the opening and made his way as fast as he could crawl backwards, to Rat Hell.

Upon his exit from the tunnel into Rat Hell, Rose was sure his beaming face could be seen even in the darkness.

"We did it!" he whispered as loudly as he dared. "We're through!"

Johnston threw his arms around Rose and hugged him as he wept openly. McDonald and Hamilton choked back tears of joy themselves, as they shook hands and pounded each other on the back.

Rose handed the chisel to McDonald. "We won't be needin' this anymore, Bedan," he exclaimed happily. "And look at this."

He pulled a small nail from inside his blouse. "It's from a horseshoe," he announced. "I found it out in the street. I was actually outside the prison!"

Rose briefly told them of his tour around the streets surrounding Libby. Then, he remembered the other men who were sleeping upstairs.

"Andrew, gather everyone in the kitchen. They'll want to know of this right away!" he directed Hamilton.

Everyone but Johnston made his way back upstairs where, while Hamilton rounded up the rest, Rose and McDonald hid the opening in the fireplace. When all had assembled, Rose looked across the group, scarcely able to conceal his excitement.

"Just thought you'd all want to know," he began, trying to appear nonchalant. "The tunnel is finished!"

Under other circumstances and in friendlier surroundings, that announcement would have been greeted with a resounding cheer. Instead, the men conveyed their joy as silently as they could, pounding one another on the back, shaking hands, and hugging the closest person. They were going home!

When the celebration had calmed down, Rose continued. "You've all done a great job. The tunnel would never have been finished if every man here didn't do his part. Now, it's time for the best part of all."

He withdrew his watch and studied it in the dim glow of the candle. "It's only three o'clock," he said. "Daylight is still three or four hours off. I think we should go now, before anything else goes wrong."

Gallagher protested. "I don't know about that, Colonel. I'm as anxious as anyone to get out of here, but that doesn't give us a whole lot of time to get past the fortifications before daybreak."

McKean agreed. "We'd probably do better with a good night's rest, too, Colonel. We've all been workin' pretty hard without much sleep."

Hamilton agreed with Rose, wanting to get out of Libby as quickly as possible. The two originators of the plan, however, stood alone in their desire to leave immediately. After much discussion, it was agreed that the escape would take place the next night. They also agreed that each of them could inform one other person of the plot, although by now it was becoming apparent that many already were aware of the tunnel and were merely awaiting its completion.

Final logistics were discussed, and Harrison Hobart, Lieutenant Colonel in the Twenty-First Wisconsin Infantry, agreed to be the last man out. His job would be to maintain order among the second group to leave, allowing one hour to lapse before he led the second group out. One man from that group would have a similar task, with each man in that group being allowed to tell one other person about the escape. All agreed that, if the escape could be handled systematically and orderly, a maximum number of men could take part. If need be, a second escape could be effected the next night, using the same system of one man from each group telling one other person.

With the escape plan finalized, the men were too excited to go back upstairs to sleep. They chattered animatedly among themselves in the kitchen.

"Which way you headin' when you get out?" Randall asked Hobart.

"Well, I ain't rightly sure," was the answer, "But the Colonel told us a long time ago to try to get to Miss Van Lew's if we could. I'm thinkin' that might be the way I head."

"Yeah," agreed McKean. "I hear tell she has a secret hiding place in the roof of her portico. If that's true, we can stay there till the Rebs get tired of huntin' fer us."

"Not me," said Garbet. "That's the first place the Rebs are gonna look. They'll know ole Crazy Bet is gonna put some of us up. They're bound to tear her place apart lookin' fer anybody that escapes. Me, I'm goin' the opposite direction."

For several minutes they debated the merits of trying to get to Van Lew's mansion. Several planned to go there, others were not so sure. The discussion ended with each knowing in his own mind the direction he intended to go.

"Our pays oughtta be buildin' up pretty good, don't you think?" Garbet asked nobody in particular, during a lull in the conversation.

"You're right about that," agreed McDonald. "They are holdin' our pay, aren't they, Colonel?"

Rose had not considered this before, having grown used to infrequent pays while on the march anyway. "I don't know for sure," he offered. "I imagine they will, but I never thought about it."

"They'd have to, don't yuh think?" Garbet said. "I hope they give it to us all at once. Let's see, a hundred and five dollars a month for eight months, what's that work out to?"

As Garbet tried to compute his pay, others fantasized about how they would spend their windfall. Rose listened, then broke in.

"I hate to be the one to throw cold water on all this spendin'," he said, "But, fact is, we'll probably all be sent back to our regiments to finish our terms of service."

Major Fitzsimmons of the Thirtieth Indiana looked astonished. "They can do that?" he asked.

"Can, and probably will," answered Rose.

"Not me," replied Fitzsimmons. "I think every one of us here has done our duty. I ain't all that fond of fightin' in the first place. I just want to go home. I'll resign if they do that to us. I intend to forget the war, and especially Libby Prison, as quick as I can."

"Not me," countered Hamilton. "I don't never want to forget Libby. If we forget, then the last six months will be wasted. I want to remember everything so I can tell my children, and their children. This place must never be forgot."

"What about you, Colonel?" asked Garbet. "You gonna try to forget?"

Rose looked at his friend from his own regiment. "I'll try to forget some things, Davy, that's a certain. There's things about this war I don't want to remember."

"Like what?" Garbet persisted.

"Well," said Rose. "Like the actual fightin', for one. Some people look at the war as something exciting or romantic. Anyone who thinks that, should see it up close. Smell it. Taste it. They should feel what it's like to run across a battlefield while someone's shootin' at you, all the while you're tryin' not to step on bodies, or pieces of bodies. They should experience the sensation of slipping in puddles of blood. They should see the piles of amputated arms and legs layin' outside a field hospital, or smell the rottin' flesh, or taste the gunpowder. If they did, they'd soon realize that war isn't romantic. It's terrifyin', and I hope none of us ever has to experience it again. I guess that's the part I'm hopin' to forget."

Garbet and the rest drew silent, looking thoughtful. All had experienced what Rose had just described. Some had already spilled their own blood. Finally, Garbet broke the silence.

"Reckon we'll all try to forget that part," he said softly. Nods of assent went around the group.

"It's gonna be nice to be able to write a letter and know that nobody's gonna read it first, or scratch out somethin' you've written," McDonald mused.

"You're right about that," agreed Hamilton. "I ain't never been one fer writin' long letters, but I gotta admit I had trouble fittin' everything I wanted to say into the six lines we was allowed."

"And how 'bout gettin' packages that haven't been opened by someone else and rummaged through?" commented Rose.

"Yeah," several chorused in agreement.

"I plan to ask my wife what all she sent me while I was in here," said McDonald. "It's gonna be interestin' to find out what I never got."

"I hear that one of the boys recognized one of his old suits on a guard once," said Garbet. "His wife sent it and the guard helped hisself before he distributed the package."

"I heard that, too," said Hamilton. Turning to McDonald, he said, "Major Turner's about your size, Bedan. You maybe oughtta take a quick look at his wardrobe before you leave. You might see somethin' you recognize."

Several of the men laughed.

"If he wore it, I don't want it back," said McDonald.

They laughed again, all agreeing that the Turners would be among the things they wanted to forget.

"No disrespect intended," said McKean, "But has anybody thought about how we'll get Colonel Streight through the tunnel? I don't know if he's gonna fit."

McKean's point was well taken. The tunnel was only about eighteen inches in diameter, and Colonel Streight, even with the shortage of food over the past several months, looked to be much wider. All agreed that Streight should be among those given the opportunity to leave.

"If I know Colonel Streight," said Rose, "He's gonna find a way to get through."

Hamilton grinned mischievously. "Maybe we could go out in alphabetical order."

Confused looks greeted his suggestion.

"I'll ask the question everyone else wants to," said Rose. "How will that help him?"

"The way I remember my letters," said Hamilton, "Streight would come right after Sanderson. If Colonel Streight knows that's Sanderson right in front of him he'll probably chase him clean through to the other end and never touch the sides."

Forgetting where they were, a loud guffaw arose from the men. It was no secret in Libby that the two men hated each other. Before Rose could calm the men, a guard quickly appeared at the doorway from Cary Street. Walking his post, he had been passing the window at the precise moment the laughter rang out.

"What are y'all doin' in here?" he demanded.

They drew quiet immediately. Rose spoke up. "Couldn't sleep, for some reason. We all came down here to talk so we wouldn't disturb anybody upstairs."

The guard did not appear suspicious. "Don't be makin' so much noise, then. Y'all are gonna wake 'em up anyway with all that laughin'."

"Sorry," said Rose. "We'll be sure to be more careful."

The guard withdrew from the doorway and resumed his pacing. Inside, several grown men giggled like school boys who had put something over on their teacher.

"This might be a good time to call it a night," suggested Rose. "We are all getting a little silly about now. I think we all know what we're gonna do. Everybody can tell one person, but no more. Let 'im know we're ready to go. I know who I'm gonna tell, and I'll fill General Dow in, too. He should know about it, even if he decides he doesn't want to leave."

"I'll talk to Colonel Streight about it," offered McDonald.

"Good," replied Rose. "Does anybody have any questions?"

Not getting any replies, Rose dismissed them with instructions to assemble in the kitchen the next night, prepared to make their exit from Libby.

"Jim, remember what I told you about bein' ready to leave here on short notice?" Rose asked Gageby.

"Sure do, Colonel," was the reply.

"Well, you were right about the tunnel," said Rose. "I wish I coulda told you that when you asked, but I just couldn't. I hope you understand."

"That's alright, Colonel," replied Gageby. "When can we go out?"

"Tomorrow night," was the answer.

Gageby appeared speechless. He knew his departure would come on short notice, either by escaping or through an exchange. Twenty-four hour notice was far better than he had ever hoped for.

"Thanks, Colonel," he finally was able to say, as he shook Rose's hand. "I really appreciate you tellin' me about it."

"I'm glad I could finally tell you the truth, Jim," said Rose. "I wanted to a couple of times, but it just wasn't possible. Anyway, we came in here together, we're gonna go out the same way."

Rose filled Gageby in on the details of where and when to assemble, and how the escape would take place. He then responded to Gageby's questions about how the tunnel had been dug and who had been doing the digging. Finally, when all Gageby's questions had been answered, Rose stood up.

"I've got to tell General Dow," he said. "Remember, though. Don't say anything to anyone until tomorrow night, just before you're ready to leave. And then, only one person. We can't risk having the Rebs find out about this now. We've come too far."

"You can count on me, Colonel. And thanks again, in case I don't get to see you tomorrow night."

"You're welcome, Jim," said Rose. "We'll meet again in Pennsylvania!"

Shaking hands discretely, Rose left Gageby and sought out Dow. He found the old man dozing against a post, oblivious to a raucous card game taking place just beside him.

Rose woke Dow, and asked if he could have a word with him somewhere away from the card game. They made their way to a secluded corner nearby.

"General," Rose began, "I just wanted to let you know we've been workin' on a tunnel. We're gonna go out tomorrow night and we want you to go along."

Rose did not expect Dow to respond with a great deal of excitement, and he wasn't even sure the old man would want to be a part of an escape attempt, in light of his marginal health, but he was totally unprepared for the reaction he got. Dow shook his head and said, "No, thanks, Colonel, I won't be going. And I think you should reconsider your plans, too."

Surprised by Dow's request, Rose did not respond immediately. Seeing that Rose was not going to reply at once, Dow went on. "Elizabeth Van Lew was here yesterday. You remember all the excitement a day or two ago? All those bells tollin' and all the soldiers runnin' around out in the street?"

Rose nodded. The prisoners had spent several hours watching the activity, each offering his own opinion on what it actually meant.

"Well, Miss Van Lew tells me that Ben Butler's forces have gained Bottom's Bridge. That means we've got troops not too far from here. The thinkin' is, maybe they're ready to move into Richmond."

"That's good news, sir," responded Rose. "But do we know that for a fact?"

"No," admitted General Dow, "'We don't. But if they do, we could all be free soon anyway, without takin' the risk of escapin'.'"

"On the other hand, General," said Rose, "If we wait, and the troops don't come, then we've missed our chance."

"Give it some time, Colonel," said Dow. "Then, if nothing happens, you can still go out."

"If the Rebs don't find the tunnel in the meantime," said Rose, going on to explain that he had reason to believe the guards were getting suspicious.

"And I have reason to believe that help will be on the way before much longer, Colonel," Dow said sharply. "Miss Van Lew tells me that she has found out that the Confederates are getting nervous about having so many prisoners in Richmond. They plan to move us further south soon. She sent a ciphered letter explaining this to General Butler, and she suggested a raid on Richmond with at least thirty thousand cavalry and ten or fifteen thousand infantry troops. General Butler always has had a lot of faith in Elizabeth, and if she suggested that, you can be sure he's gonna consider it real strong."

"But listen to what you just said, General," Rose protested. "If the Rebs plan on moving us deeper into the south, we should try to get out sooner, rather than waitin'. Once we're moved it's gonna be a whole lot harder to reach Federal lines. Unless General Butler's plannin' on makin' his raid within the next day or two, I'm afraid we're gonna have to make our own move."

"Colonel Rose," said Dow in an authoritative voice, "I can't stop you from trying to escape. But you should know that I am strongly against it. If you escape now, you could jeopardize possible future exchanges."

"I don't believe that for a minute, General," Rose shot back. "First, I'm not sure when the next exchange is gonna take place, and neither are you. For all we know there may never be another one. And if there is, I fail to see how our escape could harm any negotiations. We have a right...no, a duty, to escape. And we're gonna do it. I had hoped it would be with your blessing, and that you would come along with us."

"I can't give you that blessing, Colonel," said Dow in a resigned tone. He could see that Rose was not going to be swayed. "And I won't be goin' with you. I've been told that negotiations are under way right now to exchange me. I don't want to risk that."

Rose could not believe what he was hearing. "So that's it?" he whispered as loud as he dared. "You might be exchanged, and you want us to stay here in Libby until that takes place? I've got as many as thirty people ready to crawl out through that tunnel tomorrow night, and you want me to tell them they can't go because you might not be exchanged if they do?"

Dow looked sheepish. He hadn't meant to tell Rose about his possible exchange because he knew Rose would interpret it just the way he had. However, Dow really did believe that additional men could be a part of the exchange, and he truly didn't want to jeopardize that.

"Well, General," continued Rose, "If you want my people to hear that, you're gonna have to tell them yourself. I won't do it. They've worked too hard for this. They deserve this chance. And I won't take that away from them. I'm sorry you feel the way you do. You're still welcome to come along if you change your mind."

Dow appeared deep in thought for several moments, then reached out his hand. "I apologize if I sounded selfish, Colonel. That isn't the way I meant it. I just don't think it would be wise for me to try an escape right now. But I'll be with you in spirit. And, you do have my blessing. I hope you make it safely home."

Dow's change of tone caught Rose momentarily by surprise. Then, he took Dow's offered hand and shook it.

"Thank you, General. I apologize, too," he said. "I'm just pretty keyed up about this, I guess. I didn't mean to pass judgment."

"I understand, Colonel," said Dow. "I really do. Good luck. You'll be in my prayers."

Rose squeezed Dow's hand once more, then turned and departed. He had hoped the old man would come along. Sadly, he wondered if he would ever see him again.

Chapter Twenty

The long awaited night finally arrived. The group gathered nervously in the kitchen, keyed up for the trip home. Nobody spoke. Nobody had to. Everyone knew what the others were thinking.

Rose and Hamilton looked at each other.

"You ready?" Rose asked tersely.

"Let's go," answered Hamilton in a subdued but determined voice.

The fireplace was opened. Each man spoke briefly to Hobart, who was staying behind to lead the second group, then entered the opening. Finally, all had gone through the wall except Rose.

"Harrison," he said, shaking Hobart's hand, "I want you to know I appreciate all you did here. And I especially appreciate you stayin' behind to take the next group out."

"Glad to be a part of it, Thomas," replied Hobart. "We'll be right behind you."

Bidding each other good luck, Rose entered the fireplace. Once inside, he could hear Hobart already beginning to close up the opening.

Rose stealthily crossed Rat Hell to the tunnel opening, where the others had gathered. He found them huddled in the shadows, awaiting his arrival. As he had done with Hobart, he thanked them and warned them to be careful.

McDonald spoke up as he shook Rose's hand. "Colonel," he said, "We've all decided that you should be the first one to go, then Andrew. You two have been in on this from the first, and we feel it's only right."

Rose glanced around at the others, now murmuring their agreement in the dim light of the candle. He smiled. "Thanks, Bedan," was all he could say as his emotions overwhelmed him.

196

With one last look around his surroundings, he entered the tunnel, followed quickly by Hamilton and the others. The passage through the tunnel was uneventful, and as he crawled along Rose reminisced about the hours he had spent in this underground hole. It was not something he ever wanted to do again, but now that it was almost over he was glad to have been a part of it.

One by one they crawled out of the tunnel, those who had already exited remaining at the tunnel's mouth long enough to help those coming behind. Seeing that all had passed through safely and were gathered with him, Rose slowly opened the gate wide enough to peek out. The sentinel was walking toward them. Rose closed the gate quietly and waited. The escapees crouched in silence. Garbet looked up at the blackened windows of Libby and waved to the unseen faces he knew would be watching their progress.

The sentinel came within twenty paces of the gate, then turned. As he marched away, Rose counted his steps. Thirty-eight...thirty-nine...forty. The man stopped and turned again, returning to his turning point near the gate. Again Rose counted his paces, this time satisfied that he knew when the guard was nearing the end of his route.

The next time the sentinel turned away from the gate, Rose turned to his friends and whispered, "See you up North!" He then calmly stepped out onto the street, followed closely by Hamilton.

As the others watched, they walked briskly away, unchallenged. When they were safely out of the glare of the street lamp, three more made their exit through the gate, watching the sentinel carefully as he neared his turning point.

So it continued until all had been able to safely leave in small groups of two's and three's. Leave while the sentinel has his back turned, close the gate and wait while he marches back. Repeat the process when he turns again. In a matter of minutes the first group had all been able to walk away from the empty lot, making their way on the first leg of their journey to the North...to homes and families.

"Look at that. Did you ever see anything more beautiful?" said Lieutenant Robert Bradford of the Second West Tennessee Cavalry.

Bradford was looking out the window with Colonel William Kendrick of the Third West Tennessee Cavalry and Captain David Jones of the First Kentucky Infantry, watching the steady flow of men out the gate. The three were to act as a rear guard, leaving just before dawn.

As they watched, another small knot of men exited through the gate.

Jones snickered. "Look at that!" he said. "Those guards don't have any idea what's goin' on right behind their backs."

"Let's just hope none of 'em turn around," said Bradford.

"What if they do?" said Jones. "All they're gonna see is a couple of drunks headin' home after a night on the town. You think those sentries care about that?"

"Probably a little jealous, is all," said Kendrick.

The three snickered at the thought.

"The Rebs usually put those street lamps out around midnight," Bradford went on. "Should make it a little easier to sneak away."

"What time is it now?" asked Jones.

Bradford took out his watch and lit a match. "Almost ten," he said.

"Another six hours before it's our turn," said Jones. "I don't know if I can last that long."

"Yeah, me too!" agreed Bradford. "These last few hours are the worst part."

"It don't make it any easier watchin' those fellas goin' out, either," said Jones.

The three watched apprehensively. It was going to be a very long night.

"I don't know," said Kendrick, after a brief silence. "Some of them are a little too bold, for my blood."

"How do you mean?" asked Jones.

"Just watch 'em," Kendrick answered angrily. "Some of 'em act like this is a lark, waltzin' out into the glare of that street lamp. They aren't even tryin' to stay in the shadows."

"Maybe they figure they look less suspicious that way," suggested Bradford.

"Less suspicious?" snorted Kendrick. "It's only gonna take one guard to get suspicious enough to stop them and ask who they are and where they're goin'. Once that happens, the rest of us are doomed to stayin' in here till the war's over."

The three watched anxiously for several minutes, their silence broken only by an occasional oath as yet another escapee indiscreetly walked nonchalantly out into the street.

"They keep that up and this escape'll be over long before it's our turn to go out, that's for sure," declared Kendrick.

"What do you think, Colonel?" asked Bradford. "You wanna go now?"

"I'm thinkin' we should," answered Kendrick. "What do you think, David?"

"I'm for it," replied Jones, a worried look crossing his face.

"Let's do it, then," stated Bradford. "Gather your things and I'll meet you in the kitchen."

The three parted company to prepare for their departure.

Inside the kitchen, a major problem was developing. The plan had allowed each man to tell one other, with that man also being permitted to tell another just before he departed, and so on. This was done to control the number of people converging on the fireplace at any given time. In some manner, however, word had leaked out. Before the escape had progressed very far, hundreds of anxious prisoners were now alerted to the breakout.

The throng quickly filled the kitchen, each man pushing to be first in line at the fireplace. Chaos reigned, and the situation deteriorated rapidly. Fights broke out as the desperate men pulled one another away from the fireplace so they could enter instead.

Hobart vainly tried to restore order, then realized the futility of his effort. Seeing he could no longer control the desperate prisoners, he begged them to at least remain quiet, to avoid alerting the guards. Failing that, he decided to enter the tunnel and make his escape while the opportunity was still there. Opening the fireplace, he was immediately followed by the frenzied crowd. From inside the wall he could hear those above him fighting and clamoring to be next in line. He feared that few would be able to escape before the commotion drew Captain Turner and his guards.

The prisoners were so desperate to escape from Libby that they were anxious to leave immediately, whether prepared for the journey or not. Many had no chance at all of success, trying to leave with no warm clothing and no idea of where they would go once they were outside the walls. Still, they were willing to risk everything for the chance to be free once more.

The scene became more frenetic by the minute. The stronger prisoners quickly dominated the weaker ones, often bullying their way to the front of the line. Many were knocked to the floor, only to be stepped on by others pushing their way to the front. Several were injured, and others were in danger of being crushed or trampled by the mob.

The normally placid kitchen area was a mass of motion, with people clamoring to get past one another to reach the fireplace. The scene was a strange model of incongruity, as men pushed, shoved, fought, and generally milled about, but with relatively little noise. Everyone recognized the importance of keeping the guards from learning what was happening, but still wanted to make their own case for being first through the fireplace. Often, that case was made with a fist or a well-placed forearm. Men whose mannerisms would normally be best described as mild mannered had now degenerated into enraged animal-like creatures who would be ashamed of themselves tomorrow.

"We ain't never gonna have a chance at gettin' near the front this way," a grizzled captain complained to his companion.

"Don't be so sure," said his friend, a sandy haired young lieutenant whose nose was already bloodied in the melee. "We got as much right to get out of here as the rest. Maybe more than some. We've been here a lot longer than some of those up front."

Struggling to maintain his balance in the shoving throng, the captain inquired, "You have any ideas how we can get up there?"

"Sure do," said his friend. "Get back against the wall here and stay out of the way." With that, he cupped his hands around his mouth and shouted as loudly as he dared without bringing the guards in, "Guards coming! Guards coming!"

The cry went from man to man, quickly reaching the front of the line. The men stampeded for the stairs, knocking down anyone who was unfortunate enough to be in the way. Those who had been pushed aside by many of the men fighting their way to the front of the line were pummeled again by the same men on their way back. The scene became even more disorderly.

Two people were knocked off the narrow stairs as the mob rushed up to their quarters. Those onto whom they fell, in some cases their own mess mates, roughly flung them aside like rags, intent on reaching safety themselves before the dreaded guards made their presence known.

The lieutenant who had raised the original alarm flattened himself against the wall, as did his friend. The headlong rush for the stairs threw others against them, and they protected themselves as well as they could while doing their best to stay out of the maelstrom. Agitated prisoners flailed madly about as they tried to clear a path. The only thing they feared more than not being able to escape was being caught in an escape attempt, and the panic stricken men cared little who they pushed out of their way in their crazed state.

When the crowd had thinned to the point where it appeared possible to move against the flow, the captain and lieutenant inched their way along the wall, occasionally lashing out to fend off another maddened prisoner trying to reach the stairs. A few other prisoners had recognized what was happening and followed the two as they fought their way, like salmon swimming upstream to spawn, to the fireplace.

Several who had fled upstairs quickly learned the alarm had been a false one, and slowly made their way back to the kitchen. Those who had been near the front when the alarm had gone out were in foul moods, as would be expected, and were even rougher in their efforts to get to the front of the line a second time.

The clamor continued throughout the night as the men jockeyed for positions. Only the first light of dawn brought the drama to a close, and those who had not yet entered the fireplace vowed to be first in line the next night. They would not be bullied out of their rightful place two nights in a row!

* * *

Wells had prepared himself physically for his eventual escape. He hadn't known when it would be, or how, but he was sure it would happen. It was only a matter of time. He was not surprised when he received word that the tunnel was ready and an escape was imminent.

"I knew it!" he said to himself. "There was a tunnel!"

The daily long walks around the prison were now going to pay off. Only one thing concerned him, and that was his lack of suitable footwear. His shoes were badly worn, and would not serve him well in the wet weather. Most likely, his path to freedom would take him through some of Virginia's thickest swamps. In the freezing temperatures of a February night, he knew his feet would freeze, making his chances of a successful escape remote. Without a good pair of boots, he may just as well remain inside Libby.

He had tried to persuade a friend to trade his boots, but had not been successful. At the time, Wells had not yet learned of the tunnel, nor of the escape. He did know, however, that the boots would be necessary at some point.

"Come on," he had begged his friend, who was taking his boots off for the night. "You know how I like to walk all day, and look at my shoes." He had held his feet up for the man to see. The sole of one shoe was nearly gone, and the other wasn't much better. "I can't walk much longer in these. You don't do any walkin'. Why won't you let me have them?"

"They're mine, that's why," the owner of the boots had grumbled. "I don't have to give you a reason."

"Look," Wells had pressed on. "I just got a package from home. It's got coffee, some shirts, vinegar...you can have all of it. Just trade me for the boots."

"I ain't interested in tradin'!" his companion had insisted. "Now, leave me be. I ain't interested in no shirts or vinegar, either. I'm keepin' the boots."

Wells would not be denied. "For what?" he had asked, hoping to wear his companion down with his persistence.

The man had steadfastly waved his hand in Wells's direction in disgust, shaking his head.

Picking up one of the boots, Wells had said, "Look at this. They fit me better than they fit you." Slipping his foot into the boot he had stood up. "See! I told you. Perfect fit. Just like they was made for me."

"Gimme back my boot," his friend had spat out angrily, lunging at Wells.

"Some friend you are," Wells had replied. "Keep yer boots. Wear 'em to yer grave, fer all care." Then, as an afterthought, he said, "And don't come 'round askin' fer no vinegar, either."

On the night of the escape, Wells helped himself to the boots, telling himself that he would send them back once he had reached safety. He also found a cap which would serve him well during his flight to freedom. Without it, he may not survive.

Following the instructions he had been given, Wells proceeded to the kitchen. When he arrived he was totally unprepared for what he saw. To his eyes it appeared that nearly everyone in the prison had crammed into the room. Every direction he turned his head he saw men fighting, men who had been friends that very afternoon.

Wells paused to think about the route he should take to get to the fireplace, but was roughly pushed forward by the crowd already gathering behind him. He would have no choice of routes. He would have to go where the crowd took him.

As he stood in line he considered the exit route. How ingenious! The fireplace. Nobody ever suspected, even though they stood around it every day. He had to give Rose and Hamilton credit. They not only had come up with a way out of Libby that nobody had ever thought of, they had also done a good job in keeping their plan a secret. He shook his head in awe as he thought about it.

The line moved slowly, and he felt himself being pushed first to the right, then to the left. Reaching inside his coat, he felt the reassuring forms of the maps he had made of the area, just for this eventuality. He had no idea how close he was to the fireplace. He only knew he was in danger of being crushed if he didn't soon get there.

Then, he heard the dreaded words. "Guards coming! Guards coming!"

If possible, the pandemonium became even greater. Now he was being shoved from both front and back, as the confused men tried to get back to the stairs. Seeing a small opening, he quickly squeezed through. He found himself next to the wall, the lights of the street lamps on Cary Street beaming on the fireplace just ahead of him.

The decision was made for him. He was this close. There was nothing going to keep him from getting out now. As the others pushed their way toward the stairs, Wells worked his way to the fireplace and entered the opening. He had no idea where he was going, but he was on his way.

He slid through the small entrance to Rat Hell, falling the last several feet when he unexpectedly came out of the hole in the wall. Squealing rats ran in all directions when he hit the straw. He pushed one off his face as he scrambled to stand up.

"I never knew there were this many rats in the world," he thought, "Let alone in Libby!"

He tried to get his bearings, but in the black nothingness of the basement he had no idea where he was. He could see nothing, but he was able to grope his way forward until he encountered another prisoner. At least, he hoped it was another prisoner.

"Who's this?" he inquired as he grasped the unknown man's arm.

"Plympton White," came the answer. "Who are you?"

"It's me...Wells!" said Wells, recognizing the man's name. "Where are we heading?"

"Can't tell," said White, "But there's a line right in front of me. I'm just followin' them."

They shuffled forward to their unknown destination. As they approached the tunnel entrance he could hear those just in front of him whispering. "Here it is," someone said.

"It ain't very big. We're gonna have to do some squeezin'." "Duck down. You have to get down on your belly."

Then, he felt White drop to the floor. Reaching out, Wells felt the wall. He ran his hands down the wall until he felt the opening, just as White's thrashing boots disappeared into the tunnel.

Wells quickly got on his hands and knees and squeezed into the tunnel. He couldn't turn back now, even if he wanted to. He could hear White just ahead of him, and someone was striking his foot from behind. Wells wriggled his way ahead, still not knowing where he was going.

With the tunnel crammed full of escaping prisoners, the air flow was effectively reduced to nearly zero. By the time Wells felt the tunnel rising, he was afraid he was going to pass out. He reached the surface just in time. He felt someone's hands under his arms, lifting him out the final few feet. The rush of cold night air washed over him, reviving him as quickly as it had revived Rose the previous night when the tunnel had punched through.

Wells halted momentarily, reaching down to assist the man behind him. He then followed White's shadowy form to the gate. The two paused only momentarily, then went through the gate, turned left, and calmly disappeared into the night.

Chapter Twenty-one

"Beggin' the Major's pardon, but it looks like we may have a problem on our hands, sir!" said Adjutant Latouche. Latouche had been hastily dispatched by Captain Turner when the Clerk of the Prison was unable to reconcile his count. He knew there had been no repeating this time, though. Ross was coming up short by the same number on every count: 109.

"What kind of problem is that, Adjutant?" Major Turner asked testily. Why did these things always have to happen first thing in the morning, before he had a chance to clear his head and think straight?

"Missing prisoners, sir."

Turner sighed. Escaping prisoners were becoming such a bother again. For a while he thought he had it under control, but the last few weeks had seen an increase in the number of men trying new ways to get out of Libby. What would it be this time? Two more men walking out while wearing dresses? A bribed guard?

"How many this time, Adjutant?" he asked wearily.

"Close as we can tell, sir, there's 109 of 'em missin'," came the answer.

The unexpected number quickly garnered Turner's attention. That many men didn't walk out dressed as women!

"How many?" he asked incredulously.

"About 109, sir," Latouche answered meekly, not knowing what to expect next. Turner's temper was legendary, and he had been known in the past to hold the messenger responsible for any bad news conveyed, simply because there was nobody else in the immediate vicinity to blame.

"How in God's name did 109 men get out of here without anyone seein' them?" Turner bellowed.

"We don't know that yet, sir," answered Latouche, thankful that Turner had refrained from swinging his fist at him, so far at least.

"Well, find out, man! Find out! Don't just stand here makin' excuses! Look around! Do somethin'!" Turner was beside himself with rage.

"Yes, sir," stammered LaTouche. "I... I'll do just that, sir. Right away, sir!"

"And tell Ross I want to see him," screamed Turner. "Now!"

"Yes, sir," said Latouche, scrambling to get out the door before Turner threw something.

"And quit sayin' yes, sir, Adjutant!" Turner spat out with contempt. "Just go do it!"

"Yes, sir," said Latouche over his shoulder, not knowing what else to say.

"Corporal!" Turner bellowed, summoning the corporal of the guard.

The young guard ran into the room. He had seen Turner in this state too many times in the past to risk becoming the recipient of another tongue lashing for being too slow.

"Yes, sir!" he said in his best military tone.

"Corporal, I want you and Captain Turner to take your men and tear this prison apart from top to bottom to find those missin' Yankees," ordered Turner. "Then, get the dogs in here. I want them trackin' those men within the hour. And get word to someone to start ringin' the bell in Capitol Square. If we have Yankees out there runnin' around, the good people of Richmond have a right to know it. And be quick about it!"

"Yes, sir," the young guard said, saluting on the run. In his haste to get to his task he nearly ran headlong into Erastus Ross, on his way to answer Turner's summons. Ross turned to watch the guard sprint out the door, and Turner spied Ross while he was still standing there, shouting at him before he had a chance to even say, "Did you call for me, Major?"

"What's goin' on here, Ross?" Turner shouted. "Can't you keep these men under control?"

Ross did not like Turner to begin with, and he was in no mood to listen to another of the major's tirades this early in the morning. He struggled to keep himself under control.

"All due respect, Major," he began, "My job is just to count them that's here. It's your job to keep 'em under control."

Turner was livid. "I know what my job is, Mr. Ross," he screamed. "I don't need you to tell me. Now, where are those Yankees?"

Ross studied Turner for a moment. It was not difficult to tell that there would be no reasoning with him today.

"Well, Major," said Ross, "I can't tell y'all where they is. I can only tell y'all where they ain't. And they ain't here!"

"Don't you think I know that, Mr. Ross?" said Turner, almost out of control with rage. Ross saw no reason to answer.

Turner began to pace. "Do we know who they are, Ross?"

"Yes, we do, as a matter of fact," said the clerk. "Got their names right here for y'all to look at. Not that it matters much who they are. They still ain't here."

Turner glared at Ross as the clerk handed him a handful of papers. In his anger he grabbed them from Ross, tearing them in the process. Having to hold the torn papers edge to edge so they could be read did not improve his mood. His eyes scanned the list, stopping when they came to Colonel Streight's name.

"Streight!" he spat out venomously. "I should have known he'd be in on something like this!" He crumpled the paper and threw it onto the desk. Whirling around, he said to Ross, "Is there anything else you'd like to add to this conversation, Mr. Ross."

Ross looked at him for several seconds before answering, the look of disgust on his face telling Turner what he needed to know. Finally, Ross spoke, "No, Major. Don't reckon I do."

"Then get out of here and help look for those missin' Yankees. I swear I can't figure out how someone could misplace 109 prisoners and then stand around jawin' about it."

Ross, as a civilian under no obligation to salute Turner, turned to leave.

As an afterthought, Turner called to him, saying, "First, though, get me General Dow. I want to find out just what he knows about this."

Ross exited without saying anything, leaving Turner to wonder if the clerk had heard his last command. Turner got his answer within minutes in the person of the general from Maine.

"Lose something, Major?" asked Dow smugly. His mouth curled in a slight grin. Turner hated him almost as much as he did Colonel Streight.

"This is very unprofessional, General," said Turner. "Your men got out of here somehow, and I want to know how they did it."

Dow was amused to see Turner so upset.

"I'm just as shocked by this as you are, Major Turner," lied Dow. "I didn't know anything about this until the count came up short this morning. Do you know who the men are who escaped?"

"Yes, I do," spat out Turner, "And so do you. Several of them are colonels, includin' your friend Streight. A colonel wouldn't sneak out of here without tellin' you first. We both know that. Now, let me ask you once again. How did they get out, and when?"

Dow was enjoying this conversation more than any other talk he had ever had with Turner. He wasn't about to let Turner off the hook.

"Major Turner," he said softly. "If I knew about this, and I'm not sayin' I did, mind you..., but if I did, do you really think I would tell you anything?"

Turner looked at Dow with no attempt to hide his bitterness. "No, I don't guess you would, General," he said. "A Yankee would never do anything that honorable, not even a Yankee general."

Dow did not fall for Turner's attempt to lure him into saying something to prove he had honor. "You want to think I have no honor, Major Turner, that's fine with me," he said. "Doesn't bother me a bit. It might if I had any respect for you, but we both know I don't, so there's no sense in pretending."

"Well, General," said Turner, slowly beginning to calm down. "That there is somethin' we both agree on, then, ain't it? Neither one of us cares much for the other, I mean."

Dow simply nodded his agreement.

"As long as we both agree on that, then," said Turner, "We can go on with our conversation." He stood and walked to the window. Dow watched him as he stared out at the street for several seconds.

Without looking away from the window, Turner continued. "Y'know, General, I gotta say one thing about you Yankees. Y'all ain't got any honor, but y'all are good at what ya do. We've added iron bars to these windows, increased the number of guards out on the street, done any number of things, just to improve security. And still, 109 of y'all were able to get out. I gotta admire that."

Dow smiled but refrained from speaking. The major appeared to be leading up to something. Dow decided to let him continue.

"Every newspaper in Richmond's been tellin' us about General Morgan and how he escaped from your Yankee jail up in Ohio," Turner went on. "Now I guess they'll have somethin' to say about this. Unfortunately fer me, it probably ain't gonna be very complimentary."

Dow smiled. "I would think it would be very hard to find anything complimentary to say about a prison administration that lets 109 men escape, don't you, Major?"

"They're only out temporarily," snarled Turner as the bells on Capitol Square began their mournful toll. "Y'all hear those bells? Every person in Richmond is gonna know those men are out there. Someone's gonna see 'em. And the dogs are gonna be trackin' 'em very shortly, if they aren't already. Can't none of them get back to your lines before we catch up with 'em. Y'all will be seein' 'em again before nightfall, General. I personally guarantee it!"

Dow smiled again. "I wouldn't count on it too much, Major," he said. "Next time you see those boys'll be when they come back here with their regiments and let the rest of us out."

"I'll blow this place up before I let that happen, General," promised Turner. "I'll fill the basement with explosives and turn every brick in here to powder. And you prisoners, as well, I might add."

Before Dow could respond, the grimy face of one of the guards appeared in the doorway. "Major, sir," he said tentatively, "I think you better come out here and take a look at somethin'. Captain Turner thinks he found out how the Yanks got out!"

* * *

Just before dawn, it had become apparent to many of the prisoners that they would not have sufficient time to go out through the tunnel. A large crowd was still gathered in the kitchen, and it was getting dangerously close to daylight. There would be insufficient time to get clear of the city. They would have to wait until another night. Disappointed, they settled down to close the fireplace opening.

"Guess we'll have to wait 'till tomorrow night," said one dejectedly. He had a young son he had never seen, and his heart had been set on leaving last night. He had to get home!

"I been here nine months, already," responded another. "Another day ain't gonna make much difference."

"I guess you're right," said the first man as he placed the last brick into place. "That just gives the Rebs one more day to torment us, though."

"And to search the prison to find out how the others escaped," said the second.

That was something the first man had not considered. If the guards found the tunnel, there would be no further escapes. At least not through this particular tunnel.

The two worked silently, cleaning up the area. Then, a thought came to the first prisoner.

"Y'know," he said, "If we convince the Rebs the escape took place some other way, they'll quit lookin' for a tunnel."

"They aren't gonna believe anything we tell 'em about an escape," responded his friend.

"Maybe they won't believe anything we say, but they will believe anything they find," said the first with a grin. "What if they find a window with the bars out, or a hole in a wall? Don't you think they'll be sure they found the way out?"

The second quickly agreed, and a plan was hatched to throw the guards off the track, even if only temporarily.

"What are the bells ringing for, James?" Elizabeth Van Lew asked one of her servants.

"Don't rightly know, Miss 'Lizbeth," said the old man, a former slave. "I'll just go and see what I can find out, if y'all would like."

"Would you please?" Elizabeth requested. "Perhaps General Butler has dispatched his troops as I suggested. Richmond may be about to fall!"

"Yes'm," the old man said. "Sho' 'nuff would be a happy day, wouldn't it?"

"That it would, James," she agreed. "You go and see what's happening. Let me know right away. And send Thomas in, would you please?"

"Yes'm," said James as he hurried away.

Thomas, a young black man in his early twenties, entered the room. "James said you wanted to see me, Miss Elizabeth?" he asked.

"Yes, Thomas," Elizabeth replied. "I have a job for you. Do you hear the Capitol Square bells?"

"Yes, ma'am," Thomas answered.

"I've sent James over to find out what it's all about," she said, "But I have a feeling that the Yankees may be on their way."

"Will we be leavin', Miss Elizabeth?" Thomas asked apprehensively.

"Oh, no, Thomas," Elizabeth said with a laugh. "If they come, or maybe I should say, when they come, we will be celebratin', not leavin'! But, at any rate, I have something I'd like you to do for me. Go up to the roof and take a good look at our flag pole. It's been so long since we've used it that I want to make sure it hasn't rotted."

"You plannin' on flyin' a flag again, ma'am?" asked Thomas.

"Not just a flag, Thomas," she said. "I am going to fly THE flag! The stars and stripes! I have a huge flag hidden away upstairs that I smuggled through on my last trip to Washington. I've been waitin' for the day when I could use it. I'll have Sarah fetch it when the time is right. As soon as we know for sure if those bells are right about the Yankees coming!"

Thomas's face broke into a huge grin. "I'll go check it directly, Miss Elizabeth," he said, hurrying out of the room.

Within the hour James had returned. He rushed into the room as quickly as his old legs would allow.

"Miss 'Lizbeth! Miss 'Lizbeth!" he was shouting before he even saw the lady of the house.

"What is it, James? Calm down and tell me," she said.

"You were wrong, Miss 'Lizbeth!" James said excitedly. "The Yankees ain't comin'. Leastways, not the whole Yankee army!"

"What do you mean, James," Elizabeth asked. "If General Butler is not coming, just what is going on that they are ringing that bell?"

"The Yankees...some of 'em done broke out of Libby!" he blurted out. Her face brightened. "Do you know who they are?" she asked.

"No, ma'am," answered James. "Didn't hear no names. But they's an awful lot of 'em, that much I did hear. More than a hundred, I heard one man say!"

"More than a hundred?" Elizabeth exclaimed. "That's wonderful! That means at least some of them are going to probably try to come here. We must get ready for them!"

"Yes, ma'am!" James agreed eagerly. He then laughed and said, "Oh, my, Miss 'Lizbeth. If y'all could only see all those Confederate soldiers runnin' in every direction. Ever'where I looked in town I seen soldiers runnin'. I swear, I think some of 'em was jest runnin' around 'cause everyone else was runnin'. Jest runnin', they was. No place in particular. Jest runnin'."

Elizabeth laughed with James at the thought. She could imagine the scene. She knew how excited Major Turner could get. This would have him near apoplexy!

Escaped prisoners had come to the house on a regular basis in the past, but usually they only escaped in small groups, or even alone. If all of this latest batch came, it would tax the facilities, to say the least. But they would manage.

"Get everybody moving, James," said Elizabeth. "We'll need to get out everything we have stored, for that many men. I'm sure they won't all come here, but even if we only get a few, they will need food, warm clothing,..., you know what we always gather. And we'll have to prepare the secret room in the attic!"

"Yes'm," said James, as Thomas returned to the room.

"Flag pole's in usable condition, Miss Elizabeth," he said. "Should I ask Sarah to fetch the flag?"

"Not yet, Thomas," she answered. "It isn't what I thought. But it's good news, just the same. There has been a large prison break over at Libby. We have to get ready for possible guests."

"More escaped prisoners? Yes, ma'am," said Thomas, his face lighting up. "Shall I prepare the summer house?"

"Yes," agreed Elizabeth. "That would be a good idea. And be sure Mrs. Green is aware of what has happened. Tell her we will probably be needing her help once again." Mrs. Green was an old friend who had assisted Elizabeth in moving escaped prisoners on many previous occasions. They had initially conspired to help escaped slaves get to the North by way of the underground railroad, but had gradually expanded their system to include the men who broke out of Libby, Belle Isle, and the other prisons in and around Richmond. The two had developed quite an extensive network of friends who served as guides and providers of safe houses.

With all the servants setting to their appointed tasks, there was little more to do for the time being. Not much would happen today, but after darkness fell she would be very surprised if she didn't hear the familiar tentative knock on the door. Perhaps, this time, it may even be General Dow himself. She hoped so. She had grown to like the old man, and was concerned for his health.

Although she had done this countless times in the past, she was always nervous about it. Yet, the element of danger excited her. It gave meaning to her life.

She sat down by a window. The first prisoner would be here within the next few hours. There was nothing more to do now but wait.

* * *

"What do ya make of that, Major?" said Captain Turner.

The two Turners, accompanied by a retinue of guards, were looking up at a window on the top floor of the prison. A makeshift rope, consisting of several strips of blanket tied together, was swaying in the morning breeze. It extended from the window to a point only about ten feet above the ground. The window had not yet been barred, and it would have been easy for a man, or 109 men, to squeeze through the window and slide down the rope of blankets.

Major Turner seethed as he looked at what appeared to be the avenue of escape.

"Gotta admit, Major," said Captain Turner admiringly, "It's simple but ingenious."

Major Turner looked at him. "I don't have to admit anything, Captain. The only thing I can think of right now is that 109 men were able to slide down a rope and escape, right under the noses of your so-called sentries. Do you have any idea how long it would take for 109 men to slide down that rope, let alone walk away with nobody seein' 'em?"

Captain Turner had not considered that. He knew immediately that he was in trouble. He cast his eyes downward, dreading Major Turner's next salvo. He didn't have to wait long.

Major Turner's eyes blazed. "Where were your guards while all this was goin' on, Captain? Sleepin' again?"

"No, sir," replied the captain. "I'm sure of that. We got that problem all broke up, I'm positive."

"Then there's only one other explanation, Captain," Major Turner shot back. "Your guards were bribed."

"Oh, I don't think so, sir," said Captain Turner defensively.

"Then you tell me how it happened," the enraged major shouted. "Couldn't have been any other way. I want every guard who was on this side of the prison last night to be arrested! Search 'em for greenbacks! Throw 'em in a cell 'till they decide to tell us the truth!"

Despite their protests, the guards were summarily arrested. Protesting their innocence and correctly insisting that nobody had come down that rope while they were on duty, each man was searched. No greenbacks were found.

The furious Major Turner insisted that the men be imprisoned until they confessed their part in the escape. The perplexed men became the unwitting victims of those whose captivity they had been charged with supervising!

Chapter Twenty-two

"General Wistar," the young captain said crisply.

"Yes, Captain?" answered the general, looking up from his desk at his Yorktown headquarters.

"General, one of our scouts just returned. He reports that the pickets are bringing in two men who claim they are escaped Union officers. The pickets found them wandering around outside town."

"Escaped?" exclaimed the general. "From where?"

"The scout didn't know, sir. He said they were in pretty bad shape and weren't able to talk too well. The pickets are bringing them in now, but he came on ahead to let us know about it."

The general scratched his chin thoughtfully. "Well, let's assume for now they're tellin' the truth," he said. "Get some blankets and some hot food ready for them. We'll talk when they feel up to it. But don't take your eyes off them until we're sure they aren't spies."

"Yes, sir," said the aide, saluting sharply.

Wistar returned the salute, the signal that the aide could leave. When he closed the door, Wistar walked to the window and peered out, looking at nothing in particular. He was confused. He had heard of no officers being captured in the vicinity recently. That would mean that these men, if they were legitimate, had to have escaped from a prison camp. But if they were really officers they would most likely have been kept near Richmond, and that was fifty miles away. Few could survive such a trip in the dead of winter, especially if they had been prisoners. In Wistar's experience, most prisoners were too weak to walk very far even under ideal conditions. He could not imagine a prisoner walking from Richmond to Yorktown, particularly when it would not have been safe for him to travel a direct route.

Wistar got his answer within an hour. As his aide had reported, the pickets arrived with two bedraggled men in what looked like the remnants of Federal uniforms, although they could have been blue rags. The men had already eaten, ravenously by all reports, and had been given time to get warm. They entered General Wistar's office in a nearly exhausted state, but still feeling better than they had in months.

"Welcome to Yorktown, gentlemen, "said Wistar.

"Thank you, sir," the two arrivals answered.

Wistar looked them over from top to bottom, then back again. If these men were spies, they certainly had gone to a lot of trouble to look like authentic escapees. Although still not sure, Wistar was beginning to believe their story.

"Who are you?," he asked. "What are your names?"

"I'm Captain Wallick, Fifty-first Indiana, sir," said the taller of the two. He also appeared to be the one who was in the better condition. "This here's Lieutenant Harris of the Third Ohio. Like we told your pickets, General, we escaped from Libby Prison about five days ago."

"Libby Prison, you say?" said Wistar, deciding to test them with some phony questions to see if they were really who they said they were. "How is my old friend, Congressman Ely?

The two looked at him quizzically, Wallick finally answering, "Congressman Ely was released some time ago, sir."

"Is that a fact?" said Wistar, reigning surprise. "Well, I'm glad to hear that. He shouldn't have been in there in the first place."

The two men stood silently, not feeling obligated to answer.

"Please forgive me, gentlemen," said Wistar, sliding a chair over to Harris and turning to reach for another one. "Would you like to sit down?"

"Thank you, sir," said Harris. "I'd like that a lot."

"I'll bet you would," said Wistar as the two plopped wearily into the chairs. Then, looking at Wallick, Wistar said, "Fifty-first Indiana, right? How about my friend, Colonel Thomas. Haven't seen him since Bull Run. He still in Libby?"

Wallick wanted to ask this man if he truly was General Wistar, but refrained. He certainly wasn't very conversant on either Libby or the fifty-first. "Beggin' your pardon, sir," said Wallick, "But the Fifty-first wasn't at Bull Run. And our colonel is Colonel Streight, not Colonel Thomas. I don't know a Colonel Thomas, leastways not at Libby. How 'bout you, David?"

"Can't recollect 'im," mumbled the exhausted Harris.

"Well, no matter," said Wistar, feeling better about these men now that they had passed his little test. "Maybe I'm thinking of someone else."

"Yes, sir," said Wallick.

"Tell me," said Wistar, "How did you two get out of Libby?"

"There was a tunnel, sir," said Wallick. "We didn't dig it. Colonel Rose did, but we all used it."

Did you say 'all'?" asked Wistar, raising his eyebrows in surprise. "Are you saying everyone in Libby escaped?"

"Not everyone," said Wallick, patiently, "But quite a few. Colonel Streight was one of them. He'll be along shortly, if I know the colonel."

"What about General Dow? Did he get out?" asked Wistar, taking notes as he talked.

"No, sir," said Wallick. "General Dow was a little too weak to make the trip. I mean, he's not real sick or anything. He's just...well, you know. He's not real healthy. But not sick, either, mind you."

Wistar chuckled. "I understand, Captain. I know General Dow. He may have been too weak to make the trip, but don't let his appearance fool you. He's a tough old bird. He'll get along fine."

"Yes, sir," said Wallick, happy that he didn't have to try to explain further.

"Well, do you men need anything?" asked the general. "Other than some new uniforms, I mean. Food? Something to drink?"

"No sir, we're fine," said Wallick. "Your men already fed us."

Harris merely shook his head, too tired to do any more.

"Do you feel up to telling me how you got here, or would you rather rest?" Wistar asked.

"Yes, sir," said Wallick. "We can talk now, if you'd like."

"How 'bout you, Lieutenant?" Wistar asked Harris. He was genuinely concerned about Harris's condition. Wallick's too, for that matter, but Harris was showing the strain of spending five days and nights outside.

"I'll be fine, General. Just a little tired, but I can rest later," he answered.

"Good," commented Wistar. "Then, if you feel up to it, tell me how you were able to get here."

"Maybe I should do that, David. Is that alright with you?" Wallick asked his friend.

"Go right ahead," replied Harris, hoping to minimize any unnecessary exertion.

"Well, sir," began Wallick, "It's like I said. We crawled out through this tunnel Colonel Rose and some of the others dug. It was impressive, I don't mind tellin' you, General. Through a stone wall and clean under the street. Never saw anything like it. At any rate, we crawled out and just walked away when the sentries had their backs turned."

"And you said this took place about five days ago?" interrupted Wistar, still taking notes.

"That's right," said Wallick. "I don't exactly know how many got out, but it was quite a few, like I said earlier. David and me teamed up by accident, just because we got out of the tunnel at the same time. So we left together. We hid during the day and traveled by night. Came close to being seen by some Reb cavalry a few times. We figured they was out lookin' for us, though, and we kept a close watch for 'em."

"What did you eat during all this time?" inquired Wistar.

"Not much of anything, except for the one night when a black family took us in. We didn't stay there too long, other than to eat. They was pretty nervous havin' us around. They said they'd be in real trouble if the Rebs found us there, and we didn't want to cause them any problems. They fed us, then the old man took us around a Reb picket line. If he hadn't helped us, we probably would've stumbled right into 'em. Couple other nights we got us some clams out of the river, but we didn't have nothin' to start a fire with, so we ate 'em raw. Other than that, we didn't eat anything until your men fed us."

"You didn't even have a fire to warm yourselves beside, anytime during the five nights you were travelin'?" asked Wistar, amazed that the men had not succumbed to the elements.

"No, sir," replied Wallick. "It probably would've been too dangerous to build one anyway. Rebs were lookin' pretty hard for us. They would've spotted a fire pretty quick."

"Yeah, I guess that's so," agreed Wistar. "Anything else?"

Wallick thought for a moment. "Nope. I can't think of anything else. Can you, David?"

"Well, we ran into your pickets. Watched 'em for about twenty minutes or so to make sure they were ours. The rest I guess you know," said Harris.

Wistar stood up. "You two have had quite an ordeal," he said. "You should probably get some rest. I'll have one of my aides try to round up some new uniforms for you. Just let us know if you need anything."

"Thank you, sir," the two said in unison. They stood and prepared to leave.

"Feels good to be on the Union side of the line again, sir," said Harris.

"Amen to that," agreed Wallick.

"We're just as glad to have you back," said Wistar. "Now, while you two get some sleep I'll have some troops out lookin' for your friends. By the time you wake up, maybe we'll be fortunate enough to find a few. But, I guess I don't have to tell you, the path for them will be hard."

"Yes, sir," answered Wallick. "But every last man out there was able to get through several months of Libby. They'll be tough enough to make it."

Wistar smiled. "I have no doubts, judging from you two," he said admiringly.

Wallick and Harris saluted, waited for Wistar's return salute, and left the room for their first sleep in a bed in several months.

* * *

"There's a scout here to see you, sir," said the aide. "Says he has some important information, but he won't give it to anybody but you. Should I send him in?"

Wistar looked up at the aide. The general had been busy with eleven more escaped prisoners who had arrived since Wallick and Harris. He also had received a telegram from General Butler stating that Butler had twenty-six escapees at Fort Monroe. That made thirty-nine men who had unbelievably made the trek from Richmond. He rubbed his eyes and sighed before answering the aide.

"Go ahead," he replied. "Send him in."

The aide opened the door and summoned the scout, who had been waiting just outside. The man waited until the aide was gone before speaking. Wistar studied the man carefully. He knew this scout from previous reports, reports which had always proven to be factual.

The scout, tall and lean, stood respectfully at attention until given the signal by General Wistar to relax. He removed his hat, his long, curly hair dropping almost to his shoulders. His face was thin and rugged. Weatherbeaten, some would say. Yet it was a friendly face, with twinkling blue eyes and a ready smile. "General Wistar," the man said softly, "I apologize for barging in here like this, but I have some news that I think you may be interested

"And what might that be?" asked Wistar.

"Well, sir, "the scout began, "I don't know if you've heard yet, but there was a big escape from Libby Prison a few days ago."

"Yes," replied Wistar. "I'm aware of that. I have a detachment out right now trying to find some of them. We have about thirteen of the escapees here already. At least that's the last count I have. The way they're rolling in here we may have more by now."

"Thirteen?" said the scout. "That still leaves a lot of them unaccounted for."

"How do you know that?" asked Wistar, his curiosity piqued.

"I saw a Richmond newspaper the other day," said the scout. "Said about 109 men got out. You got thirteen. That still leaves a bunch, don't it?"

"General Butler has twenty-six of them at Fort Monroe, but, as you say, that does still leave a bunch," said Wistar. "Did you bring a copy of the paper with you?"

"No, sir," the scout admitted. "Wasn't mine to take, and I couldn't find another one. I waited around till the feller was finished, so I could pick it up, but he took it with him."

"You know this territory pretty well, don't you?" asked Wistar.

"Like my own property, sir," the man stated proudly.

"If you were on foot, coming from Libby, what route would you take?" asked Wistar.

"Well, sir," the man said, rubbing his chin with his hand, "I believe I'd try to follow the Chickahominy as close as I could. Trouble is, all the usual crossin's are watched real careful by Hume's scouts."

Wistar agreed with the route, but felt the Union presence in the area could offset Hume's troops. "We aren't the only ones out lookin' for the escapees, y'know. General Butler has cavalry patrols roaming up the Peninsula to the Chickahominy, and I think he has a gunboat cruisin' the Chickahominy and the James. If any of the prisoners can get that far, either Butler's troops or mine should be able to find them."

"Yer right, General," agreed the scout. "But, there's a lot of Rebs'll be out there lookin' fer them, too. They're gonna have to be careful. They probably know about the scouts and pickets at the upper fords and bridges. But...if they can come down parallel with Charles City Road, and if they can find boats on the Lower Chickahominy, they got a chance. Only trouble is, the Rebs take those boats about as fast as they're put there, to keep runaways from usin' them. They could still do what a lot of the darkies do, and swim across. But I don't know as I'd want to be the one doin' the swimmin' this time of year."

"What you are sayin' then is, that they have a better chance of gettin' here safely if they don't try to cross at the upper end of the Chickahominy, and even then they'll have to be lucky. Am I hearin' you right?" asked Wistar.

"Yes, sir," answered the scout. "That's the way I see it."

Wistar sat quietly, thinking about the best deployment of his troops. Finally, he spoke. "You aren't very encouraging, you know that, don't you?"

"Ain't tryin' to be discouragin', sir," said the man. "Just tellin' you how I see it, and how I'd try to get here. One thing's sure, though. It ain't impossible. If it was, you wouldn't have any of 'em here, now would you?"

"No," agreed Wistar. "I guess you're right about that. But it still doesn't sound real good. If one-fourth of 'em get through, I'll be surprised. The Rebs are gonna have a pretty well-organized effort to get 'em back, and those men who escaped aren't gonna be in the best physical shape, either."

"One-fourth, you think?" asked the scout.

"Just a guess, but I can't see too many more makin' it safely to our lines," confirmed Wistar.

"Well, General," said the scout. "I ain't the best person around with ciphers, but if you got thirteen of 'em, and if General Butler has twenty-six, that's thirty-nine men already, and they're just startin' to arrive. You're already over one-fourth, the way I figure it."

"Yes, I guess you're right, at that," said Wistar, giving consideration to the numbers. "This is one time I'm glad to be wrong. But I'm still afraid they won't all make it."

"Maybe not, sir," said the scout, "But they're off to a pretty good start, you gotta admit."

* * *

Within twenty-four hours of the arrival of Wallick and Harris, Wistar has calculated that possibly fifty of the escapees have somehow managed to reach Union lines. Maybe he was wrong. Maybe, by some stroke of good fortune, every one of them was going to make it to safety.

"Telegram from Colonel Shaffer, sir," said the young aide, interrupting Wistar's thoughts.

"Thank you, Captain," said Wistar, taking the telegram and tearing it open. Colonel John Shaffer was Chief of Staff of the Army of the James, and a telegram from him merited rapid action. Wistar read it carefully, then smiled. "He's gonna do it!" Wistar said out loud, not realizing the captain was still in the room. "That devious rascal is gonna do it!"

"Sir?" queried the Captain, not sure if he was expected to respond or not.

Wistar looked up in surprise, seeing the captain. "Oh, I'm sorry, Captain," he apologized, still grinning. "It's just this telegram. It says that Colonel Abel Streight is safe but hiding somewhere in Richmond. Colonel Shaffer says Abel's friends want us to announce to the press that he has made it back safely to Union lines. 'For obvious reasons', Colonel Shaffer says. I'll say it's obvious! The Rebs hate 'im. They won't care if the other 108 get away if they can recapture Abel. So if we announce that he's safe, maybe they'll quit lookin' for 'im. When that happens, you watch and see if old Abel doesn't just come marchin' in here some fine morning. I can almost hear his voice already, tellin' me how this place should be run."

"Yes, sir," replied the Captain.

"He's probably sittin' somewhere right now, just watchin'those Rebs huntin' for 'im," exclaimed Wistar. "He's probably darin' 'em to find 'im. I almost wish I was there with 'im, just so I could watch."

The Captain smiled, obviously enjoying seeing his general in such a good mood. "How should we announce it, sir?" he asked.

"What's that, Captain?" asked Wistar absentmindedly, still thinking about his friend Colonel Streight and the consternation he must have brought to the Confederate prison authorities.

"The message that Colonel Streight is safe, sir. How should we announce it?" the captain repeated.

"Oh," said Wistar, coming back to reality. "Well, I guess we should just tell the Associated Press agent. He can take it from there."

"Yes, sir," said the captain, preparing to leave.

"One more thing, Captain," said Wistar. "After you've gotten in touch with the agent, gather the rest of the staff and come on back in. There's something I want to tell all of you."

"Yes, sir," repeated the aide, closing the door behind him.

Wistar paused, thinking again about Colonel Streight. Then he read the telegram once more. The escape was going extremely well.

* * *

The knock on the door woke him. Wistar apparently had dozed off. He hadn't slept much since the prisoners had begun arriving.

"Come in," he responded drowsily, rubbing his eyes.

It was the captain returning, with the rest of the staff following behind.

"I got the message off to the Associated Press, sir," the captain stated. "And here's another telegram from Colonel Shaffer. You may want to read this before you say anything to the staff."

Wistar took the telegram and read it. His expression became grim as he absorbed Colonel Shaffer's words: "Richmond papers of 12th, received, say 109 prisoners escaped, and that 25 were recaptured, none less than 20 miles from Richmond. All of them must have crossed the Chickahominy. Have you anything further in regard to them. Many of them must still be secreted in the woods." Twenty-five recaptured...the words echoed inside his head. They would not all make it safely back, after all.

Wistar stood, tossing the telegram onto his desk. He surveyed his staff, all good men. He did not speak immediately, choosing instead to look into each face, every pair of eyes. Finally, he sighed, then spoke softly.

"Gentlemen, I asked you all to come in so I could give you some good news. However, this latest telegram from Colonel Shaffer is to the contrary. I must be fair with you and tell you the bad news as well. Colonel Shaffer reports that 25 of the escaped prisoners have been recaptured."

A soft murmur went through the assembled staff, a murmur of disbelief, of disappointment, of anger.

"But," continued Wistar, "He also reports that every one of them got at least twenty miles from Richmond before they were caught. They must have given the Rebs fits! I don't know who these men are, yet, but I'm extremely proud of them. And you should be, too."

The men stood in silence, watching their leader as he struggled with his emotions.

Taking a deep breath, General Wistar clasped his hands behind his back and continued. "The good news is that as many as fifty of the prisoners may have reached the safety of our pickets. And there are still a lot of them out there. Between our troops and General Butler's, I'm sure we'll find more of them very shortly."

He paused as the men expressed their pleasure at this latest update.

"Now," he went on, "For what I originally called you all in here for. This is confidential, but I trust all of you enough to know that it won't leave this room."

He paused again, groping for the proper words that would convey the importance of what he was about to say. He walked around to the front of his desk and leaned against it.

"Gentlemen," he began, "Within the next few weeks, our army will be conducting the largest rescue mission ever undertaken. A mass rescue of all the prisoners in Richmond is going to be attempted. The raid will be made on every prison in Richmond, and will result in the release of thousands of our boys, officers and enlisteds alike. This escape that just took place was made by 109 brave men who didn't have any way of knowing about the coming rescue. It's up to us to see to it that as many of these escapees are successful as possible. If we can do that, every one of you is going to be a part of history. This escape is going to be a fitting prelude to the raid, and some day you will be able to tell your children and their children that you helped in their rescue. I predict, gentlemen, that this escape, and the coming raid, will demoralize the Confederacy so badly that you will see the end of the war very shortly. And history will show that the tunnel those 109 brave officers dug was the start of it all!"

Epilogue

Of the 109 who escape from Libby Prison on February 9, 1864, 48 are successful in reaching Union lines. Few of those who make their way out through the tunnel do so without being bitten by the rats in Rat Hell. Among those reaching safety are Hamilton and Wells.

The prisoners who were unable to get out through the tunnel would report that they were told the next day by several guards that the guards had seen the men exiting through the gate but didn't bother them. They assumed it was their own men sneaking out after stealing items from the prisoners' packages.

Colonel Streight, as was feared by several in the tunnel digging party, does get stuck in the tunnel. He strips most of his clothes off to pass through the tunnel, pushing them ahead of him as he makes his way through. He becomes wedged at the point where the tunnel begins its upward climb, but with the help of others he is able to free himself and get through the tunnel successfully. Along with three others, he makes his way to a house near Howard's Grove, where Union sympathizers hide him for more than a week. With the newspapers announcing that he has safely made it to Union lines, the Confederate army quits looking for him, at which time Mrs. Green leads the four out of the city to Blackstone Island, in the Potomac River. There, they are rescued by the USS *Ella*.

When the initial announcement of the escape is reported in the Richmond *Examiner* on February 11, 1864, the bitterness of the Confederates toward Streight is emphasized. The newspaper reports the escape as follows: "The following is a list of the principal officers who escaped, and their rank. Among them we regret to have to class the notorious Colonel Streight."

Several of the men would report having been aided in their flight by black families, who feed and shelter them, and in some instances act as guides. At least one, Wells, is helped by a farmer who had fought for the Confederacy. Telling Wells he is aware that Wells has escaped from Libby Prison, he nonetheless cannot bring himself to turn a hungry man away. Wells and Lieutenant Randolph are rescued by a detachment from the 11th Pennsylvania Cavalry. When rescued, both men are delirious from fatigue, cold, and hunger, and Wells is unable to remember his own brother's name.

Two of the escapees drown in their attempt to reach Union lines, and the remaining 59 are recaptured, including Colonel Rose. Rose is captured by several Confederate soldiers wearing stolen Federal uniforms. Seeing the men, he believes he has been rescued and makes no attempt to get away, realizing his mistake when they point their guns at him. Several others who are recaptured would tell similar stories, with many of them within sight of Union pickets when recaptured.

The recaptured prisoners are placed in the cells in the basement of Libby Prison, getting only minimal rations while confined there. Ice and water from the James River often washes into the cells during high tide, forcing the prisoners to live in up to two feet of water. Rose himself spends 38 days in the dungeon, subsisting on a diet consisting exclusively of corn bread and water. When released from his cell, his hair, beard, and clothing are covered with mold from the dampness. Rose would be exchanged for a Confederate colonel on April 30, 1864, rejoining the 77th Pennsylvania Infantry on July 6 and serving with them until the end of the war. He would then serve in the regular army until 1894.

Those who knew Rose before his imprisonment would see a major change in his personality after his release. They would report that his generally calm demeanor had been lost forever, replaced by a more emotional disposition. He would be described by close friends as being somewhat paranoid as a result of his experiences in Libby, suspicious of others, easily upset, and given to periods of depression.

General Dow would be exchanged on March 14, 1864, some five weeks after the tunnel escape, for W. H. F. Lee, Robert E. Lee's second eldest son. Dow, raised in a Quaker family, would be dismissed from the Society of Friends for having taken part in the war. Although his fellow prisoners feared for his health, he would live until 1897, when he died at the age of 93.

After the war General Dow and Colonel Streight would accuse Lieutenant Colonel Sanderson of revealing escape plans to the Confederates. Sanderson would be arrested for aiding the enemy and dismissed from the army without a trial. He would demand, and get, an investigation of the charges against him. An informal commission would find him innocent of the Libby charges, as well as charges of cruelty at Belle Isle.

Of the prison officials, General Winder would die of a heart attack on February 7, 1865. He is replaced by Brigadier General Gideon Pillow. Major Turner would flee to Mexico after the fall of Richmond. Eventually he returns to New Orleans and becomes a dentist. Erastus Ross, the prison clerk, would become a clerk at Richmond's famed Spotswood Hotel after the war. The hotel was to burn down in the mid-1870's. Ross would die in the fire.

Elizabeth Van Lew hides several prisoners in a secret room in her attic. Although the Confederates search her home, they never discover either the room or the escapees. After the war, Van Lew would be appointed postmistress of Richmond by President U. S. Grant, as a reward for her work as a spy. Her neighbors, however, would treat her with disdain for the rest of her life, often crossing the street to avoid talking to her. Van Lew would die in 1900, at which time her home would be torn down to make way for the construction of a school. The demolition workers discover a secret tunnel which historians believe had been used by Van Lew to move escapees and runaway slaves out of Richmond. Van Lew is buried in Shockhoe Hill Cemetery in Richmond. The site of her home is unmarked.

The outside help for which the Libby prisoners had hoped, and which had been announced by General Wistar to his staff, would arrive some three weeks after the escape in the form of a raid led by Brigadier General Judson Kilpatrick and Colonel Ulric Dahlgren. As the raiders approach Richmond, prison officials place 200 pounds of powder inside the prison and threaten to blow it up if an escape is attempted. The planned escape never materializes, as Dahlgren is killed, and Confederates say papers found on his body outline plans to free all the prisoners in Richmond and kill the members of the Confederate government. Union officials would deny the plot. Dahlgren's body is put on public display in the York River Railroad Station, where it is desecrated and ultimately buried without so much as a coffin. Elizabeth Van Lew would get the body secretly moved and properly buried, and Jefferson Davis himself would eventually have the body returned to the young man's grieving family.

Shortly before the escape, Confederate General John Hunt Morgan, who himself had recently escaped from a Northern prison in Columbus, Ohio, visits Libby Prison. His tour reveals to him the conditions in which the prisoners are living, leading him to raise charges against the commissary department. A subsequent inquiry would uncover that the quartermaster had misappropriated money paid by the government to feed and care for the prisoners. He would be relieved from duty.

Libby Prison would continue as a permanent Confederate prison for only a few more months after the escape. In May, 1864, most of the men still imprisoned there would be moved to a new prison near Macon, Georgia. One of those transferred would be 2nd Lieutenant John Mitchell of the 79th Illinois Infantry. Mitchell had been one of those who had dug the tunnels, and would have gone out with the first thirteen. However, he fell victim to the rigors of his effort, collapsing before the escape began. He would remain unconscious for several days, not regaining his health until long after the escape was history.

Prior to their departure for Macon, the prisoners would destroy their remaining rations, furniture, and anything else that they thought could be of use to their captors. Their new prison, a three-acre enclosure on a fairground just east of Macon, would become known as Camp Oglethorpe. No records of this prison have ever been found.

After Richmond was taken over by the Union, Libby ironically became a prison for captured Confederates. It subsequently would revert to its original use as a warehouse. It would be purchased in 1887 by a group of Chicago businessmen, who would have it razed and shipped by rail to Chicago, where it is reconstructed to house a Civil War museum. It would open in 1889 and become especially profitable during the 1893 World's Fair. It would be torn down again in 1895, with many of its materials used in the construction of the Chicago Coliseum and the Chicago Historical Society's Civil War Room. Many of the remaining bricks and timbers are purchased by State Senator Charles Danielson, who uses them to build a barn in Starke County, Indiana. Over the years the barn draws a great deal of attention until its owners have it razed for the final time in 1960.

The tunnel would be quickly discovered by Confederate authorities, but it would be some time before they would learn how the prisoners had been able to pass from the kitchen to Rat Hell. The admiring Confederates would put the tunnel on display, billing it as the "Great Yankee Wonder."

Appendix

Complete records of the individuals involved in the escape have never been found. Several attempts at tabulating the names of the participants were made in the late 1800's and early 1900's, but by that time several of the participants had died. Those still alive had forgotten many details, or never knew them in the first place. As a result, early lists were highly inaccurate and incomplete. In fact, based on those earlier lists, scholars have not been able to reach agreement on exactly how many of the escapees were successful and how many were recaptured, although the total number who attempted the escape is generally accepted at 109. Published estimates of the number who were successful in reaching Union lines range from 48 to 59. A comprehensive study of files, letters, and records has resulted in the following tabulation of 107 names, believed to be the most accurate listing available of those who participated in the mass escape from Libby Prison on February 9, 1864. Unfortunately, the names of the remaining two escapees, those who drowned, are believed lost to history.

ADAMS, WESLEY R., Captain, 89th Ohio Infantry, Company K

Captured at Chickamauga, September 20, 1863. Successfully escaped at age of 26, reaching Union lines at Williamsburg on February 19. Escaped with Lt. Edgar Higby and Lt. Edward Scott. Suffered from nervous debility, diseases of the stomach and liver, and jaundice as a result of his confinement. A farmer as a civilian, he also served in the 27th Ohio Infantry and the 175th Ohio Infantry. Promoted to colonel November 9, 1864 and resigned on November 16, 1864.

BASSETT, MARK M., 1st Lieutenant, 53rd Illinois Infantry, Company E
Captured at Jackson, Mississippi, July 12 or 13, 1863. Recaptured on his fourth night out after the Libby escape. Transferred to Macon, Georgia May 7, 1864, and from there to Columbia, South Carolina, from where he eventually escaped. Promoted to captain but not mustered. Discharged April 12, 1865.

BEADLE, MARCUS, 1st Lieutenant, 123rd New York Infantry, Company I
Captured at Gettysburg, July 2, 1863 while on a night reconnaissance of the enemy's works. Recaptured after Libby escape attempt. Was 29 years old at time of escape. Hospitalized February 20, 1864 for rheumatism. Transferred to Macon, Georgia, May 7, 1864 and from there to Columbia, South Carolina. Escaped February 14, 1865 at Winnsboro, South Carolina. Mustered out June 8, 1865, near Washington, D.C. Had been wounded previously at Chancellorsville, May, 1863. Also had prior service in First United States Infantry as provost, from January 10, 1861 to June 29, 1862. Worked as a brickmaker in civilian life.

BENNETT, FRANK T., 2nd Lieutenant, 18th U.S. Regulars, Company F
Captured at Chickamauga, September 19, 1863. Recaptured after Libby escape, transferred to Macon, Georgia, May 7, 1864. Released December 10, 1864, suffering from Bright's disease and rheumatism. Age 24 at time of escape attempt. Brevetted 1st lieutenant June 26, 1863 for gallantry and meritorious service at Hoover's Gap, Tennessee, and captain September 20, 1863 for gallantry and meritorious service at Chickamauga. Also served in 2nd U.S. Cavalry, 9th U.S. Cavalry, 36th U.S. Infantry, and 39th U.S. Infantry, retiring from military service as a major. Was active in the Libby Prison minstrel troupe. He later required surgery for what was described at the time as a large tumor, and died June 21, 1894 in San Francisco, of cerebral apoplexy, at the age of 54.

BOYD, JOSEPH FULTON, Lieutenant Colonel, 20th Army Corps
Captured at Dunlap, Tennessee, October 2, 1863. Successfully escaped from Libby with Lieutenant Colonel Harrison Hobart and Lieutenant Colonel Theodore West. From Ohio, he also served as quartermaster of volunteers for the 20th Army Corps, chief quartermaster of the 23rd Army Corps, chief quartermaster of the Army in the Field, and chief quartermaster of the Department and Army of the Ohio. Promoted to colonel, June 21, 1865. Brevetted brigadier general, USV (War Service) March 13, 1865. Was given special mention in official reports of the Battles of Stones River and Chickamauga for his devotion to duty, gallantry in action, and intelligence on the field. Mustered out March 13, 1866.

BOYD, MATTHEW, Captain, 73rd Indiana Infantry, Company B

Captured at Rome, Georgia, May 3, 1863. Successfully escaped from Libby at age of 26, rejoining his company on April 21, 1864. His resignation was requested and received July 25, 1864 for alleged incompetency. Boyd chose not to dispute the charges. Died August 8, 1893.

BRADFORD, ROBERT Y., 1st Lieutenant, 2nd West Tennessee Cavalry, Company B

Captured at Jackson, Tennessee, June 29, 1863. Successfully escaped from Libby. Had also been captured December 20, 1862 at Trenton, Tennessee, being paroled the next day. Was captured a third time just six weeks after escaping from Libby, at Union City, Tennessee on March 24, 1864. He escaped three days later at Trenton. Died while still in service February 3, 1865 at Paducah, Kentucky, of pneumonia.

BROWN, JAMES P., 2nd Lieutenant, 15th U.S. Infantry, Company F

Captured at Chickamauga, September 20, 1863. Recaptured after Libby escape at age of 19. Transferred to Macon, Georgia, May 7, 1864, and from there to either Charleston or Columbia, South Carolina, from where he was paroled. Brevetted 1st lieutenant for gallantry and meritorious service at Chickamauga. Promoted to 1st lieutenant August 15, 1864 and to captain of Company A on August 15, 1867. From Ohio, he had also served in 8th Ohio Infantry from April to August, 1861. Had suffered wound of throat, date and place unknown. Died June 9, 1875 of consumption.

CALDWELL, DAVID S., Captain, 123rd Ohio Infantry, Company H

Captured at Winchester, Virginia, June 15, 1863, with nearly his entire regiment. This was his (and his regiment's) first battle. Escaped from Libby at age 42. Rejoined his regiment March 30, 1864. Elected by other prisoners to serve as unofficial chaplain of Libby Prison. Discharged July 24, 1864.

CHAMBERLAIN, HENRY B., Captain, 97th New York Infantry, Company I

Captured at Gettysburg, July 2, 1863. Successfully escaped from Libby at age of 27. Wounded at Weldon Railroad, Virginia, August 19, 1864. Mustered out February 25, 1865. Served in marines (1857-1859), 34th New York Infantry (June to November, 1861) and as lieutenant in the 108th U.S. Colored Infantry from August 17, 1865 to March 21, 1866. Died June 20, 1877.

CLARK, TERRENCE, Captain, 79th Illinois Infantry, Company A

Captured at Chickamauga, September 20, 1863. In both original and final tunnel groups. Successfully escaped. Promoted to major, March 21, 1864 and to lieutenant colonel, September 5, 1864. Resigned January 24, 1865 and became a highly successful banker in civilian life. Died of heart disease December 19, 1909 in Metcalfe, Illinois.

COLLINS, JOSEPH P., Major, 29th Indiana Infantry
Captured at Chickamauga, September 20, 1863. Successfully escaped from Libby. Had also served as captain of Company D. Was mentioned in official report of the Battle of Stones River for "...fighting nobly and gallantly ..." after he took command when his lieutenant colonel became separated from the regiment. Was also singled out in the *Official Records* for his coolness and general gallantry at Chickamauga. Died of typhoid fever October 5, 1864 at Chattanooga, Tennessee.

CRAWFORD, HENRY B., 1st Lieutenant, 2nd Illinois Cavalry, Company M
Captured at Hernando, Mississippi, June 19, 1863 while on a scouting mission. Recaptured after Libby escape. Was 41 years old at time of escape. Transferred to Macon, Georgia, May 7, 1864 and from there to Charleston, South Carolina. Exchanged March 25, 1865. Promoted to captain and discharged June 24, 1865. Had been hospitalized November 9, 1863 for rheumatism and again July 21, 1864 for dysentery, both for unknown periods of time. Was a physician in civilian life. His name appears in some records as Henry P. Crawford, and in others as H. J. Crawford.

CUMMINGS, THOMAS, Captain, 19th U.S. Infantry, Company A
Captured at Chickamauga, September 20, 1863, where he was also wounded. From Pennsylvania. Recaptured after Libby escape. Paroled March 26, 1864. Brevetted major September 20, 1863 for gallantry and meritorious service at Chickamauga. Cashiered December 31, 1869, reinstated on unassigned list March 28, 1870. Resigned July 15, 1870.

DAILY, WILLIAM A., 1st Lieutenant, 8th Pennsylvania Cavalry, Company H
Captured at Warrenton (Sulphur Springs), Virginia, October 12, 1863. Recaptured after Libby escape. Age 26. Transferred to Macon, Georgia, May 7, 1864, and from there to Columbia, South Carolina, from where he was paroled December 10, 1864. Returned to regiment January 18, 1865. Had also served as 2nd lieutenant in Company M, and had been charged with being AWOL while on march, from June 18, 1863 to July 12, 1863. Mustered out January 23, 1865, to date January 15.

DAVIS, GEORGE C., Captain, 4th Maine Infantry, Company F
Captured at Gettysburg, July 2, 1863. Successfully escaped from Libby. Age 22 at time of escape. Suffered wounds at Fredericksburg while leading his company in the assault on Marye Heights, December 13, 1862. Mustered out with regiment. Died in 1911.

DAY, ROBERT H., Captain, 56th Pennsylvania Infantry, Company D
Captured at Gettysburg, July 2, 1863. Recaptured after the Libby escape. Transferred to Macon, Georgia, May 7, 1864, and was moved from there

to Columbia, South Carolina. Sent north December 8, 1864 and was discharged January 10, 1865. Had been wounded in hip and back at Second Bull Run, August 29, 1862.

EARLE, CHARLES W., 2nd Lieutenant, 96th Illinois Infantry, Company C

Captured at Missionary Ridge, Tennessee, September 22, 1863. Successfully escaped from Libby and was rescued by the 1st New York Rifles. Promoted to 1st lieutenant January 8, 1865. Also served as adjutant. Brevetted captain for gallantry and meritorious service at Chickamauga, Resaca, Atlanta, Franklin, and Nashville. Mustered out June 10, 1865 and became a physician in Chicago.

EDMONDS, CHARLES L., 1st Lieutenant, 67th Pennsylvania, Company D

Captured at Winchester, Virginia, June 15, 1863. Recaptured after Libby escape. Transferred to Macon, Georgia, May 7, 1864 from where he escaped in August, 1864. Age 39 at time of Libby escape attempt. Employed as a foundryman before war. Mustered out December 18, 1864. Died in Philadelphia on March 12, 1890 of injuries suffered in a fall from B & O Railroad bridge at age of 55. Buried in National Cemetery at Germantown, Pennsylvania. Name appears in some military records as Charles L. Edwards.

ELY, WILLIAM GROSVENOR, Colonel, 18th Connecticut Infantry

Captured at Winchester, Virginia, June 15, 1863 when surrounded during retreat. Approximately 800 of his men, including 33 commissioned officers, were captured. Recaptured after Libby escape. Paroled March 21, 1864. Had his horse killed under him and was wounded in throat at Piedmont, Virginia on June 4, 1864. Wounded again at Lynchburg, Virginia, June 18, 1864. Discharged September 18, 1864. Also served in 1st Connecticut Volunteers and 6th Connecticut Volunteers, and commanded Second Brigade, Second (Milroy's) Division, Eighth Army Corps. Wrote history of the 18th Connecticut Volunteers. Brevetted brigadier general, USV, March 13, 1865.

FALES, JAMES M., 2nd Lieutenant, 1st Rhode Island Cavalry, Company D

Captured near Middleburg, Virginia, June 18, 1863. Was on special duty in command of Company D when captured but normally was assigned to Company F. Recaptured after Libby escape. Transferred to Macon, Georgia, May 7, 1864, escaping again a month later by jumping off train while being transported to Charleston, S.C. Recaptured again. Returned to Libby Prison via Danville Prison, February 18, 1865. Paroled February 22, 1865 and admitted to hospital for unknown ailment. Mustered out March 6, 1865. Had also served as sergeant in Company E.

FISHER, BENJAMIN FRANKLIN, Major, U.S. Signal Corps
Captured near Aldie, Virginia, June 17, 1863. Successfully escaped from Libby. Forced to march at bayonet point for two hours when he arrived at Libby, for resisting confiscation of his war souvenirs. Wounded in wrist and stomach when shot by Libby guard for standing too close to window. Had also served in 3rd Pennsylvania Volunteer Infantry. Served as chief of Signal Corps. Appointment expired July 28, 1866, but not relieved from duty until November 15, 1866. Promoted to colonel December 3, 1864. Brevetted lieutenant colonel August 1, 1864 and brigadier general U.S. Volunteers (War Service), March 13, 1865. Died in 1900.

FISLAR, JOHN C., 1st Lieutenant, Indiana Light Artillery, 7th Battery
Captured at Chickamauga, September 20, 1863. Was selected by Rose and Hamilton to be a part of both the original and final tunnel groups. Successfully escaped from Libby at age of 24. Mustered out December 7, 1864.

FITZSIMMONS, GEORGE W., Major, 30th Indiana Infantry
Captured at Chickamauga, September 20, 1863. In both original and final tunnel groups. Successfully escaped from Libby. Had also been captured and exchanged at Stones River, December 31, 1862. Recommended by his lieutenant colonel for court-martial, alleging that Fitzsimmons was intoxicated during the Battle of Chickamauga, and that he hid behind a tree until captured, rather than attempting to rally his troops. Resigned July 21, 1864.

FLANSBURG, DAVID S., Captain, 4th Indiana Independent Battery, Light Artillery.
Captured at Chickamauga, September 20, 1863. Was wounded at time of capture. Was from Michigan. Recaptured after Libby escape at age of 32. Transferred to Macon, Georgia, May 7, 1864 and from there to Columbia, South Carolina. Still a prisoner, he died at Columbia on November 15, 1864 of dysentery.

FOSTER, ELI, 2nd Lieutenant, 30th Indiana Infantry, Company G
Captured at Chickamauga, September 20, 1863. In final tunnel party only. Successfully escaped at age of 34. Reached Union lines wearing a Confederate uniform, for which he had traded with a slave to become less conspicuous while traveling. Was told by Major General Butler himself to get a "more Christian-like uniform" from the quartermaster before departing. Mustered out September 29, 1864.

GAGEBY, JAMES H., 2nd Lieutenant, 19th U.S. Infantry, Company A
Captured at Chickamauga, September 20, 1863. Recaptured, with Lieutenant Adam Hauf and Captain Edmund Smith, at Charles City Cross-

roads after escape attempt and placed in cell for eight days upon return to Libby. Transferred to Macon, Georgia, May 7, 1864, and from there to Charleston and Columbia, South Carolina. Brevetted 1st lieutenant for gallantry and meritorious service at Hoover's Gap, and captain for gallantry and meritorious service at Battle of Chattanooga. Released on parole May, 1865. Had also served in 3rd Pennsylvania Infantry, April to July, 1861. Transferred from 19th U.S. Infantry to 3rd U.S. Infantry in 1869. Promoted to major of 12th U.S. Infantry, July 4, 1892. From Pennsylvania. Died July 13, 1896 and is buried in Grandview Cemetery in Johnstown, Pennsylvania with mother and two sisters, all of whom drowned in the Johnstown Flood of 1889.

GALLAGHER, JOHN, Captain, 2nd Ohio Infantry, Company B

Captured at Chickamauga, September 20, 1863. In both original and final tunnel parties. Successfully escaped from Libby at age of 31. Mustered out with regiment on October 10, 1864. Although Andrew Hamilton claimed Gallagher was a stone mason, he was actually a carpenter in civilian life. Name also appears as Gallaher in some records.

GALLAGHER, MICHAEL, Captain, 2nd New Jersey Cavalry, Company H

Captured at Fairfax Courthouse, Virginia, October 18, 1863. Successfully escaped from Libby, only to be killed at Egypt Station, Mississippi, December 28, 1864. Buried at Corinth National Cemetery, Section C, Grave 1.

GAMBLE, SAMUEL, 1st Lieutenant, 63rd Pennsylvania Infantry, Company D

Captured at Harper's Ferry, Virginia, July 19, 1863. Recaptured after Libby escape and transferred to Macon, Georgia, May 7, 1864. Escaped again that same month. Had been wounded at Fair Oaks, Virginia, May 31, 1862 and at Peach Tree Creek, Georgia, July, 1864. Discharged April 26, 1865. Died in Pittsburgh, December 31, 1904.

GARBET, DAVID, 2nd Lieutenant, 77th Pennsylvania Infantry, Company G

Captured at Chickamauga, September 20, 1863. In both original and final tunnel parties. Recaptured. Transferred to Macon, Georgia, May 7, 1864. Paroled March 1, 1865. Promoted to 1st lieutenant July 7, 1864 and to captain March, 1865 while still awaiting muster as 1st lieutenant. Discharged March 15, 1865.

GATES, JUNIUS, Captain, 33rd Ohio Infantry, Company K

Captured at Chickamauga, September 20, 1863. Recaptured after escape from Libby, at age of 30. Transferred to Macon, Georgia, May 7, 1864, from where he escaped in November, 1864. Had been placed in hospital December 26, 1863 for rheumatism and hepatitis. Had also served as 1st lieutenant in Company F prior to his promotion to captain of Company K. Mustered out with company, July 12, 1865, and returned to his profession as a school teacher.

GAY, FREEMAN C., 2nd Lieutenant, 11th Pennsylvania Infantry, Company K

Captured at Gettysburg, July 1, 1863, where he was wounded. Recaptured after Libby escape attempt when the skiff he was using to cross the Appomattox River capsized. He remained in the water for approximately 30 minutes, immersed up to his chin. Was taken back to Libby and thrown into dungeon in his wet clothes, where he remained for two weeks. Transferred to Macon, Georgia, May 7, 1864 and from there to Charleston, South Carolina. After several months, moved again to Columbia, South Carolina, from where he escaped. After 18 days he was recaptured near Guilders Creek, East Tennessee. Was placed in stockade at Columbia. Caught typhoid around October 15, 1864 and was confined for six weeks. Sent to Rolla stockade, and from there to Goldsboro, North Carolina, from where he was paroled March 1, 1865. Had also been badly wounded at Antietam (in neck) and Fredericksburg (bad wound of right hip when hit by shell). Was sent to Washington for four weeks to recover from hip wound suffered at Fredericksburg, but he would be partially paralyzed after his recovery. He also suffered from seizures after release from prison. Discharged by special order, May 28, 1865. Was from Greensburg, Pennsylvania. Worked as a farmer before the war and as a clerk after. Died October 11, 1900.

GOOD, GEORGE S., 1st Lieutenant, 84th Pennsylvania Infantry, Company I

Captured at Mine Run, Virginia, November 30, 1863. Recaptured after Libby escape. Had also been wounded and captured previously at Chancellorsville, May 3, 1863. Paroled and exchanged on April 30, 1864. Discharged December 31, 1864.

GREBLE, CHARLES E., 1st Lieutenant, 8th Michigan Cavalry, Company E

Captured at Knoxville, Tennessee, November 18, 1863. Recaptured after escape from Libby at age of 29. Transferred to Macon, Georgia, May 7, 1864. Transferred again to Columbia, South Carolina, from were he is believed to have escaped. Returned to regiment, April 21, 1865. Promoted to captain, August 31, 1863 and mustered November 21, 1863. Discharged July 20, 1865 at Pulaski, Tennessee. He suffered from rheumatism as a result of his time in Libby, which resulted in partial paralysis. He died on February 27, 1879.

HAGLER, JACOB S., Captain, 5th Tennessee Infantry, Company F
Captured in Morgan County, Tennessee, May 21, 1863. Was recaptured after his Libby escape and sent to Macon, Georgia, May 7, 1864. Paroled March 1, 1865. Age 41 at time of escape attempt. Name appears as Haglen in some records.

HAMILTON, ANDREW G., Captain, 12th Kentucky Cavalry, Company A
Captured at Jonesboro, Tennessee, September 20, 1863. In both the original and final tunnel parties, leading escape attempt with Colonel Rose. Successfully escaped from Libby. Commissioned as major on November 1, 1863 while in Libby, but never mustered in. Resigned June 5, 1865. He is believed to have been a murder victim a few years after the escape.

HANDY, THOMAS, Captain, 79th Illinois Infantry, Company F
Captured at Chickamauga, September 20, 1863. Was recaptured and sent to Macon, Georgia, May 7, 1864. Believed to have also been transferred from Macon to at least one other prison camp. Paroled December 10, 1864. Mustered out May 29, 1865. Died August 10, 1870 and is buried in Marshall, Illinois.

HARRIS, DAVID H., 2nd Lieutenant, 3rd Ohio Infantry, Company E
Captured at Rome, Georgia, May 3, 1863. Successfully escaped from Libby at age of 26, reaching Fort Monroe on February 14, 1864. Born in Wales, he worked in Cincinnati as an iron worker in a rolling mill. After his escape he suffered from general debility, rheumatism, catarrh, stomach disease, heart disease, liver disease, kidney disease, and impaired eyesight. Mustered out June 21, 1864. Died at age 70 on March 13, 1908.

HATFIELD, JOHN D., 1st Lieutenant, 53rd Illinois Infantry, Company H
Captured at Jackson, Mississippi, July 12, 1863. Successfully escaped from Libby, reaching Union lines near Washington, D.C. Promoted to captain, March 29, 1865. Had been shot in lower jaw October 5, 1862 in a skirmish at Hatchie Bottom, Tennessee. Mustered out July 22, 1865.

HAUF, ADAM, 1st Lieutenant, 45th New York Infantry, Company H
Captured at Gettysburg, July 1, 1863. Recaptured with Lt. James Gageby and Capt. Edmund Smith during Libby escape attempt after being run down by bloodhounds. Spent several weeks in cells after his return to Libby. Age 31 at time of escape. Transferred to Macon, Georgia, May 7, 1864 and from there to Charleston, South Carolina and Columbia, South Carolina, from where he was exchanged March 1, 1865. Suffering from general debility, rheumatism, scurvy, and dysentery, he was discharged March 11, 1865. Had been born in Germany and said that his name was really Hanf, but that it had been transcribed incorrectly and he finally

tired of trying to get it corrected. Listed his occupation as "segar" maker. Also served in 5th New York State Militia. Suffered from chronic alcoholism later in life.

HAYES, EDWIN L., Lieutenant Colonel, 100th Ohio Infantry

Captured at Limestone Station, Tennessee, September 8, 1863. Recaptured after escape from Libby, at age of 44. Transferred to Macon, Georgia, May 7, 1864, and from there to Andersonville, Georgia and Charleston, South Carolina, from where he was paroled and exchanged August 3, 1864. Was one of several prisoners moved into the line of Union bombardment while at Charleston, in a Confederate attempt to halt the artillery fire. As result of his prison diet he suffered from dysentery and chronic diarrhea, which caused severe hemorrhaging and loss of blood. Promoted to colonel, January 2, 1865, but not mustered. Brevetted brigadier general, January 12, 1865. Had also served as captain in 44th Illinois Infantry (aka North Western Rifles) earlier in the war, suffering wounds at Pea Ridge, Arkansas. Resigned May 20, 1865. Was appointed governor of North Carolina during Reconstruction. The oldest remaining Union general, he died at Glen Ridge, New Jersey on January 1, 1917.

HENRY, JOHN, Major, 5th Ohio Cavalry

Captured at Hernando, Mississippi, June 19, 1863 with 75 of his men, while leading a demonstration. Was accused by some of gross carelessness for allowing his detachment to become surrounded and surprised. Recaptured after Libby escape attempt and paroled April 30, 1864, at age of 35. Promoted to lieutenant colonel March 1, 1864. Was honored in official records of Colonel W. H. Morgan for his skill and assistance in establishing a defense in a skirmish at Davis's Mill, December 21, 1862. Granted leave June 26, 1864 for treatment of severe neuralgia and lumbago acquired while in prison. Mustered out November 18, 1864. Returned to professional lecturing after war.

HIGBY, EDGAR J., 2nd Lieutenant, 33rd Ohio Infantry, Company C

Captured at Chickamauga, September 20, 1863. Successfully escaped from Libby with Captain Wesley Adams and Lieutenant Edward Scott, only to be killed three months later on May 14, 1864 at Resaca, Georgia at age of 20. Buried at Chattanooga, Tennessee.

HINDS, HENRY H., 1st Lieutenant, 57th Pennsylvania Infantry, Company A

Captured at Gettysburg, July 2, 1863 when his company was overrun at Sherfy House, near the peach orchard. Recaptured after escape from Libby at age of 22. Transferred to Macon, Georgia, May 7, 1864. Placed on list of sick, suffering from bronchitis, and transferred to Columbia, South Carolina. Paroled March 1, 1865. Was wounded at Chancellorsville. Promoted to captain and discharged on May 15, 1865.

HOBART, HARRISON C., Lieutenant Colonel, 21st Wisconsin Infantry
Captured at Chickamauga, September 20, 1863. Successfully escaped from Libby with Lieutenant Colonels Theodore West and Joseph Boyd, reaching Union lines after five days and six nights in the swamps. Promoted to colonel, March 1, 1864 and to brigadier general of U.S. Volunteers, January 12, 1865. Mustered out June 8, 1865. Had also served as captain in 4th Wisconsin Infantry in early part of war. Before war had been leader in Wisconsin House of Representatives and a candidate for governor. Considered the father of the Homestead Law, adopted by many states. After the war, served as president of the Libby Prison Tunnel Association. Selected by escapees, along with Col. William McCreery, to be spokesman at group meeting with President Lincoln after the escape. Died January 26, 1902.

HOOPER, J. HARRIS, Major, 15th Massachusetts Infantry
Captured at White Plains, Virginia, July 26, 1863. Successfully escaped from Libby. Returned to his regiment March 28, 1864. Had been commissioned as lieutenant colonel, July 4, 1863 but was not mustered. Had been declared missing in action at Ball's Bluff, Virginia. Wounded December 13, 1862 at Fredericksburg, Virginia and June 22, 1864 near Petersburg, Virginia. Had prior service as a private in 13th New York State Militia from April 13, 1861 to August 6, 1861. Age 24 at time of Libby escape. Mustered out July 28, 1864.

IRSCH, FRANCIS, Captain, 45th New York Infantry, Company D
Captured at Gettysburg, July 1, 1863. Recaptured with 2nd Lieutenant Edgar Schroeders after Libby escape. Awarded Congressional Medal of Honor for heroism at Gettysburg, for "...gallantry in flanking the enemy and capturing a number of prisoners and in holding a part of the town against heavy odds while the Army was rallying on Cemetery Hill." Transferred to Macon, Georgia, May 7, 1864, from there to Danville, and from there to Charleston, South Carolina. Paroled March 1, 1865. Age 23 at time of escape. Discharged May 15, 1865. Had been hospitalized for unknown length of time on April 26, 1863 for unspecified illness.

JOHNSON, ISAAC, Engineer, USS *Satellite*
Captured in Rappahannock River, August 23, 1863. Recaptured after Libby escape and transferred to Macon, Georgia, May 7, 1864. From there he was moved to Savannah, and then to Charleston, from where he was paroled. He would report that he never had a blanket while in Libby, and had gone for 145 days without meat at one stretch. Found guilty of cowardice during capture of his ship by Naval Board of Inquiry, with several other officers. The hearing found that he had stayed in his cabin and offered no resistance during the capture. Resigned December 30, 1864. From New York. Also served on USS *Cambridge*. Was lost at sea in March, 1866 on the steamship *Juno* of the Murray Ferris Line. All on board perished in the accident.

JOHNSTON, I. N., Captain, 6th Kentucky Infantry, Company H

Captured at Chickamauga, September 20, 1863. Originally believed to have been killed in action, and was reported as such by Brigadier General W. B. Hazen. Successfully escaped from Libby. In both original and final tunnel parties. Had been severely wounded in face at Shiloh, April 7, 1862 while leading a charge. Mentioned in Colonel W. C. Whitaker's official report on Battle of Stones River for gallant conduct and efficient service. Mustered out with regiment on December 31, 1864, at Nashville, Tennessee.

JONES, DAVID, Captain, 1st Kentucky Infantry, Company D

Captured at Graysville, Georgia, September 10, 1863 in skirmish with Confederate cavalry. Successfully escaped from Libby and returned to duty on April 9, 1864, following a short leave to recover from the rigors of his imprisonment. Mustered out with his company on June 18, 1864 at Covington, Kentucky.

KENDRICK, W. P., Colonel, 3rd West Tennessee Cavalry

Captured at Corinth, Mississippi, June 10, 1863. Successfully escaped from Libby. Little is known about Colonel Kendrick, as his regiment did not exist as it is listed, and his name does not appear on any Tennessee regimental rosters. The information concerning his escape was taken from the Libby Prison register and other sources, all of which list his name and regiment in this manner. He is known, however, to have written a letter to President Lincoln just 12 days after the escape, telling him of conditions at Libby and Belle Isle and imploring the president to do something before more prisoners died.

LUCAS, JOHN, Captain, 5th Kentucky Infantry, Company F

Captured at Chickamauga, September 20, 1863. Recaptured after escape from Libby. Transferred to Macon, Georgia, May 7, 1864. Transferred to Camp Asylum at Columbia, South Carolina, from where he escaped on November 29, 1864. Reached Union lines at Lenore Station, East Tennessee. In both original and final tunnel parties. Discharged January 13, 1865. Originally listed as killed in action at Chickamauga. Age 27 at time of escape attempt. Had also served as adjutant of his regiment.

McCREERY, WILLIAM B., Colonel, 21st Michigan Infantry

Captured at Chickamauga, September 20, 1863. Wounded when captured, placed in hospital upon arrival in Richmond. Successfully escaped from Libby at age of 27. Resigned on September 14, 1864, due to disability resulting from six wounds received at various actions and skirmishes, including three at Winchester. Also served in 2nd Michigan Infantry. Entered politics after war. Served as president of Libby Prison Association and as life-president of the 21st Michigan Infantry Association. Selected

by escapees, along with Lieutenant Colonel Harrison Hobart, to be spokesman at group meeting with President Lincoln after the escape. Died December 9, 1896. Buried at Flint, Michigan.

McDONALD, BEDAN B., Major, 101st Ohio Infantry

Captured at Chickamauga, September 20, 1863. Successfully escaped from Libby at age of 33. Rescued by USS *Ella* at Blackstone Island in the Potomac River, February 28, 1864, with Capt. William Scearce, Colonel Abel Streight, and Lieutenant John Sterling. Two days prior to his rescue, February 26, 1864, his regiment promoted him to lieutenant colonel. In both original and final tunnel parties. Wounded at Franklin, Tennessee, November 30, 1864. Mustered out with regiment June 12, 1865.

McKEAN, NINEOCH, 1st Lieutenant, 21st Illinois Infantry, Company H

Captured at Chickamauga, September 20, 1863. Successfully escaped from Libby. In final tunnel party only. Awarded Congressional Medal of Honor in 1890 for gallantry in 1863. His citation reads "Conspicuous in the charge at Stones River, Tennessee, where he was three times wounded. At Liberty Gap, Tennessee, captured colors of 8th Arkansas Infantry." Resigned July 2, 1864. Name also appears as Nineoch McKeen and as Nineveh McKean, in various records.

MILES, DAVID, Lieutenant Colonel, 79th Pennsylvania Infantry

Captured at Chickamauga, September 20, 1863. Recaptured after escape attempt and transferred to Macon, Georgia, May 7, 1864. Moved from Macon to Charleston. Was one of several prisoners moved into the line of Union bombardment while at Charleston, in a Confederate attempt to halt the artillery fire. Exchanged and paroled August 3, 1864. Brevetted colonel, March 13, 1865. Wounded in left thigh at Bentonville, North Carolina, March 19, 1865 while leading a charge, and was noted in the official battle reports for fighting energetically and skillfully. Mustered out with regiment, July 12, 1865.

MOORE, McCASLIN, Captain, 29th Indiana Infantry, Company D

Captured at Chickamauga, September 20, 1863. Recaptured after escape from Libby. Age 30 at time of escape attempt. Transferred to Macon, Georgia, May 7, 1864, and from there to Columbia, South Carolina, where he was placed on list of sick and convalescent with what was described as "debility and fever." Paroled at Charleston, South Carolina on December 10, 1864. Mustered out May 2, 1865 on surgeon's certificate due to a generally debilitated condition which the surgeon attributed to exposure, starvation, and chronic diarrhea. Worked in private life as a miller.

MOORES, ARCHIBALD, 1st Lieutenant, 4th Kentucky Mounted Infantry, Company E

Captured at Chickamauga, September 20, 1863. Recaptured after escaping from Libby and transferred to Macon, Georgia, May 7, 1864. Age 26 at time of escape. Transferred again to Columbia, South Carolina, from where he escaped on November 29, 1864. Promoted to captain August 7, 1864 while still in prison, and was mustered in to date July 21, 1864. Had been wounded in head at time of capture at Chickamauga. Mustered out March 14, 1865, to date December 22, 1864, when he reached Union lines.

MORAN, FRANK, 2nd Lieutenant, 73rd New York Infantry, Company H

Captured at Gettysburg, July 1, 1863. Recaptured after tunnel escape and transferred to Macon, Georgia, May 7, 1864. Escaped five times from different Confederate prisons but recaptured each time. Age 21 at time of escape attempt from Libby. Finally released from prison March 1, 1865 in Wilmington, North Carolina. Promoted to captain, March 30, 1865. While in Libby was active in the Libby prison minstrel troupe. Discharged May 15, 1865.

MORGAN, CHARLES H., 1st Lieutenant, 21st Wisconsin Infantry, Company F

Captured at Chickamauga, September 20, 1863. Recaptured after Libby escape attempt. Escaped again from train transporting him to Charlotte, North Carolina, February 15, 1865. Promoted to captain of Company H, May 1, 1865. Had also been captured at Chaplin Hills, Kentucky, October 8, 1862 at which time he was paroled. Mustered out June 8, 1865. Served as congressman after war.

MORTON, CHARLES H., Lieutenant Colonel, 84th Illinois Infantry

Captured at Chickamauga, September 20, 1863. Recaptured after Libby escape attempt at age of 40. Paroled March 14, 1864. In a mentally debilitated state when released, those who knew him said he was never the same after imprisonment. Mustered out as colonel, June 8, 1865. Honored for his gallantry at Stones River, Chickamauga, Atlanta, and Nashville. Owned a real estate business. Also served as county clerk and police magistrate. Died under mysterious circumstances July 26, 1880 and is buried in Woodland Cemetery, Quincy, Illinois. Death was ruled a suicide brought on by his mental infirmity, but some officials intimated that he may have been murdered.

MULL, DANIEL H., Captain, 73rd Indiana Infantry, Company A

Captured at Rome, Georgia, May 3, 1863. He was recaptured after his escape from Libby. Transferred to Macon, Georgia, May 7, 1864 and from there to Charleston, South Carolina. Paroled from Charleston December 10, 1864. Mustered out May 27, 1865.

PHELPS, ITHAMER D., Captain, 73rd Indiana Infantry, Company K

Captured at Rome, Georgia, May 3, 1863. Recaptured after escape from Libby at age of 33. Had wandered through Chickahominy Swamp with fellow escapee Major Ivan Walker, an old friend from before the war, for five days in freezing weather. He was recaptured when he refused to abandon Walker, who had become disabled and begged Phelps to continue on without him. Placed in dungeon upon return to Libby. Was approved for exchange in May, 1864 but instead was transferred to Macon, Georgia, and from there to Charleston, South Carolina. In October, 1864 he was moved to Columbia, South Carolina, from where he was finally paroled on March 1, 1865 with unknown disability. Discharged at Nashville July 1, 1865. Refused to apply for pension as long as he felt he could work, despite his illnesses which were acquired in prison. He was so admired by his fellow citizens that they regularly elected him to public office so that he would have an income while he was ill. Served as sheriff of LaPorte County from 1866 to 1870, and became partner in an insurance business around 1874. Born in Canada. Before the war he had served as an officer of the Northern Indiana State Prison. Died April 11, 1900 at LaPorte, Indiana, of diarrhea and dyspepsia and was buried in Pine Lake County.

PIERCE, WILLIAM P., Captain, 11th Kentucky Cavalry, Company A

Captured at Marysville, Tennessee, November 14, 1863. Recaptured after escape from Libby. Exchanged April 30, 1864, suffering from dysentery. Transferred to 12th Kentucky Cavalry. Had served as adjutant before promotion to captain. Was mentioned in *Official Records* for his action in pursuit of the enemy at Creelsbourough, Kentucky, and for his part in the capture of Brigadier General John Hunt Morgan in July, 1863. Discharged January 3, 1865.

RANDALL, WILLIAM S. B., Captain, 2nd Ohio Infantry, Company C

Captured at Chickamauga, September 20, 1863. Successfully escaped from Libby at age of 30. Participated in final tunnel party only. His skull had been fractured when he was struck by minie ball at Stones River, December 31, 1862. Mustered out October 10, 1864.

RANDOLPH, WALLACE F., 1st Lieutenant, 5th U.S. Artillery, Battery L

Captured at Winchester, Virginia, June 15, 1863. Successfully escaped. Had been wounded at time of original capture. Brevetted captain June 14, 1863 for gallantry and meritorious service in defense of Winchester, and major March 13, 1865 for good conduct and gallant service during war. Promoted to captain July 28, 1866; to major of 3rd U.S. Artillery April 25, 1888; to lieutenant colonel, March 8, 1898; to colonel of the 1st Artillery October 17, 1899; and to brigadier general, Volunteers, May 27, 1898. Honorably discharged November 30, 1898. Had also served in 17th Pennsylvania Volunteers from April to July, 1861, and while in Libby was active in the Libby prison minstrel troupe.

RAY, THOMAS J., 1st Lieutenant, 49th Ohio Infantry, Company K

Captured at Chickamauga, September 20, 1863. Recaptured with Colonel William Ely and 1st Lieutenant W. H. H. Wilcox near Charles City court house. Age 23 at time of escape. Placed in dungeon, with no shoes, for 12 days after recapture. Suffering from rheumatism when he got out of cell. Transferred to Macon, Georgia, May 7, 1864, and from there to Charleston, South Carolina. Moved to Columbia, South Carolina when yellow fever broke out at Charleston. Promoted to captain of Company E, August 11, 1864. Escaped from Columbia December 5, 1864. Given a 60-day leave of absence by President Lincoln himself, which was extended to allow additional recovery from his rheumatism. Returned to Company K in May, 1865. Was placed in hospital a short time later, and was in and out of hospitals several times over the next several months. Had been wounded in leg and right hip at Stones River, December 31, 1862. Gangrene set in and his leg was eventually paralyzed. Mustered out with Company K on November 11, 1865. Died September 9, 1921 at Bartlesville, Oklahoma of a cerebral hemorrhage, accompanied by nephritis.

REYNOLDS, WILLIAM, 1st Lieutenant, 73rd Indiana Infantry, Company K

Captured at Rome, Georgia, May 3, 1863. Successfully escaped from Libby. Was 34 years old at time of escape. Employed as contractor before the war but was physically unable to work after war. Suffered severe head wound at Stones River on December 31, 1862. The wound, in which a two inch square piece of his skull was blown away, caused him severe pain, partial deafness, dizziness, and mental confusion throughout the remainder of his life. There is evidence that additional pieces of his skull were removed while he was in Libby. Discharged on surgeon's certificate August 8, 1864. Died October 15, 1904.

ROGERS, ANDREW F., Lieutenant Colonel, 80th Illinois Infantry

Captured at Rome, Georgia, May 3, 1863. Recaptured after Libby escape attempt. Transferred to Macon, Georgia, May 7, 1864 and from there to Charleston, South Carolina. Paroled and exchanged August 3, 1864. Promoted to colonel but not mustered. Discharged November 25, 1864.

ROSE, GOTTLIEB C., Captain, 4th Missouri Cavalry, Company C

Captured at Union City, Tennessee, July 11, 1863. Successfully escaped from Libby, suffering frostbite of the toes in the process. Promoted to major, November 16, 1864. Cashiered by General Order #223, Department of Missouri, December 12, 1864, for refusing to give up his mare

when ordered to do so by the provost, saying he had properly traded for the horse and it was his. War Department ordered this changed to honorable discharge in 1905, effective December 12, 1864.

ROSE, THOMAS ELLWOOD, Colonel, 77th Pennsylvania Infantry

Captured at Chickamauga, September 20, 1863. Originally escaped while enroute to Libby but recaptured near Weldon, North Carolina. Led the February 9, 1864 tunnel escape. Recaptured within sight of Company K of the 11th Pennsylvania Cavalry. Suffering badly from scurvy, he was exchanged for a Confederate colonel April 21, 1864. Many who knew him prior to his capture said later that he suffered from a personality change as result of his imprisonment, becoming uncharacteristically irritable, emotional, and suspicious. Wounded at Kenesaw Mountain, Georgia, June 26, 1864. Brevetted brigadier general July 22, 1865. Mustered out December 6, 1865. After war served as captain in 11th U.S. Infantry. Brevetted major, March 2, 1867 for gallantry and meritorious service at Liberty Gap, and lieutenant colonel, March 2, 1867 for gallantry and meritorious service at Chickamauga. Also honored in official reports of the Battle of Stones River for having taken command of his regiment when commander was wounded, and for "...keeping the regiment together and setting a good example by leading the attack." Transferred to 16th U.S. Infantry in 1870. Retired March 12, 1894 and died November 6, 1907 in Washington, D.C. of cerebral hemorrhage. Buried in Arlington National Cemetery.

ROSSMAN, WILLIAM C., Captain, 3rd Ohio Infantry, Company F

Captured at Rome, Georgia, May 3, 1863. Only one other man from his regiment was captured this date. Recaptured after Libby escape attempt at age of 28. Transferred to Macon, Georgia, May 7, 1864. Transferred again to Charleston, South Carolina, from where he escaped on November 4, 1864. He did not reach Union lines at Dalton, Georgia, until December 6, 1864. Discharged December 7, 1864.

ROWAN, CHARLES E., Captain, 96th Illinois Infantry, Company F

Captured at Chickamauga, September 20, 1863. Successfully escaped from Libby, being rescued by 1st New York Rifles. Honored for his gallantry at Atlanta in September, 1864 and for his gallantry and meritorious conduct before Nashville, December 16, 1864 when he pursued and captured many of the enemy, with only 20 of his own men. Age 24 at time of escape. Brevetted major, March 6, 1865. Mustered out June 10, 1865.

SCEARCE, WILLIAM W., Captain, 51st Indiana Infantry, Company K

Captured at Rome, Georgia, May 3, 1863. Successfully escaped at age 26. Rescued February 28, 1864 by USS *Ella* at Blackstone Island, in Potomac River, with Major Bedan McDonald, Colonel Abel Streight, and Lieutenant John Sterling. Wounded in thigh at Nashville, December 16, 1864. Promoted to major May 15, 1865 and to lieutenant colonel June 1, 1865. Worked as a farmer in civilian life. Discharged December 13, 1865 on surgeon's certificate for chronic bronchitis and other ailments resulting from the time he was confined in Libby.

SCHROEDERS, EDGAR, 2nd Lieutenant, 74th Pennsylvania Infantry, Company D

Captured at Gettysburg, July 1, 1863. Recaptured, with Captain Francis Irsch, after Libby escape attempt. Age 29 at time of escape attempt. Transferred to Macon, Georgia, May 7, 1864. Transferred again to Charleston, South Carolina and then to Columbia, South Carolina, from where he was exchanged and paroled March 1, 1865. Transferred to Company I on September 16, 1864. Promoted to 1st lieutenant, July 1, 1865. Mustered out August 29, 1865. Had been in hospital in December, 1863 for diarrhea and scorbutus, and in January and February, 1864 for unknown illness. Received disability pension for total deafness in left ear and partial deafness in right ear, and depressed scars of the scalp and face, resulting from scurvy, which gave him excruciating headaches during cold and damp weather. Also suffered from rheumatism and an injury to his right leg suffered when his horse fell on him at Chancellorsville May 1, 1863. Served in Company K prior to promotion to 2nd lieutenant of Company D, and in the 103rd New York Infantry from January to May, 1862. A native of Germany, he had served in the army there for four years before coming to the United States in 1861. Employed as draftsman and surveyor as a civilian. Died in New York on February 4, 1909.

SCHROEDTER, HUGO, 2nd Lieutenant, 82nd Illinois Infantry, Company F

Captured at Gettysburg, July 1, 1863. In hospital September 20 through 26, 1863 for unknown illness. Recaptured after Libby escape attempt and placed in dungeon on his return. Transferred to Rolla, then Charleston, South Carolina, then Macon, Georgia, beginning May 7, 1864. Was 32 years old at time of escape. Paroled March 1, 1865. Mustered out May 15, 1865. Had been placed in hospital in Richmond for six days in September, 1863 for an unknown ailment, but believed to be hemorrhaging of the lungs. Reported by other prisoners as having been sick his entire stay in Libby. He died at the age of 48 at his home in Chicago on December 17, 1880 of tuberculosis acquired in Libby Prison. Buried in Graceland Cemetery in Chicago. A native of Germany. Early reports of the escape listed his name as Schwester or Chivester, due to misreading of handwritten records. Worked as a liquor dealer.

SCOTT, EDWARD S., 2nd Lieutenant, 89th Ohio Infantry, Company G

Captured at Chickamauga, September 20, 1863. Successfully escaped with Captain Wesley Adams and Lieutenant Edgar Higby, at age of 21. Promoted to 1st lieutenant, March 19, 1864. Wounded July 20, 1864 at Battle

of Peachtree Creek, Georgia. Appointed adjutant September 20, 1864. Mustered out with regiment June 7, 1865.

SCUDMORE, GODWIN, 1st Lieutenant, 80th Illinois Infantry, Company A
Captured at Rome, Georgia, May 3, 1863. Successfully escaped from Libby after wandering in the swamps surrounding Richmond for several days and nights. Promoted to captain but not mustered. Mustered out August 31, 1864. Name appears as Scuttermore or Scudamore, and his first name as Goodwin, in various records.

SEELEY, HORACE B., 2nd Lieutenant, 86th New York Infantry, Company K
Captured at Gettysburg, July 1, 1863. Recaptured after escape from Libby. Transferred to Danville, Virginia May 7, 1864 and from there to Columbia, South Carolina. Wounded May 10, 1864 at Po River, Virginia in what may have been another escape attempt, and was placed on sick list for loss of great toe. Paroled March 1, 1865. Promoted to 1st lieutenant, July 2, 1863 and to captain, May 15, 1865. Developed rheumatism and kidney disease in prison, requiring hospitalization after his parole. Mustered out June 27, 1865. Died August 10, 1904 in Addison, New Jersey.

SIMPSON, JOHN D., 1st Lieutenant, 10th Indiana Infantry, Company H
Captured at Chickamauga, September 20, 1863. Recaptured after escape attempt. Transferred to Macon, Georgia, May 7, 1864, and from there to Columbia and Charleston, South Carolina, where he was placed on the list of sick and convalescent prisoners, suffering from general debility. Paroled December 10, 1864. A nephew of General Robert Anderson, he served as an aide to General Fry and General Steadman. In final tunnel group only. Discharged December 19, 1864.

SMALL, MELVILLE R., 1st Lieutenant, 6th Maryland Infantry, Company H
Captured at Harper's Ferry, Virginia, July 19, 1863 while in process of a court-martial for unspecified charges. Recaptured after Libby escape attempt. Paroled April 30, 1864, returning to his regiment on June 7, 1864. Served as adjutant of 6th Maryland Infantry. Died of complications from wounds of left leg suffered at Cedar Creek, October 19, 1864.

SMITH, EDMUND L., Captain, 19th U.S. Infantry, Company G
Captured at Chickamauga, September 20, 1863. Recaptured with Lieutenants James Gageby and Adam Hauf after escape attempt. Transferred to Macon, Georgia, May 7, 1864, and from there to Charleston and Columbia, South Carolina, from where he was paroled. Awarded brevet major, September 20, 1863, for gallantry and meritorious service at Chickamauga, for having taken command of the 19th U.S. after the commander was badly wounded. Resigned his commission July 23, 1867. Died September 11, 1891.

SPOFFORD, JOHN P., Lieutenant Colonel, 97th New York Infantry
Captured at Gettysburg, July 1, 1863. Recaptured after escape attempt from Libby. Transferred to Macon, Georgia, May 7, 1864, and from there to Charleston. Was one of several prisoners moved into the line of Union bombardment while at Charleston, in a Confederate attempt to halt the artillery fire. Paroled August 3, 1864, suffering from rheumatism and general debility. Age 45 at time of escape. Promoted to colonel, February 18, 1865. Mustered out July 18, 1865 at camp in Field, Virginia. Promoted to brevet brigadier general USV (war service) March 13, 1865. Had been wounded in the side, with a fractured rib, at Hatcher's Run, February 6, 1865. Died August 28, 1884.

STARR, GEORGE H., Captain, 104th New York Infantry, Company D
Captured at Gettysburg, July 1, 1863. Recaptured after escape attempt from Libby at age 24. Transferred to Macon, Georgia, May 7, 1864. He escaped from Macon in July, 1864 but was recaptured and transferred to Columbia, South Carolina. Eventually escaped again October, 1864. Was aided in his flight to Union lines by a woman who had two sons in the Confederate army, telling Starr that she hoped someone would do the same for her sons if they were ever captured. Mustered out January 6, 1865.

STERLING, JOHN, 1st Lieutenant, 30th Indiana Infantry, Company A
Captured at Chickamauga, September 20, 1863. Successfully escaped from Libby. Age 28 at time of escape. Rescued by USS *Ella* from Blackstone Island, February 28, 1864, with Major Bedan McDonald, Colonel Abel Streight, and Captain William Scearce. Mustered out September 29, 1864.

STREIGHT, ABEL D., Colonel, 51st Indiana Infantry
Captured at Rome, Georgia, May 3, 1863. Successfully escaped from Libby. Rescued by USS *Ella* from Blackstone Island, February 28, 1864, with Major Bedan McDonald, Lieutenant John Sterling, and Captain William Scearce. Suffering from what was described as general debility at time of escape. Returned to duty in May, 1864. Took command of the First Brigade, Third Division, Fourth Corps on November 17, 1864, relieving Colonel John A. Martin. Promoted to brevet brigadier general, March 13, 1865. Resigned his commission March 16, 1865. Erroneously credited for many years with being the mastermind behind the escape. Died May 26, 1892.

SUTHERLAND, LEWIS, 1st Lieutenant and Adjutant, 126th Ohio Infantry
Captured at Germantown Ford (Locust Grove), Virginia, November 27, 1863. Recaptured after attempting escape from Libby at age of 33. Lost his boots while fording a stream during the escape and wandered several days in sub-freezing temperatures in his bare feet. Confined in basement

cell for eight days and nights upon his return to Libby, resulting in severe rheumatism. Transferred to Macon, Georgia, May 7, 1864 and from there to Charleston and Columbia, South Carolina, from where he attempted another escape on November 1, 1864. He was run down by bloodhounds and returned to Columbia, from where he escaped again three weeks later, this time successfully. Reached Union lines at Knoxville. Promoted to captain, June 27, 1864. Discharged June 17, 1865. A farmer, he died of dropsy in 1904 at Smithfield, Ohio.

THOMAS, JOHN W., 1st Lieutenant and Adjutant, 2nd Ohio Infantry

Captured at Chickamauga, September 20, 1863. Successfully escaped from Libby at age of 23, reporting back to his regiment April 20, 1864. Erroneously listed in Libby records as G. W. Thomas of the 10th Wisconsin Infantry. Had been promoted to 1st lieutenant to replace W. S. B. Randall, another Libby escapee, when Randall was promoted to captain. Killed July 20, 1864 in battle before Atlanta.

TILDEN, CHARLES W., Colonel, 16th Maine Infantry

Captured at Gettysburg, July 1, 1863. Successfully escaped from Libby. Brevetted brigadier general, March 13, 1865. His command was honored for gallantry and steadiness while under fire at Fredericksburg, the regiment's first battle. The 16th Maine and Colonel Tilden's leadership were held up as an example for more veteran regiments. Had also served in 2nd Maine Infantry in 1861 as a 1st lieutenant and captain. Captured again at Weldon Railroad, August 19, 1864. Escaped while enroute to Libby Prison for the second time, rejoining his regiment three nights later. Badly wounded February 6, 1865 at Hatcher's Run, and was officially recognized for returning the next day to lead his regiment despite his severe pain. Mustered out June 5, 1865. Died in 1914.

TOWER, MORTON, 1st Lieutenant, 13th Massachusetts Infantry, Company B

Captured at Gettysburg, July 1, 1863. Successfully escaped from Libby at age of 23. Suffered from chronic diarrhea as a result of his confinement. Promoted to captain, October 23, 1863. Mustered out August 1, 1864 as captain of Company C.

URQUHART, SAMUEL A., Captain, C. S., 6th Corps

Captured at Chantilly, Virginia, October 15, 1863. Recaptured after Libby escape attempt and sent north, March 21, 1864. Brevetted major, July 7, 1865 for efficient and meritorious service, and was ultimately promoted to colonel. After war he served as vice president of Libby Prison Tunnel Association. Mustered out July 7, 1865.

VON MITZEL, ALEXANDER T., Major, 74th Pennsylvania Infantry
Captured at Gettysburg, July 1, 1863. Successfully escaped from Libby. Promoted to lieutenant colonel, May 11, 1864. Mustered out October 15, 1864. Born in Germany. Had also spent 10 days in Libby after being captured at Chancellorsville, May 3, 1863 before being paroled on May 13, 1863. Died February 24, 1877 in Baltimore.

WALKER, IVAN T., Major, 73rd Indiana Infantry
Captured at Rome, Georgia, May 3, 1863. Recaptured after escape attempt from Libby, and was exchanged and sent north April 30, 1864 from City Point, Virginia. Was recaptured in Chickahominy Swamp with his old friend from before the war, Captain Ithamer Phelps. Promoted to lieutenant colonel. Resigned July 4, 1864. Name appears in some records as Ivin Walker or Irvin Walker. Had been hospitalized three times while in Libby: in November, 1863, December, 1863, and again in February, 1864 immediately after recapture. Was employed in civilian life as warden and merchant.

WALLACE, ROBERT P., 2nd Lieutenant, 120th Ohio Infantry, Company E
Captured in hospital at Raymond, Mississippi, May 24, 1863, while recovering from diarrhea and camp fever. Admitted to hospital for six weeks on arrival at Richmond, for treatment of severe diarrhea. Recaptured after Libby escape attempt at age of 28. Readmitted to hospital on March 19, 1864. Transferred to Macon, Georgia, May 7, 1864, and from there to Charleston and Columbia, South Carolina. Escaped from Columbia November 19, 1864. Promoted to 1st lieutenant, March 21, 1864 but not mustered. Had served as color bearer for his regiment, and was the first to scale the heights at Fort Hindman, Arkansas, temporarily planting his colors on the breastworks. Hospitalized several times while in Libby, and suffered from chronic diarrhea, rheumatism, impaired vision, indigestion, stomach disease, affliction of the heart, and nervous debility. Transferred to Company D, 114th Ohio Volunteers, November 27, 1864. Mustered out June 29, 1865. A farmer, he died December 29, 1920 at the age of 85.

WALLBER, ALBERT, 1st Lieutenant, 26th Wisconsin Infantry, Company I
Captured at Gettysburg, July 1, 1863. Successfully escaped from Libby at age of 23. Promoted to adjutant of 26th Wisconsin, March 10, 1863 but not mustered. Discharged April 3, 1864 for chronic dysentery and severe frostbite of the toes, suffered during the escape, that prohibited walking for three months. Died in 1911.

WALLICK, WILLIAM, Captain, 51st Indiana Infantry, Company G
Captured at Rome, Georgia, May 3, 1863. Successfully escaped from Libby, reaching the Union lines at Williamsburg and getting to Fort Monroe on February 14. Suffered from sciatica as result of his imprisonment. Also ex-

perienced nearly total deafness in both ears as result of exploding shell. Was 30 years old at time of escape. In original tunnel group only. Discharged December 14, 1864 at Nashville. Worked as carpenter. Died August 31, 1892.

WASSON, JOHN, 2nd Lieutenant, 40th Ohio Infantry, Company G

Captured at Chickamauga, September 20, 1863. Recaptured after tunnel escape, at age 24. Confined to dungeon at Libby after his return. While in prison he contracted indigestion, rheumatism, heart disease, and other ailments, which left him in weakened condition. Transferred to Macon, Georgia, May 7, 1864 and from there to Columbia, South Carolina, where he became ill with typhoid fever after his arrival. Paroled April 10, 1865. Promoted to 1st lieutenant but not mustered. Mustered out April 13, 1865. Died September 4, 1912.

WATSON, WILLIAM L., 1st Lieutenant, 21st Wisconsin Infantry, Company G

Captured at Chickamauga, September 20, 1863. Wounded at time of capture. Recaptured after Libby escape attempt at age 21. Transferred to Macon, Georgia, May 7, 1864. Sent from Macon to Columbia, South Carolina, from where he escaped on December 8, 1864. Promoted to captain, January 14, 1865. Also had been captured at Chaplin Hills, October 8, 1862 and paroled the next day at Harrodsburg, Kentucky.

WELLS, JAMES M., 2nd Lieutenant, 8th Michigan Cavalry, Company F

Captured at Athens, Tennessee, September 27, 1863. Successfully escaped from Libby at age of 26. Promoted to captain of Company M, May 12, 1864. Taken prisoner again August 3, 1864 on Stoneman's Raid to Macon and Lovejoy and exchanged September 28, 1864. Appointed acting assistant inspector general, First Brigade, Sixth Division, April, 1865. Discharged July 20, 1865 at Pulaski, Tennessee.

WEST, THEODORE S., Lieutenant Colonel, 24th Wisconsin Infantry

Captured at Chickamauga, September 20, 1863. Wounded when captured. Successfully escaped from Libby with Lieutenant Colonel Harrison Hobart and Lieutenant Colonel Joseph Boyd. Prison confinement brought on rheumatism and Bright's disease. Promoted to colonel, March 4, 1864. Wounded again at Resaca, Georgia, May 14, 1864. Resigned May 12, 1865. Had also served in 5th Wisconsin Infantry. Worked on railroad as civilian, and died at Asbury Park, New Jersey on August 15, 1889 at age of 49. His body was cremated at Hollywood Cemetery in Los Angeles.

WHITE, ALBERT BENTON, 1st Lieutenant, 4th Pennsylvania Cavalry, Company F

Captured at Warrenton (Sulphur Springs), Virginia, October 12, 1863. Recaptured after Libby escape attempt. Transferred to Macon, Georgia,

May 7, 1863. Transferred from Macon to Camp Asylum at Columbia, South Carolina. Paroled March 1, 1865. A teacher by profession, he was 22 years old at the time of the Libby escape attempt. Mustered out March 27, 1865.

WHITE, PLYMPTON, 2nd Lieutenant, 83rd Pennsylvania Infantry, Company D
Captured at Point of Rocks, Maryland, June 17, 1863. Recaptured February 13, 1864 after Libby escape, having been run down by bloodhounds. Put in cell for five days after returned to Libby. Transferred to Macon, Georgia, May 7, 1864 and from there to Charleston, South Carolina, where he died, still a prisoner, on September 13, 1864. Had also been wounded in hand at Malvern Hill, July 1, 1862.

WILCOX, W. H. H., 1st Lieutenant and Adjutant, 10th New York Infantry
Captured at Elk Run, Virginia, October 13, 1863. Recaptured after Libby escape attempt. Transferred to Macon, Georgia, May 7, 1864, and from there to Columbia, South Carolina and Charleston, South Carolina. Paroled December 10, 1864. Suffered from chronic rheumatism and heart disease after getting out of prison, and was deaf in his right ear. Served as quartermaster of his regiment. Had suffered leg wound at Gaines' Mill, June 27, 1862. Mustered out by special order, February 21, 1865. Lost all the toes on his left foot in a 1902 railroad accident at the Broad Street Station in Newark, New Jersey. Died in Newark on September 6, 1916 of cardiovascular and renal disease.

WILKINS, JAMES E., Captain, 112th Illinois Infantry, Company I
Captured at Riceville, Tennessee, September 25, 1863. Recaptured after escape from Libby at age of 32. Transferred to Danville, Virginia on May 7, 1864 and from there to Macon, Georgia. Escaped by leaping from train while enroute to Macon and reached Union lines after traveling 20 days in enemy territory. Suffered from rheumatism and chronic diarrhea resulting from his confinement. Mustered out June 20, 1865. Died June 9, 1901 as result of accident in Carl Junction, Missouri which fractured his skull at the base of his brain.

WILLIAMS, LEANDER, 2nd Lieutenant, 73rd Indiana Infantry, Company K
Captured at Rome, Georgia, May 3, 1863. Successfully escaped from Libby. Promoted to 1st lieutenant September 1, 1864. Remained in Union service for more than a year after the escape from Libby, mustering out with his regiment July 1, 1865.

WILLIAMS, WILLIAM A., 2nd Lieutenant, 123rd Ohio Infantry, Company H
Captured at Winchester, Virginia, June 15, 1863. Successfully escaped from Libby at age of 37, rejoining regiment on March 24, 1864 after a short leave to attend to affairs at home and to recover from minor illnesses acquired while in prison. Discharged July 24, 1864.

Bibliography

Abbott, Allen O. *Prison Life in the South.* New York: Harper and Brothers, Publishers, 1865.

Armstrong, William M. *The Civil War Diary of Arthur G. Sedgwick.* Publisher, place, and date unknown.

Bates, Samuel P. *History of the Pennsylvania Volunteers.* Harrisburg: B. Singerly, State Printer, 1871.

Bates, Samuel P. *Martial Deeds of Pennsylvania.* Philadelphia: T. H. Davis and Company, 1876.

Beers, Henry Putney. *Guide to the Archives of the Government of the Confederate States of America.* Washington: The National Archives and Records Service, 1968.

Beyer, W. F., and O. F. Keydel, editors. *Deeds of Valor.* Stamford, Connecticut: Longmeadow Press, in association with Platinum Press Inc., Woodbury, New York, 1992.

Bill, Alfred Hoyt. *The Beleaguered City.* New York: Alfred A. Knopf Publishers, 1946.

Blakeman, A. Noel, editor. *Personal Recollections of the War of the Rebellion, Addresses Delivered Before the Commandery of the State of New York, MOLLUS.* New York: G. P. Putnam's Sons, 1897.

Bliss, George N. *Prison Life of Lt. James M. Fales.* Providence, Rhode Island: Soldiers and Sailors Historical Society, 1882.

Boatner, Mark Mayo. *The Civil War Dictionary.* New York: David McKay and Co., Inc., 1959.

Boggs, Samuel S. *Eighteen Months a Prisoner Under the Rebel Flag.* Lovingston, Illinois: Bobbs Publishing, 1887.

Botkin, B. A. *Civil War Treasury of Tales, Legends, and Folklore.* New York: Random House, 1960.

Brockett, Dr. L. P. *Camp, Battlefield, and Hospital.* Philadelphia: National Publishing Company, 1866.

Byrne, Frank L. "A General Behind Bars: Neal Dow in Libby Prison," reprinted in *Civil War History,* June, 1962.

Cable, G. W., et al. *Famous Adventures and Prison Escapes of the Civil War.* New York: The Century Company, 1906.

Caldwell, David S. *Southern Prison Life.* Dayton, Ohio: United Brethren Printing Establishment, 1864.

Cavada, F. F. *Libby Life: Experiences of a Prisoner of War in Richmond.* Philadelphia: Lippincott, 1865.

Cesnola, Louis Palma di. "Ten Months in Libby Prison." New York: Reprinted from the United States Sanitary Commission *Bulletin,* March, 1865.

Chapman, Adjutant General Chandler P. *Roster of Wisconsin Volunteers: War of the Rebellion, 1861-1865.* Madison, Wisconsin: Democrat Printing Company, 1886.

Commission of Inquiry, United States Sanitary Commission. *Narrative of Privations and Sufferings of United States Officers and Soldiers while Prisoners of War in the Hands of the Rebel Authorities.* Boston: Littell's Living Age, 1864.

Committee on Veterans' Affairs, United States Senate. *Medal of Honor Recipients 1863-1978.* Washington: U.S. Government Printing Office, 1979.

Connecticut, State of, Adjutant General's Files. *Record of Service of the Connecticut Men in the Army and Navy of the United States During the War of the Rebellion.* Hartford: Press of the Case, Lockwood, and Brainard Company, 1889.

Coulter, E. Merton. *The History of the South, Volume 7: The Confederate States of America, 1861-1865.* Baton Rouge: Louisiana State University Press, 1950.

Crabtree, Beth G., and James W. Patton, editors. *Journal of a Secesh Lady - The Diary of Catherine Ann Devereux Edmondston, 1860-1866.* Raleigh: Raleigh Division of Archives and History, Department of Cultural Resources, 1979.

Domschcke, Bernhard. *Twenty Months in Captivity.* Rutherford, N.J.: Fairleigh Dickinson University Press, 1987.

Dornbusch, C. E. *Regimental Publications and Personal Narratives of the Civil War.* New York: New York Public Library, 1961.

Dyer, Brigadier General Elisha. *Annual Report of the Adjutant General of the State of Rhode Island and Providence Plantations for the year 1865.* Providence: R. L. Freeman & Son, 1895.

Earle, Charles Warrington. *Libby Prison Life and Escape.* Rockland, Illinois: Maine Bugle-Campaign III, 1896.

Glazier, Willard W. *The Capture, the Prison Pen, and the Escape.* Connecticut: H. E. Goodwin, Publisher, 1868.

Goodnoh, E. C. *From Rat Hell to Liberty—The Famous Tunnel Escape from Libby Prison.* Place and publisher unknown, circa 1900.

Graf and Hoskins, editors. *The Papers of Andrew Johnson, Volume 6, 1862-1864.* Knoxville: University of Tennessee Press, 1983.

Hamilton, Maj. A. G. *Tunnel Escape from Libby Prison.* Chicago: Publisher unknown, 1893(?).

Hartpence, William P. *History of the Fifty-first Indiana Veteran Volunteer Infantry from 1861 to 1866.* Cincinnati: Robert Clarke Company, 1894.

Hayes, G. A. *Under the Red Patch.* Pittsburgh: 63rd Pennsylvania Volunteer Regimental Association, 1908.

Heitman, Francis B. *Historical Register and Dictionary of the United States Army, 1789-1903.* Washington: U.S. Government Printing Office, 1903, and Urbana: University of Illinois Press, 1965.

Hesseltine, William Best. *Civil War Prisons.* New York: Frederick Ungar Publishing Co., 1964.

History Committee, The. *History of the Eleventh Pennsylvania Volunteer Cavalry.* Philadelphia: Franklin Printing Company, 1902.

Hobart, Harrison C. *Libby Prison — The Escape.* Milwaukee: Read before the Commandery of the State of Wisconsin, MOLLUS, 1891

Hoehling, A. A., and Mary. *The Day Richmond Died.* San Diego and New York: A. S. Barnes & Company, 1981.

Hooper, J. Harris. "Twelve Days Absence Without Leave." *Overland Monthly.* Vol. V. Date unknown.

Hutchins, E. R. The *War of the 'Sixties.* New York: Neale Publishing Company, 1912.

Illinois, State of, Adjutant General's Files. *Report of the Adjutant General of the State of Illinois, 1861-1866.* Springfield: H. W. Rokker, State Printer and Binder, 1886.

Indiana, State of, Adjutant General's Files. *Report of the Adjutant General of the State of Indiana.* Indianapolis: W. R. Holloway, Printers, 1865.

Johnston, I. N. *Four Months in Libby.* Cincinnati: Printed at Methodist Book Concern, R. P. Thompson, Printer, 1904.

Jones, Katherine M. *Ladies of Richmond.* Indianapolis and New York: Bobbs-Merrill Co., 1962.

Jones, Virgil Carrington. "Libby Prison Break," in *Civil War History.* Vol. 4. The State University of Iowa, 1958.

Kelsey, D. M. *Deeds of Daring by the American Soldier.* New York, Akron, and Chicago: Saalfield Publishing Co., 1901.

Kent, Will Parmiter. *Story of Libby Prison.* Chicago: The Libby Prison War Museum Association, circa 1900.

Long, E. B., with Barbara Long. *Civil War Day by Day — An Almanac.* Garden City, New York: Doubleday and Company, 1971.

Maine, State of, State Archives, Military Service Files. Augusta: Department of the Secretary of State.

Massachusetts, State of, Adjutant General's Files. *Massachusetts Soldiers, Sailors, and Marines in the Civil War.* Norwood, Massachusetts: Norwood Press, 1931.

McCreery, William B. *My Experience as a Prisoner of War, and Escape From Libby Prison.* Grand Rapids, Michigan: West Michigan Printing Company, 1896(?).

Military Order of the Loyal Legion of the United States. Register of the Commandery of the State of Pennsylvania, April 15, 1865 - September 1, 1902. Philadelphia: Press of John T. Palmer, 1902.

Missouri, State of, Adjutant General's Office. Jefferson City: State Archives.

Mitchell, John. "Tunneling Out of Libby Prison." Appearing in *The Confederate Veteran.* Vol. XVII, 1909.

Moran, Frank E. "Escape from Libby Prison." Reprinted in *Civil War Times Illustrated.* October and November, 1970.

National Archives. *Record of Federal Prisoners Kept in Libby Prison, September 24, 1862 - March 25, 1865.* Record Group 249, Miscellaneous Records, Volume 100.

National Cyclopaedia of American Biography. New York: D. T. White and Company, 1893.

New York, State of. *Annual Report of the Adjutant General of the State of New York for the Year 1900, Ser. No. 24.* Albany: James B. Lyon, State Printer, 1901.

New York, State of. *Annual Report of the Adjutant General of the State of New York for the Year 1902, Ser. No. 32.* Albany: The Argus Company, Printers, 1903.

New York *Times,* February 15, 16, 17, 20, 21, 23, March 1, 11, 1864.

Official Army Register of the Volunteer Force of the United States Army, Volumes 1 through 9. Washington, D.C: Adjutant General's Office, August 31, 1865.

Official Records of the Union and Confederate Armies in the War of the Rebellion. Series 1, Volume X.

Official Records of the Union and Confederate Armies in the War of the Rebellion. Series 1, Volume XVII.

Official Records of the Union and Confederate Armies in the War of the Rebellion. Series 1, Volume XX.

Official Records of the Union and Confederate Armies in the War of the Rebellion. Series 1, Volume XXI.

Official Records of the Union and Confederate Armies in the War of the Rebellion. Series 1, Volume XXIII.

Official Records of the Union and Confederate Armies in the War of the Rebellion. Series 1, Volume XXIV.

Official Records of the Union and Confederate Armies in the War of the Rebellion. Series 1, Volume XXVII.

Official Records of the Union and Confederate Armies in the War of the Rebellion, Series 1, Volume XXX.

Official Records of the Union and Confederate Armies in the War of the Rebellion, Series 1, Volume XXXII.

Official Records of the Union and Confederate Armies in the War of the Rebellion. Series 1, Volume XXXIII.

Official Records of the Union and Confederate Armies in the War of the Rebellion. Series 1, Volume XXXV.

Official Records of the Union and Confederate Armies in the War of the Rebellion. Series 1, Volume XXXVIII.

Official Records of the Union and Confederate Armies in the War of the Rebellion. Series 1, Volume XLII.

Official Records of the Union and Confederate Armies in the War of the Rebellion. Series 2, Volume III.

Official Records of the Union and Confederate Armies in the War of the Rebellion. Series 2, Volume V.

Official Records of the Union and Confederate Armies in the War of the Rebellion. Series 2, Volume VI.

Official Records of the Union and Confederate Navies in the War of the Rebellion. Series 1, Volume XXV.

Peele, Margaret W. *Letters from Libby Prison.* New York: Greenwich Book Publishers, 1956.

Pennsylvania Shiloh Battlefield Commission, The. *The Seventy-Seventh Pennsylvania at Shiloh.* Harrisburg, Pa.: Harrisburg Publishing Company, 1908.

Petersen, Eugene Thor. "The Grand Escape." *Michigan Alumnus Quarterly.* LXIV, 1957/58.

Phisterer, Frederick. *Statistical Record of the Armies of the United States.* New York: Charles Scribner's Sons, 1883.

Prowell, George R. *History of the 87th Pennsylvania Volunteers.* York, Pennsylvania: The Press of the York Daily, 1901.

Publishing Committee. *A Brief History of the Fourth Pennsylvania Cavalry.* Pittsburgh: Ewens and Eberle, Book and Job Printers, 1891.

Richmond *Enquirer,* February 12, 16, 1864.

Richmond *Examiner,* February 11, 12, 16, 20, 1864.

Richmond *Times-Dispatch,* June 30, 1935

Roster Commission, The, State of Ohio. *Official Roster of the Soldiers of the State of Ohio in the War of the Rebellion.* Cincinnati: Wilstach, Baldwin and Co., 1886.

South Bend (Indiana) Tribune, September 17, 1961

Stryker, Adjutant General William S. *Record of Officers and Men of New Jersey in the Civil War.* Trenton: 1876.

Turner, William Dandridge. "Some Wartime Recollections." *American Magazine.* LXX, 1910.

Warren, Daniel C. *Luther Libby's Warehouse and the War: Richmond's Libby Prison.* Place, publisher, and date unknown.

Washington (D.C.) Daily National Intelligencer, February 18, 20, 22, and 23, 1864.

Wells, James Munroe. "Tunneling Out of Libby Prison." *McClure's Magazine.* Volume XXII, 1903/04.

Wilkins, Capt. William D. "Forgotten in the 'Black Hole': A Diary from Libby Prison." Reprinted in *Civil War Times Illustrated,* June, 1976.

Williams, Eric. *The Book of Famous Escapes.* New York: W. W. Norton and Company, 1953.